FALLEN ANGEL

KAT TURNER

CITY OWL
PRESS

FALLEN ANGEL
Coven Daughters, Book 4

CITY OWL PRESS
www.cityowlpress.com

Cover Design by MiblArt. All stock photos licensed appropriately.

Edited by Tee Tate.

For information on subsidiary rights, please contact the publisher at info@cityowlpress.com.

Print Edition ISBN: 978-1-64898-346-7

Digital Edition ISBN: 978-1-64898-347-4

Printed in the United States of America

PRAISE FOR KAT TURNER

"A fledgling witch finds love with a mature rock star in the midst of occult danger in Turner's magic-heavy debut and series launch. Turner sets up a promising world that readers will be pleased to return to in subsequent installments. Paranormal fans should check this out." – *Publisher's Weekly*

"*Hex, Love, and Rock & Roll* is clever, witty, and captivating from chapter one. Helen and Brian pull you into their world and refuse to let you go. It is utterly a bewitching love story that has it all: chemistry, mystery, *love*, but most of all–rock and roll." – *Jaqueline Snowe, author of the Shut Up and Kiss Me series*

"In *Blood Sugar*, readers can expect Turner's trademark snark mixed with magical and metaphysical mysteries, a well-paced plot full of unexpected twists, and two layered and complex characters winning their happily ever after." – *Janet Walden-West, author of Salt + Stilettos*

"I adore Cynthia and Raven! The chemistry between them is off the charts and they are both such badasses. *Fallen Angel* is pure paranormal joy. From the scintillating opening scene to the satisfying ending, it grabbed me and didn't let me go. Kat Turner has not only provided readers with a fascinating new addition to her series, she's given them a story and characters that feel distinct and fresh. I loved every moment of it." – *Rosanna Leo, author of Darke Passion*

"*Song of Virgo* is an intense and perfect combination of magic, mystery, and love!" – *Jaqueline Snowe, author of the Shut Up and Kiss Me series*

"Absolute magic. *Hex, Love, and Rock & Roll* delivers thrilling suspense, steamy chemistry, and a sexy British front man. Anyone who's ever had a crush on a rock musician or wished on a star will fall in love with this debut." – *Mary Ann Marlowe, author of Some Kind of Magic*

ALSO BY KAT TURNER

COVEN DAUGHTERS

Hex, Love, and Rock and Roll

Blood Sugar

Song of Virgo

Fallen Angel

＊

COVEN DAUGHTERS ORIGINS

Embers

For Mark, my real-life romance hero.

ONE

WHERE DOES MAGIC COME FROM? WHERE DOES IT GO?

The errant thought tapered into a fuzzy memory as quickly as it arrived, but not before rocking Cynthia Fields. She rode a wave of ripples that shook her like déjà vu.

Standing at the side of some California highway as the relentless beat of a midday sun baked her skin, she stared into the blue dome of a sky, certain that a thread of magic stitched her into the fabric of the mystical unseen.

A trio of vultures circulated above, scouting for carrion in their endless black loop of death, yet her realization filled her with a renewed zest for life.

The thought of magic had not originated in her own mind. She'd made contact with a witch who shared her bloodline. The spell that she'd cast to mind-meld with one of her long-lost coven sisters had worked. Now, all she had to do was gather and assemble all six witches in the same place, and the prophecy would commence.

But first, she had to get to Hollywood. And figure out what exactly the fabled prophecy was all about.

She held her hand up to her forehead, craning her neck to see around the side of the mountain where the two-lane highway curved behind a hill. Cars tended to come around the bend fast, meaning she had to be ready to signal quickly.

A bead of sweat slipped down her temple, the acrid taste of dust chalky on her tongue. She'd only been hitching for an hour, but dehydration was a consistent threat in the Northern California climate. As she reached for the hook securing her water bottle to her hiking pack, a coil of brown and tan patches camouflaged to blend with the rocky landscape caught her attention.

She came face-to-face with a small rattlesnake who regarded her with beady eyes. The nub capping its tail shook in a blur, cutting the still air with a tell-tale buzz.

Cynthia grinned at her new pal. Sister Folly was visiting her in serpent form, a good auspice and sign that her journey was unfolding according to the prophetic plan. The chaos and fire witches resided in southern California. They had to be there. She crouched on her haunches and met the snake's predatory stare with a question, "Where does magic come from? Where does it go?"

The low bleat of a truck horn aborted her communion with the visiting familiar, and she leapt to her feet. The silver plate of a big rig's grill barreled right toward her, the sixteen-wheeler lengthened by a typical cargo load. It honked again, and she stuck out her thumb.

The truck ground to a halt, kicking up dirt and rocks under its wheels. Cynthia squinted to get a look at the driver, letting out a breath when she spied feminine features and tousled gray hair.

Cross-country hitchhiking was a harrowing crapshoot, and she'd rather not have to use her air magic to leach the oxygen from the lungs of another sleazy guy who assumed she was some hooker or runaway that he could rape and discard without consequence. Dead bodies were logistical nightmares, and the the two she'd dealt with were plenty.

The trucker's passenger window slid down before the driver hollered in a gravely, smoker's voice, "Where ya headed, blondie?"

Cynthia tipped her chin in goodbye to the snake before sidling up to the side of the truck. "Beverly Hills."

The woman laughed, brushing some items off the passenger seat. "No offense, but you might need to grab a shower before your audition."

Once she gathered those two keys to the Coven Daughters Prophecy and set her part of the phased plan in motion, nobody would care what she looked or smelled like. They'd be too busy hailing her for saving the world. "Yeah, well, I'm not exactly going there to see my name in lights." Not in the conventional way that the trucker assumed, at least.

The trucker leaned forward, brows raised, and opened the door. "Okay, I'm interested. Get in."

Cynthia stepped up without hesitation, sticking her hiking pack on the floorboard beneath the dash as she settled into her seat and buckled. The truck's cabin was tidy and smelled like the pine tree air fresheners that hung from the rearview window, promising a pleasant ride in one sense. But as she glanced to her sandaled feet, she spotted a cluster of religious pamphlets in all different shapes, sizes, and levels of printing quality.

Uh-oh. She gritted her teeth, bracing herself for a long trip involving proselytizing and gushing declarations to a lord and savior. Not the best topic of conversation for an advanced witch with two killings on her conscience and a predilection for the darker aspects of the craft.

The driver revved the engine and got them moving, the truck taking several seconds to return to full speed. "You think you're in for a lecture about the salvation of your eternal soul, don't you?"

Cynthia looked to her driver, a woman so petite and whisky-thin that the belly of the big rig swallowed her whole. The lady practically needed a booster seat to reach the steering wheel. As they whizzed by a green mileage sign posting over ninety miles to Los Angeles, she resolved to humor the little old lady in the big truck. She'd endured far worse in her travels, from high-pressure sales pitches that verged on threats to unnerving screeds about ex-wives ranted by psychos with thinly veiled misogyny issues.

"We can talk about whatever, or not talk at all. Thanks for picking me up." Politeness never hurt, and occasionally religious conversations lent fresh insights to Cynthia's understanding of the magical tome stuffed into her backpack.

"I collect those. Those papers at your feet. Which isn't to say I believe what's printed in them."

Cynthia used the toe of her hiking sandal to sift through a few pamphlets. There were some from a few different sects of Christianity, a couple of Buddhist ones, and some of unrecognizable origin. Her interest piqued, she asked as casually as possible, "Why?"

The lady pulled a fast-food cup from the middle console and slurped the dregs through a straw. "Now that my grandkids are older, I think that I'd like to go back to college and study world religions. People are always shoving these into my hands at truck stops. Figure I can make the most of it by getting a head start, and accepting them is less awkward than saying no."

A fondness for the truck driver emerged as an unspooling warmth in Cynthia's chest. She might be a staunch follower of the Left-Hand Path, but her sinister predilections of the diabolical sort didn't stop her from harboring an affection for industrious types.

Spending the past five years roaming around the country in a tireless, dogged search for clues to the prophecy, including an off-grid stint living among animal shifters in the Peruvian jungle, had instilled in her a healthy appreciation for improvisation and thinking outside the box. Talking to people, she'd come to learn, fed her mind more than any book or article. "Nice. Which concepts interest you the most?"

Intellectual analysis of the subject matter might spark clues. The likelihood of a revelation was certainly higher than if she'd met some jolly, boring convert droning on about salvation.

The truck hugged a hairpin curve, the driver slipping Cynthia an odd, sly look. "What's your name, dear?"

Cynthia beat back a frown, forcing herself to exert dominance over her stubbornly expressive face. Thirty-three years alive and she still hadn't mastered her poker mask. She'd inadvertently given something to this woman to make her think that she had the upper hand. Not that it mattered. They weren't there to lock horns, and all that Cynthia needed at the moment was a lift to Beverly Hills. Appeasing the trucker didn't come with a cost. "Cynthia. You?"

"My given name is Denise, but I work under the nom de plume Nerissa. I have five other aliases that I rotate, depending." The words hung like runes in the space between them, codes to unlock destiny.

Where does magic come from? Where does it go? This time, Cynthia wasn't able to discern whether the questions came as memories of her own thoughts or the implantation of someone else's. As the engine moaned out its rumbling song of monotony, she stared at her chauffer's sharp-cut profile.

Cynthia had never been particularly good at circumspection or indirection and lacked the finesse required to play situations cool. Rarely was there time to meander, in her estimation.

Bluntness worked the same as air itself, blowing away clutter and dust, clearing out stagnation to make room for new energy. "You're part of the network, aren't you?"

That's what the esoteric tome sandwiched between a t-shirt and some dirty socks called the alliance of magic users supposedly scattered around the globe. The coven daughters were the most central to the prophetic unfolding, but their mentors, guides, accomplices, conduits, and foils all played roles.

Now all Cynthia had to do was figure out how Denise-Nerissa fit in.

The woman tipped her chin at Cynthia's bag. "You didn't even need to ask, now did you? What all have you learned from that book in there?"

Chemical reactions set off sparks in her bloodstream. She'd amass as much as possible over the next hour or two and do her best not to push too hard and drive Denise-Nerissa into a shutdown. "Am I the first person whose book you've seen? Either normally or through an extra-sensory ability?"

A long, agonizing pause emphasized the whizzing noise of tires spinning over pavement in endless loops. "No, I've seen them all, at one point or another. I've played crucial roles in ensuring that all six tomes make their ways where they need to be." Her tone dropped an octave lower and went flat, as if to suggest that this reunion of book and rightful owner was not an altogether positive development. "Whether by my own design of free will or through auspice and synchronicity, I can't be certain."

Frustration, dread, and irritation fought for control of Cynthia's emotions. Her research into the Coven Daughters Prophecy led her to conclude that the six witches finding their respective books was good. Otherwise, humanity had a holographic prison universe, a future of high-tech mind control technology, and some scary-ass energy harvesting programs waiting in the wings. "You seem troubled about this."

The trucker clarified, "I'm worried. Wary. My dreams are telling me that there's a twist coming. This conclusion we're marching towards isn't all neat and tidy." She sighed like the exhale weighed a ton. "My problem right now if that I can't figure out what the book represents on a deeper level. At first, I concluded that they were instruction manuals, but they also contain elements of warning. And language written in code, which suggests a need to hide or pass off the knowledge in covert form."

How much to hold back versus what to reveal? This woman seemed on the level, for real, but one never knew. A few varieties of scammer, fake, and lying nutcase had crossed Cynthia's path since she'd started opening up about her relationship with witchcraft and journey into the far corners of occult belief. She went with vague yet honest. "Directions written in code strikes a chord. Have you had any hunches?"

The vehicle approached an intersection, then a ramp that led them on to a sparsely populated highway. "I used to think they were lost texts of the Book of Revelations. I spent a lot of time with one of them before releasing it to the whims of the universe. It wasn't suited for me, apparently."

"You used to think they were lost books of the Bible. But now?"

An icy, knowing, blue-eyed gaze came Cynthia's way. Denise-Nerissa merged onto a new highway clogged with traffic. "I think that their origin is not of this world, and they have the power to control us if we aren't careful. These books have an agenda that seems separate from our own. At times in conflict, at times in accordance. All but the chaos sister is supposed to avoid working with the sixth section of the book, but I have a feeling that's a moot point in your case."

A chill slipped up Cynthia's spine. She couldn't quite land a read on Denise-Nerissa, whether she was being completely earnest or playing some game of misdirection and subterfuge, and to what end. But they'd come together by the machinations of fate or destiny, landed side-by-side in this truck on route to Beverly Hills, so Cynthia's best bet was to treat the older woman as an ally until proven wrong. "I believe that. I also believe that the Coven Daughters have agency. More than we may even know. And yeah. I've worked with the sixth circle. I've never been one to follow the rules"

"Rules exist for reasons."

"To be broken with intent. I believe in that adage."

"What do you seek?" They passed rows of palm trees, the ocean offering glittery peeks of its waters from over a cliff.

"Chaos and fire. Chaos is easy. The chaos witch is one of my opposition elements in the hexagon sisterhood. I think that she manifests as a serpent of some kind and is connected to snakes. I saw a rattlesnake back where you picked me up and have reason to believe it was a familiar visiting me with a message." In any other context, she would have felt like a crazy person spewing tinfoil hat drivel, but this driver knew the score.

Yet, the sober look on the older woman's face plunged Cynthia into dread-laced doubt. "Be careful. Nothing in this system is easy or obvious, ever, and thinking so infects the practitioner with virulent hubris." The driver pushed a button on the radio and scanned through static and pop songs.

"Why do you say that?" She wiped her palms on her lightweight cargo pants.

"Experience." Denise-Nerissa settled on a news program and turned up the volume. "Everything that's important in this world is something that we don't see. Take that for what it's worth."

Denise-Nerissa would have to do better than dropping a passive-aggressive hint by turning up her radio. "I'm not sure what it's worth, actually. Does it have to do with why you have five aliases? Six names total, one for each Coven Daughter, right?"

The older woman turned the volume dial higher, filling the cabin with dry talk of geopolitics. "Excuse me. I'd like to catch my show."

"This talking head garbage is all surface-level theater. You realize that, right? Besides, you're the one who just told me that the important stuff is unseen."

Denise-Nerissa slowed to let a motorcycle pass. The helmeted pilot, drenched in leather, flashed a quick wave of thanks. For some odd reason, the signal pleased Cynthia. Must've been the unexpected element of it, violating expectations. She watched the biker shrink to a black dot on the horizon.

"I'm tired of turning over rocks. Every time I did, I wasn't actually helping. I ultimately did something concerning that I can't seem to reverse," the old woman said.

"Oh, come on. You can't dangle that and not follow through."

"Sure I can. Don't test me."

"What'll it take to get you to talk?" Everyone had a price, financially or otherwise. Everyone wanted something and responded to incentive to get it.

"You're slick, aren't you?" Begrudging respect infused the rhetorical question.

"Lady, I've been living the nomad life for five years. I've gotta be savvy and pragmatic."

"Fine. I'll give you one piece of my story in exchange for a promise."

"What is it?"

Denise-Nerissa held a ferocious stare until traffic forced her focus back to the road. "Promise me."

"How can I make a promise without having the terms?"

"You're a practitioner of the Left-Hand path of air magic, correct?"

"Yes. How did you know that much detail?"

"Advanced members of the network, myself included, we see. You'll be more than capable of fulfilling your obligation to me in exchange for what I'm about to give you."

Cynthia balled fists so as not to fidget with her messy ponytail. She might be digging herself a hole here, but what choice did she have? She hadn't picked up any new leads in weeks, and the Beverly Hills excursion was itself a faith-based launch into a blind alley. If she wasted a chance to glean insights from this stranger in the truck, she'd kick herself. "Okay. I promise."

"If you find one or both of the Coven Daughters out here, I need you to facilitate an introduction to me. Don't lose touch. We need to be in regular contact and make a plan to meet once we have all six of you assembled. I'd stick by your side, but for various reasons, I can't."

The plan didn't sound terribly daunting, but it didn't make much sense, either. "You picked me up because you knew who I was. What I was."

"Of course. I've been tracking you through remote viewing and astral travel. Managed to pin down a rough read on your coordinates and come get you. But my spells to locate the others are failing. Fire and chaos are elusive, and I can't figure out why."

"Are you connected to earth, spirit, and water in addition to me?"

"Yep."

If true, this fact alone warranted keeping Denise-Nerissa close and opening lines of communication.

Cynthia's insides jumped. "What's in it for you if you collect the entire set of us?"

The trucker's jaw tightened. "I'm invested in this prophecy the same as you are. Plus, it's starting to look like a combo spell of the daughters is required to undo a mistake I made. There's discussion in the books of a practice called partner work. I'd ask to see your book, but I don't trust myself with those texts anymore."

"This has to do with what you initially didn't want to tell me." Though air conditioning blew from the vents in a generous stream, Cynthia's face heated. She sensed herself already drifting into the deep end, and Denise-Nerissa with her cryptic talk wasn't the flotation device she would've chosen. But the trucker was a lead and the only tenable one at the moment. "The concerning action that you can't reverse."

Denise-Nerissa nodded with intent. "After I identified my first coven daughter, I got too eager and enthusiastic about tracking down the other five. I used spirit magic spells to scatter myself. Long story short, I broke my consciousness apart and implanted it in six bodies. It didn't entirely work out according to plan, so now a little bit of me shares a physical form with parts of the original host." She patted her jean-clad leg. "The original trucker lady is in here with me. Name's Denise. We've learned to share. She's a real good sport."

An icky feeling made Cynthia's skin crawl even as excitement chased through her. This was no doubt the work of possession magic, the entire dark underbelly of the system. "You want to gather back into your original form. Leave Denise and whoever else and go back to being strictly Nerissa."

"Yeah. And dispatch the hitchhiker."

Cynthia reached for the mace on her key ring. She'd try a non-lethal solution before resorting to magic.

Denise-Nerissa snorted. "Not you, silly. It's not in my best interests to harm you. When I split my psyche, I let in something else. A traveler from another dimension. I assumed I was advanced enough to prevent this side effect of psyche splitting spells, but as they say, assumption is the mother of all fuck ups."

"I see. And I'll do my best to help."

Without warning, Denise-Nerissa veered onto an exit ramp and drove toward a gas station. "I appreciate it. We'll exchange contact info here."

Cynthia's stomach hardened. "We've got to be an hour away still."

"Yeah. Sorry, hon, my contracted route extends to the east. This is as far as I can get you without getting poor Denise fired." She pulled up in the refueling area and turned off the ignition, stilling behind another truck with pinup girl silhouettes on its mud flaps. "Gimmie your number, please." She reached under the seat and pulled out a cell phone. "This way's more polite than stalking you through the astral plane."

Cynthia rattled off her digits, and Denise-Nerissa texted her with a ding, cementing their connection. Though bummed to be stranded again, she supposed that she should count the day's development as a win, having wrangled a lead on a possible node in the Coven Daughters network. Unless the old lady was full of shit. "I'll be in touch if it's worth reaching out. Thanks for the lift."

"Be safe and all of that nonsense." The trucker winked.

"Never. Safety's overrated." After returning the tease, Cynthia hopped down the big step onto the pavement and shut the truck's door.

Once she got her pack secure on her shoulders, she blazed a path across the parking lot, figuring that she'd pause for a decent meal at the truck stop diner before gathering her bearings and plotting her next move.

She passed a row of motorcycles, pausing by the line of chrome beasts when one machine struck her as uncanny, like something she'd ridden in a dream or when spellbound in astral travel. How did she know of this mysterious motorcycle?

TWO

WITH BLACK WAVES OF HAIR TO MATCH HIS LEATHER PANTS AND jacket, the man four booths down damn near stole Cynthia's breath. And for an air witch who had literally stolen the breath from multiple people, that was saying a lot.

A smattering of other patrons populating the roadside eatery were effectively invisible to her, apparitions with dim halogen lights flickering off their burgers and waxen faces. Not him. He was real.

She chewed on a bite of her chicken sandwich, the meat surprisingly juicy and flavorful for greasy spoon fare. The man was more than real, he was magnetic. A dark light of fire amidst cardboard cutouts. Cigarette smoke curled around his devilishly pointed facial features like brimstone clouds from hell.

His three companions, their goth aesthetics extreme enough to disguise their genders from immediate identification, arranged some kind of card spread on the tabletop. Empty plates and cups crowded the edge of the table to make way for their Tarot-like game. She craned her neck for a closer look at the cards, catching only blurs of color.

The stranger looked on, pushing a card now and then even as he stared into the distance. She wondered what he was doing, thinking. He was so invested in the occult pursuit that he shared with his motley crew.

Was he like her, someone who flirted with the dark parts of the universe and courted its esoteric mysteries?

Whatever he was or wasn't, she couldn't stop looking. It was as if the world collapsed into the orbit of her gaze.

He had an air of blasé cockiness about him, with his shoulders taking up half of the seat back and his casual, unapologetic smoking. Cynthia plucked a piece of fallen lettuce from her plate and bit into it, savoring the crunch. Was he an actual demon? A sexy one? Witches and shifters were certified real, but who knew what other creatures stalked the night and roamed the streets?

A tired-looking waitress with gray roots and a major mustard stain on her apron hustled to the table, slapping her note pad against her palm. The obnoxious, rapping sound shattered Cynthia's reverie. "Can I get you anything else?"

"No, I'm good." Cynthia pointed a French fry at the table full of skinny, androgynous bodies draped in dark fabrics and silver jewelry. "Have you ever seen that crew before?"

The waitress glanced discreetly, bunching her tanned forehead. "Why, you in some kind of trouble?"

Best to sidestep the quagmire of that question. She folded what remained of her bun in half and munched. Mayo mixed with pan drippings coated her taste buds with a pleasurable tang. "No more so than usual. Send the hot one with the long hair and nice bone structure a strawberry milkshake. Put his tab on mine."

Mostly she wanted to see how he looked with his long-fingered hand wrapped around the wholesome drink. Fantasy fuel. The bad boy in the diner, Mr. Motorcycle, cruising for a nice girl to corrupt. Cynthia wasn't nice or good by any stretch, but she was always up for a bout of corruption with a tasty stranger. Her lower belly warmed. I'd been awhile since she'd indulged an anonymous quickie, and what better way to distract herself from the witchy predicament for a few minutes?

The waitress snickered while making note with a blue ballpoint. "Sure thing." At least she didn't bemoan the fallen state of the detached, cynical hookup generation or whatever.

"Thank you," Cynthia said sweetly.

The server laid down the bill along with a helping of side eye and ambled off.

The man tousled his black waves, chin tipped up as he watched the game with that half-interest of his. All smug and disaffected, ensconced in cool. His left ear was pierced, his neck as long as a swan's. A tattoo on the inside of his wrist intrigued her.

She squeezed her thighs together, the tingle between them building. Might be about time to get lost in a dark, sensual dream with the stranger. There were many intoxicating fantasies that she could project onto the man in black while he drove into her. In all of them, his composed veneer cracked at the moment of climax as he shouted and ripped the towel dispenser from the bathroom wall.

The double doors leading to the kitchen swung open, two silver flaps ejecting the waitress. She took a curvy glass filled with a hot pink confection and topped with a swirl of whipped cream to the man in black's table.

Cynthia bobbed her foot, anticipation bubbly in her midsection. This was fun. She liked to color her world with action and make exciting things happen. Life was too short to wait around for the good stuff to come to her when it was relatively easy and certainly worthwhile to be the architect of one's own destiny.

She was a witch, after all. The ultimate example of a woman with agency.

In a flash of languid, graceful movement, he snagged the milkshake and sauntered her way. His hips, ruler-slim under pants as snug as a coat of latex, rolled in a dirty invitation. He slid into the booth opposite her and stared as he pulled a sip through a wide, full mouth. A pressed white t-shirt hugged his slim chest. Up front, his leather jacket fit like a tailored blazer.

His companions didn't even notice his swift departure. Maybe he picked up random women in restaurants all of the time. He certainly was attractive enough. Not that she cared or felt any inkling of jealously. She wasn't angling to crush the female competition or take the guy off the market.

Pink liquid slipped up the clear straw as he stared at her with an air devoid of affect. As expected, he was beautiful in way that eschewed gender conformity and was also a bit frightening to look at. Cold, with his coal-black eyes, nose and cheekbones as carved as ice sculptures, and wild hair billowing like a banshee flying through the night sky. "What do you want?" he asked in a low, neutral voice before taking another sip.

Arrogant, sexy son of a bitch. Yeah, this was for sure not his first rodeo. "You looked interesting. I'd like to get to know you." She wanted to fuck him, but occasionally men balked at such bluntness. Women were supposed to flirt and tease, tempt with promises while dangling the precious pussy out of reach, and all of that bullshit.

"What do you want to know?" His slight sneer was epic. Omg, had she been transported into the movie *The Lost Boys*? She'd obviously won some kind of karmic lottery.

"Your name, for starters."

The smirk he let out plumbed the depths of her dirty mind, and a gleam in his eye suggested that he was on board. "Isn't it more fun without it?"

"Nah. A few broad strokes help me construct a scenario."

"It's Raven."

Boom. Surreal. And awesome. "Seriously?"

"Seriously."

Her heart slammed in hypnotic beats of lust to swell her chest. "Meet me in the ladies' room in five minutes." She threw two bills on top of the ticket, enough to provide the waitress a decent tip.

Raven plucked a soft pack of smokes from his jacket pocket and lit up, blowing a rail out of each nostril as he stared at her with a combination of hunger and something more destabilizing that she couldn't place. It wasn't threatening but challenged her equilibrium by complicating the version of him that she'd written in her mind. "Nice to see you're generous," he said. "Lots of people aren't."

She shrugged. "Like attracts like. I put abundance into the world and get it back. My motivations are purely selfish."

He tapped ash onto the floor and puffed another drag. "You believe in magic."

"Don't you?"

The ember of his cigarette tip burned into gray particles. "It's never been a matter of belief or non-belief for me. It's just a thing that *is*."

That sealed the deal. Cynthia didn't mess around with boring people anymore, unless she was riding out an extended dry spell and so horny that it hurt. The ones who were a little skewed, in the know, or otherwise quirky made superior memories. She swept him into the coils of one more round of eye contact before gliding to a bathroom that was tucked a few feet past the empty buffet station.

Inside, she checked her reflection in a streaked mirror. The rind of dust on her skin wasn't exactly kissable, so she splashed cold water on her face before popping a breath mint. Two stalls, plenty of room. The main door didn't lock, but who cared? She'd never see anyone here ever again, and accidental exhibitionism got her off now and again.

The door swung open, Raven moving with purpose as he closed in on her. He acted fast, confidently, clamping firm hands on her waist and pressing her back into the door. He was even more beautiful at kissing distance. So mesmeric that she couldn't stop staring.

"You have a condom?" he asked in a sultry voice, his scent a heady swirl of cigarettes, woodsy bath product, and the animalism of leather. Before she could answer, he brushed his lips against her neck, nibbling preliminary kisses, and wedged a knee between her legs to rub her center.

Maybe someday she'd share more meaningful, tender sexual experiences with another person or even learn to make love for once. Might be nice, but today was not the day for mushy daydreaming. "In the side zipper pocket." She kicked her pack with the side of her foot.

He crouched long enough to open the compartment and free the string of six remaining condoms. Face-to-face wouldn't work with both of them in shoes and pants, so she flipped around and arched her ass. Better this way anyhow. No risk of catching feelings from a purely transactional, physical exchange when eye contact and kissing were factored out of the equation.

His zipper gave with a metallic zing, a sound that sped her breathing and peaked her nipples into tender points that chaffed against her bra. She undid her own pants and shoved them to her knees along with her underwear.

"Look at this perfect ass," he murmured in a filthy tone. His hands were on her butt, massaging, kneading the flesh in big handfuls and the right amount of pressure. "Bald pussy, too. Nice. I've been needing someone like you to take the edge off."

She looked over her shoulder, emboldened by the power she wielded over him with her firm body and the lower lips that she kept free of hair. She liked the slippery, depraved feeling of being waxed bare underneath her panties, a bad girl's calling card. His hard, curved cock was his only nudity, sheathed up and jutting its approval from the split "V" of his open pants. No underwear. Seemed to suit him. "Someone like me, huh? What's that supposed to mean?"

He smirked again, giving his length two languid pumps. "Whatever you want it to mean."

There was a quiet part that neither was saying aloud. They weren't people to one another, they were characters, constructs of the other's mind. Suited her fine. "Well, then likewise. I'm ready, by the way. Let's get this going before someone walks in."

Instead of surging forward to penetrate, he slipped his index finger into her seam and played with her. She gasped at the initial rush of pleasure when his flesh brushed her clit. "You like that?" he asked.

She'd never turn down a good fingering, and one-offs didn't tend to be generous with their offers to satisfy her. In other words, big sex partner points for Raven. Cynthia rocked her hips back into his touch and widened her stance to accommodate him. "Very much."

"Hard or slow? Teasing torture or a fast orgasm?" He slid two fingers into her opening, to the first knuckle, withdrawing before spreading her moisture around.

She didn't recall the last time a man had asked her what she was into. Hell, she usually had to help herself along or even get out her vibrator. More points to Raven. Maybe she'd have to get his number just in case. "Hard and fast. Just get me off as efficiently as possible. No bullshit."

"That's hot. I like you. Assertive." His first and second fingers slid upward to target her clit. He rubbed in fast, big circles.

The pressure buildup hit immediately. She heard herself gasp, bucking into him as a promise tensed below her navel.

"There you go," he purred in his dirty voice, working her over. "I feel your clit getting swollen and big now, tender. You're hungry to come, aren't you?"

"Yeah," she panted, feeling her hips thrust back and forth. Bliss built, climbing higher, the rush to her peak spurred by his words. The ability to concentrate on anything other than bursting fell away, and her vision blurred. "I'm super close already."

A growl of male satisfaction arose deep in his chest. He sped his strokes, changing the motion to a flurry of up and down slides. A few more of those finishing moves, and she erupted, her cheek pressed into the cold door, moans rushing from her throat as the sensation of pure relief overcame her senses. He kept going until she had no more to give, and her spent knees shook.

Next came methodical motions as he withdrew his hand from her crotch and tacked his warm palms on her hips, pinning her in place. His tip butted her opening. She bit her lip, ready for more, her body still buzzing when he pushed in to fill her up. From then, his thrusts were quick and deliberate, long and deep.

Without seeing him, she attuned to his smells and sounds, how he vocalized more with every thrust until he grunted on each stroke.

She bounced her ass against him, urged on by his building arousal, chasing the possibility of a second climax when his pumps became erratic and want for rhythm. This went on for a bit until his pace sped to a frenzy and he let out a long, decadent moan—just as someone pushed the door, knocking Cynthia into Raven as he came.

"Oh, shit!" some random woman called out over the shouts of Raven's triumph.

The whole ordeal, the taboo of intruding on a hapless stranger while being intruded upon, set Cynthia off again. She shook as a follow-up climax made speedy work of her in a series of lush ripples, barely noticing as the door lurched back to its closed position like the third party couldn't get away fast enough.

Raven pulled out, and Cynthia took the cue to pull up her pants while he threw the condom in the trash and fixed his zipper. "That was fun." Tone buttery and satiated, he dropped a peck on her cheek. "Can I walk you out?"

"No need." She hiked her pack over her shoulders, stealing a final glimpse at him. A healthy flush had spread over his pale cheeks like blood on snow, and the look in his ebony eyes was surprisingly kind for a man who'd just used her to get his rocks off in a truck stop bathroom. "I don't really have feelings that you have to protect against emotional trauma. We fucked in a down-market Denny's. Gentlemanly aftercare not required."

"And somehow that means that I can't talk to you for five more minutes?"

She rolled her eyes even as an odd, gooey sensation bloomed under her ribs. Raven didn't look like a nice guy on the surface, but she struggled to resist the allure of novelty. "Whatever. Sure. What do you want to talk about?" Cynthia left the bathroom and crossed the dining hall on route to the parking lot. A cute, middle-aged brunette sitting at a table caught her eye and cringed, her red-faced male companion staring at his shoes.

Cynthia grinned at the woman and refused to drop eye contact first. She had nothing to hide and felt no shame in how much she enjoyed her wild, vibrant sex life.

At Cynthia's side, Raven matched her brisk clip. "How about your name?"

Eh, whatever. He'd gotten what he wanted just fine without it, but apparently the lissome, long-haired goth was chronically polite. There were worse qualities. She pushed off into the balmy dusk outside, smells of gasoline and fried food mingling with rock music over the sound system. Finding her motivation to hitchhike rejuvenated, she said, "Cynthia."

"Where's your car, Cynthia?" A gust blew his hair so it flowed like a cape behind him, concern drifting through his pitch.

They paused by the fleet of motorcycles, polished speed demons charging the air with power and danger. "I don't have a car." Four big rigs were parked in the rest area for trucks. Surely one was heading toward Los Angeles and wouldn't demand cash or ass as the ticket to ride. "I'm hitching."

"You're fucking kidding me right now, Cynthia. Tell me you're joking."

A snap of annoyance jolted her into confrontation mode. She stared Raven down, meeting his stern glare with a defiant glower of her own. This sort of male posturing clownery had happened a couple of other times, with prior hookups, and she did not abide. She was free. Nobody's property. Many men had been inside her, but none got to claim her, thank you very much. "Miss me with that alpha male crap, big guy. We fucked. Had sex. It was fun, but fun doesn't mean that you've bought yourself the right to boss me around until we go our separate ways. Do I make myself clear?"

"Take my bike." He grabbed the handlebar of the motorcycle on the end, an admittedly mouthwatering beauty polished to shine and embellished with red accents.

She freaking *loved* riding bikes, especially ridiculously imposing, American-made hogs like Raven's. Amusement at the idea faded as confusion set in. "That makes no sense. Why didn't you just offer me a ride?"

"Because I can't guarantee that you won't hitchhike again after I drop you off. This way you have a more permanent sense of safety. A defense against murderers, at the very least."

She scoffed. Where did this guy get off playing hero? He was probably full of shit anyway or riding some sleazy power trip involving paying for the time spent in her vagina. "My knight in shining armor. Thanks, but no thanks, buddy. I'm not a hooker."

"Just take the motorcycle, Cynthia." He fished in his pocket and pulled out a key ring with three keys on it, his tattoo coming into full visibility when he stretched out his hand.

She tapped the ink, a looping symbol rendered in black ink and juxtaposed against blue veins crossing the delicate, ice-white skin of his wrist. "What's this mean?"

"Why are you stalling?"

Maybe because the situation was so outlandish by now that the rational part of her mind was scrabbling for purchase, desperate to order her world by any means necessary. As if decoding the tattooed symbol would, in itself, send in a raft of sense-making context. "You offered to give me your motorcycle. I'm allowed to ask you whatever I want." To balance the scales of power, she supposed. Accepting a huge gift like that would put her in his debt, literally and/or energetically.

"It means chariot in Sanskrit." He jingled the keys. "Your chariot awaits. Take. Please."

"What will you do, ride on the back of someone else's?"

Raven played a pause that lasted too long, beat after beat of silence dangling in the wind. She wished that she had the skill to read minds, because she'd love to crack the one in front of her like a walnut. "You're fucking with me."

No more words from him. His arms sucked inward, absorbed by his center mass, and before too long his shoulder blades jutted out from behind in a grotesquely oversized mutation. He shrunk, darkened, glossy black wings taking the place of the bones protruding from his back. Facial features morphed, a beak grew from his strong nose, and in the parking lot sat a raven.

Ascending into flight with a mighty, flapping wingspan, Raven picked up the key ring in his beak. He hovered in the air—such an intricate network of feathers—and shook his head to make the keys tinkle.

Cynthia wasn't stunned or freaked, she knew firsthand that animal shifters were a thing, but why was one crossing her path here and now, under these circumstances? She'd been told that all shifters now lived in Peru. She had no reason to question that fact. But apparently, someone had been mistaken or lying.

Didn't matter now. She had a fix on transportation and maybe another magical person to cross paths with at some point in the future. Besides, hitching kind of sucked. She opened her palm and thrust it forward. Raven dropped the keys into her waiting hand and flew off into the night.

Bemused and baited on Raven's hook, she rubbed each of the three keys between her thumb and forefinger. A third item occupied the ring, and she brought it close to her face and stepped toward the restaurant to catch some of the castoff light. The lemon-yellow, plastic oval had a crude drawing on it, a crescent moon with a face that dripped with stars.

The cursive words "Moon Heart" sat beneath the picture along with a phone number whose area code she didn't recognize. Okay. Possible clue to track down Raven, if the urge ever struck. Cynthia mounted her new motorcycle.

Beverly Hills, I'm coming for you, baby.

THREE

Forty bucks. Not exactly broke, but far from flush, especially in Los Angeles. The troublesome thought bounced around in Cynthia's head as she slowed her speed upon approaching a roadside sign that glowed with cheap promises of a place to crash. The engine's rumble fell to a low purr as if her new ride tacitly agreed to stop at the seedy motel in the middle of nowhere.

Nothing about her situation was ideal, but she'd cope, adapt, and lean on her main survival strategies. She'd find some gig work during her stint in The Golden State. She could sew and throw pots. Until employment opportunities cropped up, she'd cast another spell to conjure some money out of thin air.

She licked a film of grit off her teeth and pulled into the motel parking lot, anxiety setting in as she snagged a spot close to the office. She had to stop doing those money spells and find legitimate employment. Her recent onset of recurring nightmares was a sign that money magic came with a cost. Nothing valuable in life was ever free.

After dismounting, Cynthia walked a short stint across cracked pavement to the office, pausing to draw in a deep breath and glace up at the place's looming sign. Surprisingly bright and cheery, the blue word "motel" was flanked by golden stars and bulb lights in some nod to

Hollywood glamour. At least none of the bulbs were burned out, and there were no cliché flickering letters or other Bates Motel murder vibes. Maybe she'd get lucky, and the rooms would be clean, even though the doors faced the outside. Cleanliness soothed Cynthia's tired soul. After weathering the literal and figurative mess she grew up in, she's come to value order and tidiness.

She supposed it was good that the modest parking lot was nearly full of jalopies and rusted trucks. More people around to hear her if she had to scream.

A bell dinged some musical melody she didn't recognize as she pulled the door to the main office. Halogen lighting made the space murky and nauseatingly violet, but at least the area was neat and smelled like orange-laced bleach. Photos of actors and maps to stars' homes lined particle board walls in an aggressive reminder of locale.

Behind the scuffed desk, a bald black man in a gray mechanic's jumper sat in a junky office chair, hunched over a crossword puzzle. He was rapt, his forehead scrunched in concentration, and she brought her finger to the button on a little silver bell before deciding it would be an asshole move to ring it right in front of him. She stood there awkwardly and thought about clearing her throat or whistling but nixed those strategies, too. Not like she was in a hurry or running from anyone at the moment.

Cynthia might be brash, but she hated to act rude, especially to working class folks. She'd come up hard with parents who worked three jobs between the two of them, learning real quick not to interrupt or steal their few pilfered moments of leisure time. This dude deserved a minute to finish his puzzle.

The man spoke in a mild voice, "I need a seven-letter word for catastrophe. Starts with 'D'."

It was kind of amusing, how he'd let her know that he'd seen her. Whimsically nerdy and a bit socially challenged but not creepy. Funny, too, the word he needed, a coincidence pointing to a serendipity. Cynthia often understood her life path as an amusing series of catastrophes, a rocky and wild ride of her own making.

"You sure it doesn't start with a 'C'?" She thought back to the practice vocabulary tests she'd taken for graduate school applications before choosing to focus on her powers instead of higher education. "Debacle."

"Ah." He sat up straight and waved a black ballpoint in the air. "It fits. Thanks."

"Crossword with a pen, eh? Bold move." She took out her wallet.

The man swiveled his chair to face her. A name tag sewn onto his uniform read "Mike." Mike looked past her. "You here alone?"

If only people knew that they didn't need to worry about her well-being. Plenty of human compassion had come her way during her travels, enough to grow her shrunken heart to a near-normal size, but relentless concern was tiring all the same. "Yep. Is forty bucks okay for one night?"

Mike scratched the side of his head. "Yeah. That works. Look, I'm gonna level with you. There are some rough characters that come through here. Lots of partying, drugs, prostitution. There was a gang bust in room seventeen last week. A man was stabbed in the—"

"Thank you, Mike, but I can take care of myself." She laid her last two twenties between the bell and a cartoonish, laminated map of downtown L.A.

"Okay." Drawing out his word, Mike took the money and grabbed a key off a hook behind him. "You meeting friends in the city?"

Yeah, sure, if all went well, they'd end up friends. Two friends, a chaos witch, and a fire witch, to complete a magical trio. Maybe they'd play jump rope or hopscotch after rescuing the universe. "Sisters."

"Family's important." Mike pressed a button on an old-fashioned cash register, making the drawer pop open with a ding, and handed her two softened dollar bills. "Get yourself a soda. You look thirsty."

Paternalism ground her gears, but when it came to men, far worse treatment was possible. She accepted the singles, slid them in the vending machine, and made her choice. A plastic bottle of diet soda hit the tray with a thump, the impact sending her awareness to her thick tongue and dry, scratchy throat. "Appreciate it."

"That's your ride?" He jutted his thumb at her gracious gift from Raven.

She twisted off the cap of her beverage and enjoyed an icy, fizzy drink of sweetness, caffeine perking her up in an instant and reminding her how long the day had been. It'd feel good to crash in a bed, no matter how creaky the springs. "Sure is. Isn't she a stunner?"

Mention of the bike and visualization of a bed caused her thoughts to slide to Raven, his onyx waves and devil-may-care stride, the way he looked right through her while *seeing* her, something her casual sex partners rarely did. They gawked and stared, those men, but for all of their lustful, appraising gazes, they never *saw* her. She thought of Raven some more, wondered where he'd gone. She missed him, even, as she disguised the true nature of the silent intermission by drinking more soda.

Mike grumbled, pulling his lips back to show a good set of teeth. "I'm here for four more hours, so I'll keep an eye on it. The guy who comes in after me won't be nearly as diligent, so if I were you, I'd try to be up with the sun."

The soda burned her esophagus as she absorbed his point. "You think it might get stolen."

He smoothed the seams of his folded newspaper. "Like I said, this place tends to house those on the more unsavory end of the spectrum. Just warning you to sleep with one eye open."

Well, worst-case scenario, she'd be hitting up one of her fellow motel patrons for a ride—or practicing the advanced flight spell that she hadn't yet nailed. "Thanks, Mike." She left the office, walked to her room, and worked the key into the lock. After some coaxing and jiggling, the bolt yielded with a click. She flipped on the light, smelling copious cleaning products that masked a stale miasma of ancient cigarette smoke.

The room was as expected. A double bed with a faded, thin bedspread occupied most of the room. The dresser supported a microwave and coffee pot, and above the bureau hung a midsize plasma screen television. At the end of the room, a bathroom mirror and sink faced her.

Not glamourous, but not rat infested or trashed, either. No sounds penetrated the walls, so perhaps the partiers and hooligans that Mike had mentioned had blown past and settled on a different flop house. All in all, adequate for a night's sleep. Cynthia threw her backpack on the bed and crashed beside it, staring at a popcorn ceiling as she rubbed an achy upper-body muscle.

First order of business was to freshen up, then study her spell book. If she confirmed her hunch about the location of the two witches, she wasn't about to roll up to them fumbling her way through spells. She'd arrive well-dressed and prepared for the interview, so to speak. She peeled herself off the mattress and went to inspect the bathroom.

The shower was grungy and small, but adequate. A robust stream of hot water washed away the day. After, she rubbed her body dry with a frayed scrap of a towel, taking solace in the blessing of privacy and a decent shower. Cynthia liked to think that her relatively positive disposition had kept her functional in the years since she'd lost her parents.

She and the universe had a deal. She gave thanks and didn't bitch, and in return more blessings manifested. Her nakedness caused mild heebie-jeebies, so she dumped her backpack and pulled a sweatshirt over her head before tugging on some pajama bottoms. The spell book with its leather cover sat among her mundane things, sticking out like an uninvited guest.

Ten years had passed since she'd slipped the tome off a top shelf at a used bookstore and felt the sinister, heady pull of its power. The ladder under her feet had quaked the second she touched the spine, static electricity zapping her fingertips. Her dark little heart had known right then that the words in those pages were written just for her, and she had to have it.

But looking at it still carried the same vaguely scary, forbidden rush as that first day at the bookstore.

She split the book to the section she'd used to chart the locations of the fire and chaos witches. Their respective symbols, a triangle, and a hand with curly fingers, were inked on a page of parchment that was translucent, like tracing paper, one of a few pages made that way.

She pulled her folded map of the United States from the spot where she'd tucked it. After unfolding, she slid the creased map with the worn edges under the translucent paper. Sure enough, the symbols both sat over Los Angeles.

Her strategy could be wrong, but right now it was all she had. "What are you trying to tell me, hm?" She caressed pages as if touch could coax more meaning from the rough pulp beneath her skin, as if answers from the encyclopedia were a mere stroke away. "Do you want me to find my sisters and kick this prophecy into high gear?"

Three knocks on the door made her jump and lose her breath. Adrenaline fizzled across her chest and down to her toes. Jeez. For all of her power, she still hadn't shaken the human impulse to startle. "Yes? May I help you?" In a stupid reflex, she checked to ensure that the flimsy chain lock was engaged. Not like a few inches of cheap metal would keep out anyone who really wanted in.

"Hey there, it's Mike." The voice matched, and his tone was calm. She exhaled. "Thought I'd make a couple of recommendations, in case you're hungry." Three menus slid under the door. "I recommend the pizza place."

She hopped off the bed and stooped to retrieve the slips of paper. One menu had handwritten notes on it. Mike sure was meticulous, Mr. Crossword with a Pen annotating his top food picks. "Thanks."

But as she gathered her lists of dining options, it became clear that the note on the pizza menu had nothing to do with food.

Watch out for the folks who just checked in next door. I can't prove anything, but they don't sit right with me. Your room connects with theirs, so make sure it's locked. I'd push the dresser in front of it if I were you. "Thanks again, Mike. I'll look into this."

"You bet."

Cynthia returned to her bed and scooted against the headboard, hauling the book to her lap, but failed to get into the magical study zone. Shady characters next door, eh? She had no desire to cause a scene or make trouble for Mike or anyone else, but curiosity was already getting the better of her. A peek wouldn't hurt, just to investigate.

The door that joined the two rooms lacked a knob and instead opened with a deadbolt-style latch. She pressed her ear to the wood, making out muted voices. Dropping to the floor to peek under the bottom didn't help, as the crack didn't offer enough space to see more than carpet.

Teeming, jittery, and more than a little juiced by the prospect of an adventure, Cynthia slid on the flip flops that she kept in her backpack. She grabbed her key and the room's plastic ice bucket, tucking her magic book under her arm before stepping out into the night. She never let the book out of her sight, and it stayed on her person if possible.

A quick glance at the office confirmed Mike had his back to her. Good. No need to worry him or rope him into a potential *debacle*. Well-meaning people didn't believe that she was more than capable of fighting her own battles. Cynthia might look like an angel, but she fought like a dirty demon.

Around the bend sat the ice machine, stuck at the end of the row of rooms by the edge of the parking lot. Beyond lay scruffy land, darkness, and the whoosh of the Interstate. Stagnant air spun warm clouds all around her skin, the atmosphere dry and foreboding. This armpit of the L.A. outskirts was creepy, no doubt about it, but the likely proximity of two sister witches and a brush with danger made it exciting.

Bad girl, always looking for trouble. Her mama's voice rang out in the usual way, somehow both loving and brittle with a crust of contempt.

Trouble comes for me eventually, mama. I just hurry it along.

She stuck her bucket under the chute and pushed a button, the rattle and hum of ice production loud enough to draw attention. She loved getting up to shit at night and didn't have to worry anymore who got in her way.

Back before she took off, saying goodbye to life in small-town Missouri and a boring clerical job in favor of witchy pursuits and the nomad's way, she was a regular fixture in girls' nights out. She and her gaggle of girlfriends from work and the gym used to wax philosophical on the things they would do if all men magically disappeared for twenty-four hours. The top choice was wander, alone at night, exploring forests and rural roads and shot-out wastelands of urban decay. Sometimes with headphones in for inspiration.

The bucket filled with frozen chunks, and Cynthia shook it to make more noise in case some son of a bitch was lurking, turned on by the thought of her fear. *Come and get me.*

She liked to think that she was living her best life now, roughing up psychos and stalkers on behalf of those old friends and women everywhere.

No action tonight, however. Night saturated her visibility in both directions, heavy and desolate. She rounded the corner.

A figure dressed from stocking cap to boots in black clothing stood in the middle of the sidewalk, watching. A jolt of excitement pierced her. Raven?

"Hey there." She sauntered closer, her hope sinking when she saw that the features were different. Smaller nose, dimpled chin. Not as stunning as Raven, but eerily handsome. "Nice night."

"We're watching you." He spoke with even smoothness as silver-tongued as the devil. "Following you."

She shoulder-checked him as she passed. "Yeah, that's not creepy at all. Protip. I'd cut that stalker shit out. Hunting me won't end well for you, and I'm not talking about a squirt of drugstore pepper spray. Excuse me."

He grabbed her forearm in a hard clamp, rough enough to startle but not hurt. "Listen. We mean you no harm. Please. Come talk."

She wrenched out of his hold, unable to deny the striking resemblance to Raven. Similar style, build, mannerisms. But she didn't recall this particular person from the restaurant. "What for? I'm not looking to make any new friends."

He smiled like he held the trump card. "That wasn't the case earlier, now was it?"

If he was talking about Raven, why did he care? Unless someone wanted the bike back. "I'll talk to you, but you need to give me some idea what this is about and promise me that I won't end up wrapped in plastic in the trunk of your car."

Never gonna happen, of course, but she wasn't one to show her whole-ass hand when she didn't have to. People gave up more when they thought they held the ultimate advantage. The illusion of free and unencumbered choice was empowering, tricking others into thinking that they could speak and act with impunity.

"I highly doubt it, death dealer."

Her blood ran cold. "What did you just call me?"

"You heard me."

She shook her head. Crap. Was he family of one of the two men she'd killed? Shocking to think that either of those scumbags had kinfolk hell-bent on avenging their murders, but sometimes loyalty ran as deep as arterial blood. "I don't know what you're talking about."

"We want to talk to you about your magic. That's all."

The pale skin of his face was so dewy that it nearly glowed in the night. The man had an ageless, uncanny quality and could have been anywhere between eighteen and fifty depending on the angle. Come to think of it, Raven had a similar aesthetic. "Who's we?"

She'd never taken down multiple adversaries. He wasn't acting hostile or even unsettling, but plenty of people excelled at hiding their intentions. With any luck, they were dealing with a Denise-Nerissa type of psyche splitting situation, or he was a narcissist with a habit of referring to himself with the royal 'we.'

"Come on." He motioned his hand in a scoop. "I'll introduce you."

Well crap. She had to concede that she'd come out to the ice machine in search of more interesting happenings to spice up her night, and now she'd found them. The universe had delivered yet again, ponied up in response to the wishes she'd willed into fruition. "Alright. Nobody better go haywire on me."

"We wouldn't dream of it." He led her to the door adjacent to hers and unlocked.

The room was identical to the one she'd rented, with only a different style of bedspread distinguishing the setups. The two people sitting cross-legged on the bed, a spread of cards arranged in rows between them, captured her focus.

She recognized the cards as the ones from the diner, an a-ha that made her heart jump into her throat. But the individuals were distinct. Similar overall look of gothic androgyny, but not the same faces.

Puzzled, Cynthia turned to the one who'd led her here. "Does the reason why you want to talk to me about magic have anything to do with those cards? Because I have a feeling that they aren't playing Gin Rummy."

Her new friend laughed with light mirth and caught her fingers—cold touch—before leading her into the belly of the room for a closer look. If he got crazy, she'd steal his breath first, hopefully buying enough time to run while prepping a spell for the other two. But nobody was acting malevolent. The card players were rapt, like she was invisible.

Speaking of invisibility, that was another cool magic trick that she could pull of with relative ease, but that was an issue for another day.

"Watch carefully," her new friend whispered. "The game play."

The individual with their back to her, black cape trailing off the bed, turned over cards with a brown hand. The images on the cards were weirdly unknowable, words in some other language paired with crude color drawings of people, animals, and symbols. The opposite sides were painted with a coating of red gloss. Some tiny symbol in the center finished the design.

The cape wearer flipped another with deliberate precision. The illustrated side showed a buff, shirtless man with at least five animal heads. Wolf. Bear. Bird. Snake. Nature imagery filled the background: trees and a brook. Both the sun and the moon hung in the sky.

She clamped her teeth together to stop her jaw from going dumbstruck slack. What she wouldn't give to look through these cards for patterns and meaning.

Her brain was kicking with strategies for how to get them to agree to let her take pictures when the person opposite the cape-wearer changed. Their features morphed, back and forth, back and forth, cycling between a few humans and the animals in the picture. When the process halted, a brand new person sat on the bed.

Cynthia turned to the man who'd led here here. "That's remarkable. But I don't understand how I fit in."

"Let me call Raven." He walked to the motel room door, opened it, and stuck two fingers in his mouth. An eardrum-melting whistle sliced the air. "He needs to be here when we discuss your magic and its role in the Deck of Deceit."

FOUR

COMING FACE-TO-FACE AGAIN WITH QUICKIES AND ONE-NIGHT-STANDS was always weird, but watching a former lover fly straight towards her was downright shocking. Cynthia really needed to rethink her jaded stance on having seen it all.

Raven's feathered form cut a path through the night, swooping over the parking lot until he stopped at the threshold of his companions' room. He hung in midair, flapping wings that spanned so wide they nearly touched the cars flanking them, before descending to the ground and transforming to a man. He had on different clothes, a Henley the color of ash and dark jeans, both fitted to show off his ropes of lean muscle.

She cleared her throat, bemused and intrigued and a little embarrassed. Here was a prospective second-round hookup looking the portrait of a music video fallen angel while she stood before him in her ugliest sweats. "Good to see you again." She meant it, he was fine as hell. But as the events of the last several hours played through her mind, irritation set in. "You knew about my magic and followed me. Or had me followed. Not cool. Tell me what's going on."

"I can explain." He breezed into the room and looked her in the eye, his scent evoking a memory both erotic and oddly tender. He took up space, commanding, sucking out ambient oxygen to leave a vacuum in his wake. "There's a line of connectivity linking our magic, and we might be able to help you find what you're after." Raven pointed to the man in the hat who'd blocked her path by the ice machine. "This is Ether."

Ether waved hello.

Raven gestured to the bed. "That's Portia in the cape."

"Check this out." Portia flipped her hood down to reveal a short, black bob. She turned a card over, and her hair turned blue and curly. "Stick with us and you can be whoever you want, whenever you want. It's a tight skill."

"The other person on the bed is Dragon," Raven said.

"Sup," Dragon said, immersed in the cards.

The shifter goth crew all seemed super nice, but still. What the actual fuck. Cynthia tossed everyone a friendly nod before turning to Raven. "There is absolutely no way that you're done explaining."

Ether ambled to the bed to join Portia and Dragon, and soon all three were lost to the cards, offering a cursory scrap of privacy.

"No. I'm not. The four of us have been on the road for a long time, looking for others of our kind. We heard a rumor that there might be a shifter colony in Mexico, and we were all set to cross the border tomorrow and start roaming when Portia finds the Deck of Deceit and changes the game completely."

Hm. Sounded like quite the convenient development. Nobody in the room raised red flags, but if any situation called for healthy skepticism and an application of scrutiny, it was this one. "What do you mean, she found it?" That could mean anything, from petty theft to a claim laid by force.

Cynthia didn't need complications or drama and wasn't terribly keen on random acts of altruism, which was why she didn't ask Raven follow-up questions about his lead on more shifters. He might be thinking of the community in Peru, but she sure didn't trust his group enough to lead them there. She'd left great friendships behind in the jungle and cared about those folk deeply, even though she didn't talk to them anymore. Let these four weirdos run off to Mexico on a wild shifter chase. So what if one of them made her blood boil with desire.

Raven claimed her hand above the wrist, the pad of his thumb sending a pleasurable zing to the pulse point where her veins crossed like blue ley lines. His touch sure set her off, no denying that fact. "Nothing shady. She traded some books and a bag of crystals for it. The previous owner had no idea what those cards could do, and neither did we."

Equations assembled. The cards worked in accord with other magic. For that fact alone, they were not to be ignored. "Were you all able to shift before Portia got the cards?"

"Yes. Into one animal aspect each. That's how we found each other, through an underground meet-up. Our kind are out there, but most of us are scattered."

With Portia and Dragon still engaged, the woman's cloak gone in favor of a dress whose train flowed onto the cheap comforter in a river of crimson sequins, Cynthia took a stab at pinpointing their backstory, "You experimented with the cards, and they enhanced your powers. Augmented them. Which is why those two are over there cosplaying Jessica Rabbit one minute and *The Crow* the next."

Raven smirked his intoxicating, infuriating, bedroom smirk. "I'd argue that I get to be *The Crow*."

She glared at him, but some contradictory affect must've leaked, because he licked his bottom lip. "You aren't funny."

"Sorry." The satisfaction on his face spelled out more flirtation than remorse. "I thought that levity might be appreciated."

"Well, it wasn't. This is heavy as hell. You guys should not be playing around with magical artifacts like you can experiment willy-nilly. This stuff is dangerous and real, like a Ouija board but ten times more powerful. Those cards over there are *not* toys."

"I realize that. We feel qualified to use them, based on our research so far, but you're correct that we need guidance. The tutelage of an experienced witch, to be precise, is crucial for mapping the connection between shifting and elemental magic. That connection is there, and we're going to find it one way or the other and set the next phase this prophecy in motion."

She reeled like she'd been punched. "How do you know about the prophecy?"

Raven pointed to the spread, which now occupied the majority of the mattress. "It's all in there. Those cards. The Coven Daughters Prophecy is all over the fringes of the Internet, and we've cross-referenced those findings with the symbols in the cards and parsed what's true."

"Yeah, okay, I guess. Congrats on successful trolling sessions of Reddit's conspiracy sub, but I'm not convinced that you should be doing any of what you're doing. Not one single iota. I've been studying magic for ten years and much of it is still lost on me. Just when you think you've got the upper hand on this system, it catches up to you. And not to throw you a surprise party."

Raven's eyes burned as dark as coal embers. "I know. That's where you come in."

The burdensome honor of tremendous responsibility both elevated and sunk her. "You want me to be the witch advisor to your team."

"Precisely."

"Why me? We had a great time and all, but what tipped you off about who I am?"

He put on that lopsided smile of his, like her secrets lived in a glass palace and he stood at the threshold with a stone in hand. "The keys to the bike. It was a test."

Ugh. Had she been played? No. That never happened. Who did this guy think he was? "You're full of shit."

"Not at all. The yellow charm with the number and the moon on it? I made it. That wasn't a phone number. Come see." He took her hand and led her to the bed, making her nostalgic for what she'd assumed had been a simple, uncomplicated fuck. No such luck. A saga involving Raven was unfolding, and as kooky as it was, she couldn't bring herself to back away.

For hadn't she been searching for a fresh round of excitement in her life and lamenting a lack of experiences that *moved* her? As always, the universe had read her subconscious like a picture book and delivered, albeit not how she'd anticipated.

The cards were arranged artfully before her in crisp shapes of geometrical symmetry, an esoteric tapestry of hidden meaning both frightening and wonderful. A wellspring of potential threatened to erupt into madness. She could feel their subtle power as a dark undercurrent of pulsations. "What am I looking at here?"

Raven plucked a card and held it up. A chaotic portend of artwork damn near slapped her. A golden disc of a moon blew a gust of wind over a starry sky, and below the firmament lay a river that forked beside a tree with a snake coiling up its trunk. A white-eyed apparition stood between the streams, a fire burning at her bare feet.

This was easily the most disquieting image that Cynthia had looked at during her study of the craft. She probably wasn't supposed to be looking at the picture and would face some repercussion large or small for her transgression. Yet for all of its cursed creepiness, the picture was maddeningly meaningless. "I'm not connecting the dots."

"Look closer." He pressed his hand against her lower back, the thrill of that territorial, protective touch compounding the charge of supernatural mojo in the room.

She leaned forward and saw greater clarity in the illustration. In the cloud that burst from the moon face's puffed cheeks, numbers were hidden. The numbers on the key chain. She'd memorized Raven's number, which shamed her to admit but was a shortcut to getting the gist. "How?" She fought for her words. This was heavy-duty synchronicity in play. "How did you know to give it to me?"

"I just knew." His inflection was so sincere. He regarded her with a long look that penetrated to her marrow. "When I looked at you, I knew that you were the chosen one to guide us. The exalted witch. And once I got back inside the restaurant, I pulled this very card. So my clairvoyance was confirmed, and I knew that I couldn't let you go."

Never having been all that great with responsibility, Cynthia pinched the bridge of her nose. She'd once had furniture repossessed for non-payment. How was she supposed to teach anyone anything? And what about Denise-Nerissa? Should she alert the body jumper to this new development, or do the opposite and stay mum? "Jesus Christ."

"He is not a party to this situation," Ether interjected.

"Leave them alone," Portia whispered.

Raven laid slow, gentle hands on her outer arms, prompting her to stop touching her face. She wasn't entirely sure about him, but she wanted to keep looking at him. Keep feeling the way she felt when he looked at her. "I know this is a lot. But there are so few of us, and we're crucial to this prophecy. There are thousands, millions maybe, tirelessly researching to piece this thing together before the universe goes holographic and all earthlings end up in feeder pods for the Other Ones.

But we have the shortcuts. The keys." He pointed to the cards on the bed. "There." He touched two fingers to the left side of her chest, right over her heartbeat, his stare beating with the intensity of a separate heart of passion. "And in here." He tapped her sternum twice.

She got dizzy. It was all too much, too fast. The room spun, a stuffy and confined space choked with odd people orchestrating occult mysteries. Raven burning into her soul. Touching her. Her knees were too soft, loose. "Excuse me. I need some air." She pushed past him and out into the night, where deep breaths wrapped her in a safe haven.

Once outside, she paced, using movement in a futile effort to corral racing thoughts. Attraction to Raven notwithstanding, there was a benefit to having allies. To not going at her mission alone. They knew things. They cared. Projects worked better when folks put their heads together, assuming that her co-conspirators weren't planning to kill her in her sleep.

The door clicked shut. "I know this is a lot." Raven stepped in front of her. "And I don't expect you to roll over and accept everything that's been thrown at you today. But it's my firm belief that the most important thing we can do is stick together."

"Where did you fly off to after you gave me your bike?" She looked him up and down as if the appraisal would uncover buried truths. Given his stoicism, she suspected that her interrogation wouldn't crack much new ground.

"Scouting. I map territory through flight. Assess the grid systems of locales, highway and street patterns, and building layouts. A lot of information comes from above."

Admittedly, what he described sounded like a skill they could use when searching for the witches in Los Angeles. No doubt Raven could cover large swaths of territory quickly in his avian form, spying on people if need be. "That's how you knew I was headed here."

"Yeah. More or less."

"Why didn't you show me the cards at the restaurant and explain then?"

"Too conspicuous. The waitress was already asking questions, and if we drew someone else into our orbit, she might not forget. That's a problem. We want to be forgotten, like spirits vanishing into the night."

"Tall order. You're awfully memorable."

"You'd be surprised what people are willing to write off from those who are just passing through. But once a fleeting moment begins to resemble a conspiracy, people get invested and aren't inclined to forget."

She chanced a glance at the office, where Mike's back was turned. "You're already all over the manager's radar. So am I."

"That's how it goes. We need to leave tonight. The longer we stay, the more liable he is to fixate. And once he does, he's a problem. Once we're the subject of rumors and even local lore, discretion becomes near impossible. At that point, people get in our way."

Okay. Valid. With one topic of concern squared away, the reason for her irritation flared. "So why did you have sex with me at the truck stop, if you're all about discretion? Everyone there knew what we did."

And he was looking at her again with that way of his that made her feel both tiny and big. "Because I wanted you, and you wanted me. You're irresistible, so I didn't resist. Sometimes a risk is worth taking."

The temperature notched up a few degrees, hot wind from the canyons animating his lazy waves while those same breezes licked her skin. "Is that how you court all potential witch advisers?"

"No. I saw you. I wanted you, and I had you. Simple as that."

"Do you respond to lots of people that way?"

"No. I don't."

She respected the straightforward approach, and how somehow, paradoxically, his choosing her for a fast tryst made her feel special. One corner of her mouth bent up.

He returned the tick of lips, silent recognition passing between them. But she wasn't about to let her guard down just yet, no matter how hot the stranger and cool the paranormal ability. "I'm still not totally sold on you guys. If all you want is to get to the shifter colony, why do you care about the Coven Daughters Prophecy? Y'all don't strike me as the good Samaritan sorts. No offense."

"None taken. We aren't."

Possible lie detected. "Yet you said that you wanted to support the Coven Daughters Prophecy in order to save the world."

"Not exactly."

"Then what, exactly?" If she was going to form an alliance with these four, she'd settle for nothing less than full transparency. A pang of guilt twisted her. If she demanded openness from Raven while holding back what she knew about Peru, that made her a hypocrite. But that was a problem for future Cynthia. "What's at stake for you?"

His gaze zeroed in on the bright splash of light cast off by the office, and she stole a peek. Mike still had his back turned but was now standing and rummaging in a cabinet.

Raven pointed in the direction of the ice machine, and Cynthia walked over there with him. The spot felt totally different now, colored by the character of recent events. The motel wasn't a seedy opportunity to find senseless trouble anymore, it was a breeding ground for possibility. A possible doorway to the new life she sought, a life with her sisters.

"I'm waiting." She shocked herself with the comment. Cynthia had never waited for a man, ever. Not for anything. Not to notice her. Never to prioritize her, impress her, or bestow his blessing upon her. To surprise her? Absurd. Until now.

"Stopping the onset of the holographic universe will usher in a new reign of magic. That's why they want to pull this off so bad. To contain us, use us, channel our abilities for their own ends. But if we can subvert them? It's our time. The entire dynamic of the world will change when we make ourselves known and have strength in numbers. World leaders will lose the ability to intimidate the masses and oppress their populations. We'll form councils and governments and independent civilizations. We've already started, in Latin America. Think of the possibilities. For peace. Kinship. Family. Have you ever felt like you truly fit in? Belonged, anywhere?"

Of course not, but that wasn't the point. He was selling this too hard. "Who's 'they?'"

"I'm not entirely sure yet. A cabal working tirelessly to harness magic for their own greedy ends. To become god-like or channel the old gods in some possession ritual to assume their power, we think. There may be front companies involved. Entire industries, even. It's big. Our enemies have operatives on the ground everywhere."

"That doesn't sound good."

"It's not. But if we work together, we can stop the plan before any more life is lost."

"What's in it for you? Personally?"

"I want to reach my full potential. Find my place."

Incomplete. "There's more."

He radiated an aura that filled the darkness. Void black orbited around him. Outer space black, shadows stretching into phantom wings. "There is. They captured and killed my family during one of their rituals to siphon off our power. Ritually extinguished them. I escaped."

Her chest caved in. Vengeance was a powerful motivator, and one that clouded. Those seeking revenge tended to stop at nothing to get it, even when safety and good sense demanded a different course. She should know. Her taste for revenge had smeared two permanent stains on her soul. Now, however, wasn't the time to subject Raven to the saga. Not when it behooved her to hold back while she figured him out. "I'm sorry for your loss. I lost my parents, too."

The pain had dulled over the years, but not faded entirely. She could only imagine what Raven had gone through, and what he was going through all over again as he rehashed his pain.

"I'm sorry." He brushed her index finger with his. "What happened?"

"Car accident. Total freak thing. They were at an intersection, and a bus was coming their way. Its brakes failed, at that was it."

The sympathy in his expression crushed her. This man had such a sincere energy about him. Authentic, even though he didn't let emotions flow freely. "We can find our spirit family, Cynthia. Together. That's what they call the clan. Spirit kin. The more of us that congregate together, the stronger our powers become. And, as you likely know, we're going to need that power soon."

Perhaps at some point she'd clue him and his friends in about Peru, but now wasn't the time. Not yet. She needed a little more time to observe him, study him, run him through her tests before certifying him. He'd help her find these witches in Los Angeles, however, if there were witches to locate in the City of Angels. She was certain. Raven would not stop or give up. And if he showed a nefarious side, she'd cut him out like a tumor and go right back to her solo quest. She didn't need him, but he could help her. Overall, she was in an advantageous position. "Deal." She stuck out her hand.

When he shook, firm and warm, his gaze nearly made her shiver. In that moment, Cynthia knew with stark certainty that she'd have to keep her wits close beside her so as not to succumb to this beguiling man's spell.

FIVE

THE DOOR CONNECTING THE ROOMS HUNG OPEN, CREATING AN unguarded camaraderie. Dragon and Ether passed in a blur of black and gray capped by Dragon's cherry-red shock of hair. They chatted about exits and gas stations and other travel logistics, with Cynthia finding solace in the presence of people. After spending years on her own, the company of others was a pleasant break from solitude's grind.

She stuffed a tank top in her backpack while Portia folded clothes and placed them in an old-fashioned suitcase protected by a hard shell. Was Portia cautious like she was, forced by circumstance to grow a rigid rind of armor? "How long have y'all been traveling?" Cynthia asked.

Her relationship with the shifters might end up being temporary like the rest of what she'd shared with people over the last several years, but it still made for good vibes to have conversation and get to know folks better.

The other woman packed a pair of tall boots. She had one of those funky, eclectic styles that Cynthia envied for the creativity involved. She'd never branched out much beyond go-anywhere casuals and sturdy athletic wear. Stuff designed to travel well and withstand abuse.

"Let me check." Portia pursed her full, ruby-stained lips and pulled a battered journal from her things. She flipped pages. "Damn. It's been fifteen months now."

Down the line, she might ask Portia a question or two about Raven, but it would be too obvious to plunge in without a proper social lubricant or opportunity. She wasn't really the "gossip about boys" sort anyway and hated to think that the others might dismiss her interest in them as rooted in a crush-based ulterior motive. "The first couple of years are the hardest. Where are you from originally?"

Portia looked off into space, her features softening wistfully. "Ohio. The worst part of all this is living the lie, you know? My parents and brothers think that I moved to Montana for a nursing job. I call them once a month with fake updates. It kills me but worrying them would hurt worse." She closed her suitcase with a definitive click.

"I'm sorry. Are you a nurse?" Talk about a useful skill.

"Yeah. Trauma. If you take a bullet and end up with a gaping wound, I'm your girl."

Duly noted.

Cynthia sat on the bed, the ancient mattress creaking as it caved beneath her bottom. She pulled her pack over before sliding it on. "Does your family know what you can do? The shifting, I mean, not patching up flesh holes."

She shook her head, offering a polite chuckle at the quip. "I was the only person I'd ever met who could do this, who had an animal aspect. Felt like a freak my whole life until I met those three goobers in the other room. I wonder where the rest of our kin are. Other shifters, you know? It's so weird that there's this small number of shifters and those who want to capture and kill us. There have to be more out there."

A weight settled in Cynthia's ribs that might as well have been as large as Peru's land mass. "You'll find them."

"What are you going to do when you find the other two witches?"

Following an in-grouping wink, Cynthia said, "I guess I'll explain to them who the four of you are and why I let y'all talk me into advising you."

Portia smiled in a way that made her look younger, girlish, which in turn had Cynthia wondering about the female shifter's actual age. Mid-twenties, probably, around the age that Cynthia was when she came into her new identity.

Ether poked his head through the doorway, icy blond spikes of hair sticking out in every direction. Had he morphed, or had she just not noticed his hair? This crew was a trip. "Ready?"

Portia pulled on a strap that crossed her front until a blue velvet purse rested against her stomach. She pulled out a few crumpled bills. "Shit. You guys got any more cash?"

Ether shook his head. "Not till we hit L.A. and can start hustling. Is there enough left for a shitty hostel, even?"

"Nope." She turned to Cynthia. "You up for squat camping on the beach?"

For now, she'd keep the money magic secret, at least while the situation was not an emergency. Ether sounded confident about the prospect of hustling, and she could earn her keep doing simple magic tricks for passersby on the boardwalk if she had to. "Sure. Sounds fun."

"I dig your adventurous spirit." Portia cased the room with a panoramic glance before nodding at Ether. She afforded Cynthia another friendly expression. "You're gonna fit in great with us."

Cynthia hadn't heard a variance on that theme more than a couple of times in her life. Never got old. "I can hustle, too, if we need to scrape up petty cash. Do parlor trick type stuff."

The possibilities of air magic to promote levitation and flight were bountiful, and Cynthia had gotten creative in her harnessing of the gift. Even a basic gimmick like making everyday objects float in the air was perceived as stunningly unusual enough to draw a crowd and part them from their money.

Ether looked mildly interested. "Cool." He vanished into the adjacent room.

When Cynthia crossed the threshold, Portia in tow, she spotted Raven leaned against the wall with his stare glued to his phone. He ran a finger over the screen, totally enraptured. She watched him for a bit while Portia and Ether went outside. He was more than handsome, more than brooding. Raven exceeded space. Overflowed. One of those people who was too much, who spilled out of themselves, a rogue who resisted categorization. One who begged to be known and possessed.

"This message board poster," he muttered. "I think he might be leaving clues as to the location of the shifters. But I can't figure out why he'd construct a cipher, or if this is even real."

At any moment he could find what he was looking for and slip through her fingers before she'd even really gotten a chance to touch him. After all, he was built to literally fly away. She could give him what he wanted. *I know where they are.* "Yeah, there's a lot of misinformation on those pages."

He tucked his phone in his back pocket, an impressive feat given the tightness of his pants. "You ready?"

To camp with him on the beach and with any luck instigate a second encounter of the passionate sort? Hell yes. Not that she'd let herself seem too eager. "Ready as I'll ever be."

He started walking to the exit. "You want the bike?"

"Up to you. It's cool if you want it back. Did Portia and the others ride together?"

"Yeah." He pointed to a boat of a Cadillac whose hubcaps shone in the glow of one lone streetlight. Ether sat behind the wheel, Portia riding shotgun. Dragon got in the back and slammed the door. The immanent prospect of riding off into the night with this pack of misfits made her giddy with anticipation of new mysteries. "Plenty of room for you in there." Raven looked back at her, his mouth tilted with a subtlety nearly impossible to catch. "Unless you wanna ride with me. Front or back, either way's fine."

Her breath hitched. A spark danced over her midsection. His totally innocuous comment sounded dirty, given what they'd done and were apparently ignoring and not talking about. The duration of the remaining ride would offer prime time for private conversation. "I'll ride with you. I could go for a break from driving."

"Works for me." He mounted up as she tried not to stare at the scrumptious picture of his lithe body draped over the machine, its sculpted metal curves contrasting his lean, long legs and flowing hair, his fingers wrapped with confidence around the handlebars. "Hop on."

She was busy trying to pretend that she wasn't already red hot and ready to hop on to something more satisfying than a motorcycle when she remembered an important end to tie. "I have to turn in my key. Be right back."

A quick jog across the pavement led her back to Mike's post. But he wasn't at his desk, though his computer glowed, and a sheet of paper sat beside the keyboard. She set the key on the counter and was about to ring the bell when she heard him speak.

"I appreciate it. It's the interest payments and late fees that are killing me here. I'll catch up next month."

Her throat thickened. She glimpsed at the paper, a hefty credit card bill. Memoires of her folks having similar conversations with creditors barraged her.

Mike came out, looking buoyant in the wake of his financial victory. She was happy to see not one trace of shame. There was no shame in being poor—fuck those predatory lenders. "Bills, bills, bills. Maybe next month this place will finally give me that raise. I've only been here for fifteen years, loyal as a damn dog." He took the key and speared it on a wall hook. "You're leaving soon. Did somebody bother you?"

Little did Mike know that she was leaving with the alleged bad elements. "No. I just caught up with my sisters faster than I thought. Everything was great."

"Alrighty then. Let me get your receipt."

She began to decline, then bit back her words upon seeing an open checkbook beside Mike's credit card bill. "Thanks."

He swirled a mouse on the track pad, making an old printer buzz and clunk. Mike walked to it and watched a piece of paper lurch out inch by inch.

She whipped out her phone, working fast to bring up the setting to turn down effects noises. After sliding the dial to silent, she leaned over the counter and snapped a shot of one of his checks.

"Here you go." Mike turned around just as she jammed her phone in her pocket. "Safe travels." He handed over the printout.

"Take care. Hope you have some good financial luck coming your way soon."

Unbeknownst to Mike, he wouldn't have to hope.

He chuckled. "Hey, thanks. I need all the luck I can get."

Say no more. She left the office and ducked behind a tree, pulling up the picture of his check and concentrating on it until the account and routing numbers took root in the part of her brain that plugged in to the realm of magic. She didn't understand why her brain connected to that ethereal, ancient place and other brains didn't. Maybe someday she'd be illuminated, maybe not.

This was why gambling on the other witches felt like the right bet.

While Cynthia breathed, she dropped her inhale and exhale pattern into a low, slow state. After a while, her head went fuzzy, and she became nothing but breath flow. Air, pure air essence, moved in and out with no flesh to constrain. The next step was to put magic on the exhale and use it as a vector, a magic carpet to deliver cash to its destination with a speed that put Venmo to shame.

She dug deep and plummeted to the other place, her descent marked by a steep drop in equilibrium as she fell through space and time on her trip through layered dimensions of light and shadow. Stability came, clouds leaving her eyes to give way to clear perspective.

The magic realm changed every time, and on this particular occasion, she found herself in the middle of a prairie. A few feet in front, grasses as tall as her full height swayed, hypnotizing her with their wind song calls.

What do you seek, child? The air asked in a breezy, androgynous voice apropos to its fickle and fungible nature. Once upon a time, things had been rockier with the magic-giver. But they'd been all good since Cynthia chose the Left-Hand path.

"Money." She stroked the fuzzy brown tip of a cat tail plant. "For another who is in need."

"The Other Ones are coming." The statement echoed through the grass as a glib taunt.

Her extremities chilled, the ominous comment shaking her resolve. In her ten years of practice, she'd never heard the magic-giver reference the fabled horde of demons who teemed somewhere beyond the veil, trapped and subdued by spell walls. Those fiends were legends, maybe even fake, relegated to the pages of her tome. Why had they come up now? Best to ignore the threat. Maybe the moon phase or some other astrological event had the capricious magic-giver feeling punchy.

Sweet aromas of sunbaked wildflowers filled her nostrils as she concentrated on her breathing pattern, guiding herself back to her goal.

Soon, her exhale took on shape and texture, shimmering like heat waves over blacktop. "Please send my chosen sum to the destination of one who needs." She conjured a big number and linked the string of integers and commas to Mike's checking account digits.

"You witches." A bitter chuckle. "You take and take and take, never giving back. Soon there will be no more to take, and we will have to take from you."

What the hell was this all about? Magic was her birthright, or so she'd assumed. Payment and giving back had never come up before. "What do you want?"

She listened closely, but only the rustle of leaves struck her eardrums. On the horizon, sunlight brushed the sky a milky blue.

Finally, an answer came. "Folly requires that your collective debt be paid in blood."

Her heart rate kicked up to a fast clip that bumped in her ears. This was a new development. She'd never heard of a stipulation that the elemental sister governing chaos magic wielded that much power in the system. Of course, the supposition could be a bluff. The magic-given had bluffed before for whatever cryptic reason. "Whose blood?"

"Depends."

"On what?"

The stalks near her toes bent against unseen movement. A slinky tube of muddy colors undulated toward her. Pits of black eyes, lance-shaped head—the rattlesnake from the side of the road.

Creepy, but she gathered her cool. "You again. And accosting me in nature this time. Big Garden of Eden energy."

The serpent laughed and spoke in the same voice as the magic-giver, "Clever reference, but you're no Eve, my dear."

Hard to infer from the dry, savvy tone if that was an insult or a compliment. "Meaning what?"

"You already know."

"As in I know why I'm not Eve? Or that I'm unlike her because I have knowledge where she started out innocent?"

"Both."

Um, okay. Not helpful. "Why are you here?"

"Because you're getting closer to your sister, the chaos born, and you guessed correctly that she will present through the snake. Once you find her, collaborate to make your blood sacrifice. Your gift shall appease Folly for a time. If you fail to choose a sacrifice, then Sister Folly will choose for you, or allow the Other Ones free reign."

Every drop of moisture leached from Cynthia's mouth. Heavy, disturbing energy filled her mind. "You just said that when it comes to whose blood is spilled, it depends. Now you're saying I have to choose."

"Good girl. You listen well."

She scowled at the curved length of scales and muscle staring up at her from its low station in the dirt. Ironic, how such a low born thing flexed power on her, a powerful witch, like the dumb, squashable reptile was some kind of dragon. "That doesn't make any sense."

"Such is the nature of chaos and the will of Sister Folly, my darling of the air. Eventually, we all have to pay." The snake crumbled into chunks of mottled flesh, then a delicate lattice of blanched bone, then a fine mist of ash to complete the rapid decomposition.

Shaken but not spooked, Cynthia returned her focus to the money spell. At least her impending effort was rooted in altruism. The chaos snake was wrong. She wasn't wantonly taking from a place of greed. She was using magic to help others. There was a chance that the visiting serpent was toying with her, too, misdirecting for one hidden reason or another. Random, inexplicable stuff happened in the magic realm. That was just how things worked, with occult matters often hidden behind a thick veil of secrecy that Cynthia might never shred.

She might never fully grasp the entirety of how magic operated, but she was able to use it for good. So, she did.

Concentrating, pulling, gathering, she drew up the energy that pulsed in the legendary place and set it on her breath. Once the force was there, she called upon her memory to snag Mike's checking account number and the amount intended for him and rested those figures on top of the magic wave. She inhaled until her lungs burned with fullness, held her breath until the edge of a blackout crept close, and blew.

Cool relief coursed through her as the air spell shot through the magic realm and pierced the barrier to the everyday world, sending a big deposit to Mike's bank. A flash of numbers in her mind along with a vision of his name and the name of the bank confirmed arrival.

Dizzy and lightheaded in the wake of the spell, she shook off unease and brought herself back to the motel lot. Tree bark scratched her back, the night engulfing her in its dense glimmer. Ozone tinged the air, and the temperature had dropped a few degrees. A bright blotch flashed far off in the sky. A storm was coming. Time to move.

She jogged to where Raven waited on the motorcycle.

He revved the engine, making it roar and rumble. "Settled up?"

Time moved differently on the magic plane. Her trip there had felt like fifteen minutes, but in the everyday world probably amounted to fewer than five. Just as well. She didn't feel compelled to open up to Raven. She answered with motion, throwing her leg over the bike and maneuvering into position, surprised at how strong and solid the back of his body was. All muscle, compact and efficient.

Made her wonder what his torso looked like nude, how that skin-on-skin sensation would make her feel, as she looped her arms around the firm front of him.

"Here." He nudged her arm with a helmet that he'd procured from presumably the car.

"Do you have a spare?"

"Nope."

"What about you?"

"I can shift in time if something happens."

She canted her head, awash in skepticism and affection. "So why wear one at all?"

"I don't tempt fate."

She slid the hard shell over her skull, foam padding making for a snug fit. "You're missing out."

A silky wave of his hair tickled her cheek, seductively teasing. "You're a lot. Has anyone ever told you that?"

"Frequently."

He turned his head to the front of their ride, but not before she caught him bite his bottom lip.

She grinned stupidly under her face shield, confident that he wasn't able to see her leak of girlish delight in the attention that he paid to her, and in his gesture of care.

The motorcycle's machinery unleashed a big groan of readiness as he spurred the metal steed to life, gasoline fumes blooming into a smelly fog all around her. She loved that smell. It reminded her of warm summer nights out in the country. High on nostalgia mixed with the enjoyment of the moment, she burrowed into him a little deeper.

They got moving, sliding down the dark tunnel of highway, taillights of the Cadillac glinting off his handlebars.

She would have been content to stay in comfortable silence, lulled by the motor and the romantic monotony of the lost highway, when Raven dropped a bomb. "Once we're on the beach, show me how to travel to the source of magic."

She pretended not to hear him. How had he known?

SIX

THE OCEAN WAS ACTIVE, ITS WATERY TONGUES LICKING THE SHORELINE in big laps as night-black swells rolled in at a fast pace to suggest an impending storm. A melody of crashes carried moonlight glimmers on the crests of waves. An auspicious night to set up camp and hunker down for spell work was upon them. The energy was fertile and wet. Sister water was present. Cynthia pressed the full weight of her heel into a tent peg, staking plastic into pliant sand with one satisfying penetration.

Raven had disappeared into their second tent immediately after he and Ether had erected it, dropping the issue of his interest in learning about her magic source. He could have his space for now, but she didn't intend to let that topic die. How had he known, through telepathy? She'd get to the bottom of enigmatic Raven and his connection to her soon. But for now, she relaxed and enjoyed the air's cooling strokes over her skin. The presence of her element moved through her and all around.

Voracious winds styled the loose strands of her hair into a chaotic frenzy. She loved the feel of breezes, their playful power to shape matter to their will, and how in this place they brought to her notes of brine and fish. Sister air was afoot, dancing with water.

Awash in the joy of her senses and pride in her task, she crouched to check the tent's fixture. Tight and sturdy, securing their tent to its spot abutting a cliff.

A few feet away, Portia and Ether tugged straps on the larger tent, affixing the doorway open. Dragon, who had a fire going several feet away, poked a stick into a pile of kindle topped by a healthy dollop of orange flame.

"You two need any help?" Cynthia called over a whistling breeze.

"Nah." Portia turned to the waters; her profile serene. "I figure that we'll rest for a bit, then take the cards to the fire for a session. I'd hate to pass up an opportunity to work with you give how we have all of the elements at our disposal. That alright?"

Earth, fire, air, and water were the only obvious ones that were hanging around. The comments about elements at their disposal, serving their whims, struck her as somewhat arrogant, but she let her worry slide away in the beachside breezes. "What about spirit and chaos?"

Portia said nothing. Cynthia's heart skipped over itself, trepidation quickly turning to interest. After all, why was she here if not to experiment with witchcraft and make forward progress? The magic-giver's ramblings about too much taking had fucked with her head, but she wasn't about to shrink into cowardice after years of bold, unapologetic practice.

The metallic whiz of a zipper gave way to Raven exiting the bigger tent, ducking to clear the arched doorway. He had a small object in his hand as he strode to her in big, direct steps. "Can I show you something?"

"What's up?"

His hand found its way to her lower back again, the touch sending her soaring more than it had any right to. In under a minute, they were alone in the smaller tent. Anticipation jumped around in her middle. Of course, he wasn't talking about sex, but her dirty mind was stubborn.

Raven zipped up the entrance, both layers, shadows made by nearby flames dancing on the walls of their cave. He motioned for her to sit and found a cross-legged seat himself. Waves roared behind them as if excited, in on some scheme. "The entire prophecy is hidden in these cards. I'm positive. Your role is to help us divine it. We need to get as far in front of this as we can before we head out there and start doing spell work to find our witches and shifters."

She was more than a little hurt that Raven just wanted to talk shop and had no amorous intent. Such moping was childish and stupid, however. They'd shared no more than a fast release, a physical escape. No different than when she'd banged some guy she worked with and gone right back to being friends with him afterword. A tight sensation in her chest stayed with her as she watched him pull the deck from its battered box and assemble a layout between them. He was literally constructing a barrier. "Sure." The word came out harder than she wanted.

"Great." He distributed more cards in a pattern known only to him.

No mooning over quickies. She'd never indulged such feeble irrationality before. "I take it that you set them down intuitively, since you aren't using any kind of booklet or guide?"

His fierce stare snapped up to her, the sheer potency fixing her in stasis. "Is there a better way?"

This was the first time that Raven had asked her advice, consulted her, and she welcomed the transition into whatever collaborative territory they suddenly inhabited. "I'm not sure. I've never seen cards like this before, let alone touched them. But I'm willing to try a reading and see if my magic influences or informs the messages in any way. If I'm supposed to be advising you with these, I should probably at least handle them and get a feel for their energy."

With magician's grace, he swept rows of rectangles into a single stack. "Any fix on the odds of consequences?"

"Oh, probably high," she deadpanned. "But we aren't here to play it safe and be risk averse, are we?"

He winked, a tiny eyelid kiss joining the outer corners of his eyelashes. "Hey, we used protection last time."

She heard a dumb noise burst from her lips. Her cheeks heated. Must've been Dragon's fire. Not a crush stirring, please no.

"I meant the helmet. Clean up your mind." He extended his hand, offering the card deck in what felt like a gesture of kinship and trust. Or maybe she was thinking wishfully.

"Sure you did." She snatched the heavy paper stock, an ache made of

smutty thoughts taking root between her legs. The ocean, the fire...
they'd sure have a helluva backdrop, in this primal setting. But he was
right. They had work to do and a track to stay on. "I'm going to flow
through this and follow my instinct, calling upon my magic for
guidance."

She split the deck, bent each half with a thumb, and released her
stacks to the full fall of accordion sounds. Delighted by the juicy smack
of air against cardboard, physical and unseen colliding under the force of
the universe, she shuffled.

Raven watched. She watched him watch, unable to ignore the bulge
to the left of his zipper.

"Talismans." He shifted his hips. "Charms and objects. There are
hints here and there about members of the prophesized coven enhancing
their powers through use of personal objects."

Cynthia cut the cards again, forming an ephemeral intimacy with the
peculiar heft of their paper, how they were denser than typical Tarot or
playing cards. Worn and smooth to the touch, these babies were
softened from use. She wondered by whom, in whose hands, and in
whose rooms and homes they'd lived. If those same users had touched
the stiffened parchment inside of her book. "The theory being that my
magic binds to these cards?"

"Could be. Or the keychain supplied the link between the cards and
your magic. Or the cards are sentient, using an object to reach out and
connect to you. Lure you in."

Sounded vaguely sinister, but sinister was her jam.

"Let's see what we can find out." She made a fan from the spread,
smoothing the rectangles over lumpy ground, taking stock of the symbol
stamped in the middle. A hexagon with that squiggly-fingered hand in
the center of the polygon. The sigil for chaos. A flare of light from
outside turned Raven's face into a shadow play. It was as if the burst of
fire reflected in her mind. "It's us." She traced the pattern. "Each plane
and connecting point in the hexagon represent one of the four
traditional elements, plus spirit and chaos."

"I figured. But I can't make sense of the print in the middle. I
thought at first that it symbolized chaos, but it makes no sense why

chaos is slapped in the center when, as you say, it also has a distinct point in the figure like everyone else."

"Beats me. Shall we pull some cards?"

He tipped his chin down once.

Her pulse quickened, an acceleration marked by a muted sense of dread that they were meddling with forbidden forces. But they'd come this far. She'd made big strides in her cross-country pursuit of answers and vowed never to give up. She wasn't about to surrender just when she'd found a good lead. What would she do if she gave up, go back to her apartment and dead-end job in the ghost town of Storyville, Missouri? She'd rather jump off the cliff towering above their heads.

She flipped the first one that called to her and laid it down. The picture showed cave drawings of winged and horned beasts, primitive yet fearsome renderings evoking a medieval aesthetic. "These could represent the shifters. The origin of you guys." An idea struck. "Why don't you pull one?"

Raven did. The second upturned illustration was of rows of oval-shaped tanks lining a wall. Bodies floated in them, connected to tubes. Some lacked arms, other legs, still others still had no limbs at all. On a few, the eyes appeared to be sealed or glued shut. Cynthia grimaced, her body growing cold.

He tapped the picture. "Reminds me of a post I came across on the message board. About a plot to dupe people into moving into these pods so their souls can be easily harvested."

Her stomach soured, clammy sweat sticking the backs of her thighs to the tent material. Harvesting souls made her think of the magic-giver's warning about Other Ones. They struck her as the soul-harvesting sort. "You mentioned something similar earlier. I gotta say, it sounds like a conspiracy theory."

"The implication being that any of this adheres to simple logic? Please."

"Touché," she said. "I'm going to be totally honest with you, I'm feeling a little blocked right now. If we're going to do this, I vote that we take a big step forward."

Part of her hoped that she'd scare him off, goad him into saying 'forget it, let's take a walk on the beach and chat like normal people.' But another part of her, the temptress on her left, was rather eager to notch this card reading business up to the next level.

"Are you're about to propose what I hope you are?" He leaned forward.

"You said that you wanted to travel to the magic source. I'm game. But I have a question for you first."

"Ask me anything."

"Right before we left the hotel, how did you know that I went somewhere else with my mind?"

The sound of his inhale whooshed in her ears, as if he gathered steam in preparation for dropping a bombshell. The stormy ocean's sonorous song seemed to mirror his breath. "While I was waiting for you to come back from the office, I had visions of you in another realm. Disjointed snippets. Like a montage playing. I knew that you had magic, obviously, and the things I saw coincided with a psychic link process that I'd studied. I put the pieces together."

"Be more specific. What did you see?"

"First, I saw you falling. After that, things got fuzzier. The best I can describe it is that the visions reminded me of reliving a dream. But I was reliving your dream through my point of view. There was a field. A snake. A powerful entity, a deity even, speaking to you through the wind about otherworldly powers. That's how I knew that I'd connected to you specifically—the presence of wind magic was so significant."

Damn. This guy was sharp. Adept at inductive reasoning. Made sense. People committed to missions tended to be good detectives. "So why do you want to go there? What's in it for you, if you even have the ability to access what we're talking about?"

"You already know the main reason. Finding the shifters." He steepled his hands below his chin. "But the more I learn, the more invested I become in the prophecy and figuring out the shifters' part in it. I want to test a theory. We already know that shifters bind to witch magic, at least in some form. If I can follow your perspective to the magic realm, I think that I'm able to piggyback off the magic. And you being an air witch, various forms of flight and consciousness throwing are theoretically in your purview. In layman's terms, the practice is referred to as remote viewing or astral travel. Whether those two are one in the same, I can't say for sure."

She was starting to feel not great about this. Instrumental. Used, more so than any casual sex had ever made her feel. Her arm muscles tightened, and she began to cross her arms over her chest before stopping to pretend to pull a thread. "You want to see if you can take some of my magic to remote view the location of the shifters and therefore save yourself the effort of flying all over the place in search of them."

He knitted his eyebrows together. "When you put it that way, it sounds craven and gross. That's not my intent."

"Whatever. I don't care. We're here to help each other out, right? Quid pro quo. So what's in this for me?"

"Cynthia, please."

"Please what?" She flinched at the hurt, defensive uptick in her tone and got ahold of herself. "This is a bargaining situation, so I'm bargaining. You should know that when I was there, in the magic realm, I received a pretty scary warning about taking and taking without giving back. So perhaps we should both be mindful of our greed here."

She could tell him where in Peru they lived and send him on his way. But then she'd be responsible for giving up her former community. And Raven would be gone. He'd leave her and drop off the planet like her parents had, and she'd again be all alone. Sure, she was being selfish, but everyone worked better collaboratively, and teamwork conferred mutual benefits.

Or maybe you're just pathetic and lonely, holding on to people at any cost.

"You're right." He locked his jaw. "I apologize. The way I asked came out wrong and sounded awful. We've been searching for so long, one promising lead after another going dry, and I got too eager. I lost sight of your feelings, and I'm sorry."

"It's not about my feelings. I told you, I don't have any." The ooze of the lie saturated every syllable. "It's about practical precautions."

"Okay. I hear two valid points from you right now. One, that in order to do this big favor for me, you need to see a gesture of good faith that I'll reciprocate in some way. Does that summary adequately capture what your saying?"

Some of the built-up negativity drained away. Raven was capable of active listening, a good quality in a travelling companion. Or ally. Or friend, or whatever he was. She was being smart to keep him close. "Yes."

"Secondly, I hear you saying that it's unwise of us, me in particular as more of a novice, to trample through magic without a firm grasp of the risks. Accurate?"

"Essentially. Though I'll admit that I don't have a complete handle on all of the risks myself."

"What's your inclination on the best way to proceed? Because the others are out there preparing a ritual to bring your magic and these cards into union. All three of them lack the apprehension chip and have restless spirits. Well-intentioned, but impulsive."

That could be an issue. With any luck, though, she and Raven would return from the magic realm with insights to share. "I'll take you to the magic realm on two conditions."

"Name them."

"One." She held up her index finger. "We go there and ask for advice. We back up, present our situation, and seek council on how to proceed. Humble ourselves. See if a little more genuflection and a little less hubris endears us to the magic-giver and helps to dial down their irritation."

"Damage control. Okay. I can get behind that. What's number two?"

"I need an action plan on how exactly you're helping me find my coven sisters. Something concrete. I'm tired of hearing about the message board, and offering to fly around the city on a scouting mission isn't enough."

"I have an idea. Hear me out."

She waited, the cards spread out between their legs becoming more of a bridge than a wall. "Shoot."

"We'll learn how to summon them, or at least leverage your magic to psychically connect with them. I'm convinced that's possible based on my tie to you, but we'll aim to find out for sure from the magic giver. As you said, we've gotta do some PR. So we'll go to the realm, glean as much insight as we can, and come back up here armed and confident."

Her pulse raced again, this time with excitement. He spoke so earnestly and had a natural way of cultivating trust. For all of his enigmatic qualities, Raven didn't strike her as deceitful or shady. In no way did he project that peculiar guarded, insecure trait that leaches out of someone with secrets to hide. "Then we go out there to the fire and get to work."

"Precisely."

"What about the others? Are they content to do any sort of spell as long as there's a vague promise of pinpointing the shifters?"

"Basically. They operate from the principle that enhancing power is always good. So yeah. When it comes to the ways of the occult and esoteric practice, those three are up for anything with anyone by any means. Shortsighted in some ways, but I'll admit that we've come a long way by taking chances."

Now there was a motto, encased in Raven's final line. Cynthia might have to be the one to reign in the practice if things got too crazy, lest she be accused of unduly influencing Raven or even corrupting him with her wiles. The other three had to be forming some theories on what was going on in the tent.

Pros and cons aside, going to the magic realm was Cynthia's top option. "Okay. Good enough for me. I can't guarantee that this will work, I'm flying by the seat of my pants here, too, but let's give this a shot."

He lured her in with that stare of his, not quite smiling, but definitely observing. That look fascinated her, its combination of introspection paired with a misfit's gift for assessing the world from an outside viewpoint. "Flying's what we do best."

She liked the "we." A lot. And she liked the whole entire concept of flying together, the romanticism and escape that such a notion entailed. Too much and to a dangerous extent, Raven's dream-spun world of motorcycle beaches and black-winged flights bathed in the farthest, edgiest reaches of magic tempted her. Tempted her to let the walls around herself crumble so she could feel everything again.

Before she thought too much about the danger of her encroaching feelings, she dragged her pack to her side and pulled the strings. "There's a spell in here for partner work that we can try first."

SEVEN

WHEN WAS THE LAST TIME THAT CYNTHIA HAD HELD HANDS WITH another person? High school? Some naïve time before the first big heartbreak, back in the days of unwrinkled skin and idealistic beliefs in true love. Before she'd hardened her tender side and chosen to enjoy herself by having sex like a man. Not that all men wanted fast and impersonal fucks. Unfair to pin her attachment issues on an entire gender.

Raven's hands, warm and firm, secured her like an anchor as she mentally and emotionally prepared for partner work. She'd expected his touch to be cool, his grasp aloof, but the man was full of surprises. A glance at her open book steeled her focus. Pages filled with inked calligraphy and drawings full of ancient secrets stared her down. She did her best to summarize the mysteries, "So the gist of this is that, if you're bound to me while I cast a spell to draw from one of my opposition elements, you have the ability to pull from that element's opposition."

"A chain reaction." He craned his neck. "Does it mention shifters specifically?"

She thumbed through a stack of warped, stiff pages that must've been nailed by a spill. "Sort of. There's a section on familiars and creature work that covers this type of collaboration. Apparently, witches can do partner work with familiars or humans with animal aspects. That bond is what gives me the ability to pull from an opposition element in the first place."

His expression morphed. Though she was only guessing at his his inner state, she swore she caught downright wistfulness. "Are we bonded?" His question validated her guess, and the entire thing was both scary and exhilarating.

"I mean, for the purposes of the spell, sure." No crushes. No pining. "Yes."

"Good. I'm glad that you think so." No mistaking the full stretch of his mouth, which in turn brightened her. Positive affect could only help magic work go according to plan. "Have you ever done this before?"

"A partner work spell?" She hoped that her palms hadn't started to sweat. "Or bond with someone?"

"Both." He held her a little tighter.

"I've never tried this," she confessed. "And to the bonding thing, I was close with my parents, but I kind of checked out after they died. I mean, I had friends, but no great love or anything like that. Most of my life, it's been me and only me. I like it that way, so I don't need your pity."

"None to give. I can respect a loner."

"So why did you even ask?"

"I wondered if we should try to get to know each other a little better. For the efficacy of the spell. It seems to me that a prerequisite for building a strong bond is feeling close to someone on a personal level."

She laughed even as she squeezed his hands on some affectionate impulse that she'd had no idea that she possessed. "You state a valid case. So, Raven, tell me about yourself." An over-affected tone of interest mocked the idea that they were on a date, sending a message.

He countered her cynical move with an earnest one, painting a background portrait made of both broad strokes and compelling tidbits of detail. Three years her junior, Raven was from Seattle. Family life had been healthy enough but stifling in its conformity, with Christian parents who questioned the morality of his penchant for all things goth. Two sunny, popular brothers who excelled at sports and loved parties, never struggling to fit in like Raven had, made for painful sibling contrast. He'd spent many solitary nights in his bedroom, lulled by the song of nonstop northwestern rain as it bathed the pine trees beyond his window, until one day he dropped into a meditative state and shifted.

"That's when I renamed myself." He stroked the outside of her thumb with the pad of his, a tiny intimacy that lodged a lump in her throat. "Mom and Dad refused to honor it in public, didn't want their church friends thinking that I'd been swayed to sin by the devil. But the day I changed was when Matthew died, and Raven was born. I still have an inkling that I was adopted but nobody would tell me. I was so different on every level."

"It sounds alienating."

"I mean, in a sense, yes. Absolutely. But the upside is that I've always been able to be myself. Never had an option to choose otherwise."

"Way to look on the bright side. I assumed at first that you'd be all broodiness and gloom."

"I like when our assumptions are upended. Things are more interesting when you go against them now and then," he said.

"So maybe you shake things up on purpose to keep people guessing?"

"Sure. Why not?"

"Cool. Works for me. Let's wrap up our bonding session with lighter fare. What's your favorite food?" she asked.

"Anything free. I don't eat poultry. I'm sure that you can guess why."

"Too general, which is cheating."

"Ha. Okay. I'll pick sushi."

Classy and refined yet accessible enough to not be snobbish. A notch in the positive column for Raven. "Why?"

"I like the simple elegance of it. Artistic. Reminds me that for all of our evils and foibles, humans are capable of creating beauty in something as mundane as sustenance."

"Deep answer. Now I want sushi. Maybe we can get some for lunch tomorrow and you can educate me on the simple beauty of a California roll and its supreme power to redeem the many ills of humanity. All hail our lord and master sashimi."

He scowled, but crinkles reached his eyes. "I bear my soul, and you sarcastically make fun of me. Rude."

Not in a mean-spirited way, just as a self-protective measure to handle that she'd asked him out on a date. If she had armor on, a stab of a rejection wouldn't land. "Well, let's be real. You're only able to get away with saying something like that because you're hot. If you were ugly, pontificating on the praises of raw fish would've been a douche-tastic comment of the highest caliber."

"Hot, eh?"

"Um, obviously. I chose to fuck you."

"That you did." His voice dropped, and she could damn near see the memories flooding his mind. "Lucky me."

"Now who has a gutter mind? Okay. Focus time. For you to access a witch's element, I first have to—"

"Whoa, nelly. Unfair."

"Excuse me?"

"Bonding goes both ways. You haven't told me hardly anything about yourself."

Vulnerability sucked, but unfortunately, he made a good point. For the sake of the spell, she best open up as much as she could. A successful foray into the craft necessitated full disclosure.

Cynthia talked about her travels, the people she'd met, and the strange happenings with Denise-Nerissa. She rounded out the nomadic chapter of her story with some obligatory, boring stuff about her upbringing in Missouri. He laughed with mirth when she talked about her imaginary childhood friend, empathizing based on his own history with loneliness but conceding that the life of an only child had to have major drawbacks.

"Nah, it was alright," she said. "My folks were wonderful, and there were no other kids around to steal my toys. I read constantly; I stopped by the local bookstores so often I practically lived there. Never shook that habit. That's how I ended up meeting my craft book, spending an afternoon in my favorite shop. I'd read *almost* everything in there and made it a project to comb through the books on the highest shelf."

"That's dedication."

"Thanks. Speaking of the craft, shall we?"

"We will after you share what it is that you're keeping secret."

He stomach vaulted to her throat. Shit. He knew about Peru somehow. "What makes you think I'm holding back?"

"When you got into the specifics of your journey across the country, there were gaps. Missing pieces. And you got quiet in a couple of places. Then your voice changed, like it was kind of...clipped but also shaky. But look, if it's none of my business, just tell me to back off. You don't owe me your story, for the sake of the spell or anything else."

He clearly wasn't talking about Peru. He meant the *other* stuff. Why keep secrets? Elusiveness might mess up their partner work, to echo his legitimate concern. Besides, if he saw her in all of her nastiness, he might dismiss her as a romantic prospect, freeing her to be her true self without fear of being hurt. "You wanna know the worst of it? Okay, Raven, brace yourself." Now, her palms were definitely damp. Her head emptied out and she became one with her senses as mind and body prepared the confession to end all confessions. "I've killed two people."

Calm neutrality stayed on his face—he didn't flinch or balk or drop her hands—and she exhaled a wad of tension. She'd never admitted her private shame to anyone, and the catharsis had a detoxifying effect on her emotions.

"Why?" Raven asked.

Such a basic question, yet so profound in its import. Tremors shook her as the first incident flooded back, striking as raw and immediate as it had at the time. Man One, as big as a refrigerator, panting sour breath. Pathetic excuse for an erection stabbing her inner thigh as he groped her breast like she was dead meat with no nerve endings. Asphalt cold on her cheek. Froth on his lips as he wheezed, clawing his throat before falling as heavy as a log on top of her and slowly expiring. She hadn't meant to go that far.

She hated that she still laid awake now and again, blaming herself for exiting that stupid Nebraska dive bar via the back door leading to the alley. But she liked alleys, dammit, and was high and buzzed and wanted to go for a fucking stroll without having to worry about the same damn thing all women worried about once twilight fades to black.

"They tried to rape me." The words burned her tongue, but at least she got to spit the poison out after years of holding it in to fester and corrode.

More flashbacks mounted a merciless assault. Man Two, slamming her head into that grungy toilet seat after he'd followed her into the gas station bathroom and locked the door. Her heel had slid across the freshly mopped linoleum as she'd tried to run, leaving her with a rolled ankle as insult to injury. She'd bitten and kicked him, slammed her good foot into his instep before registering with dismay that he liked when she fought back and got off on the pain and struggle. He'd yanked her shorts and underwear to her ankles when she finally turned to her last resort.

Droplets tapped against the rounded slopes of tent material before weeping streaks down the sides. She'd been so immersed in talking with Raven that she hadn't noticed the onset of rain. The staccato sound pattern offered a bit of solace, a rhythm to concentrate on while Raven held silence, his chest rising and falling.

"Despicable wastes of air. They deserved it. Retributive justice was served, if you ask me."

"Self-defense, at least." A sting bit her nose. Her throat was so thick, but she refused to cry. Refused to crumple into a pathetic remnant of herself. She was here to be strong. He was interested in her specifically for her powers and abilities and had kept her around this long for what she could do. "Or I told myself that it was self-defense. I probably went overboard. I tried other methods to subdue them first."

"It wasn't your fault. None of it was, in any way, your fault."

"I know," she snapped, pain lancing her chest as the wave of emotion pressed forward.

"I'm sorry. I'm sure you already know that."

She blinked rapidly, wiping the corner of one eye until the unshed tears dried, and went back to holding his hand. "Don't apologize. There's a little, um, trauma still in me I guess, but it felt good to talk about it. I'll be okay. Thanks for listening."

"Any time. Anything you need, and I'm here."

"Can we move forward with the spell?" A discreet sniff banished any residual threat of a weeping episode. "I need to be done with the topic of what happened. At least for now. I think I still need to do some processing on my own."

"Of course. You were breaking down the process of partner work."

"Yes. So yeah, it's a chain reaction. I'm able to draw from one of my opposition elements, which in my case are earth and chaos." She flipped to the hexagon chart that showed each elemental witch's two neighbors.

"Once I stir you into the mix, you can pull from an element adjacent to the one I tapped."

His eyes slid from left to right over the page. "So I get chaos or earth's neighbor. Fire or water, respectively."

Smart guy. "That's my assessment, too. We keep the system moving so that one element taps into the next, and so on, until we complete the circuit."

"Makes me doubly curious what the sign in the middle represents."

She sighed. The longer she fixed on those branches of curls, the more indecipherable it became, fingers bleeding together into a boundless, endless, knot of questions and unknowns. "You and me both. Maybe we aren't supposed to figure it out. But I don't like that it has this effect of halting our momentum."

"Ditto. I say we press on."

With that settled, she outlined another facet of her theory on partner work and the act of hailing sister elements. "I'm spit-balling a little on this, but I think that I'd be best served drawing from chaos. That piece of the six-fold magic system is the element most strongly connected to the manipulation of one's own mind and other minds. Splitting your psyche to be in multiple places—or bodies—at once. Sharing bodies and perspectives with others, infiltrating dreams." She gulped. "Thought manipulation aka mind control."

He raised one eyebrow. "Sounds dark and creepy."

"In the wrong hands or without control, sure, but every element has multiple purposes and applications."

"What's your theory on why this is what we want to use?"

"If we go to the magic-giver with leverage, demonstrating what I'm capable of, that instills confidence. Works to our benefit. Since we want to find my coven sisters, if I use chaos magic to get to the source place, the magic-giver will see that I'm serious and competent. The giver needs to see how I'm capable with the sixth circle. If we can cultivate respect in the magic giver, they'll be more likely to offer insight on how to proceed."

"Okay. Fair enough. I will say that I like the idea of working with fire, since the others have a fire going on the beach. If I'm enhanced with the strengths of that element, there's a chance that will guide us when we bring the cards into the picture. A sympathetic ally."

"Sound theory, sound theory. Plus, the clues I found point to my fire sister being nearby. So you taking on fire magic stands a chance of establishing a stronger bond with her." She pawed through more pages. Damn, there was so much material to cover. Tons of script, much of it in languages she'd never seen, let alone had the education to read. And etchings of all kinds, words and symbols crowding every piece of paper. Ten years poring over this thing, ten years of late nights spent scribbling notes and stopping every two minutes to Google, and she'd barely made a dent. But if she only studied and never practiced, she risked spending a lifetime obsessing over material that she'd never use. As her mama used to say, the perfect was the enemy of the good. "Based on what I've gleaned from the fire section, the fire element has a couple of primary functions. Blockage and destruction."

"Blockage as in a firewall. An insurmountable boundary."

"Bingo. All of this magic can be deployed, from what I can tell, on numerous planes of existence. The literal, physical realm. Wildfires, a burning building, sources of heat and/or light. The basics."

"And the advanced?"

"Damming up thoughts and mental processes so the target of the spell can't reach conclusions or reason from point a to point b. Forgetfulness. Memory stuff. Clouding up those brain faculties with flames and smoke. Hot emotions can ruin logic by circumventing the executive function of the brain, so our prefrontal cortex shuts down. Oh, and there's also a counter-spell application of fire when used in this way. The firewall you mentioned. Protecting one's mind against the efforts of others to spy on your thoughts, read your mind, or otherwise infiltrate."

"Shit. That's all serious stuff. And we haven't even gotten into the destructive properties yet."

She chuckled in reverence to the mighty prowess of Sister Fire. "Right. That's where we get into straight-up razing, literally or figuratively. Tearing down a structure or system and starting over. A wipe out. Incinerating whatever the witch wants to make disappear. From spontaneous combustion to amnesia, fire's got you covered."

"You're remarkable, you know that? Your mastery of this complex system is impressive. You have reams of encyclopedic knowledge at your disposal."

She narrowed her eyes at him, her salty expression exaggerated enough to send the signal that the compliment landed at least partially. "Flattery will get you nowhere."

"Not one single place?"

"Head in the game. Keep brainstorming." Sure was fun to finally have someone to brainstorm with, she had to admit. Mind melds like this were unheard of to her, a wonderful fright of a surprise.

"I wonder if fire can protect us as we try to find the inner states of the other witches. Keep out any undesirable elements. Psyche splitting and the like can't be foolproof."

"Checks out. Or smokescreen scramble any hitchhikers who try to get in." Possession by Other Ones, malevolent beings from hidden realms, and God knew what else was an ever-present risk when working with magic.

"Okay. Let's do this." She moved a chunk of pages, opening to the section on partner work, and re-read a portion before brushing up on the part dedicated to chaos magic. "Sister Folly, I, an Air Born, humbly call upon your guidance. As I travel to the magic realm with my pair-bonded companion, one with an animal aspect who shall touch the element fire, please imbue me with your gifts. We wish to scout the locations of my chaos and fire sisters so we may commence the sacred prophecy of the Coven Daughters."

A peal of thunder tumbled over the ocean, the wind picking up to screech an ominous song and slash streaks of water against the walls.

"Someone's listening," Raven said.

"Air and Water are in consort," Cynthia whispered, unsure why she was whispering. Perhaps awe had stolen the bulk of her voice. "Spirit might be in there, too. Let them flow through us." She geared up to read more, "Send us to the magic realm graced with the talent to see through another. Bind me to my coven sisters of fire and chaos by linking our minds, shrouding us in a cloak of fire so we may remain unscathed."

A snap broke deep in her hindbrain with an effect that was a cross between a sound and a physical jolt. She reeled, her neck cracking back as if dashed by whiplash, and blacked out before coming to with a spinning head and faint nausea.

Red blobs swam in her vision. Once the spinning subsided, she pinpointed the source of the color blobs: her own feet. Stilettos slicked in a crimson gloss so shiny that she damn near caught her reflection stared up at her. She'd never wear impractical heels like those, as she often found herself walking long distances.

Confused, she touched her hips and stomach. Thin, flimsy material clung to her. Some kind of fuck me dress designed to be hiked over hips had been put on her. No underwear. A stone hung from a chain around her neck, an onyx cube that warmed to her body heat.

Her attire was weird enough, but her surroundings had the hooker couture beat in the bizarre category. All four walls, plus the ceiling and floor, were pure obsidian and polished to a sheen rivaling the shininess of her shoes. Her heels clattered against the tile as she took a few steps, prepared to accept whatever the capricious magic realm had to offer up. Which, among other things, she hoped was Raven. "Hello?"

Raven failed to materialize, but a door in the floor slid sideways to make an opening in preparation for someone's—or something's —entrance.

EIGHT

THE RATTLESNAKE FROM THE SIDE OF THE ROAD WAS BACK LIKE A BAD penny, rusty and crusty and twice as ugly.

"Tell me what you seek, air born." It slunk to her, eerily uncanny when framed against an enclosure as dark as the spaces between stars.

Thinking fast, she mobilized some verbiage from her book. "I seek my sisters fire and chaos. I wish for their personhood to join with my own so I may see and live as they do."

"And why should I abide?" Scales scraped against tile with a tiny noise of friction.

"The prophecy demands that we unify. My partner and I came here with chaos magic. We're capable of harnessing Sister Folly's expertise to locate my sisters and persuade them accordingly." She hoped that mentioning Raven would trigger the visitor into revealing his whereabouts, because she was getting worried.

A dry, rough trail brushed against her ankle before the spirit creature slithered to the other side of the room. "I'm not sure that you're ready to claim your place in the prophecy."

Icy worry settled in her stomach. "Why would you say that?"

"Your conscience isn't clear. You practice the Left-Hand path and dance with the darkness, yet you've allowed guilt and shame to put a saddle on you. Only when you embrace your nature and ride the air unencumbered will you truly connect to your fellow sisters in the light triad, and to those who contrast you in the dark trinity."

Shit! She'd forgotten all about the trinity and triad aspects of the coven. Cynthia, along with her water and earth siblings, was a member of this light triad. The other three belonged to whatever the dark trinity was.

Unfortunately, she knew fuck all about what either trio did or was about. Two minutes in and the magic-giver had smacked her down and held up a mirror to reveal her stupidity. All she could think to do was come clean. "I'm sorry. I'm really trying here. I read and read, I study that book until my eyes are about to fall out, but I miss stuff. I need help. I feel like I need to practice, but when I do, I make mistakes due to my knowledge gaps. It's a catch-twenty-two, and I'm here to ask your guidance on getting out of the maze."

"I admire your drive and honesty." The serpent laid in an s-curve opposite Cynthia. "I'll allow you one ritual to glean a little more on the triad and trinity, since you were derelict in your duty to study. But once is all. I'm not here to tutor. You must find your mentor, child."

Another issue loomed large. She had to call Denise-Nerissa soon, in the morning, even, and deliver the latest updates. Maybe a chat with the elder would help. "Message received. What's the ritual?"

"A song of fire and chaos, of course, since you seek those sisters with the aid of your partner. If you tap spirit, you've unlocked the rites of the trinity and ascended one rung in the prophetic ladder. Good luck."

"Wait—"

The magic-giver didn't wait. The serpent bit down on its rattle-capped tail and spun, eating its end in an infinite loop. The fleshy blur turned to dust, then a cloud of smoke. Raven formed from the ashes.

He wore all black, a button-up shirt and slacks, monochromatic save for the skinny red tie slashing down his front like a streak of blood.

He walked to her, footsteps echoing, his strides commanding and his gaze intent.

Foreign heat licked her up and down, all over, buzzing in her ears. All she managed to do was stare at him. "Do you know?" she whispered, beside herself, packing so much into that question without even fully comprehending the extent. "Fire and chaos?"

Once he reached kissing distance, Raven responded by cupping her cheek in his palm. "We connect, now. I feel it in me, with me, all around me. We share the force to create spirit. We can conjure the third prong in the dark trinity through the union of fire and chaos."

Gah, this sounded ominously akin to a fertility ritual, and the last thing she wanted to deal with was a surprise pregnancy. Too bad the magic-giver hadn't stuck around for a question-and-answer session. But they weren't in this place physically, so it was safe to bet that biological rules didn't apply, as was custom in the magical realm. Her gut told her to push on, so she did.

She tilted her head back, allowing him more access, registering the intent as he brushed fingertips down her throat, leaving a trail of tingles in his wake. Sex magic, initiated. While many questions buzzed in her brain, she managed to shut off her mental chatter and simply feel her way through the process.

She stepped closer, bringing them eye-to-eye, locking in with the depths of his dark-eyed stare that was rich and dense with lust. The magnetic pulses yoking them reverberated in some cosmic, unreachable place, letting her know that she was seen by something bigger, a presence orchestrated by design.

When their lips met, she let go, dissolving into the kiss and all it had to offer. He kissed her with tenderness at first, sucking her upper and lower lips by turn, urging her against him until their bodies rested flush. He was firm, solid, and evidence of his excitement pushed stiffly against the flimsy screen of cloth on her skin. As she allowed her hands to roam to his lower back, allowed herself to move them into a hug, it struck her how she'd never really shared such closeness with another person.

Magic or no, means to an end or not, the moment was special, and she'd savor every second. A re-do with someone she'd had her usual sort of romp with, a joy of rediscovery and a first time, was a beautiful paradox of harmonic discord.

His hands tangled in her hair, threading loose strands, as his lips worked hers. Tongues came out to play, in tandem, strokes traded as warmth and the fresh, clean taste of him took over.

She could have kissed this man for hours, made out with him forever and ever like some high school kid, living in the moment with no endgame and no pressure. You know, for the sake of the ritual. Not in a mushy romantic way.

He guided her backwards in a graceful and sensual dance, the kiss unrelenting, mouths crushed in consort as their breath flowed as one. She was that breath, the ephemeral and invisible substance which she commanded, except now she surrendered.

Her feet were moving, heel taps clicking against hard floor, and soon she found herself being lowered. The spell faltered for a moment, and she grasped his arms, breaking the kiss to look behind out of fear of falling.

She should have trusted him not to drop or throw her. A cube had risen from the ground somehow, a block to match the walls in shade and shine, as high as a table and with enough surface area to support two bodies. She fingered the smaller cube dangling from her neck, fascinated.

He asked, "Do you want to do this? If not, that's okay. We can say the words and go right back to that tent if this is too much."

Too much, absolutely. Too much risk of so many things. Power. Magic. Her heart. Breaking for him. Too much steered her to the precipice of uncharted territory. Too much was going to win. She touched his face like he'd touched hers, showing him a little more of herself, revealing her hidden places through her mirrored gesture. "Yes. I want to do this."

He claimed her mouth again, fiercer than before, a claiming met with a confession. They'd fall together, here, in this desecrated place of buried secrets and irresistible nightmares.

The slab met the backs of her thighs, cool and hard with a sharp-edged slice, as he lowered her with one strong arm. Finding herself in a very familiar position tipped her body into arousal. Chilled air slipped up her arms. Tense, damp heat where the scandalous hem of what passed for her dress grazed her mound. She watched while he slid the fabric to her waist in a single, fluid glide, his stare staying on her face even though her pussy was right there.

She caught a whiff of herself, mixed in with subtle notes of opium and lilac that'd come with the realm. Sex was in the air. The stage had been set, prepped. Took some of the pressure off, how their impending act had a predetermined quality to it, as if similar moves had been made here before, several times over.

Metal tinkled against metal as he undid his belt, zipper. She bent her knees and planted her stiletto soles on the hard platform, the pose wanton and whorish and, she supposed, apropos.

When he pushed in, though, he filled her up in a long, deep stroke. If he wanted to rush, he didn't show it. They began to move, Raven folding forward to gain leverage, gripping the sides of the altar as he thrust his hips.

His lips brushed her neck, dry and fluttery, the quickening sounds of his breath heightening her excitement. The sounds of a lover's breathing as he approached the peak had always turned her on, an effect that was magnified by actually liking the other person.

She gripped the taut muscles of his upper arms, matching him pump for pump with her bouncing bottom, her insides stretched with the glorious pressure of a cock inside of her.

"Can you come this way?" he asked, voice choppy and labored.

"Not usually, but that's okay."

"Do you want to come?" He let out a groan that made her a little jealous. She did want to come now.

"Yes." Might as well get off on this. Ecstatic release seemed to bode well for the magical element of their congress. "I want to come."

"Good." The one word was so arrogant in its assuredness, so unexpectedly smug, that she felt her walls clench around him. A sexually confident partner got her going every time, and Raven's second performance was already shoring up his status in the quality category. "Because I want you to come for me."

With that final declaration, he maneuvered his hand between their bodies to rub her clit. He stroked efficiently, up and down with two fingers, and around six brushes in, she felt the tell-tale buildup of base need. She clamped down on the hard knot of muscle in her palm, wishing she could feel his skin under cloth.

But a few more ministrations later, she didn't care about anything except climax, arching her back as she threw her head back to stare at the abyss of darkness surrounding her on all sides.

She heard herself pant, watched her chest heave under the red scrap that showcased her pebbled nipples. Then, she was gone, hurtling, as release unraveled to the fanfare of mindless shouts and exalted eruptions that rolled through her in waves.

He went off as she rode the orgasm, his pumps rapid and greedy, moaning on every push. When he surged forward, crying out, she'd about reached the end of her finish but for a white light in the middle of the ceiling. The glow brightened and dimmed, expanding and contracting as it merged with the rhythms of her breath and heartbeat. The longer she gazed, the quicker she realized that the light she was seeing wasn't merely a side effect of sexual pleasure.

"Hello?" a woman's voice said. "Are you down there?"

"Yes," Cynthia shouted, her wail a swirl of red alert and ecstatic frenzy. "Yes, yes, yes."

"Follow me upward. Visualize a rope."

The climactic relief tapering into aftershocks, she concentrated on the throbbing blob at the apex of the room until the sphere with ragged edges lengthened to a phosphorescent tentacle.

The coil slipped down through void space, impossible as it broke all physical laws while affirming metaphysical ones, dripping right down upon her face.

Cynthia's perception drifted and went muzzier the longer she looked, and by the time the tip of the rope poked her between the eyes, she wasn't sure what was real, a dream, magic, getting off, or hallucination. But what did it matter? She'd asked for all of this and stayed open for any outcome. All she could do was follow the lead of what was given.

Burrowing, digging with intent, the column of energy rooted a stronghold in her forehead, stretching bone and connective tissue to their achy limits. She squinted, unable to see a single thing other than a blinding glare. Whether Raven was still inside her or had moved aside was unclear.

"What now?" she slurred, the pressure of invasion becoming acutely uncomfortable, unnatural to a frightful degree.

"Up. Up. You have to move up, Cynthia. Get out of where you are."

Her pulse slammed at the bossy, clipped manner of the woman's speech. Was Cynthia somewhere bad, duped into harming Raven and herself?

"What about Raven?" her speech came out labored and as wetly sticky as mud.

"Move, move, move!"

Friend or foe, truth, or trick? Maybe one of these days, some guidance or rush of insight would blast her into epiphany. But today wasn't that day. Today was for winging it, as usual. Cynthia drew on every available reserve of her air magic, corralling the power to propel and fly, and shot herself up the twenty-foot length of megawatt lifeline.

Spins, flips, and tumbles hurled her to and fro until she came to with her feet on solid ground. Moist sand. Night outside, crashing ocean, the smell of a storm that'd moved on—she was back on the beach. But the tents and fire were gone. So was Raven. No sign of his posse. She jerked her head left to right and back again, fumbling to make a frantic determination about whether to call out or stay silent. Well, great. What now?

Far off down the shoreline, movement stirred. She craned and strained to see, but there wasn't enough light despite a juicy tangerine slice of half moon flinging blue rays upon lazy waves. Who or what was there? Probably just some dumb bird. She took quick stock of herself. At least her regular clothes and sandals were back on, and she wasn't freezing in the ritual dress. Maybe she'd try to manifest that rope again. Use it as a flashlight.

The figure moved closer, closer, until it became undeniable that what walked along the sandbar at a brisk clip was a person. The person came into better view, a common loosening of relief setting in when Cynthia made out a woman. Thick waves of brown hair, sweatshirt and jeans. Youngish, as in early thirties. Okay.

"Hi," Cynthia said once the woman approached her personal space bubble and stopped her walk, for there wasn't much else to say.

"Congratulations. You summoned me. Your bump and grind ritual worked." The mystery brunette stuck out a palm, offering a shake.

Nonplussed, Cynthia accepted, finding the stranger's handshake confident enough to suit a business leader. "You're Spirit, aren't you?"

That was her best guess, since the magic-giver had brought up Spirit as a new factor in the equation.

"In the flesh. And I was in the middle of a nice dream when you came calling, so this better be good."

"Truth be told, I don't have a lot of clarity to bring to the table right now. I'm operating without direction, doing what I can do connect with the coven and carry out this prophecy."

"Wanna walk and talk? I hate standing around," the visitor said.

Cynthia could relate to the itchy, restless feeling borne of staying still too long. The urge to move was the germ of wanderlust. "Yeah. Sure." They took off, strolling side-by-side, frothy wetness cooling Cynthia's toes before a robust tide sucked the ocean back in.

Felt like a metaphor, one step forward and two back. But at least she wasn't walking her crazy pants zigzag path alone at the moment.

"The more I try to move away from the witch life, the more the witch life finds me." Spirit pulled a hair tie from her wrist and bound her waves in a loose bun.

"Why do you want to move away from the witch life?"

"I made some mistakes similar to yours. Operating without direction. Recklessness. Impulsivity. And let me tell you, that can be deadly with this craft. The risk of possession and infiltration lurks around every corner. As does the threat of conjuring things that you don't want. Things that will hurt you and the ones you love."

"Yeah, I'm starting to get that, but this is our destiny. We can't outrun our fate."

"Fate and destiny are two different concepts."

"Oh?" Praise be to the universe for sending up someone to talk about this stuff with. Not a mentor, but better than the jack nothing she was used to. "Do tell."

"Fate is what's done to us. Predetermined, the invisible hand that moves things along according to its own will. Destiny is the sum of our choices, vibrations, and manifestations. What we, consciously or subconsciously, ask the universe to give us."

"So what is me summoning you?"

That earned a big, fat sigh. "I'm not sure. But I will say that this is the first time such a thing has worked, at least that I've been party to. I tried to teleport somewhere with another witch once, and we failed."

Cynthia's spine straightened as her attention snapped to this woman's delicate, pretty profile. "You connected with another one of us? Who? How?"

"Water. And she came to me on a mission. But like I said, the effort was a flop. We lost touch."

Water. Damn. If Cynthia could get a lead on this water witch, she'd have two members of the light triad, counting herself, plus this spirit witch. And she just knew that she was closing in on chaos and fire. Best not to appear too eager and spook Spirit, though. Her best bet was to keep Spirit close and fish around for info on Water bit by bit. "Operation Collect All Six" belonged in her back pocket for now. "Can you describe to me how exactly I summoned you? You said you were dreaming. Did I reach you there? And in such a way that you sensed my duress?"

"Essentially. Stop me if you already know this from your research, but there's a realm called the astral plane. It covers a lot. Other dimensions, dreamscapes, how reality appears when we are altered by craft work. My theory is that we witches always go there when we dream, or maybe I just end up there because I'm spirit born. Who knows. But you came to me from a very low, very fallen place, and I knew that I had to get you out of there ASAP."

Uh oh. "What do you mean, low and fallen?"

"A realm with low vibrational frequency. Hell dimension, maybe. I don't have the specifics pinpointed. But there are layers and levels to the astral realm. We can't easily control where we go when we travel there, or what else we might find. Which is why we have to have each other's backs."

"Is Raven okay?"

"Yeah. I'm walking you back to your tent. Sorry I couldn't drop you off at your door. I'm far from perfect at this stuff either."

Cynthia liked her newly introduced coven sister. They had imperfection in common. "What's your name?"

"Helen. You're Cynthia, right?"

"How did you know?"

"Raven called you that when we all crossed astral paths."

"So, uh, can I summon you again?" Ugh. Awkwardness alert, like asking someone out on a friend date.

"Sure. Yeah. We can keep working together. I'll be perfectly honest with you, I'm not super comfortable with this prophecy stuff. But I do like the idea of a witchy reunion. And I'll concede some credence to the idea that we can't outrun our destiny."

The beach narrowed to a tight, rocky passageway where a cliff stuck out to kiss the ocean. Cynthia stepped in front of Helen in a demonstration of courtesy through courage, in case some undesirable element awaited them on the other side of the bluff. But beyond the towering rocks, pebbled shore pockmarked by seaweed globs funneled open to an expanse of sand. Two tents and the crackling tendrils of a fire beckoned the same as a makeshift home. Four bodies ringed the flames, holding hands. She had no idea how Dragon had kept it burning, but trivial inquiries lay at the back of her mind. "This is me. Thanks, Helen."

"Yeah. You bet. Can I give you a piece of advice?"

"Please do. I'll take any help that comes in."

"Until you connect with your mentor and are sure of her competence, be super careful about going to the astral plane. At least read up on it. There's a lot of darkness there, smart and cunning darkness with its own agenda."

"Okay. I can't promise that, but message received."

"Well, we pulled off a summoning. So that's good news."

Which, fingers crossed, would lead to a repeat. Cynthia sensed Helen checking out as she prepared to leave, so she dropped the question that'd been bugging her since the snake spoke in the cubic room. "What do you know about the dark trinity and the light triad?"

Helen slashed a hand through her hair. "Oh, man."

Cynthia's heart skittered. Her mind cleared of thoughts. "Please. Tell me what you know."

"It has to do with whatever we've been put here to halt. All I know is that the crux of the idea reduces to combatting a holographic projection of some sort. Half of us merge into light, the other half dark, and those opposing forces create a dialectical tension that synthesizes into some new type of magic. And *that* magic is the only one capable of neutralizing this hologram. Whatever that is."

The hologram concept had come up before, and it wasn't good. At least now Cynthia could compare Helen's account to what she'd already heard from Raven's crew. She played it a bit on the dumb side in the interests of gleaning as many details as possible. "What's the story with the hologram?"

"Beats me. Look, if you want to come find me sometime I can show you my book, and we can compare notes. I'd like that, actually, to try in-person collaboration again. But I have to get back home now. Life calls, and I have to get up and go to work in the morning. All that jazz."

So much for picking up details. "Yeah. Of course."

Helen turned to the ocean. "Sister Water, I, a spirit born, humbly request your assistance. Please send me quickly through the astral further and deposit me home." Before Cynthia even had a chance to say goodbye, Helen walked into the dark waters, where she was soon engulfed by a swell.

She shook off the strangeness, chalked the ordeal up to a victory, and walked to the circle around the fire with a whole lot of new developments to report. From the looks of things and based on the droning beat of a collective chant, a project involving spells cast upon those weird cards was already well underway.

NINE

Someone had laid out the cards on the sand, enclosing both the fire and the circle of practitioners surrounding it. The whole presentation had a clockwork, celestial aesthetic that rendered ritual magic tangible through a stark visual.

Cynthia stepped over the threshold just as Raven awoke from some swaying trance. Everyone else was rocking back and forth, repeating a low-toned chant in unison.

"Thank God. You made it." He looked absolutely flattened with relief, which admittedly pleased her. He cared. "Join our circle." He dropped Ether's hand and took hers. The other man was so spaced out that he failed to notice that he'd been ditched.

"What is this?" Apprehensive but not wanting to cause a disruption, she picked up Ether's palm before the guy noticed. His snapping out of it didn't seem to be a risk, though, not with his sealed eyelids and strange movements. What was everyone doing?

"Did you have an encounter with Spirit?" Raven whispered, tugging her in his direction.

Ether resisted the pull generated by Raven, drawing Cynthia into his orbit. Soon she fell into a tug-o'-war pattern where she lacked total control over her faculties, jerking like a passive hand on a Ouija board.

Made sense now, how monotonous, collective motions promoted surrender.

"I did contact Spirit." She cast a sideways look at the fire, those pointed curls of flame kissing a vast night sky to make a menacing light flanked by the bizarre cards. "And just so you know, she warned me to pull back on things like astral travel and visiting realms until I have a mentor. It's not safe."

Raven pulled a quizzical, amused face that showed his naughty side. "Since when are we in this to play it safe?"

A spray of sparks shot from the flame in a burst of iridescent glitter chased by heady crackles. It was as if the element had agreed with Raven, underscoring his point with an impeccably timed "oh, snap."

"Okay, but we don't want to go somewhere evil and get stuck there. Or end up possessed, or unleash some force we can't control."

"That's why you're here." A yank on her fingers underscored his claim. "Your connection with your coven sisters is the exit strategy. That's what provides us whatever protection we're able to scrounge up. The more of your kin you can bind with, bond with, the better."

A low, steady drumbeat of voices merged into a reverent choir. The sounds seduced her with their call to join the group, enticing in their plea to merge with the hive.

However, she had to question, what was in all of this for her? She could contact the other witches without the shifters. Surely, she didn't need them. They needed her, or thought they did.

What if they realized she was of no use to them? She leaned in close to Raven, close enough to catch his scent, and dropped the bomb that she'd been stashing inside, "What if I told you that I know where the rest of your shifter kin live?"

There. Now he was free to discard her at his leisure, store that nugget of victory info in his pocket, and head south on his bike. Commence the countdown to emotional disengagement, now that his pretense for feigning romantic or sexual interest in her was obliterated.

He pulled her close with a tug forceful enough to snatch her full attention and drum up some energy in her loins. The inferno warmed her, a sensual contrast to crisp sea breezes. Raven's face was inches from hers. Her breath caught as she fell to rapture.

The artistic angles of his face were framed by ebony waves in free fall. She waited.

"I know," he said with the smooth assuredness of someone who could predict the future.

What mind game was this? "There's no way you know that."

"Why do you think we did this in the first place?" He used his body weight to urge her in the direction he wanted her to go until she faced the fire. "Look inside. Really look. See. Forget yourself and give in."

Shades of orange dominated the canvas of combustion, interspersed with bursts of crimson and white-tipped peaks. But as her mind melted into the element and her breathing slowed, a broader spectrum of color painted the spaces where her thoughts once lived.

There were florid purples and the gentlest shades of robin's egg blue, rivers of lemon splashing onto banks as green as the jungle canopy.

"Follow the rainbow." A stage whisper rose above the drone of chanting before dissolving into the wind. "Fly, air born."

And there she was, back in Peru, dumbstruck and blinking like an idiot. Cynthia stood in the middle of the wild, the depths of night where nature reigned, surrounded by monkey chitters and the croak of bugs.

Nostalgia swelled her heart when she recognized the humid, earthen scent of her former home, the residual traces of burning wood that someone had used to cook signaling the nearness of human inhabitants. She thought she might cry as she breathed in the smell of the closest thing she'd found to home. Close, but no six-fold sisterhood cigar.

Her resolve wavered further when she spotted the ramshackle outhouse by the edge of the creek. She wasn't as far in the trees as she'd thought. The jungle was tricky like that. A short hike and she'd be back at the cabins. Her old cabin. They'd take her back.

It'd be easy. Simple, to abandon her harebrained quest, quit chasing witches through astral hellholes inhabited by riddle-spouting rattlesnakes and return to the bosom of those who'd cared about her once upon a time.

"This is why we need you." Raven's voice, all calm and wise came to her.

She turned to spot him poised between two trees, their thick vines drooping down to frame him like twisted serpentine brackets. "You don't need me at all. You can come here any time, and they'll take you in. They love all shifters. The camp is hard to find, but not impossible."

There. She'd told him just enough to where he could run with the tidbit and figure out where the shifters lived, if he chose to pursue the lead. Let that clue serve as a loyalty test, to see how quickly he'd jump at the chance to use her as his steppingstone on the road to his goal.

"You misunderstand. You're part of our circle, Cynthia, as our destined witch. We don't just want to go to the shifters to fit in. We want to take *you* with us."

She squinted, blinking away blotches. "Why? They'll accept you without me. If you can prove you can shift, they'll take you, and you can all run free in the jungle."

The community technically vetted people, but they'd gotten good at sniffing out phonies and mostly done away with their once-rigorous stance on screening. Besides, let Raven and his buds prove themselves once they put the pieces together based on her hints. She wasn't particularly eager to stick her neck out and vouch for them when she barely knew them.

Knowing Raven in the biblical sense didn't count for much. It wasn't like she'd even given up Peru yet, not technically. Raven and the others might discern the true location, but at least she had plausible deniability. Cowardly? Sure. But at least this way she wasn't a traitor who had betrayed the only family who had ever truly accepted her.

He shook his head. "It's all so much deeper than that. The ritual we started after you and I did the spirit ceremony revealed things. Big things that we already suspected and have now confirmed. All witches and shifters must be congregated in one locale for the prophecy to commence. Every single magical being on this earth must meet under a portal. We need strength in numbers gathered in a nodal network to charge the energy field with our magic. Only then can the Light Triad and Dark Trinity collaborate."

She rubbed her face with both hands until she gave up on the notion that she could make everything he'd just said make tidy sense. "I can't promise that I can deliver witches to you, if that's what you want. I don't think Helen—Spirit—is all that interested in being recruited into this prophecy, for starters."

He took three steps closer to her, entering conversational space, and caught both of her hands. "There's this recurring theme that comes up when I try to talk to you about the prophecy and our destinies. Whatever I say, you counter it with pushback about how you're not as useful to me as I think you are."

Some scabby, protective plaque inside of her began to crumble. She jutted her chin at him and tried real hard to toughen her heart. "So what? Maybe I'm not."

"Missing the point yet again. I don't want to *use* you."

She snorted even as his rebuttal struck her somewhere buried and vulnerable. "Of course you do."

"I don't, Cynthia, I really don't. I want to collaborate with you. Join with you for our mutual benefit and the benefit of all of our kind." On a pause, he swallowed so hard his Adam's apple bobbed. His next words were too soft, wide, open, "I want to be with you."

No. The final sentence was too much. She couldn't afford to risk the destruction of losing herself to a heady temptation like that. People left. People disappointed. True closeness was a lie, or at least a fantasy that never lasted too long. "I don't think I'm ready to get into all of that."

"Fine. Fair. Tell me what you want. Deep down."

Nah. She doubly wasn't ready to bear her soul or have the onus of confession thrown back on her. It was his turn to answer questions. But, as long as he was in a forthcoming place, she could meet him halfway or at least entertain his proposition. The Peru secret wasn't blown, but the scaffolding around it had crumbled to an extent that she felt safe demanding more honesty from him. "I want to know what's in this for you. Why do you want witches and shifters corralled in some big, dysfunctional paranormal reunion? What's your skin in the game with this prophecy?"

He held a gravid beat of silence. Haunting nocturnal ballads blew through the wilderness, making absence of speech all the more pronounced. "If we don't do our part, if we neglect to abide the tenets of our destiny, the world as we know it ends. Or, more accurately, plunges into a low frequency realm. And a lot of shifters will die before the descent happens."

"Die how?"

"Sacrificially. So their negative energy can be harvested to expedite the descent. They'll die like my family died."

"Says who?"

"Says me. Says the prophetic voice in the astral realm while speaking through me. Look, I can't tell you how you're supposed to label it, I can only tell you what I witnessed. Visions came to us after we joined in the fire circle. Our minds are linked. Those visions were commensurate with themes that Portia read in the cards." He closed another foot of space and brought her bundled hands to his chest. "You are a crucial component of our circle, Cynthia. You round us out. We can't connect to the witches without you, and your coven can't fully play your part in the prophecy without us. Think symbiosis. Synthesis. Collaborative flow. Destiny rewards it. Fate demands it."

"So the name of the game is to get five other witches plus myself in the same space as the shifter community."

"Yes. To do partner work with the assistance of shifters—your book talks about shifters, right?"

Technically, the tome referenced familiars and humans with animal aspects. As far as she could tell, this was close enough to draw a confident parallel. Which he would not know unless he read it. "So you went through my things, or what?"

"No. I made educated guess based on the visions I told you about. I'm correct, aren't I?"

"Essentially."

"Okay." He cocked his head, tilting his ear upward as if listening to some sign available only to him. "We need to get back up there soon. After our last two excursions I think I've got a pretty good idea of realm travel and how long we can be gone before we get lost."

"You're trying to tell me that P—where the shifters live is a realm and not real? Or that we're in a shadow realm like where the shifters are?" Now she was a little spooked. This was all a lot. Had she been in a real, physical place when she'd lived in Peru, or some matrix-like facsimile of the three-dimensional world?

"No, not quite. I guided us to a physical place to show you what I knew about it. The basics of geography, terrain, and climate. But Portia and the others are elsewhere. In realms. And since we're spellbound at the moment, we're operating as a conjoined entity. If the clock runs out and someone gets stuck, we all might."

They'd built a symbiotic chain link of sorts, interdependent, with their metaphysical systems bound by magic. Her fate was glued to whatever Ether and company were currently up to. Just ducky. "Yeah. Good call. Let's jet." Her training had taught her that teleportation happened by calling upon the nearest sister element for help. A gaping cubby cleaving the base of a giant tree would work just fine. "You teleport with your phone by chance? We'll use the flashlight app to check in that hole for anything that likes to bite and then go in. I can get us home that way."

"Cynthia." He spoke her name the same as a plea.

She was in for a big ask or major reveal, she could feel magnitude coming down the pipes. After winning a battle not to bite her lip or play with her hair, she asked, "What?"

"I need to know that you're in this with me. A united front. That you care and are committed."

It sure sounded like he was asking for so much more than her loyalty, that his request, at least subconsciously, came from a thirst for closeness. Which was not to say that she lacked such an urge but catching feelings didn't play a part in the equation. They couldn't. There was too much at stake, which he'd already outlined bluntly. "Yes. I'm dedicated. I mean, what else am I gonna do? But you need to know that I don't get involved with people. I hope that you aren't seeing this as a lead in to a relationship or whatever, because I don't do relationships."

His expression was stoic. Too damn stoic, because despite herself she really really wanted to get a reaction out of him and was disappointed in her failure to trigger pushback. "Okay. Got it. You don't do relationships. This is a strictly business arrangement for the sake of the greater good."

"Don't make me out to be a Pollyanna." The instant she finished her sentence, a bone-chilling cross between a hiss and a screech joined the usual mating calls. She shivered, reluctantly writing off the noise as the war cry of some mama cat or whatever. "I'm in this for me. To form my coven. We can help each other by aligning our goals. Quid pro quo. That's all."

"That's all." He let go of her hands, leaving her with a sad, empty sensation where the pleasure of his touch once filled her up. "We'd better be careful not to keep crossing those blurry lines."

Was this guy fucking with her? She swore she caught a lilt in his voice, smug and taunting as he'd let go of her and watched her face likely fall in the wake of his faux rejection. She rubbed her thumb and forefinger together. "I mean, we can still have sex. As long as it's just sex, and for the furtherance of magic rituals only. Strictly instrumental."

"Strictly instrumental." A corner of his mouth quirked. "I agree to your terms, boss." He squinted and brushed his temple. "Now we really need to go. I'm losing Dragon, and he could pull us down any second like a drowning person shoving their rescuer under."

"Follow me." Circling his wrist, she led him to the hole at the base of the trunk. "You end up with your phone?"

He reached for his back pocket and excavated a cell. "Yeah. Did you know that we can only teleport with people and things that we are physically touching?"

"Nope." She crouched as a slim beam of ice-blue light came on and scratched over the bumpy hollow of the abyss. Bugs squirmed in dirt, but no nesting animals with a penchant for biting or stinging occupied the belly of the tree. "You learn something new everyday. Get in."

"See? We make a good team."

She shot him an askance look. Raven better not attempt any goalpost moving on the terrain of their engagement. Sex and mystical collaboration: sure. Feelings: nope. "Don't test me, birdman, or I'll put you on the express highway to Hell."

"I'll be on my way to the promised land."

A laugh jumped from her throat. Yanking him along, she sunk to her knees and crawled inside the tree. "Shut up and get in this gross pit with me."

"You're infinitely persuasive, Cynthia." Raven joined her, the space so cramped that their knees touched.

It was a weird, innocent sort of intimacy, like children playing in the woods, and the tenderness of the posture plus some buried, nostalgic memory made her heart softer than it had been in awhile. "Hold my hand again and invest the sum of your concentration on the words I'm about to speak." She'd hate to leave him here with whatever had been shrieking bloody murder a moment ago. Once they'd grabbed on to each other, she pressed her palm against the cold, rough bark an inch above her head. "Sister Earth, I, an air born, humbly call upon your guidance. Please send me and my companion back to the ground on which we camp so we can reunite with our compatriots and guide them out of the astral further."

Her perception went weird, contracting and expanding. Claustrophobia worsened the vertigo. Her head swum as dizziness set in, walls collapsing to box her in in a suffocating crush. She managed to draw a few thin, short breaths, nowhere near enough oxygen to fill her lungs or quell the incessant uptick of fear. She smelled her sweat. Her heartbeat fluttered, her pulse suddenly thready. *Can't breathe.*

Fuck, it was like being buried alive. She was being buried alive. A scream tore up her throat and died on her tongue. Was she shaking, having a seizure, dying?

"It's okay," Raven's assurance soothed like balm. His grasp, warm and firm, tethered her to life and stability. As if to emphasize his grounding role, he interlaced their fingers in a knot so strong and tender as to seem unbreakable. "You have command of all of these elements. Earth is close to physical death, so teleporting through it is intense, but it's all an illusion."

Her palm glued against his, she clutched him. Clung. If she'd had her wits about her, she would have been embarrassed. But she had bigger tacos to grill. *It's all an illusion.*

When words didn't come, she mentally recited the incantation to teleport through earth.

Dirt filled her mouth, stuffing her with panic. Her nostrils sealed. Lungs burned, desperate, clawing, crazed. Some primal scream echoed through her skull, her heart, and she was sure that she'd died or gone insane when she woke up standing on the beach, gasping like a stuck fish.

"You did it." Raven brought her knuckles to her lips and kissed, probably breaking one of their rules, but she was too blasted to care.

"Thanks." She choked out, her surroundings returning as globular blotches of light and color before coalescing. Portia and the other two men, all alert, looked on. The fire raged.

"We did it," Portia squealed, jumping up and down and taking Ether and Dragon with her.

"Did what?" She only kind of wanted to know. Mostly, she wanted to go lie down in the tent as nausea clamped down on her insides and flooded her mouth with saliva.

Ether turned to her, and he was not himself. The soul beyond the supposed windows was not his.

"We meet again, hitchhiker." Denise-Nerissa spoke. "This wasn't quite what I meant when I asked you to call me, but it's fine. I've always fantasized about slipping into a male's skin."

TEN

Everyone had taken a seat on the sand, Cynthia included, and listened rapt as Denise-Nerissa spoke of her possession experience. Or Denise-Nerissa-Ether spoke of his/her possession experience. Whatever. The situation was muddled to an alarming degree. For now, though, the name of the game was focusing on their newest companion to figure out as much as possible, how to help.

"Is Ether in there with you?" Cynthia asked, worried about the fate of her new acquaintance.

"Yes." Denise-Nerissa rubbed Ether's commanded palm over the center of his skinny chest. This was all so weird. "He consented to this possession, for the sake of the ritual. So your friend is calm, alert, and learning as we speak."

"Learning what?" Cynthia tried not to stare at the uncanny weirdness of the blended person. Features and a voice that didn't quite fit together plus some ineffable X-factor assembled into a creepy composite that was robotic and aloof.

An unsettling sneer struck her as energetically divorced from both Nerissa and Ether. "The ways."

Gee, thanks.

"Is he okay?" Portia asked, her tone soft and genuine, the shocking nature of the spell's outcome seeming to have depleted her earlier enthusiasm.

"The footprint of his consciousness has shrunk to make space for me," Denise-Nerissa admitted. "But he is at peace and will fully restore when the time is right."

A collective sigh of relief joined the breeze. The wind had picked up, crisp against Cynthia's cheeks and spritely enough to make a dervish of her hair. A shiver rippled over her skin, those sea gales penetrating her lightweight clothing. Spooky energy contributed to a dark bite in the air. She reached for Raven's hand on some impulse and pulled back in time to play with her nails instead.

No affection. Cuddly stuff might blur lines. Sex for ritual magic only. Her rules. Her lines.

Cynthia scooted a few inches closer to the fire, seeking both warmth and a closer look at their multifaceted companion. Possession wasn't to be taken lightly. It'd behoove her to keep an eye on the person formerly known as Ether. "What should we call you?"

"Nerissa is fine for my purposes. But if you need to refer to me as Ether as means of cover, I understand." What were once his elfish features remained largely unaltered, save for a regal, more standoffish slant to his expression.

Even for someone who had known Ether for a short time, it was evident that another spirit now wore his flesh. Cynthia shifted her weight on the lumpy sand, tracing idle fingertips over the goosebumps that'd erupted on her forearm.

Raven took off his jacket and draped it around Cynthia, surprising her with the tender, quiet gesture of care. She tried not to be too blatant with how she hugged the warm leather to her body, smelling and feeling traces of him in the item of clothing.

"So is his form the seventh body you're split up into?" She slid her arms into his sleeves and zipped up. A little baggy, but in a good way, like a boyfriend's varsity jacket.

Yikes. Cynthia mentally slapped herself for that ridiculous, goo-goo girly thought. The body-hopping situation was a big deal with severe ramifications for their mission. No time for silly fantasies.

"No," Nerissa said. "I left one of my other forms when I jumped into your friend's and returned that body to its original inhabitant. That's what fascinates me, actually. That I can inhabit six. No more, no fewer. We all can grasp the symbolism inherent, I presume."

Everyone nodded in unison. Raven asked, "Did you pick the people whose bodies you move into based on any kind of discernment or system? Did you have agency in the process, or did they, or both?"

Smart question. Cynthia peeked at his profile, sharp cheekbones and a strong nose cut in relief against smooth skin fit for a nineteenth-century aesthete. Erudite and refined while somehow also masculine. The look of a poet. Handsome *and* intelligent.

Get. A. Grip!

"Why Ether?" Dragon interjected. "Don't get me wrong, we're thankful that you're here, but why did you flow into him after we finished the spell to conjure a prophetic key?"

Portia shot her pal a guilty look that made Dragon wince. "Somehow we combined our energy to offer up one of our bodies tonight. A Russian roulette of sorts. Ether drew the short straw."

Raven shrugged. "Or the long straw. Depending on your perspective. Who says that possession is bad? Sounds like a chosen one situation to me."

Dragon and Portia bobbed their heads, Raven's reasoning seeming to have absolved them of internalized culpability.

Cynthia schooled a goofy smile out of existence. Raven was optimistic with a leadership streak, too. She cringed at herself. Murdering this budding crush in its infancy was gonna be tough as hell.

Denise-Nerissa took a turn, "I used to think, based on my research, that there were six individual coven mothers. One for each element. But now I'm not so sure. Perhaps it's only me, bouncing from body to body, inhabiting skins of magically inclined individuals who prepare the road for me to meet the Coven Daughters."

"You didn't answer his question about Ether," Cynthia said as politely as the situation warranted without crossing a line into combativeness. "Why his body and not someone else's?"

"I'm aware that I didn't provide you answers. Truth is, I don't know. It's possible that my movement is entirely in the hands of fate. Or destiny. Or that spells cast to facilitate my possession are imprecise and, to a degree, random. I can tell you that each person I ended up in was open to receive me in some way. Even if only by living as a receptive beacon to the esoteric. Denise the trucker had gone down more than a few new age rabbit holes along her spiritual journey. The four of you, of course, had Ether the shifter. Another person along the way had some psychic gifts. For all I know, that may be the extent of the connection."

Two principles from Nerissa's explanation stuck out and did a runaround in the grooves of Cynthia's brain. Fate versus destiny. She tapped her bottom lip. Helen had mentioned the distinction during their walk along the shore. Surely it was no coincidence that Nerissa evoked such a similar notion. "Were any of the people you possessed witches?"

"Not unless you count Ether."

"Do you know any other witches besides Cynthia?" Raven asked. His knuckles brushed Cynthia's, causing her heart to skitter. She didn't rip her hand away. It was almost physically impossible to do so, on this diabolical, unseasonably cold summer evening when she longed for the comfort and support of a sympathetic person.

"Personally?" Nerissa didn't wait for anyone to clarify, "When you rule out the dabblers and wannabes, I've known two that I'd classify as having observable supernatural abilities. Both in my hometown. My coven daughter and a woman who works in an arcane magic shop. Surely there are others here and there who practice the craft with varying degrees of seriousness and competency, but I'm only aware of those two as formidable practitioners of exceptional power." She paused, coughed, and when she spoke again, her voice was roughened and raspy. "The shopkeeper claims to have had a brief encounter with a young woman whose mind she was able to read—ability to access thoughts is a relatively failsafe tell that a witch is dealing with kinfolk connected to an ancient bloodline. Not sure if this young woman is affiliated with the Coven Daughters Prophecy." More coughing.

Cynthia sprang to her feet and jogged to the larger tent, where she'd seen Raven place a big red cooler. She popped the lid, relieved to see lots of bottled waters. She snagged one and ran it to Nerissa.

"Such a considerate young lady." Nerissa twisted off the plastic cap and downed a big gulp. "Where was I? I've lost my train of thought, I apologize. All of this possession and body-jumping has made me a wee bit featherbrained."

After reclaiming her seat beside Raven, a tad bit closer to him for the sole purpose of stealing some of his body heat, Cynthia recapped. "We covered how may people you possessed, and you speculated that they were all open to metaphysical or spiritual things in some way. You mentioned two other legitimate witches besides me."

Soon, Cynthia would have to look for an inroad to broaching her encounter with Helen. She'd tread carefully for a bit first, let Nerissa talk as much as she wished. The last thing she wanted was to come off as overeager, pushy, or desperate. Any skewed energy like that risked overwhelming Nerissa or looking like an ambush ought to be avoided. Best to practice her underused life skill of holding back and using an abundance of caution.

"Right, right. As soon as I rented a space in your friend Ether, I left someone else behind. Physically, I vacated their body. More than on that literal level, though, I gained a stronger connection to and affinity for this element." She pointed at the fire. "Perhaps because it was so heavily incorporated in a ritual to move me. I can't be sure, but I am now tied to this flame with a cord of steel."

Cynthia's interest level kicked up. Now they were getting somewhere. The bit about elements was juicy. She played with the cuff of Raven's borrowed leather sleeve to keep her body busy. "Can you elaborate any more? Whatever you have to share or are willing to share will help."

"I've garnered a philosophical appreciation that I lacked before. For example, three earthly elements are inherent. Free-standing, if you will, fully constituted of their own accords. Except fire. Fire must be summoned through a combination of her sisters. She's a sum. An endgame who is constructed with the efforts of her accomplices."

"Oxygen and earth," Raven supplied. "Like rubbing sticks together."

"There's a touch of chaos in there, too," Portia added. "The genesis of the spark. The destructive aspect."

"Even spirit is involved." Cynthia's mind raced as connections clicked. "The will to create something out of nothing, to harness and claim, springs from a determined spirit. Prometheus was motivated by sheer force of will. The drive to take a powerful force from the gods."

If the seats on the sand had had edges, all would have been perched on their respective precipices. Portia picked up the conversational ball. "Water as well. Dryness or moisture plays a central role. For fire to flourish, the conditions have to be set. Just so. She's mighty, but fickle."

Cynthia found herself snapping her fingers repeatedly, an old tic she'd used back in high school to marshal her thoughts when they began to spin out of control. "The ultimate example of collaboration, the end result of partner work. Fire can't *exist* without partner work."

Someone slurped down a massive inhale, the sound of heightened emotion igniting a bright light in Cynthia's mind. Her speech tumbled out at a rapid clip to keep up with her developing thoughts. "Chaos, Spirit, and Fire make up the Dark Trinity. They're alike, fundamentally. They must be. These three elements are ungrounded in some way, all detached from the earth, or represent a whole that exceeds the sum of elemental features." She dug her fingertips into her temples. Her heart thudded. "There's more. I can feel it."

Raven leaned forward, closing space on Nerissa though his gesture was mostly symbolic given the flame between them. "She's right. There's more. What is it, this excess that we're dealing with? Interdependence? Agency?"

Portia got a word in edgewise, "What does this mean for finding the fire witch? I'm not sure that I follow."

"As for the fire witch, I'm not positive. She may only manifest with our direct intention." The fireside glow reflected off Ether's pale platinum locks while shadowing his face, creating an artsy effect. In a flash, Nerissa stood on Ether's lanky legs. "It does us no good, though, to tumble down rabbit holes. Endless pursuit of one topic will only frustrate and confuse us. Such *folly*, I believe, is the influence of chaos magic that is constantly in play."

Cynthia's heart sunk. Was Nerissa preparing to leave? Worse, what gave with the warning about chaos magic slipping in to screw them up? She didn't need any more problems. "You're saying that you feel chaos magic right now?"

"Yes. Absolutely." A whistle pierced the wind, one that Cynthia may have only imagined. The effect was the same. "I feel her," Nerissa's tone dropped to a lower, scarier one. "She's here right now with us. Sister

Folly is here, sowing chaos. Disillusionment. Discontent. Error and misdirection. She wants to get inside of me." Nerissa stumbled, buckling forward toward the raging fire.

Portia gasped, bolted up, and grabbed her arm before she fell. "Is she making out clear words or phrases?"

Nerissa shook her head, her legs still wobbly, her face slack with stupor. "She wants in. At first, she'll give you things. Then she'll borrow, and finally she'll take. Don't attempt to counter her with your hatred or scorn, for any attention will make her stronger."

Cynthia's blood ran frigid. "What do we do?"

Nerissa dropped to her knees and screamed, a brain-melting cry that echoed across the water and banged off the cliff walls like the howl of a scorned siren.

Her chest tight and her world shredded by the shriek, Cynthia jumped up and made a break for the tent. There had to be some spell in her book for undoing possession. In the book or in those damn cards that created this mess in the first place.

She'd staggered over a few feet of sand when Nerissa called out with choppy breath, "Wait."

Her leg muscles locked in place, her entire body trapped in paralysis. Fight or flight instincts warred for dominance. Run to the tent? To the fire with mace? Scream? Look back in calmness?

"I'm fine," Nerissa called. "I've expelled the unclean spirit. For now."

Cynthia turned around. Nerissa was shaking in the wind, Portia rubbing her arm, the whole display a strange look on Ether's imposing stature and edgy aesthetic. "Are you sure?"

"I'm sure." Nerissa straightened her spine, waving her hands in time with the stubborn wobble that shook her voice. "Did the rest of you feel it? Something wasn't right, and then the fog lifted. I was taken by a nearly insurmountable force. The sensation was sickening. Horrid. But it's over now. It was bad."

Portia glanced at the sand as if trying not to stare.

"I felt a change," Dragon said in a hesitant way that failed to inspire confidence.

Cynthia locked eyes with Raven, who said nothing. She hadn't felt an intuitive transition from bad vibes to good. On the contrary, Nerissa continued to act weird and doth protested too much.

With Nerissa's behavior combined with Portia and Dragon's eggshell walk, the whole scene had an aura of off-ness to it. She had no reasonable counterpoint to make and offered a noncommittal noise. "I trust you, Nerissa," she lied. Or rather, she distrusted the byproduct of the fucked up possession experiment and *definitely* distrusted Folly and her chaos magic. Which didn't change the fact that it would be to her benefit to learn about Folly and her wiles in pursuit of the chaos witch. "But I'll admit that I still feel unsure of what's happening. Give me something I can use. Direction. A tip."

Nerissa covered her mouth with the back of one hand as a small, haunting moan escaped her lips. "She's going to continue to try and infiltrate us and release the Other Ones. We won't be able to control her. The only one capable of gaining command of Folly's magic is your chaos sister." She swooned back and forth before marshalling her faculties. "It's speeding up. Shifting. Merging. Do you feel it? The tissues of the universe are fraying in preparation for the Other Ones' ultimate takeover." Some different, slick presence spoke through the Ether body and Nerissa voice, "Don't worry. In exchange for allowing the Other Ones to feed, the holograph will surround us in a cage of light for our eternal salvation."

Raven stood abruptly and backed up a few paces to reach Cynthia. He circled an arm around her waist and pretended to look at the tent while muttering, barely audible, "She's unraveling. We need to go. Run. On my signal, take what you can carry and run to the motorcycle. Portia and Dragon will follow."

Cynthia's throat thickened. She hated feeling helpless and defeated more than anything in the world, yet here she was. "This is so colossally fucked."

"I know. Now, Cynthia."

"No," Nerissa bellowed in a new tone, mannish and guttural with a protracted vowel. Her normal speech returned, "You must not leave me in here with Her. You summoned me. You prepared me. You knew what to expect. Yet you conspire to abandon me when the situation becomes complicated."

"Nobody wants to abandon you," Raven shouted over the wind and fire. "What we don't want is to do any more damage. You need to get control of what's inside you and offer some assurance that you'll be able to keep it dormant for us to even begin to consider the possibility that this might work out. Those are the terms. The bare minimum for our continued loyalty."

"I'll try. Bring me your cards and Cynthia's book." Nerissa doubled over, clutching the sides of her head as series of seizures made her writhe and twist. "I have an idea. For how to both banish Folly from the frontal position my consciousness and put her to work in a less dominant area. Quick!"

"I don't like this," Raven said.

Portia and Dragon looked to him.

"Me neither," Cynthia's mouth dried. She watched in horror as Nerissa succumbed to her episode, her vocalizations alternating between wails and maniacal laughter. "I hate the idea of surrendering my book. A lot. But what else do we do? She's here now, and deteriorating, but if we can fix this we might have a shot at making her involvement productive or beneficial."

Raven's jaw clenched. His nostrils flared, his gaze bouncing between the tent and a spot adjacent to the fire where the cards, packed up in their box, sat. "Every word she's saying could easily be a trap laid by Folly. What if she gets so clever that we can't even distinguish the possession from Ether or Nerissa anymore?"

"I'm aware. If we can find a way to work with her, though, there's a lead on both the fire witch and the chaos witch. She brings so much. I wouldn't have gotten to that theory about summoning fire on my own."

Nerissa stilled on her feet, going as rigidly motionless as a robot. "Losing...control. Fast. Now! B...book. Cards. Must...halt...gah!"

"Fuck!" Raven hissed, balling his fist like he itched for a target to hit.

"How else?" Cynthia turned to face him head on, suddenly regarding him as a longtime ally, a comrade in battle instead of a fast fling. It was an odd feeling, watching her relationship with someone evolve in real time, and a strange sensation that she lacked the luxury to analyze. "How else, Raven, are we supposed to nail down a solid lead on those chaos and fire witches? You said yourself that linking up with them is the most important element of this craft. From how I see it, we're out of options. And not to cast aspersions, but this summon and possess plan was dreamt up and executed by *your* people. So here we are. Bed made. Lying down in the shitty mess. Let's figure it out before Folly goes haywire and turns us all into zombie incubators for these Other Ones or whatever it is that she's fighting for over there."

They locked gazes for a few seconds, the seductive, intense energy they shared becoming wilder than the night itself.

"Fine. Portia. Hand Nerissa the cards."

Portia scooped up the deck and forked them over.

Nerissa crouched to a squat, movements ungainly but purposeful, and made fast work of spreading, sorting, and pulling.

Cynthia battled a wave of queasiness as she ran to her book, held it tight, and ferried the tome to Nerissa.

A broken "Thank you" croaked out of Nerissa's mouth, shaky fingers splitting pages to receive the blessing of firelight.

The next several seconds were a spinning blur of chants, fast hands slapping over paper, and the stunning materialization of six silver lights in the sky that hovered low and fantastical over the belly-up tome. Nerissa's language, foreign and forceful, was impossible to ignore, a taboo lifeline of terror.

The six balls of light coalesced into one blurry globe that bled iridescent spillage over the paper. Nerissa drew her hand back as if preparing to pitch a baseball and flung her arm forward with fingers spread wide. The glowing blob followed the force of her throw until a luminescent splatter blasted one of the cliff walls, faded to a faint glimmer, and died.

Nobody said a word. Nerissa's pants and gasps filled silence. Finally, after several agonizing seconds, the old lady in Ether's body spoke with jubilant exhaustion, "I did it. I did it."

"Elaborate," Cynthia stammered, a mix of chemicals raining down on her faculties. Her stomach churned with worry and a dull headache set in. "What did you do?"

"Go see for yourself." Nerissa pointed at the cliff wall. "I transmuted Folly into a messenger sigil. From here on out, she, in the form of the sigil for chaos, will follow us on our journey and deliver important communications on what to do next."

Cynthia ran to the rock. A ghostly shimmer of residual light from the magical ball painted the stone with some kind of shape. She squinted and leaned close. No mistaking the Coven Daughters sigil, that familiar polygon with an element symbol marking each side of the hexagon. The shape, as far as Cynthia knew, represented the six witches bound together in fate to their respective elements. The one in the middle was different, though. No hand with scrawled, squiggly fingers.

One four-letter word, penned in sloppy text with awkward spacing between the letters, replaced the normal mark.

Cynthia felt her lips divide. Reading that word somehow managed to simultaneously confound, irritate, and amaze her. Perhaps because of the auspiciousness it signaled, the sense of coming full circle in return to a magnetic place whose pull she never managed to resist.

She'd been hailed by otherworldly forces to return to a sacred place, accompanied by a man whom she couldn't quit despite how hard she fought those feelings. The irony was not lost on Cynthia as she read the word over and over.

P E R u.

Someone wasn't about to let her wiggle out from under the weight of her own lie.

ELEVEN

CYNTHIA HAD A *LOT* OF QUESTIONS, MANY OF THEM LOGISTICAL. Unfortunately, Nerissa had passed out, crumpled onto the sand, and taken the fetal shape before surrendering to slumber. Portia and Dragon had carried her to the larger tent where she snored softly, tucked in a sleeping bag patterned with cartoon characters.

Cynthia stooped and retrieved her precious spell book, a quick leaf through prompting a rush of relief. None of the pages had been damaged or marred in the frenzy. A girl had to count blessings when they came scant. She glimpsed again at the tent, where Portia and Dragon had bundled themselves in blankets next to Nerissa and were doing their own thing with the cards. "Are those two an item? Or are all of you, like, a polyamorous collective?"

The question and hypothetical that it presented stoked an odd pang in her gut. The tents felt farther away than they were and so did Raven, even though he stood right by her. She clutched her book tight to her chest, hugging a treasured friend.

Raven touched her forearm as she rose. "Hey. Are you okay?"

Okay was a relative term given the circumstances, but there was no point in cutting him down when he was trying to be nice. "Yeah. Fine. That was a massive drama dump that Nerissa treated us to. I hope she sleeps thought the night, cause I don't wanna wake to her standing over me speaking in tongues."

He tucked a strand of her wayward hair behind her ear, making her shudder with a ripple of pleasure. "Wanna talk about it while the fire's still going? I've got booze and the ingredients for roasted marshmallows. We can decompress."

A cackle busted out. Raven was so random. "Sounds cozy enough to bring me right back to Girl Scout camp."

He quirked a single, tidy eyebrow. "You were a Girl Scout?"

"Hell yeah." She flashed the three-finger salute. "Where do you think I got my independent streak and entrepreneurial zest?"

He was grinning at her now, sexy and warm with his perfect teeth. "Independent streak is obvious. What's up with the entrepreneurial zest?"

She pointed to a sloppy wad of seaweed that the ocean had deposited a yardstick's distance from her foot. "See that?"

He snorted. "Intriguing segue. And yes. Are you saying that you have a talent for upcycling nature's detritus into a saleable product? You make that shit into soap? Candles? Shopping bags?"

"I make it dance." She whipped up a small vortex of air, an easy parlor trick at this point, and used her focus to slide the whirlpool underneath the briny flotsam. Buoyed immediately, the sea trash sprang to life, tentacles flying every which way as its jaunty movements animated empty space. "Visitors at a pagan festival paid me a hundred bucks a pop to witness a similar spectacle last summer with balloons and shaving cream." She dropped her concentration, sending the blob to the sand with a dull plop. "They wanted to pick my brain after and take notes. I charged them for that Q&A, too. Thirty bucks per hour."

"I'd have paid fifty." He gave her a golf clap before tugging on the collar of the jacket he'd lent her. "This looks good on you. C'mon. Let's get loaded."

"Sure, why not." She liked him. What else was she going to do? Besides, hanging out was harmless. Not like they were going to fall in love. Their status was to be fuck buddies at most. If she was going on a road trip south of the border, like for real, it would actually be really cool to have on hand someone she liked to chat with and screw when the urge for fun release struck. "Get the goods." She sat by the fire once again, her book safely placed in front of her folded legs.

She could get used to having him around. Which meant that she had to stay vigilant against the intrusion of feelings, those miscreants. *What would it feel like if I let go?* Wispy daydreams of a meaningful relationship blew around the far reaches of her mind. A rush of giddy fear took her aback.

Fortunately, before she had a chance to do any potentially dangerous ruminating about what they meant to each other and future potential and blah blah, Raven sauntered over, carrying a plastic bag in one hand and a big-ass bottle by the neck in the other. He handed her a wooden skewer with a jumbo marshmallow impaled near the tip.

She stuck her cube into the belly of the fire, watching dragon's breath burn lily-white flesh to a blackened crisp. "A lot to unpack with what Nerissa said back there, huh?"

The marshmallow was reduced to a shriveled hunk of char when Cynthia finally pulled it out as a burnt offering sacrificed to the fire goddess. Every seemingly mundane action felt so damn symbolic now, guided by an invisible hand. She forced herself not to peek at the message on the cave wall.

"You like 'em well-done, huh?" Following a swig of brown liquor straight from the bottle, Raven offered her a graham cracker and four squares of chocolate.

"Yup." She smashed her marshmallow between the candy and crackers, not connecting with how hungry she was until she sniffed the mouthwatering sweetness of sugary cocoa when white goo oozed over the sides of her desert sandwich. A big bite exploded a flavor medley of spicy sweetness over her tongue, and she chowed down. "I've always liked watching them burn. So I started eating them that way. It just sort of worked out. In the aforementioned Girl Scouts summer camps, I'd pretend I was a cannibal queen who ruled a deserted island and roasted the flesh of my victims." She polished off her treat, thinking back to those twisted fantasies. How she'd met her best friends at camp, her fellow freaks and outcasts. She'd kept the cannibal story to herself, though, slipping away to rule her private kingdom as Queen Cynthia the Wicked when the normie world became too much to bear. "They were always idiot tourists, in my scenarios. Disrespectful. Stepping out of bounds. Going where they didn't belong."

"So, you killed and ate them?"

"Correct." She licked sticky residue off her fingers, simultaneously transported to a happy place and affixed deliciously in the moment.

He passed the whisky. "Demented. I love it."

She swiped the handle and washed down her last bites with a swig. Alcohol scalded her tongue and throat, sufficient to raze the lingering memory of the alluring way that Raven spoke that "l" word. Smooth and rich, like the melted chocolate. "I suppose I've always looked to my mind to shape my reality, mold the world to make it more enjoyable. Maybe that was always witchcraft latent in me, ya know? Nursing a penchant for environmental manipulation."

"Or maybe you just never fit in and searched for creative ways to take control." He penetrated the fire with his skewered marshmallow, lightly browned the blob on each side, and assembled his s'more. "I can relate."

Ugh. He'd barely cooked it. What was even the point? "Why make s'mores if you're going to eat them straight-up *raw*?" She wasn't ready to get interpersonally raw with him and hear him enumerate how he could relate to her. Better to detour away from the emotional danger zone by instigating a superficial, juvenile conflict.

He pretended to glare at her defiantly while downing half of his creation in a big chomp. "Deal breaker?"

"No." Not that they were entertaining the prospect of a deal, but it was fun to bust his balls. "I will, however, judge you mercilessly for your unacceptable culinary campfire preferences."

With a flick of his hand, he motioned for the bottle. "All good. You're hot when you activate hater mode."

She watched him drink, his full lips wrapped around the bottle and his long, moving throat suddenly sexual in its elegance. "Don't hog that. And give me some more chocolate. I'm starving."

"Bossy. What are you, a secret BDSM dom?"

Sure, whatever. She could fem-dom it up with the best of them. "I'll tie you to the bedpost and peg you till you scream if you want. Just say the words."

The food bag landed at her feet as she took the bottle, her original swig already going to her head, making her relaxed and tipsy.

He studied her in the most disarming of ways. "That's tempting. But what's even more fascinating to me is this thing you have going where you make it impossible to one-up you."

Eh. Okay. Valid. Vulnerability wasn't her jam and conceding in any manner was a form of being vulnerable. "Keep up with me then, birdman." Easier and safer to snark, snipe, parry, jest, and provoke. A big slug of alcohol went down easier this time, her brain swimming, her fingertips fuzzy and tingling. She pointed the spout of the bottle at the tent. "What are we going to do with her?"

"Maybe you should tell me. I thought she was your mentor."

"I don't know who or what she is anymore." She sent the whisky over to him, vowing to slow down on the sauce. Drunk Cynthia emoted excessively and relaxed her inner controls, stumbled into bold states that served nobody. Least of all her, with a past history of opening up to others culminating in getting dumped like so much trash. "Are you up for this trip? Like, for real?" All she had to do was pretend that she, too, was on a wild goose chase, at least until she trusted him enough to reveal the precise location of the shifters. It would help if she could get in touch with someone from her old community, too, to give them a heads-up.

She stared into the fire, alcohol blunting the edges of a rush as she waited on his answer. Numerous possibilities existed on the Peru front, many of them bad and involving the rejection of her returned presence. She'd walked out on the jungle shifters, why should they take her back? Cynthia was a one-off type, the sort of temporary person that others forgot, a pit stop on a journey. The sight of her washed up again on their proverbial shore might very well irritate them beyond convincing.

Besides, they were animal people, and she was a witch. Different. Other. Her heart hurt. She felt small and frozen, then mad in an amorphous way that went both inward and outward.

"What are you thinking about?" Raven asked, leaning his upper body closer. The dip between his two sloping collarbones drew her gaze. The juncture between those bones made the perfect shape for her worshipping tongue, a first point of contact to initiate a downward oral descent.

"Oh, you know." She claimed the bottle but swirled the liquid instead of hitting it up again. A whole mess of confessions and insecure feelings pressed at her surface. If Raven had been someone she didn't care about, she'd have snapped at him. Pushed him away with rudeness. Instead, she slid the bottle across the sand. She didn't need any more to drink. "I guess I'm a little overwhelmed. I don't have a passport, and I uh, don't know exactly where we're going. The first of many problems."

"We can use the Deck of Deceit to turn a gas station receipt into a passport." He moved long fingers over the whisky's glass neck, didn't have a sip, and set the container behind him. "I'm here whenever you want to talk. If you want to talk. Just as long as you know that."

There was too much to say. Too much and not enough yet, half-formed and undercooked globules of emotion as dense as marshmallows and doubly gummy. She shook her head. Or maybe she nodded. The night was so starry that firmament looked ready to spew a burst of glitter. "You ever do anything really super weird that you couldn't tell other people about that was, like, a private ritual for you?"

"Like shift my shape into goddamn avian form?" he deadpanned with perfect timing.

She laughed loud and satisfyingly, a knot within her uncoiling. "Like the cannibal cookout story I told you about. Not because you worried that you'd be judged, but because the act of sharing it would inherently drain some of its magic."

This was one of her litmus tests of sorts. The richer, deeper, and more complexly rule-driven someone's private world was, the easier she could relate to them. Relax around them. Open up, or close into herself while the other person did the same independently, paving the way for comfortable silence and a mutually agreed upon time-out spent alone, together.

Virtually nobody passed the test, with its litany of nuanced, unspoken rules and vaguely defined challenges rife with a certain snobbery.

His look was long, the silence longer. "Yeah."

"Elaborate." Her hopes (for what, specifically, she remained largely unsure) notched higher. She pecked a tiny drink of whisky.

"You know that Chariotz of Fyre band?"

"Yeah, duh." Led Zeppelin-KISS hybrid with more class and superior lyrics. Not her speed, but super popular among the factions of the hipster crowd with a soft spot for classic rock, vinyl records, and mega-spectacle stage shows with all of the old-school bells and whistles. "Did you kill one of them and cannibalize him?"

"You got me. The guitarist met a gruesome fate at the end of my beak. I pecked him to death." He winked at the end of his sarcastic comeback.

"That's a shame," she whispered, confident that no rockers had actually died by the point of Raven's mouth. "He was cute."

"No, but for real. They were my first fandom. I had all of their records."

"Uh huh." Her interest waned. This was all pretty basic so far. "I'm sure that you weren't alone."

"Sounds lame, I know. But hang on. I'd play their albums over and over in my room until the words sort of ran together, and then I'd start hearing other words. Messages in the words...like special hidden meanings hanging out underneath the lyrics, or between them. I started writing the messages down in notebooks, which was around the time that the recurring dream started."

Back on the hook, she stared at him. This was just weird enough to make her wonder what happened next. "What was the dream about?"

"A flaming wheel came out of the sky, picked me up, and spirited me to some other dimension. Sometimes it was a good place, sometimes a bad place. I couldn't get a fix on any consistent pattern, so I tried another method with my research."

She stretched her eyebrows in a mix of bemusement and invitation to continue. "I can see why you haven't told anyone else this story. Even the most hardcore groupies would have looked at you funny."

He kicked her foot. "You said that you weren't going to judge me."

"Wrong. I asked if you had a memory that you chose not to share because it was too sacred." In case his skin was thinner than she'd estimated, she added, "I'm just messing around. I'm not judging you for real, this is fascinating. I wanna see where it goes."

Unfazed, he picked up where he'd left off, "I had a hunch about how the deeper messages were working on me. Subliminal. Unconscious. I played the records backwards, and sure enough a bunch of esoteric, occulted content came out. I wrote those lines down in my books to compare notes."

Hidden occult messages in rock songs? Her curiosity took a second, steeper nosedive. He could've swiped this story from any random sixty-minutes episode circa nineteen eighty-three. "What the actual fuck. The nineteen-eighties called. They want their stereotypical Satanic panic fodder back."

"I'm serious. It gets even weirder."

She had to hand it to Raven, his tale of musical obsession put her summer camp bullshit to shame in the bizarre category. "Alright. I'm your captive audience. Enthrall me."

"What I found when I compared the two sets was a code of sorts. Directions on practices for lucid dreaming and astral travel. So I tried out my strategy that night during sleep, and sure enough, I was able to control the path of the chariot. Its destination. I travelled to a realm where I witnessed the architects of the universe constructing the reality that we live in during our waking hours. I worked with them, altering and tweaking the matrix. I saw the hologram projection. It was all around us, an enclosure like a giant honeycomb of hexagons. Each hexagon was its own realm, and all were interconnected. Along with those architects, I modified the simulation."

"Dude." Hexagons? Hologram? *Don't freak out.* He was only describing a dream. There was no reason to suspect that these events had any connection to or bearing on the Coven Daughters prophecy, despite the auspicious hints. Still, her intrigue was boundless. "Who were the architects?"

He shook his head. "Angels, maybe. Some kind of mythical creatures or ancient principalities. They were made of light and shifting their forms. It's hard to say."

"Why were they modifying the simulation with your help?"

"To keep a certain course of events moving along. That's as far as I got. Or at least what I remember."

She reneged on her pledge to cut herself off and slammed down another shot of the liquor. More details were in order. She was powerless against this story and unable to stop thinking about the implications for how Raven's account of nocturnal adventures inspired by mystical codes embedded in hard rock tunes might tie in with all of the other strangeness. "You still have the notebooks?"

"I have a few that I saved." Apprehension radiated off of his cautious answer, but he didn't shut her down either.

"Can we look at them?"

He threw a piece of debris into the flame. "It's not that I'm embarrassed by that stage in my life, but I don't know how helpful it would be to dive back down that vortex."

"I think it might be, though. Now that we're together, and slogging through this prophecy, we need all of the clues that we can dredge up."

He bumped up one of his shoulders in a shy half-shrug. "Maybe it was just scribbles in the diary of a lonely teenager."

"Or maybe you are connected to this prophecy in more ways than you can even imagine. We found each other, right? That counts for something."

All he did for the next several seconds was watch her, his black locks flowing free in the breeze. The cool acknowledgement, sleek confidence layered atop a certain reverence, activated a case of the belly butterflies. Raven spoke volumes without saying a word. He was an energetic master of the nonverbal. "Yes," he finally said. "Yes, we did."

"Let's look. Compare what you wrote to what's in my book." There was a distinct sense, lodged near the base of her spine, that the outcome that she was pushing for was about bringing them closer together. *For the mission.* As long as she continued to reinforce the clear lines of demarcation, they'd be okay. "We'll see how our systems square. We really ought to compare notes if we're planning to leave in the morning and want to feel ready to present a case to the Peruvian clan and/or the witches in case we're able to make contact."

"There's a knowledge is power element to this, you're correct."

"Especially with Nerissa going haywire. Anything magical or esoteric that we can get a fix on represents a potential strategy to help her retain her integrity. And save Ether if it comes to that."

"Okay, fine." He took her hand. "Let's do this before you oversell it so hard that your attempt to persuade me backfires."

She gathered up the trash, high on alcohol and victory. Portia or Dragon had closed their tent, the dome illuminated from the inside by a soft flashlight glow. She lowered her voice to a discreet level, "They are truly all about those cards, huh?"

Once they'd set up in the other tent and closed the door, he responded in a whisper. "That's putting it mildly. I worry sometimes that the investment level borders on obsession. That shooting energy out there in the world with nonstop occult practice that's never fully understood inherently creates blowback. Ripples in the universe that we might not see or feel right away, but that show up eventually." He slouched to dig around in an Army-green rucksack with fabric battered soft from age and use. "But who am I to caution about consequences right now?" Sarcasm dusted the rhetorical question as he pulled out a stack of notebooks with worn, creased covers in varied styles.

Moved by a sudden reversal of commitments, she laid her palm over his wrist before he opened one of his old journals. "Hey, I hear some uncertainty from you right now. If you don't want to do this for any reason, it's fine. I'm sorry if I put pressure on. I got eager to figure stuff out, but these are your private writings, and it sounds like you have some reservations. Or if it's just none of my business, that's all good, too. You don't owe me access to your inner spaces."

"I appreciate it." He set the notebooks on the red sleeping bag that'd been open and splayed over the floor of the tent for padding. "It's not that I'm feeling shy or burdened, though." Raven played with his nail bed in a way that made him look younger somehow, heartbreakingly tender.

"What's going on?" Crap, was it time to apologize? She was bad at it. Her "sorry" always came out awkward and had a tendency to make the other person feel defensive. A midgrade case of panic bloomed in nervous energy rushing into her gut. She sucked so hard at navigating subtle social situations. *Yet you subject other people to them in your dumb tests, you hypocrite.* "I screwed up, didn't I?" she blurted out in a squeaky voice. Heat crept up her cheeks. "I totally did."

"What?" He looked as mortified as she felt when his gaze snapped up to meet hers. "No. You're fine. Totally fine. You're wonderful. I apologize if I gave you the wrong impression. I just have these moments where all of this stuff exhausts me." He gestured to the notebooks with a flick of the wrist before tipping his head in the direction of the other tent where his pals pored over the cards. "Can't catch a break. There's moments where I want to pack it all away and pack my days with mundane sources of fulfillment. Even if only for a little while, like being on vacation. Sometimes I want to take a reprieve from all things mysterious, occult, or out of this world." His wistful visage made the final sentence seem like a pipe dream. "Ignore me. I'm whining."

"No you aren't. What would you do?"

He cradled his head for a second before arranging the notebooks in some order meaningful solely to him. "Learn something super practical. Say, engineering. Get a government desk job. Play fantasy football. Become exceedingly skilled at home repair."

She fought off a robust urge to hug him hard and offer whatever comfort possible. The subtext was clear. Raven longed sometimes to be a regular, boring person. Perhaps he mourned the regular, boring person that he once was—or never was. She knew that she was supposed to contribute to the conversation but failed to conjure a smart, witty, or thoughtful offering.

Raven cursed under his breath. "I ruined our moment with my lapse into self-absorption, didn't I?"

"No, it was me. I totally know what you mean. This journey isn't for the casual dabbler. It takes it out of you. We didn't choose the magic life, the magic life chose us."

He chuckled, the sparkle returning to his eyes. "Good turn of phrase there."

"I can't take credit for it, but thanks." Props to Helen.

"Ready to rock?" He picked up a book.

She opened her grimoire to the air section.

"I can't read yours the best from this angle." He craned his neck before scooting over to sit beside her.

With their bodies aligned hip-to-hip, written evidence of the phenomena that made them different and alike laid out before them, Cynthia shored up what remained of her prudence. She might have found someone similar in many ways, but all it meant was that she had to work extra hard to stay objective and professional. She'd be playing herself if she fell for Raven, springing a trap for her own stupid, doggedly hopeful heart.

TWELVE

OH, NO. HAD CYNTHIA BEEN ZAPPED BACK TO SOME ABOMINABLE dimension of evil magic again?

Hardness pressed against her cheek—no pillow, but a smooth buffer padded her face against the worst of the ground. The instant that she moved, dull aches throbbed inside her skull. She groaned, her mouth dry and sticky. Reality lurched back. She'd fallen asleep in the tent. Drank too much, too fast, with not enough good food in her stomach.

Dizzy and gross, she stumbled out of the enclosure and onto a mild, overcast beach day. Raven picked up garbage by the dead pile of ash that used to be their fire. No sign of the other three travelers or their tent. "What time is it?" she called over the short distance, nausea bolting down as her words rang out.

"Just after eleven." He jogged back, carrying one of the chocolate wrappers, empathy etched across his handsome face. "Do you need to be sick?"

"Eleven? You're kidding." She massaged the side of her head. This was why she didn't drink much. No tolerance whatsoever. Time to surrender her bad girl card. "Why didn't you wake me up?"

Under long dark lashes, his stare was playful. "Couldn't bear to. You clearly needed your rest." He ducked behind the side of their tent, where the red cooler had been stashed, and offered her a bottled water.

"I look that bad, huh? Wait. Don't answer." She screwed off the cap and gratefully chugged several gulps of the lukewarm liquid. Sharp pangs speared her stomach when the water hit her empty, foodless pit. "You got an ibuprofen?"

"No, sorry. We'll stop at the first gas station we see. And a diner too, yeah? I'm guessing that you could use a greasy burger or some eggs and hash browns."

"Yes." Her stomach grumbled on cue, the discomfort compounding the throb in her head. "Don't let me drink ever again."

"I'm holding you to that. I gotta say, I was disappointed that our research session got cut short." He pulled his backpack out of the tent and stuffed the trash inside before rolling up one of the sleeping bags.

Right. Memories rushed back in a wave of annoyed regret. They'd been about to do a serious comparison of his journals with her book when she'd gotten too drowsy to function. She winced at herself. "I passed out, didn't I?"

He tied the strings of the sleeping bag to a buckle on his rucksack. "I didn't even realize it until I looked over. I'd been droning on for awhile. Didn't realize I was that boring." He winked. "Or maybe I just got so used to your head on my shoulder that I forgot everything else."

Though she felt like a steaming pile of shit, his comment made her happy. "I hope that I didn't wreck the moment entirely. Raincheck?"

"Sure. I'd like to get a little bit outside of the city before we stop, if that's okay. We can look at pages after we eat."

A twinge bit her neck when she tilted her head to scan the small parking lot near the top of the cliff. No sign of the Cadillac by Raven's motorcycle. "The others took off already, I presume?"

"Yeah. They left around nine. The plan is to stop for the night in New Mexico and cross the border tomorrow. An ambitious number of miles to log, but we'll see how it goes."

She rubbed a sore spot near the base of her skull, watching with affection as he pulled up tent stakes and packed them. The material of their temporary home sagged, marking the bittersweet end of the seaside camping adventure. "Thanks for waiting for my hungover ass to rise from the dead. You probably could have just rolled me out of your tent and taken off."

He dragged the remaining sleeping bags from the tent, his countenance puzzled or even a touch horrified. "You seriously think that it was an option to abandon you?"

She folded her arms over her chest. "Happened before." Her own damn fault for sleeping with some asshole of a hippie drifter that she hadn't known from Adam. It was still a shock, though, to wake up in a grimy hostel with no ride out of that rural Canadian province, her wallet having departed in the pocket of the man whose cum she'd swallowed. Hitchhiking in below zero temps with no identification or money sucked serious ass.

He dropped the bedding and faced her squarely. "I'm so sorry that you were treated like that. People have been really awful to you, and you deserved so much better."

Pride bloated out to defend her as she puffed her chest even while the old hurt made her tremble deep below the surface. "I'm no victim. What doesn't kill me makes me stronger."

"I didn't say that you were a victim, but you're entitled to respect." In a swift, fluid move, he reached out and cupped her cheek in one of his palms, gazing deeply into her eyes in a way that absolutely, positively fucking leveled her. "I'll never desert you. You can count on me."

The foundation of her world shook, stone inside of her breaking up in a way both liberating and seriously terrifying. She pulled away. "Don't say shit like that."

"Why?"

"Because you tease me into thinking it's safe to open my heart. No mush allowed, remember?"

"Pledging loyalty to someone I care about qualifies as mushy? Please. I'd do the same for any friend. Portia. Dragon. Ether."

She fidgeted with the flap on the crumpled tent door. "Okay. That's cool. Whatever. And I'm here for you, too. As a friend and all." She smoothed out the fallen tent, pressing out all of the excess air before gathering the slab into a tight roll.

Keeping her hands busy was a reliable guard against the vagaries of her emotions. If left unchecked, those forces might intervene to ruin the

Raven arrangement with some awkward comment or mistimed gesture meant to deepen their bond yet doomed to drive him off.

Been there, done that, won the ugly hat. Cynthia considered herself an exalted master at the stupid games/stupid prizes racket.

"You don't have to be afraid of me."

I'm afraid of everyone that I get close to. She jammed a hand into her hiking pack and fisted the plastic baggie containing her oral hygiene kit. In a series of furious, methodical strokes, she scrubbed out her mouth with minty toothpaste. A good gargle with antiseptic mouthwash burned away any remaining threat of a confession that would make her look weak. She spit the mess on the sand. "I'm not. I could kill you if I wanted, remember?"

"I didn't mean physically."

How dare he see right through her. She wiped her mouth, slashing a mean glare in his direction for good measure. "Stop trying to read me, Raven. It may seem like there's all of this beautiful, tragic depth underneath the prickly exterior, but I guarantee you there isn't. What you see is what you get. A bitch."

He laughed with a sort of gentle amusement that shocked her so much that she failed to generate a predictable, angry reaction. "Okay. If you say so."

"Yeah. I say so." She strapped on her pack. "Conversation over." She wanted him to say something else, to press on until her defenses wavered. It was messed up and toxic to goad him by saying one thing and meaning another but gah what was she supposed to do? This was all new, weird territory. "Shut up."

"I didn't say anything."

"You were thinking it. Things. Thinking things that you wanted to say." Her face sizzled. She'd never bombed this hard. What was wrong with her—what did she want from Raven, anyway? To fuck him again, sure, but her desire encompassed more than the urge for mindless relief or even angry sex. She wanted something bigger from him, a comprehensive and life-altering rearrangement. She wanted him to break her and put her back together. "So you might as well say it. Say it to my face."

He moved like a fluid dream, closing the gap between them and taking her face in both hands. "You want to know what I want?" he whispered darkly above her, assured and totally in control.

"Y..yes. I do." She was practically out of body. She hung suspended in her chrysalis of insecurities, reflected in his eyes as limitless potential, a butterfly in his palm. All she did in the endless moment was want, crave, and stare into him in anticipation of a portend of her future. "Tell me."

Instead of telling, he pressed his lips to hers. Just a brush at first, skin-on-skin to share that initial burst of warm breath as their bodies merged in the subtlest of ways that were so intimate. Life forces mingling. Her small gasp invited him to continue.

Her nonverbal yes urged him on. He sucked on her top lip and nibbled the bottom one, sliding his tongue over hers in an invasion of stiff warmth and clean taste.

She kissed him back, rewarding his initiative, and soon the play of mouths became a crush. The kiss wasn't a sweet one, or even a lusty one necessarily, instead it was pure hunger.

Deep-down hunger, communicating buried truths and stale old lies and the weight of ages encoded in flesh not speech. Cynthia lost herself in that moment, reading the kiss as she spoke it, giving and getting, taking the assurance he offered. Felt like an eternity before he brought them up for air and stepped back, a claiming sort of mojo living in the way he pinned her with a look.

Before, Cynthia would have slapped a guy for kissing her like that, kissing her like she was his, and attempting the whole "you're mine" thing even in unspoken gestures. But this wasn't before. Before was dead and gone, leaving Cynthia in the wake of a new era.

Aftershocks quaked through her like she'd had a tiny orgasm just from making out. No man had made her feel this way before, which made Raven a mystery wrapped in an enigma delivered on a dare.

"Let's go." He swiped her hand, interlacing their fingers, and walked the two of them to the path leading up the cliff to the parking lot. "We've got some time to make up."

Luckily, she was behind him, so he couldn't see the skip in her step. She still had a decently healthy ego to maintain and was not about to devolve into a simpering mess just yet, even if the man was an exceptional kisser and exceedingly adept at taking the lead at the exact moment when she'd thrown out a submissive signal without fully knowing it consciously.

Shit. Her resistance was proving more and more futile by the hour. Must've been the residual drunkenness, making her brain wet and smooth. "So what, you shove your tongue in my mouth and now you're gonna go ahead and play Mr. Big Man Dominant for the rest of the trip, or what?"

He tossed her a smirk that had her wet in her panties. "You're the one subjecting me to your endless tests and games. I'm the one following your lead, I'd say."

She quick-stepped up the rest of the slope, sand and rocks giving way under her rubber soles, the yielding of the environment mirroring her inner surrender. "Whatever. You cool with driving first? I'm still in pretty rough shape."

They reached his bike, a lone chrome steed in a neglected parking lot filled with green shoots sprouting out of cracks in marred blacktop. He grabbed her by the hips, the sensual touch sparking a fresh fire in her sex. He spun her around so her bottom rested against the motorcycle seat. "Come here, baby." Then, he kissed her again, slower this time but still definitely a sexual kiss with lots of pressure and the beautiful, ravenous smash of limits flouted.

Also, baby?!? Why did the sound of the cocky term of endearment in his sleek voice roughened with arousal make her heart beat with big, juicy thumps? She ought to have smacked him or told him where to shove his *baby*, but instead she was melting, her legs wrapped around his waist and her arms draped languid over his back, thirstily mainlining the experience of *being kissed*. The rigid length of his erection pressed against her crotch, thrusting up and down to obliterate her mind until nothing else mattered in the universe except more of him.

She was so screwed. Lost to him, given up and given over. But it all felt so good and new, like freedom. Flying. "Raven," she moaned against his mouth. "Right here." She fumbled with the snap on his jeans, fretful for a second that he might resist her out of either hesitation about fucking in open air, semi-public venue or to thwart her urge as a show of dominance. "I'm not afraid."

Fortunately for her horny, swept-away self, he turned to neither act of resistance. "Condom," he rasped.

Wasting not one millisecond, she snagged a foil packet from the side of her bag. His pants were already below his hips when she turned around, his cock a nice long curve. She sheathed him up, hiked up her skirt and pushed her panties to the side, and guided him to her.

He pushed in, filling her with stretching pleasure. "You and your exhibitionism," he growled against her neck, his breath coming in spurts of choppy heat as he pumped in and out of her.

She was so wet that resistance was nonexistent, her body primed and swollen enough that the angle of his entry brushed her clit. "Our. You mean *our* exhibitionism. You're super into this, too."

"I'm into you," he spoke in a raspy grunt, his fingertips digging into the flesh where her legs met her waist as he thrust in a steady pace. "Whatever you want, I'm into that."

She moved one of his hands to her pussy for good measure, and he got the hint right away and started stroking her clit with his middle finger. "I want to suck you at the end and for you to come all over me."

"Where did that come from?" He rubbed her faster, harder, working her nub with intent as his thrusts sped up.

Her clit throbbed. Pressure built near her navel. "I want to be covered in your cum in the open air. Feel really dirty and shameless." Marked. Owned. A spectacle to be advertised as his.

"Oh, fuck, your dirty talk." He drew back enough to watch the penetration in all of its obscene, glistening, broad daylight glory. "You're nasty as hell and I love it."

His fingers raced across her most sensitive area. He was good, touching her just how she liked, and every word he spoke was perfect. A dozen or so more of his strokes set her off, sending her into a hard and pulsating climax that wracked her body from center to edges. Shouts sprung from her throat. If anyone was around, she didn't care, as she was totally commanded by the present moment.

He led her through the finish, not letting up until her body slackened and she sighed. He withdrew and said sharply, "Okay, okay, now, baby."

It was the *baby* that did it, that damn baby that drew her far into the fantasy, dared her to beg for more, plead for her own surrender. She dropped to kneel before him, the stringing scrape of the ground a wicked delight for her knees, and rid him of the condom.

Looking up at him, into his glazed, lust-filled face, she yanked her tank top and bra down to expose her breasts and sucked him deep into her mouth. The first taste was full of latex reminders, the fleshy base note of him rising as she slurped off the condom's remnants.

Once Raven was good and wet, she freed his organ from the cavern of her lips and tongue and stroked very slowly. With her other hand, she cradled his high, tight balls. "We aren't in a hurry, right?"

"Right," he murmured, his lips staying divided after he spoke.

The power gleaned by extending sexual torment was divine and all, but she wasn't obsessed enough with the control high to drag out his payoff forever. Not when she was chasing another high herself, almost as great as a second climax. With her goal in focus, she bobbed her head up and down on his pole, licking and slurping and flittering her tongue this way and that, tugging his balls.

He swelled even harder on top of her tongue, moaning on every stroke, pulling lightly on her hair to urge her off. She quit sucking and switched to jerking, one hand curled around his crown to bring the entire endeavor home. Sure enough, a few jacks in and he shot, painting the canvas of her breasts, neck, and chin in creamy white. The noises he made were out of this world.

"That feel good?" she asked in her sexiest voice, squeezing the tip of his prick to wring out the last drops of cum, watching in awe as they dripped onto her nipples.

"Oh, Cynthia baby." His knees wobbled some as he gaped at the sight of her covered in his fluids. "You're amazing." He offered her a hand up, and she accepted and rose.

Once the moment passed, she cleaned herself with a sock from her stuff and jammed it back in the area designated for dirty clothes.

After buttoning up, he kissed her in a sweet and gentle way. He moved his lips and nibbled the side of her mouth. "That help your hangover at all?"

Before she let herself harden up and respond with something snarky or dismissive, she threw her arms around him for a hug. "Yeah. Thanks for humoring my weird porno request."

"You kidding?" he dipped her like they were on a dance floor. "That was the most fun I've had since, well, since the day we met."

She burst out laughing, sunny and liberated in his arms. All of her scaffolding and guard rails and the rest of it were blissfully gone for that length of time spent on the shores of an abandoned California park, on a cloudy and forgettable day amid the ruins of a shitty parking lot. Because even if it vanished or got stolen or trampled, for one moment Cynthia got to enjoy the sensation of being cherished by a man she adored.

As long as she remembered that she was pretending. As long as she wised up eventually, enough to remind herself that these types of moment weren't for her, that she hadn't earned them for whatever reason, a little pretending was okay. The key to keeping her skull screwed on right would be remembering never to trick herself into believing that the game was real.

"Get on." She smacked his arm, over-affecting the buddy-type gesture as a way of checking herself. "I'm starving."

Yet as she mounted up behind him and the open road motorcycle journey wove another round of leather-clad, engine humming seduction, she let herself daydream that she actually did deserve something so good.

THIRTEEN

DARKNESS CAME EARLY, WITH TIME HAVING FLOWN BY IN A PAINTED blur of buttes and arroyos, red dirt stretching to the yawning mouths of canyons, and more cacti than Cynthia had bothered to count.

She rested the side of her face against Raven's upper back, the fabric of his leather jacket warm against her cheek and lost herself in a moment of southwestern splendor and gentle surrender that she never wanted to end. It helped that they didn't have to talk, just listen to the moan of his bike as wheels sliced through a flat expanse of two-lane highway surrounded on all sides by desert scenery and warm, arid breeze.

Rambling across the country with another person was a soothing and novel type of comfort. They were alone and together at the same time. She squeezed him tight, her body contoured to both his and the motorcycle. *This is nice. I could get used to this*.

She didn't even lash out at herself for the gooey thought, and it felt good to stop fighting. Pain plus resistance led to suffering. Didn't Buddha say something similar? Perhaps Cynthia was finally reaching equilibrium in her life, connecting to the maxims of Buddha or some shit.

Raven's hand drifted to his pocket. "They're calling," he shouted over the whipping bluster.

"Who?" She was too zoned out on contentment to give much

thought to the callers and their importance. Whoever it was didn't inhabit her and Raven's bubble of bliss and thus didn't matter.

Their speed slowed. Soon, Raven turned off into the parking lot of an abandoned gas station, gravel kicking up to clatter against metal. "The others, checking in, finally. They must've stopped for the night."

Cynthia felt her nose scrunch as an asinine wave of jealousy rolled over her. She'd forgotten about the others and lowkey, irrationally resented them for intruding upon her scared time with Raven. Her feelings were both wildly selfish and completely nonsensical, because the mission was the whole reason that she was on a bike with Raven in the first place, despite the absurd, romantic joyride fantasies that she'd been entertaining. "Awesome," she said with as much earnestness as was possible to muster. "I was starting to worry."

He didn't appear convinced. "Sure you were."

"I will have you know that I'm perfectly capable of compassion."

"I know." He docked the bike by a decrepit gas pump coated with dust. Judging by the prices, the place hadn't been in service for a few decades. "I've seen it. But you're also a terrible liar."

Guilty as charged. "Fuck you." Fortunately, her words came out with the playful lilt she intended. Releasing some of her pent-up hostility felt good, even if her style of banter and jest remained stubbornly caustic.

He dismounted and slipped his phone from his pocket in a single, graceful motion before leaning against the abandoned service island to key in the number. "Well, I suppose this place fits the bill for us." He brought the phone to his ear.

A comeback escaped her, snark and wit crowded out by thoughts of a quickie, a motorbike, and the aphrodisiac threat of cars going by. She jumped off the bike and grabbed an unopened pack of cigarettes from her backpack. In case of emergency, break glass. It seemed that every time she fucked Raven, feelings came soon after she did, and she wasn't ready to surrender to their thrall just yet. "I'm gonna go for a smoke. Keep me updated."

He bumped his chin in a short gesture of acknowledgement before routing his attention to the phone call. No protectiveness, no insistence on going with her. Raven honored Cynthia's independence and respected her ability to take care of herself. She loved that about him.

Omg, stop!

Well, it was possible to love certain things about a person without loving *them*, right?

Sure it was. She'd go with that hypothesis. Nicotine and the satisfaction of inhaling smoke would curb her emotional angst. She tore open the fresh pack of American Spirits and chucked the plastic wrapping and foil in a trash can, her garbage landing atop the crushed remains of a novelty Pepsi can that she vaguely remembered being released when she was very small.

She leaned against the side of what was once the gas station's convenience store and lit up, mesmerized by the crackling cherry tip, fluorescent red against still, dark night, and drew a drag into her lungs before blowing out a column of smoke. Mellowed by the indulgence of her sporadic vice, she strolled the perimeter of the derelict building, pausing to peek in the windows.

From the looks of things, the establishment had been cleared out in haste, the bulk of the contents vacated to leave behind a slew of overturned magazine racks spilling time-capsule-worthy glossies.

Dozens of old pop bottles covered the floor, their contents abandoned to die on the vine. By the bathrooms, two video game machines had long since gone dark. Starting in first grade, she used to walk to the convenience store near-ish to her house and play video game machines that were much like the dead relics in the store, a ritual to celebrate her independent streak. Her mom and dad always had better things to do than activate the helicopter propellers endemic to today's nervous wrecks of parental units.

"Hey baby." The familiar voice pulled her from nostalgia.

She turned to Raven, annoyed that the term of endearment made her feel all wanted and squishy. She blew smoke in his face. "Now you're actively trying to piss me off."

"*Altered Beast.*" He ignored her potshot in favor of peering into the window of the old store. "One of my sentimental favorites."

She smoked some more, enjoying their mellow bit of downtime that she sensed would end soon. "S'cuse me?"

"That was one of my favorite video games when I was little. One of my older brothers introduced me to it. In retrospect, it's no wonder that the prospect of people shifting into animals appealed to me on some subconscious level."

The suggestion in his reverie spun pleasurably through her, mingling with cigarette smoke and the rural desert's arid kiss. She thrived in these small, thoughtful, low-pressure spaces, where a minor comment opened doors to more significant topics. "Do you think that we always knew that we were different, even before we really knew?"

He stole one of her cigarettes and used hers to light the pilfered American Spirit. "Absolutely. I mean, I can only speak for myself, but I always knew that *something* was unusual about me. I knew that it wasn't normal, per se, with what I was doing with those Fyre songs." He quieted in favor of exhaling smoke, his stare fixed on some indeterminate point in a distance marked with flat, scrubby land. "I knew from the moment I saw you that destiny had brought us together through this magic, whatever it is and whatever it wants."

On anyone else, literally anyone, that destiny line would have been the cheesiest, most cringe-worthy phrase that a person could utter, an instant inductee into the bad pickup line hall of shame.

But not on him. She glanced at her dirty feet, then back up at Raven, ashing her smoke to busy her hands while she reached into her mind. "Where does magic come from? Where does it go?"

A sigh came automatically from Raven, heavy and strong, like he'd contemplated those very words, the ones that had spontaneously erupted in her and from a mind not her own. "You wanna hear my theory, for what it's worth?"

She stepped closer to him, her eyeballs arrested upon the stone-carved exquisiteness of his face. Whatever Raven said would land. She knew. "Absolutely."

"Have you ever heard of epigenetic memory?"

A corner somewhere in her brain lit up in recognition, causing her pulse to quicken. "I think so. But only regarding trauma. Isn't it when pain is passed down through generations to be stored in our bodies? For example, if our ancestors survived an atrocity, their descendants bear some physical or psychic remnant of it that manifests as symptoms."

He stubbed out the remainder of his smoke against the wall, drawing Cynthia's attention to a mess of graffiti made from spray paint and all manner of pen and marker. "Yeah. That's the gist. I think that magic comes to you and I, and others, through a process much like that. Passed down our lineage, dormant in our cells until activated by some event."

"Interesting." She finished her cigarette and ran a finger over the text of someone's poem, chewing on Raven's insightful thoughts while reading words rendered in Sharpie and surprisingly tidy penmanship. She didn't get the point or message of the poem, but that didn't mean it was bad. Ugh. She was losing her edge so hardcore around Raven that she failed to even be appropriately judgmental of bad literary graffiti. A flash of inspiration struck. "Hey. Gimmie a pen from my bag real quick."

He scoffed. "No way, I'm not your errand boy."

She batted her eyelashes in a comical yet flirty manner. "Sorry. I mean gimmie a pen from my bag real quick, *please*."

He jogged off, calling, "You're lucky you're so charming."

"Never been accused of that before." Once he was safely out of sight, she did a stupid little dance.

Raven returned with a Sharpie like the one that the other person had used to write the poem, except hers was hot pink.

She wrote on the wall, *We come from the witches you didn't burn*. Gooseflesh sprang on her arms, the spray of bumps accompanied by an enjoyable current of energy that started in her chest and spread outward. She really needed to research her lineage to see if Raven's theory checked out. Who came before her, and were they as witchy as she?

She returned the marker to Raven for safekeeping, hoping that he noticed the small gesture of trust that she intended to convey.

He tucked the pen in his back pocket. "Nice. On that note, we should get going. The others found a place, and apparently, Ether —*Nerissa*—is talking again. I'd still love to devote some time to comparing my notebooks to your grimoire."

Her heart rate jumped. "How did you know to call it that?"

He said with teasing nonchalance, "Maybe shifters also came from the witches they didn't burn. Witches had familiars, after all."

"Good point." He also had a good point about getting back on the road. Speculating wasn't particularly helpful, but his notebooks and whatever Nerissa was talking about might be. "Where did they stop for the night?"

"Up the road about twenty miles." Raven started walking in the direction of his bike, and Cynthia followed suit. "Portia said they got a better place this time. Sounds like she figured out how to transmute low-value stuff into cash, so that solves one of our practical problems, at least. Money has always been stubborn for the deck to work with, so this breakthrough is strong."

Cynthia's skin tightened. Money magic was volatile in ways she didn't fully understand, so that specific mode of problem solving could have very well generated a whole host of new issues, but she didn't see the point in bringing that up after the fact. Portia had already done the deed. "Are the doors of this motel on the inside? That's my litmus test."

"I think so."

Cynthia was all ready to head to this hotel for a serious research session when a flash of light, originating from where they'd stood and smoked, yanked her attention back to the present.

Raven grabbed her upper arm. He'd seen it, too.

"That didn't look like a flashlight," she said. The illuminated burst was too self-contained, too diffused, and lacking a clear point of origin. She turned tail and ran back to where they'd stood, her intuition as potent as her delight at the prospect of a new clue.

But by the time she reached the marked-up wall, the glimmer had darkened. "Damn." She ran her hand over obscene scrawls and phone numbers, juvenile declarations of love and random limericks, before conceding defeat. Whatever had appeared had dimmed as quickly as it'd materialized.

"Wait," Raven said, as if reading her thoughts. "I see something." He beckoned her to where he stood, a few feet away.

After some squinting and blinking, she saw what he saw. Tiny, phosphorescent flecks still danced on painted brick, glowing in the spaces between others' words.

"Okay," he whispered with reverence. "Fascinating." He pointed at a spot, drawing her focus to the poem. And, after the poem, her own script.

Except her own script had changed, and not on her or Raven's accord. In place of the comment she'd written about witches was an eerie, yet inviting, question penned in pink.

Do you really want to know? Where you come from, and where you go? This magic inside, what you reap and sow?

She glanced at Raven, feeling a battle between apprehension and temptation pour out through her stare. Folly's outreach had become clearer and more purposeful since the beach. This new development was an invitation to dialogue, which seemed like a huge step forward. To where, Cynthia couldn't be sure, but taking steps was at least proactive.

While communicating directly with Folly was undeniably reckless, such a prospect presented nearly irresistible opportunity for breaking through some of the confounding mysteries that relentlessly puzzled her when it came to magic.

Of course she wanted to know. Knowledge was power. And danger. Two of Cynthia's favorite things. "Give me that pen," she ordered Raven before she changed her mind.

"Cynthia. We both saw what happened on the beach when Ether got possessed. I'm not sure that this force is something we want to court."

She gave him a dirty look. Who did he think he was, laying constraints on her? "I can handle it."

"How do you know?"

She didn't. But when had she ever played it safe, and why start now? Hesitancy certainly wasn't going to get her anywhere when it came to cracking the code of an ancient prophecy. She had to dance with the devil to get that sweet, sweet forbidden fruit. "Just give me my damn pen back."

He sounded off his disapproval but obeyed.

She clenched the writing implement in a tight fist and scribbled her answer on the wall:

Yes. Tell me.

More words appeared, penned by an unseen author. *May I show you?*

Her heart pounded in her throat, her body flush with arousal. She aimed her pink tip at the surface, not even thinking, just acting.

Raven grabbed her wrist. "Cynthia," he hissed. "Think this through. You're about to accept an invitation to *go somewhere* with her. Think about the possible ramifications of agreeing to something like that. This could absolutely be a trap. What if she steals your soul? Kills you? What if you don't come back the same?"

This guy was starting to aggravate her in a major way. Cynthia did *not* need a protector, despite whatever nascent inklings of feelings for Raven *may or may not* have been incubating inside of her. He was not allowed to capitalize on her affection for him and hold her back, clip her wings, and make her his caged *baby*. She jerked out of his hold. "Don't even begin to think about controlling me."

He put his hands up. "I wasn't. You take everything so personally. I was just trying to offer a different perspective."

"I don't want it, okay?" Doubt wormed in, making her hand tremble as she brought the pen to the brick. She hated that he had to see her uncertainty. Her weakness. "I've come this far. I have to keep moving forward. Find fire and chaos by any means necessary."

Before he could retort, before she had a second more to change her mind, Cynthia scratched out a reply to Folly's invitation.

Yes.

Not one second passed before Cynthia's consciousness broke from her body and she was flying, sailing, reduced to a dizzying interplay of light and shadow as she rocketed into some unknown, on the fast track to the magical realm, a place that she'd never come to understand, for it was obscure and ever-changing.

When she awoke, she was on her back, the sky above a strange, unnatural shade of amethyst. Beneath her, softness offered support. She sat up and processed her surroundings. She lay on a white sand beach that lacked water. Speckled eggs the size of softballs dotted the sands, their shells colored in an array of vibrant hues.

Before she had a chance to attempt to make sense of the novelty, an egg cracked at the exact moment that a metallic screech tore through the air above with a pitch and volume that curdled her blood.

FOURTEEN

PICK AN EGG. FOLLY'S VOICE, MELLIFLUOUS AND SEDUCTIVE, DANCED through the atmosphere like the first note before a storm. *Inside, you will see destiny.*

See destiny? That would at least be a new sight. All that Cynthia saw at the moment was endless, boundless, weirdly hued sky, arched above her like an enormous violet gumball. No sign of the monster that'd loosed that heinous screech, either.

She spent another several seconds chewing over Folly's peculiar wording, enjoying the warm, if bumpy, mattress of sand supporting her body as balmy breezes licked her skin. "See destiny" was interesting wording. Not *your* destiny, or the destiny of witches, or *a* destiny.

Just destiny.

That distinction had to matter, and Cynthia was tempted to ask, but Folly was notoriously capricious, so Cynthia kept her ignorance close to the chest. Whether the answer promised actually matched the one that she'd sought was something that she'd have to figure out on the fly. Fortunately, improvisation was another skillset that Cynthia was good at.

She rose to her feet and wandered the sands, scoping out neon green eggs, pink eggs, and eggs the color of orange sherbet. All were either cracked or cracking. "Is this like in *The Matrix*, where I pick one color to stay in the delusion, and another one to see how deep the rabbit hole truly goes?"

Perhaps hiding a legitimate question in a quip would help her get some actionable information, with the secondary goal of impressing Folly with her clever movie reference.

I'm afraid that you're already far down the rabbit hole, my dear child of Air, and the only way to go is deeper and deeper, until no light remains in the pit of the oubliette. A self-satisfied cackle followed the creepy statement that did not, in fact, help Cynthia out by providing any info that she could use. She couldn't shake the nagging hunch that Folly was misleading or tricking her, but she hesitantly chalked the concern up to nerves and paranoia. Besides, she was no coward, no quitter.

"Alright, then." She crouched by a cherry red egg splattered with white dots before checking out a pastel yellow one covered in a network of obsidian veins. She picked up Black and Gold, letting it rest in her palm. The egg probably weighed three pounds, maybe four. "Hey, this one is has the colors of my alma mater. How do I know which one to pick? Just follow my intuition, or what?"

Concentrate on your question. That will lead you to your egg.

For a chaos-driven, even evil, element, Folly was being awfully patient. Maybe she wasn't bad, just misunderstood. Cynthia sure could relate. The world was tough on women who didn't fit into society's neat little boxes. "Thanks. I'll stick with this guy, I guess. He feels good in my hand." She passed Black and Gold between her palms.

Very well, Folly said with blasé detachment, like none of this meant a thing to her. She must have had some skin in the game, though, to lead Cynthia through the entire process. Or maybe she merely played the role of the unbothered guide, shepherding Cynthia to what she sought like a mentor would. The only aspect that didn't check out with this theory was the vaguely psychotic cackle. *Commune with your egg and ask your question.*

On which question to choose, well, that was a no-brainer. One specific question had been bugging Cynthia for awhile. "Where does magic come from? Where does it go?"

That's two questions.

Oops. Cynthia flinched, embarrassed at the sense of having put herself at an immediate disadvantage.

"Fair enough. Let's take it from the top, then. Where does magic come from?" She felt a bit ridiculous asking such a simplistic question, like a child who was old enough to know better asking how babies were made just to hear the answer. But, she needed to correct her lack of understanding somehow, and so far this method seemed promising. Her nerves skittered as she waited. She hoped that Folly didn't see or sense her emotional reactivity.

The oracle will take you down a path. This journey won't always be pleasant. At times, you will find yourself frustrated, angry, or unable to accept the truth. You may experience a deep sense of betrayal, but do not succumb to denial. Face these truths head on to find your answers. Do you wish to proceed?

Folly had dropped a lot in Cynthia's lap just there. How would she know to trust her? There was a strong case to be made that she shouldn't, actually, if the warnings in the book were to be believed. But unraveling the origin story of her magical lineage might very well be the missing link to finding fire and chaos and getting to the bottom of her role in stopping the prophecy. Despite how uneasy the elemental mother's portend made Cynthia, her choice was clear.

"Yes."

The egg split down the side in a jagged crack that widened into chasm. Gooey liquid, watery red with a translucent sheen, oozed over Cynthia's fingers. She didn't have but a second to indulge her revulsion at the gross-out when a lance-shaped head no bigger than Cynthia's big toe shoved its way out of the crack. The reptilian creature, white as a new snow underneath a film of bloody goop, stared at Cynthia with two pinpoints of coal-black eyes.

"Hello there." She wasn't sure what she was supposed to do, which was fine, because all she was capable of doing was staring at this completely unusual specimen, the likes of which she'd never seen in real life. Some sort of baby lizard, its entire, tiny body covered in a delicate network of scales. "Welcome to the world, I guess."

The newborn reptile opened its beak-like mouth, revealing two rows of bent-back, razor teeth, and mewled like a kitten. "Aren't you cute." She stroked the top of its head, wiping away some slime as her finger pad bumped over a series of rough, scaly ridges. "Are you here to show me destiny?"

Initially enthralled by the novelty of her surroundings, Cynthia hadn't even realized that the sun had been out until the sky went dark with a blink. Instinctively, she looked up, and at that moment the small creature in her hands squeaked again.

One glimpse above tore Cynthia's rational mind to shreds as she gaped at what she was witnessing, her horizon collapsing to the awesome impossibility above.

Ice water shot through her veins, her body turning to stone. Her feet locked in place.

She opened her mouth to scream, but nothing came out. She could only stare, reduced to gawking stupidity, frozen in the wake of the abysmal sublime.

A snow-white dragon, bigger than a blue whale, hovered in the space above her, its massive nostrils flaring a mere body's length from her face. The mythical beast flapped wings with a hundred-foot span, the force generated by the motion dashing Cynthia's hair as a tremendous *whoosh* rang through her ears.

"Uh, is this your baby?" she croaked out through a dry mouth, the newborn creature wriggling in her hand. The dragon looked pissed off, but that could have easily been its resting face, too. "I'm sorry. I wasn't trying to steal it."

In response, the dragon stretched its massive maw wide and descended upon Cynthia in a blur of pink insides, sharp, ivory teeth, and a fishy stench like a fetid aquarium.

She didn't realize that she'd passed out until she awoke in a warm, dark, wet cave that stank like decomposing meat. She choked back an urge to vomit and tried to stand, but the ground beneath her feet was too slick. She still held the egg, thank goodness. She'd never have forgiven herself, had she inadvertently crushed or stepped on the cute little curiosity. "Sorry, buddy," Cynthia pushed the words out through held breath.

The tiny dragon mewed again.

"Glad you understand." She held her nose, waving her free hand in front of her face in a desperate effort to grasp for purchase. Finally, after a few flailing efforts, her hand connected to solidity. Well, solid-ish. The wall to the side of her was wet and squishy, and soft, like the inside of warm apple pie. "This is so gross. Do you know where we are?"

Another squeaky reply.

At least they could sort of communicate despite an inability to break the language barrier. "Thanks anyway."

A flash of light about forty feet in the distance spiked her hope. When in doubt, go to the light. Cynthia started to walk, but slipped, her feet giving way beneath the juicy, unstable ground. Worried about her egg, she settled for crawling, trading upright dignity for a promise of safety in the hands-and-knees position. Her hand landed palm-down in a shallow pool of warm liquid whose origins she had no desire to learn.

More light came through the opening, vanishing as darkness again fell from above. Some kind of garage-style door, opening and closing? Whatever was producing the light source had to be better than where she currently was.

After several minutes of lurching forward in the stress position, her arm and back aching, she arrived at what must have been the entrance. A sharp end caught the hem of her shirt, filling her ears with a tearing noise as a filed point scraped her skin in a flare of pain.

"Ouch." The involuntary exclamation forced her to breathe through her nose before she could stop herself, the odor of sewage and rotten meat wafting over her in sickening waves. Stomach lurching, she puffed out her cheeks.

The baby dragon vocalized.

"Sorry, buddy. I know that this place sucks. I'm trying to get us out of here. Promise." At least if he was scared, Cynthia could attempt to offer assurance, no matter how empty.

She wrenched her shirt free from the thorny bit that'd snagged it, waiting intently for the door to open again. At last, it did, and she staggered to the exit, hacking and coughing, her stomach roiled by the unpleasant smells now sticking to her from head to toe.

Wiping gunk away from her face with the back of her hand, she blinked away fuzziness. Curved, bumpy walls that looked to be made of a pale stone enclosed her on all sides. The sound of running water trickled in the distance. Though her latest environment was dank and dark, there was enough light to make out those basic structural shapes, qualifying this place as an upgrade from the unlit sewer. And, hey, she'd agreed to this. She had no right to complain.

"You okay, pal?" she asked the baby dragon, who in the time that had elapsed had grown a couple of inches and sprouted a pair of gossamer wings, sheer as glass and boned with a network of ice-like cartilage. The gunk and eggshell remnants had been shed in the ordeal, allowing the beast to shimmer in its full resplendence. It didn't appear injured in the slightest, looking around with interest as it stretched its long neck and flapped those shiny new wings. "Not too emotionally traumatized like I am?"

The little guy (or gal) squirmed in Cynthia's hand, squeaking more than usual and flapping its wings. Its stare seemed to be fixed on some object past Cynthia, so, with reluctance offset by a commitment to seeing this whole thing through, she turned around.

And there was the big dragon again, curled up in a ball this time, a massive tail outfitted with crystalline spikes from root to tip wrapped around its prostrate body in a protective semicircle. The monster made a chuffing noise in apparent acknowledgement of Cynthia's existence, staring her down with golden eyes that blazed like twin suns.

"Hi," Cynthia said. *You might want to consider changing your diet, cause you've got a bad case of gut rot going on.* At least she had the sense not to say that part out loud, in case the reptile understood English. "Does you swallowing me and vomiting me up in your lair have anything to do with the destiny I'm supposed to be getting a glimpse of?"

The looming dragon spoke in Folly's voice, "Congratulations, you've passed the first test."

Hey, there was some good news. Cynthia had never been good at passing tests. She got distracted, and her mind wandered, leading many of her teachers to say unkind things that motivated her to give up out of spite. Her heart lifted, and she felt her backbone slide into a straight line. "Awesome. Thank you. What test was that?"

The dragon's scaly lips stretched into a toothy, diabolical smile. "This greatly pleases your pathetic little heart, passing my tests."

Fuck. She was so easy to read, wearing her people-pleasing tendencies on her face like cheap makeup. She swallowed hard, clenching her teeth.

Lying would only dig her in a deeper hole, and she was really bad at it. There were ways to play her weaknesses off as strengths. There had to be. They said it all of the time in job interview prep videos and in that one women's self-defense class she took. "Yes, it does. I want to do this right. Tell me more about this test that I passed."

The dragon slunk forward a couple of feet. A blast of breath shot from her nostrils and slammed into Cynthia's face in a sour onslaught. "You do not, you must *never*, dictate the terms of this arrangement to me, air child."

"Right." Cynthia coughed, switching to a deferential tack, "My apologies. Thank you for your generosity in determining that I was able to pass."

The dragon puffed up and threw back her massive head, showing off a membrane that flowed down her slinky neck like a mane of diamonds and icicles. "I ought to have failed you for insubordination alone."

Ugh. She had to eat shit to get through this. Whatever. She'd done worse to get her needs met. "I understand."

"Excellent." She sounded a bit like Mr. Burns on *The Simpsons*, with that evil drawl of hers. Cynthia held her small bit of defiant, mocking humor inside. The dragon opened her mouth again. "Now. Do you wish to hear how you passed my test?"

"Yes." She tried hard not to sound too eager, despite how badly she wanted to hear the secret to her success.

The dragon flicked her gargantuan tail, teasing with a pause. "You have proven to me that you are able to prioritize the protection of our lineage over your own self-preservation instincts, even in the most extreme circumstances where your safety is threatened."

Somehow both confused and walloped with a hit of clarity, Cynthia looked down at her hands. The young white dragon gazed up at her expectantly. "*Our* lineage."

"Precisely." Folly's pale, reptilian chest rose and fell on a big breath. "What did you think, that your magic came to you by chance or coincidence, or as a gift from your Christian God or his loser son?" She cackled like she had on the beach.

Cynthia's relationship with religion was a whole other can of worms that didn't seem especially relevant, so she brushed past the dis against the Christian God. "I hadn't made any assumptions, actually. Hence my ongoing questioning."

The dragon lowered her face and made eye contact with Cynthia as she said in a condescending tone that may have belied a hint of affection, "There's hope for you yet."

Even when others were impressed by her, they had to express their approval in skeptical terms. "Thanks."

"Anyway, your test. You preserved your precious dragon egg even when your own sorry, human skin was threatened. She is yours now. Your familiar. Name her accordingly, and find strength in your bond. A familiar is an unparalleled gift to a practicing witch."

A private memory amused Cynthia. This test that Folly was so damn proud of was actually pretty uncreative, like in high school home economics where the teacher made the kids carry around an egg for a week to prove that they could care for a baby one day. Folly's test was actually exactly like that, but with more extreme elements like the whole Leviathan swallowing ordeal thrown in. But hey, she got a familiar out of it this time, as opposed to a useless grade. "Thank you. I appreciate it." She really did. Cynthia petted her new familiar, enjoying the sounds of her coos and squeals, how the little one seemed to relish being petted. "Hey, Buddy, hey. We're going to have some good times together. Do you like that name, Buddy?" Basic, but classic. Buddy's happy sounds indicated that she was pleased with Cynthia's choice. "My new Buddy. What do you like to eat, Buddy? Steak? Vegetables? The blood of our enemies?"

A rumbling, low growl stirred from deep within Folly, darkening the collective mood.

Cynthia's muscles tensed. Folly was mad. The sound of her fury was evident. There was some problem.

"Don't get too comfortable. I'm not through with you."

Cynthia pressed her lips together while Buddy climbed up to sit near the crook of her neck, moving her small, clawed feet in kitten-like motions. She resented that Folly had to get right back on her bullshit just as Cynthia was beginning to feel good in bonding with Buddy. How manipulative. Not like it was in her best interests to argue, however. "Okay."

"It's not okay," Folly snapped.

Cynthia's insides clenched. She felt tiny and miserable. How was she managing to screw this up? Why did she screw up opportunities all of the time, reliably self-sabotaging her way out of all of life's best stuff? "I'm sorry," she blurted out in a high-pitched voice that she detested and had tried to lose over the years. "What can I do?"

Folly rolled those humungous yellow eyes with their vertically slit pupils. The gesture of open contempt made Cynthia feel worthless and nonexistent, yet hyper-visible at the same time, a prisoner of another's judgment. Reduced to her shame, she hung on the promise of Folly's next words, waiting obediently for this powerful, rule-making master to make her whole again.

Finally, the monster spoke, "You need to immediately solve your shifter problem."

"Excuse me?" The words tumbled out in chaos, Cynthia's head spinning around and around as she mentally flailed for the hoop she was supposed to jump through.

"You heard me." She barked loud enough to make Cynthia cringe.

Tears prickled. "But I don't understand." Every time she'd uttered that phrase, begging for help with schoolwork or life skills or insight on how to be the right, good kind of girl, someone had humiliated her for opening up in weakness, putting her dumb ass fail on display.

Uncomfortable, unhealed memories from childhood rotted just below the surface, papered over by wet leaves. Nausea smashed down, chased by a red rush of fury. She clenched a fist, dying to break something even though nothing other than the implausible target of Folly's fearsome mouth came to mind.

"Their kind are thieves," Folly finally explained. "Shifters are parasites. They take from us, the dragon witches, before they rob. First they give. Then they borrow, and finally they steal. Just a little at first, then a little more, until we have nothing left. Cut yours loose like a cancer."

Raven. The final scraps of her joy perished. Folly was talking about Raven. The first person she'd met in forever who treated her like she was worth a damn, and who she cared enough about to return the favor, was in the fiend's crosshairs. A flame of rebellion spread through her. Folly was a fabled liar who toyed with heads for fun and power. Cynthia didn't have to swallow this petty tyrant's dicta whole. "Or else what?"

Folly growled again, flexing her monstrous muscle. Cynthia stood her ground and slid her shoulders down her back. She was nothing if not outwardly tough. Acting tough had saved her plenty of times.

"Your familiar dies first, unfortunately. Then one coven sister per week perishes until you kill the shifter. The fall of the world to the Hologram Prophecy will rest squarely on your sloped shoulders. Speaking of, you really need to work on your posture, sweetie. Think about the impression you are making, walking around all hunched like that. Doormats get walked on, and a poor bearing makes a woman look pudgy."

Cheap insults aside, the reference to Buddy directed Cynthia's attention to her familiar, who was nuzzled up against her collarbone, butting a warm, dry snout into her neck. "Is that a warning, or a threat?"

She'd wondered that quite a bit, regarding witches and witchcraft.

Folly simply stared, her demonic eyes twinkling.

"You're lying. Completely full of shit. Fuck off," Cynthia blurted out before she could think. Sometimes pushback was the only way to deal with bullies. Attempting to comply her way out of tyranny hadn't worked. She angled her body so that the side opposite Buddy served as a barrier between the baby and the dragon. "If you hurt Buddy or anyone else, I'll fucking kill you. Oh, and your insults suck, by the way. You're supposedly this big, powerful dragon witch, and the best you can come up with is calling me fat? *That's* pathetic."

"You have one week from today. Figure it out."

Not one second after Folly delivered the final injunction, Cynthia was upside down and backwards as she cartwheeled through a tunnel of bright light.

FIFTEEN

C‌YNTHIA'S ARMS FLOPPED AT HER SIDES LIKE BONELESS SACKS OF JELLY. She staggered in darkness, flailing for balance or mental clarity. Murmurs rang in her ears. She tried to pry her eyes open, but the resistance proved too much. She slapped her hands in the air, frantically clawing for purchase, panic getting the best of her. Had she passed out somewhere, used magic, gotten sick?

A firm grip clamped her arm at the same time that one of her swatting palms connected to a hard, cold substance. The person's grip held tight while she breathed and allowed the sense of stability to ground her long enough to ease back into full consciousness.

Her five senses returned in a tsunami of stimuli: the smell of gasoline and outdoor, night air, a car motor, chirping bugs. Hard brick or concrete biting into her spine, a bitter taste in her mouth. Queasiness launched a violent assault, forcing her to gag in lieu of vomiting. "Where am I?" she got out, the muscles of her throat hard and uncooperative.

"At the gas station, the same place where you were before you left. It's me, Raven. I'm here. You're okay. You used magic to go to the other place, but you came back just now. You came back with...eh, you came back safe."

Right. She was at the gas station with Raven when she saw Folly's writing on the wall and went to the other place to ask the elemental sister for answers. Had she gotten what she was after? She wasn't up to snuff, her thoughts somehow both slow and racing. Spinning and dazed, she pressed her back against the wall and slid down to her bottom.

Raven sat with her. A grim, dreadful feeling nagged at the far regions of her brain. Something wasn't right on the Raven front, but she hadn't a clue what the problem was. Or maybe the off-ness had a different, non-Raven source. Her latest magical journey had been more taxing than previous ones.

"How long was I gone?" She turned to him for confirmation. Ten or so mirror images of his face floated in a kaleidoscope effect before settling down to three, then condensing into one handsomely familiar goth-guy head. "I don't feel right."

A sound like high-pitched chatter played continuously through a loop, the mishmash of voices in her head not loud enough to overpower but not quiet enough to ignore, either. Where had that come from? A residual effect of an energetically taxing experience?

Despite many years of practiced study, she wasn't savvy enough with her magic to be able to immediately assess if new developments were good or bad. This one didn't feel great.

He thinned his lips into an em-dash. "An hour. Maybe more. Do you remember any important details of your experience?"

Vague, unsettling sensation continued to bother her, but no disturbing details of what had happened on her trip emerged. She'd been on a beach. Spoken with Folly in the form of a sentient wind. Picked up a large rock or crystal? A turtle? "No, not really. And I'm sorry to have kept you waiting that long."

"It's okay, I checked in with the others and got some writing done to prepare for our going over the song notes and your book. But I'd like to get going soon, if you're feeling up to it. Spending the night in the parking lot of an abandoned gas station isn't exactly my idea of luxury accommodations."

She summoned enough positivity to reconnect with good humor. "Not even with a bottle of Jack, marshmallows, and some sleeping bags? We could make it work."

He brushed a few stray strands of hair out of her face. "I'm glad that you're starting to recover."

Physically, she was feeling fine now, and the weird, faint voiced had tapered off. Must've been her conscious mind sloughing off old bits of dream energy. Not dreams, though. She'd spoken with a dragon, Folly the dragon, in some level of reality.

Her grimoire talked about progressively immersed levels of astral travel and magical communion. Not in enough detail to where she could neatly compare her experience against what she'd read, but she had enough confidence in the similarity to venture an educated guess that she'd leveled up. "I think I went deeper into the other place than I ever have before."

He pulled a face. "No doubt."

"What are you talking about?"

He cleared his throat in a half-snort, half-chuckle. "I don't know how to tell you this." "Spit it out."

"You have a small dragon asleep on you."

She jerked her head to see what in fresh hell he was talking about.

He was not kidding. The first impossible glimpse walloped her with vertigo. The most magnificent, surreal, and jaw-dropping specimen of anything alive that she'd ever seen in person had made a bed of her.

Though small enough to fit in the palm of her hand, the sheer amount of awe that the dragon inspired made its presence feel as massive as a planet.

The tail, wide at the base and tapering to a spear-like tip, wrapped around the mythical beast in a protective curl of pearlescent flesh and bone. A network of perfect, evenly spaced spear points dotted that awesome tail, running up the spine and neck. Each sharp tip could have been carved in snow. Even in the unlit, rural night, the wondrous animal demanded every bit of available light, reflecting twinkles of glitter off its alabaster skin.

"Hey there," she whispered, barely able to push the words out of a throat swollen with tears of amazement. "Hey, buddy."

As if on cue, the dragon poked its head up from the center of its slumber coil, its eyes popping open. They were a dark color that she couldn't make out in the light, but even in the pitch black, those eyes sparkled with sentience. "Buddy." The voice was inchoate, rudimentary, and came out like a cross between a meow and and a squeak. But the dragon very clearly mimicked the term of endearment that Cynthia had spoken. "Buddy."

"Raven." Her whisper was shaky as she nonsensically turned to him for some sort of explanation, scraping the tip of her finger over the bony ridges along the dragon's tail. "What the hell is happening?"

"I'm going to go ahead and say that's a question for you to ask yourself, baby." He petted the top of the dragon's head, earning a coo and arch of the neck from the small wonder.

"Quit fucking calling me baby," she said in a feeble way, for she neither meant what she said nor had the wherewithal to act tough with a dragon sitting on her.

"Baby," the dragon repeated in its chirpy voice. "You Baby, me Buddy."

"It's learning to talk." She was too dumbstruck to be embarrassed by the dumbness inherent in stating the obvious.

"Buddy talk. Buddy eat. Buddy pwotect Baby."

A crack of energy bolted through her head, followed by a peculiar, spacey feeling. Memories began to swell and flow back into her like water over a dam. She'd acquired this dragon cub—kit, pup?—in the other place as a gift from Folly and named the little one Buddy. Buddy was a familiar to enhance Cynthia's craft of magic. But why would Folly act with such unprompted generosity? Altruism was out of character for the elemental sister of chaos.

Amorphous anxiety and dread sickened her. Something wasn't right with Folly and Buddy. Cynthia had screwed something up, made a misstep, entered some sort of Faustian bargain or incurred a debt. "Did I say anything that sounded important, while I was there?" she asked Raven. "Mutter any words, yell or scream anything, try to write on that wall again?"

He shook his head. "No. You were out cold. Why? What do you remember?"

Buddy nuzzled her neck, begging for pets. Cynthia obliged, stroking the underside of her familiar beneath the neck, though she was beginning to feel guilty and ashamed. She was at fault, blameworthy.

Or committed to something she didn't want to do. Obliged. She struggled to pinpoint the source of the negativity and came up empty-handed. "I can't get a fix on it, but I think that I may have agreed to some kind of payment for Buddy. A deal or exchange that sounded good at the first but then a condition came up that exposed the catch." She looked out into the middle distance. "But I don't know if that's quite right."

"I tell you what." Raven cupped the side of her face in his palm, coaxing her from a fruitless rumination. "It's late, and you just went through what sounds like a really heavy experience with magic. Let's get out of here, get you and Buddy to the hotel, and get some sleep. Maybe in the morning when we compare our notes, more details will come to you that you can patch together into a meaningful explanation."

Raven sure seemed eager to get cracking on this note comparison project. He'd brought it up regularly and repeatedly since they'd been on the tent in the beach. Why was he so impatient?

She came close to pressing him on this point before nixing the urge to say anything. In the absence of any founded suspicion of his motive, she'd come across as a cynical, untrusting jerk for questioning him. Pushing him away would be pointless at best and probably actively detrimental to her goal of finding Fire and Chaos.

After spinning her wheels on the chaos and fire mission for weeks, his literal wheels were the only solid lead in a while. If alienated Raven, she'd be back to where she was when she'd jumped in the big rig with Denise-Nerissa, which was essentially nowhere. And she liked having Raven around, took solace in the presence of him by her side. He was kind, thoughtful, and, above all, right. They ought to get to the hotel. "Good call. I'm ready for a real bed." She braced her feet and pushed herself upright, a quick glimpse affirming that Buddy was perched securely, chilling out in a state of calm.

Raven eased them both into a standing position. "Are you okay?"

Not really. The entire damn situation was cockeyed, but she couldn't put her finger on what'd happened in the other place that had caused her to feel this way, and the loss of significant information from her perceptual landscape upset her. "I guess, why?"

He gazed into her eyes, the full extent of his expression difficult to read in the darkness. "You got quiet for a bit. I wondered what you were thinking about, or if you were having second thoughts."

She snorted, though her outward scoff served as a flimsy shield against the disarming effect of his perceptiveness and her failures to be closed or cagey. "Nosy much?"

He kissed the corner of her mouth, a chaste or even platonic kiss that had made her wonder just how far through her he saw. "Concerned."

She didn't quite believe him. He'd all but admitted that, in her gift with the craft, she had something that he wanted. What was that? She didn't enjoy being all testy about Raven or suspecting him of having hidden agendas, especially since the strange new feelings had come up so unexpectedly.

Cynthia played off the inner turmoil with one of her time-tested tactics, a hard act, flinging her hair and walking out a couple of feet ahead to blaze a trail to the bike. "Don't worry about me, birdman. I can take care of myself." For good measure, she shined him off with a sneer.

He caught up to her *fast*, tacking his hands on her hips with a speed and force that stunned her. Before she knew what was going on, he had her pushed against the bike, his arms caging her from behind, his lips at her ear. "What if I want to take care of you? Ever thought of that?" His tone was low, edging toward a growl, his body pinning her to the wall of chrome. "What if I want to make you mine? Come on, baby. Let me in."

Desire licked up her center from navel to throat, sending shivers up her spine as her senses heightened. One potent gasp sprang from her lips as the thrill of surrender took hold. The metal warmed her palms, the hardness and strength of him igniting frightening fires in the most hidden parts of her.

How deliciously tempting, the thought of giving herself over to this man. This man who wanted her, someone wild and dangerous and free. How new. How easy it would be to surrender to him, to give it up and let go. Allow the flimsy supports around her inner spaces to simply crumble into dust as she let go, fell into his arms, and issued her plea.

Please take me. Please have me. Please love me.

What?! No! On reflex, the wall slammed down.

She whipped around to face Raven, poking her finger into her chest to push him back. "This shit stops now. I'm not your baby, or your property, or someone that you can control. I will never be yours, or anyone's else's. I belong only to me, and the next time you pull some alpha male act, you will never see or hear from me ever again. Do I make myself clear?"

He backed off. "Yeah. Sure. Got it. But you owe me one thing."

"I don't owe you jack shit." However, she didn't believe herself, despite the false confidence with which she spoke. Raven was in her debt somehow, or she was responsible for him. Again, the elusive specifics slipped through her fingers like sand grains on that damn beach. Fucking Folly. What had she done in the other place? What had Cynthia done? Embarrassed in her ignorance, she doubled down. "I'm free. Unencumbered. I do not, nor will I ever, have entanglements with anyone. Including you. *Especially* you."

He smirked, that bastard. "You consistently, blatantly, overplay your hand. You know that, right?"

Her brain was inflamed. She came so close to slapping him across the face that her palm twitched with the urge. But even Cynthia wasn't *that* volatile, and she didn't believe in violence except in self-defense. "I'm this close," she hissed through her teeth, her hands shaking. "This close." Except she didn't even really want to hit him and wasn't sure what the point of her threat was anymore.

He held his space, she had to give him that, his feet planted wide and his energy calm yet strong. "Close to what, Cynthia? What are you so damn close to? Opening up? Letting go of all of this defensiveness and anger you carry around and project onto every inappropriate target you can find? Are you *this close* to finally showing your heart to someone who cares about you? *This close* to dropping your fake veneer and being honest and real?" He balled a fist and thumped his own chest. "Because you know what? You're not close enough. Get closer. Then cross that line. Show me."

"You don't want me. Not in the way you think I do. I'm nothing but trouble. Bad. Crazy. I'm poison. I'll chew you up. Corrode you." Her own words, a mishmash of things others had said and her own internalized interpretations of their words, ripped her to shreds.

He closed the minimal space between them, bringing them nose to nose so she smelled leather, him, and traces of old whiskey. "You don't think those things. Those are other peoples' voices in your head. People who let you down when they should have lifted you up."

A mirthless laugh escaped as his attempt to connect with her dredged up a different, unpleasant problem. "Then there's the whole matter of voices in my head. A separate problem from my screwed-up personality, but one that's arguably just as destructive and harmful."

He frowned, clearly thrown off kilter by the abrupt segue. "What?"

Tightness cinched her midsection, making it difficult to breathe. Every second that passed, the unbearable sensation in her body worsened, the wages of holding distress inside taking a cumulative, brutal toll. In a last-ditch effort to expel the agony that she'd brought back from the other place, Cynthia started talking as rapidly as the thoughts came. "Something's wrong from my trip to the other place. Coming back with Buddy incurred a cost. Folly laid some term or caveat on me, but I can't figure out what it is. I think that you're involved. But whatever she said or did is weighing on me, and I'm fucking terrified beyond all measure that she's going to come to collect when I least expect it. Hurt people. Hurt you, and Buddy, and God knows who else, because of what I did. I made a bargain with her, or a mistake, some error that had a huge cost. You aren't safe. I screwed up. Like always."

The last part of what she said smarted, and before she had the chance to spin up her hurt and grief into some variation of rage, tears exploded. A sob choked out along with the waterworks, and Cynthia was beside herself, erupting into wails of remorse, regret, and sheer terror.

"Cynthia. Cynthia, baby. Breathe." He wrapped an arm around her back, pulling her close, and stroked her hair. "It's going to be okay. Is that what you were upset about when you came back, what you were holding inside? You're afraid that you made a choice that will harm someone else?"

His words made so much sense and connected so viscerally that a light practically flared bright on her frontal lobe. That was it. That was totally it. The payment for getting to have Buddy, her familiar, was that she had to kill Raven. Otherwise, Folly was going to kill Buddy and the other witches. Probably Cynthia for good measure. Folly was probably content to kill everyone eventually. "Oh, no," she wailed. "Oh, no, no. What have I done?"

"It's going to be alright," he whispered against the shell of her ear. "You aren't going to hurt me. I'm actually pretty resilient; I've been through a lot. I know that I really piss you off sometimes, but, no offense, I'm not afraid of you. I like you too much."

That startled a sniffly laugh out of her. She was still scared shitless of the Folly threat, however. "You don't understand. Folly is powerful, and evil. All that she wants, from what I can tell, is to cause as much chaos, confusion, and misery as possible while bringing out the worst in everyone whose path she crosses. I should never have entered into a one-on-one exchange with her. I was so arrogant and stupid, to think that I could handle her or win in some imaginary contest with her. You can't beat her or get the upper hand, because you never know which way is up with chaos magic. My book warned me of that."

He pulled back from her enough to bush his lips against her forehead. "We'll beat her together. I won't let you suffer like this, Cynthia. I won't stand by while this tears you apart. And this little guy?" He tapped Buddy on the nose. "I'll protect him, too."

"Her," Cynthia corrected.

"Buddy her," Buddy confirmed.

"Excuse me." Raven tickled Buddy's cheek before moving his hands to stroke Cynthia's upper arms. "My apologies. Now, I have an idea."

She calmed her breathing to normal levels, getting the tears to taper off in the process, leaving her cheeks wet and her lips salty. "I'm all ears."

"Let's get the hell out of here and get some rest. Tomorrow, we regroup. Maybe the others will be able to help. And don't forget Nerissa. She might have insights that we can use."

"Good point." Cynthia wasn't doing anyone any favors by standing around in a decaying parking lot freaking out about what Folly might or might not do. "Let's jet." The urge to get as far away as possible from that graffiti-coated brick wall permeated every cell.

Raven mounted up, and she slung her backpack on her body and got behind him, Buddy hanging on tight and nicely buttressed by the full camping pack. Raven started off slow, then gradually picked up speed until it was clear that Buddy had the strength and leverage to stay put. Soon, they were cruising, just another anonymous motorcycle careening down a lost highway.

Miles blew past in a template of desert pockmarked by the occasional ramshackle diner or lonely trailer. In the distance, a large white sign loomed. Cynthia chanced it a passing look, and the writing made her screech to a mental halt. By the time she could toss a double-take, it was too late, but it didn't matter. She remembered what it said and remembered why those words mattered.

Seven Days.

SIXTEEN

"Is that a snake?" The young woman behind the hotel reception desk, a teenager with heavy eyeliner and platinum blond hair, stared blankly in Cynthia's general direction. "Or a bearded dragon?"

"Excuse me?" Cynthia had been too distracted gawking at the indoor doors a few feet past the hotel's lobby to pay much attention while Raven checked them in. The more she thought about how badly she wanted to lie down in a real bed with clean sheets, the worse the ache in her hips got. The ride and hotel arrival had helped to calm her down about Folly's threat, but the clerk's comment unwittingly sent her right back to fretting. "Is what a dragon?"

"On your shoulder." The clerk's vocal inflection sizzled, her face betraying not one twitch of affect behind the computer monitor that she peered over. "Is it, like, a one of those dragon lizards or something?"

Oh. Right. Cynthia was carting around a literal dragon. Buddy was so unobtrusive and quiet that she blended in easily to Cynthia, but not to the others. She'd have to figure out how to become more discreet with Buddy to avoid these types of questions, especially since she swore that her familiar had grown on the ride, meaning that Buddy's days as accessory-sized were numbered. Time to buy a pet carrier. "Yeah. She's a lizard." Best to shirk specifics in case anyone in the vicinity was savvy enough to ask follow-up questions.

"Buddy dwagon."

The receptionist gaped. "Whoa. It's like a talking parrot lizard."

The comment caught the attention of another young clerk, who wandered out of a backroom area with a stack of folded towels piled in his arms. "What's a talking what?"

"Buddy dwa—"

"How much for one night again?" Raven interrupted before Buddy had a chance to restate her true identity and stir in any more unwanted attention.

The original employee turned back to her keyboard. "Well, I'll have to charge you a cleaning deposit for a small pet." She punched some keys before sliding a sheet of paper across the desk, her short, purple manicure impeccable. "Here's your bill. Sign, please."

Raven signed and settled up, handing over the requested credit card for incidentals.

In case Buddy was hungry, Cynthia grabbed a granola bar off a complementary snack platter and took off walking beside Raven. Once they were out of earshot of the worker, she asked, "Was that a real card or magic?"

"Let's just say it began its transactional life as a means to check out graphic novels at the Seattle Public Library." He guided them in the direction of the elevators.

Cynthia had her reservations about money magic and its consequences, but now wasn't the time to raise objections. The hotel was clean, welcoming, and well-lit, and Raven's business wasn't hers. He was obviously more than capable of taking care of himself. But, speaking of magic, his alleged talent with dream scribing and reality manipulation warranted further investigation for how it connected to her mission. "Did you ever try out any of the home-cooked spells in your groupie diary to test if you could alter your environment in real-time?" She ripped open the granola bar packaging and offered the snack to Buddy, who devoured the food in two bites. "You're a hungry little dragon, huh?"

As they stepped into the elevator, unaccompanied, fortunately, Raven gently elbowed her side. "That's what I get for opening up to you, huh? Relentless belittling?"

Only because she was not-so-secretly delighted that they had something as powerful as magical talent in common. And by way of books, no less. She had to be super careful that she didn't start to like him *too* much, because thanks to the whole issue of Folly wanting him dead, she might have to run him off if it started to look like he was in danger. How would she handle such a problem?

"She told me to kill you," Cynthia blurted out before she had time to stop herself, because keeping the secret and pretending that things were halfway alright somehow felt worse.

He winced. "Who?"

"The big bitch herself. She said that if I don't kill you, she'll, well..." Cynthia bent her head in Buddy's direction and slashed a finger across her own neck, exercising discretion in the interest of protecting Buddy's feelings from a scare.

"Kill me, eh? Good luck to her," he said dryly.

She laughed at his unbothered irreverence. Talking this over with Raven actually helped, took some of the teeth and out of the threat by demystifying it. For all she knew, Folly was all bluff and bluster, testing Cynthia to see how far she could push her. If she resisted the order to harm Raven, there was a chance that Folly would concede defeat and back down in begrudging admission that Cynthia had passed the latest test. There was a chance of that. Totally. "You do something to piss her off?"

"Not that I know of." His featured darkened along with the tone with which he spoke his next words, "But dabbling in the magic of this system always runs the risk of harming oneself or someone else in ways you don't expect, yeah? Boomerangs all the way down."

A current of dismay crept from her feet to her head. The smooth, seamless confidence with which he asserted those claims about the dangers of magical practice bothered her. "How would you know that magic is risky unless you looked in my book or saw another Coven Daughters book? I don't mean to be super confrontational, but I do think we're up against some really heavy stuff and need to be totally honest with each other. So if you have tidbits of insight, or anything that you ought to tell me, please do share."

He looked to the side, breaking eye contact. The elevator opened to a hall of doors. They stepped out onto orange and brown carpet patterned with interlocking hexagons. How fitting. Raven seemed to get the significance of this geometric pattern symbolism, running the toe of his boot over the outline of one pattern. "I realize that."

Two middle-aged men passed in the hallway, each carrying a wine glass and a tiny plastic plate stocked with miniature desserts. "Love your aesthetic," a silver fox said to Raven, adding as he glanced at Cynthia, "You too. Digging the rugged outdoorswoman look. And cute lizard too."

Raven smiled politely as he watched the couple enter the hallway. "Thanks."

"Appreciate it," Cynthia added. "Safe travels."

"Buddy dwagon. No lizard. Hungwy dwagon."

The other man gaped and craned his neck. "Did that lizard just *talk*, or was that pot we smoked after dinner laced?"

Fortunately, the doors closed, spiriting away the inquisitors.

Raven tugged her arm to lead her a few doors down to the room, his steps quick and purposeful.

She stayed on him, pressing for answers. "Okay, what is going on? First you're shy about the notebooks and don't want to share them, then that's all you can think about, and now you're worried about the risks involved in practicing magic. I can't keep up with where your headspace is at."

He waved a white key card over a lock box, sliding her side eye. "You're the one who just told me that your familiar adoption session with Folly ended with a bounty on my head. Don't you think I have grounds for being disturbed?" A light blinked from red to green, causing the lock to yield with a whir, and Raven pushed open the door to darkness.

"Valid," she said, following into the room and flicking on a light. The lovely suite was clean, fresh, and tastefully styled in classic décor. Perfect, save for the single king bed. Cynthia was *not* the cuddly sort and hated to share her sleeping space. Other people got in the way, physically and emotionally. "They didn't have one with two queens?"

"Nope." He set his pack on the floor. "I can take the pullout couch if sleeping together crosses a boundary for you."

She hated to act like a total diva and force him to sleep on some hard, pokey pullout to assuage her attachment issues while she hogged a whole-ass king bed.

One of these days, she'd get over her shit and learn to act normal when it came to intimacy. Today could be a good day to take a baby step. For example, it might be nice to bask in someone else's body heat. Didn't mean that she had to spoon the guy. "Whatever. It's big enough where we can stay on our respective sides."

"Glad that our bed issue is solved. I appreciate your flexibility. Are you ready to finally dive into these books?"

"Ready as I'll ever be."

"Buddy dwagon hungry." Better pronunciation this time. Buddy was a smart little thing, learning through listening.

"Hold on a sec, Bud." Cynthia threw her pack on the bed, rummaged until she found an energy bar and some trail mix, and laid the items out.

Buddy fixated on the food packages, waiting with her muscles taut until Cynthia ripped open the plastic wrapping. It was all gone in a few swallows. "I have no idea if I'm overfeeding her or underfeeding her or what. You got any baby dragon care manuals mixed in with your notes?"

Eyeing Buddy, Raven worked a stack of books and journals out of his bag and set them on the mattress. "No, but from what I can tell, you're doing something right. She's growing."

Cynthia sized up her familiar with his comment in mind. Raven was right. The dragon was too large now to fit in the palm of her hand, easily the size of a small adult cat. Twice as large as she'd been at the old gas station. "That should tide her over for awhile at least."

"I hungry. Hungry dragon hungry."

Cynthia groaned, overwhelmed by her new responsibility. She'd never been a big pet person, as living the nomadic life wasn't conducive to prioritizing the needs of another life form. Apparently, the time to adapt was now.

Raven palmed the hotel key card off the nightstand. "I'll check next door and see if the others have anything. They might've stopped for food."

It occurred to Cynthia for the first time that Raven had quietly booked the two of them their own room, a decision which both pleased and irritated her. He should've run the idea by her, but then she would have felt compelled to shoot it down on principle even though being alone in a room with him made her all glad and fuzzy, so she was happy that he chose unilaterally even though she kinda wanted to punch him for flexing the alpha move and/or throw herself into his arms, drop to her knees and...

God, she was a hot mess.

While he stepped out to check on the food situation, Cynthia read the spines of his books to distract herself from her trash heap of feelings. One text in particular stimulated her imagination. The plastic dust jacket was still on, giving the text a nostalgic, back-room-of-the-library feel. The title was written in a language that she'd never seen, though she inferred from the vowels and accent marks that the origin was of the romance variety. An Italian or Spanish dialect, perhaps?

Raven returned with two grease-stained fast food bags crumpled in his hands. "This is the best I could scrounge up for now. You like pizza? I'll order us one before it gets too late." He set the takeout bags in front of Buddy, who tore into the paper with her sharp little claws and made quick work of the burger and fry scraps before settling, hopefully sated at last, into a nap.

"Aw. Pizza and books. It'll be just like a study session." One that had a high likelihood of ending in fooling around, just like her study sessions with boys in high school had. Difference was, this time she didn't feel compelled to use sex to get the guy to like her. Raven already did like her, for whatever weirdo reason. She pointed to the book with foreign language words on the spine. "What's this one about? Some book nerds would call it sacrilege to keep the dust jacket on."

"Yeah. I just didn't want to change anything about it, it was so unlike anything other book that I'd ever seen." He pushed the books atop it aside, bringing its cover into full view.

Instantly she noticed a difference that set the book apart. Though as tall as a regular book, it was barely half as wide, as slim as a pamphlet, an unusual look for a hardback with a jacket. This volume was made to be toted, stored, tucked, carried. The cover was a rich, deep red emblazoned with a title, sub-title, and rune-like graphics. "Interesting." She opened the book and flipped pages, struck by a familiar, comfortingly dusty old-book smell. The skinny pages were filled with typed writing like any other book, the same language as the one on the spine and cover as best as she could surmise. "What's the deal with this one? Can you read it?"

"I can't read it, no." He scooted closer to her. "I still haven't found a translator who's able to work with the language effectively. The closest that anyone's been able to get is regional guesswork. It might be a dialect that was used in southern Spain or Morocco thousands of years ago and isn't living anymore, but others disagree."

Cynthia pictured a map in her head. "That's near the Strait of Gibraltar, the channel connecting those two countries. It's where the lost island of Atlantis was fabled to be." At least, that's what she'd heard on a podcast once.

"Correct. I wasn't going to bring that up. Didn't want to scare you off with any conspiracy-adjacent theories and have you lambast me as a flat-earther or Bigfoot believer."

Man, she'd better slow her snark roll before Raven's impression of her as a closed-minded ass was set in stone. "Hey, at this point, nothing's off the table." She thumbed through more of the incomprehensible text, stopping at a chunk of pages devoted to diagrams and drawings. Unease seeped through her the longer she looked at the eerie illustrations, an uncanny sensation fixing her in place. "What am I looking at here? You got context to make this less scary?"

The etchings were esoteric with ritualistic overtones that triggered her distaste, though she supposed as a follower of the Left-Hand path of witchcraft, she should enhance her tolerance or at least cerebral appreciation of such content.

They were just so death-evocative, but in an unknowable way that made them all the more upsetting. These were pages and pages of dark secrets filled with stick figures contorted into unnatural positions that would break a body, sometimes stacked or combined with other bodies to create pyramids or pentagrams. There were crudely drawn stars and hexagons, notes scribbled near points or in margins, sometimes lines slashing through the shapes. A few skulls. Naïve renderings of four-legged mammals. Many pages were splattered or smeared with unknown substances.

The hexagon with the squiggly-fingered handprint held court in the middle. "Here's our link." She viscerally recoiled from the larger than life sigil of her magic system even while she was breathlessly drawn to it. Story of her witchy life. "Did you know this was here?"

"Yes. It's come up a few times. The theory that I'm starting to put together is that your symbol can act as a seal to stop the prophecy, but only under precise circumstances and if other conditions are met. And then, there's this. Check it out." He arranged three banged-up notebooks in front of her, worn-down relics with doodled-upon covers. Raven opened all three, showing pages filled with notes and drawings resembling those in the odd, slim book. "This one is the dream content." He pointed at the one closest to him. "I think that, based on my experience and work with lucid dreaming, that the keys toward steering our reality in accordance with this prophecy—being the architects of it—are in here. Have a look and tell me what you think."

Her feelings too mixed up to be clear to her anymore, she took the notebook. The words he'd written aligned with what he'd told her about his visions, so at least there was alignment.

He'd etched, with a high degree of artistic talent, a wheel with spokes. More of those rune-type symbols, ones she recognized from his Atlantis book, filled the pie-slice spaces in between spokes. She touched his notes, then caressed the slender book, then rubbed her own temple as she fed all of the information into her brain. "I wonder if the Coven Daughters symbol isn't just a seal, but is some kind of skeleton key to drive the prophecy and work with the material of the universe. I say this because each of the witches, as far as I can tell, uses our piece of the symbol to cast spells and manipulate reality according to one's will. Which is the essence of witchcraft, really."

Then there was the issue of the inevitable consequences that arose from partaking in the aforementioned reality manipulation, but that was a whole other matter.

Raven bobbed his head with rapt enthusiasm. "We've gotta be on the right track, as far as I can tell. There were references to witches that came up in the songs, and in the dream instructions. I saw symbols that evoked this." He pointed to the sigil in the skinny book. "That's when I knew that I needed to find a witch to take this to the next level. Connect the dots. See if it all adds up as much as I was starting to suspect."

Suspicion rang a bell inside of her like a phone call from a long-lost frenemy. There he went talking about her use value again. Why did he care so much, anyway? Not like he could bring his parents back to life. Raven's motivations remained hard to pinpoint. Was this obsession for obsession's sake at this point, a personal quest to apprehend the universe's mysteries that had grown into its own insatiable beast? "I still don't get what's in this for you. What do you want, revenge? Or, if this is a spiritual mission that revolves around uncovering the meaning of life, I promise that there are easier ways to achieve enlightenment."

He turned to her, his gaze burning into hers with passion. "Revenge isn't quite the right word, but yeah, this all started from a place of seeking justice for shifters. And of course to find the others of my kind and reunite with them. But my purpose has grown since then. Something is being kept from us, Cynthia, something huge and transformative about our place in the world. You mentioned enlightenment, and I think that's a good word to use, but it's not personal elevation that I'm seeking. I really feel here like we're on the cusp of a new age of enlightenment, and that if we keep pressing, compiling as much information as we can, and combining our powers, we'll have a major breakthrough. Our time is coming."

She glanced between him and all of the books. They deeper she went, the deeper that they went, the more dangerous the entire project seemed. Dangerous by virtue of being so much bigger and more ancient than they were, and dangerous in its association with forces whose morality was dubious at best, bankrupt at worst. "What you're saying sounds good, but also vague. I worry. I worry that these spirit beings like Folly want us doing this, you know? Running down rabbit holes until we're so deep that we have no idea where the light source ought to come from, let alone if one is there for us to see."

Déjà vu rippled through her. Folly had spoken words nearly identical to Cynthia's, referencing endless, unlit, pre-dug tunnels that they'd dart around in like blind rabbits. Or was that the power of suggestion or Folly messing with her mind or—gah! Cynthia waved her fingers in front of her face. "I just don't want us to lose track of our original point. I'm worried that the more we pour over notes and references, and the more that I use magic to connect with the other place, the more this becomes all-consuming, and consumes vital pieces of us. Which can't be healthy." She traced the circumference of the wheel he'd sketched. "Spinning our wheels is a good way to go insane."

He muttered in acquiescence. "You're right. We should stick with the original plan to connect with the shifters in Mexico and see if we get lucky and find any other witches there or shifters who can speak of their whereabouts."

Anxiety ran amok. She hadn't been honest with Raven, and now she was reaping what she'd sown with that lie. While going over some ideas for how to handle the fruits of her falsehood, she looked closer at the wheel. Flames curled around the outer ring in sharp tendrils. A fiery ring was significant to him, and probably should be to her as well, given that she'd set out on this whole crazy scheme determined to learn the secrets of fire and chaos.

Maybe she was interpreting fire too literally and ought to turn her inquiry to those important players in the game who used fire so crucially in their brand and symbolism. "I wonder if we should try to make contact with someone in Fyre instead, you know? They're significant, given your experiences with the music and its connections to your dreams and symbols that crop up in my witchcraft. I'm sure there's a way to reach them through their manager or agent."

Raven regarded her with disbelief. "You want to change the plan *now* and get in touch with these band members? What would we even say to them that wouldn't sound psychotic? Besides, we're halfway to Mexico."

Unable to look at him, she pretended to read some entries in his dream journal while she hastily confessed the truth, "There are no shifters in Mexico."

SEVENTEEN

CYNTHIA HELD HER BREATH AS IF FREEZING THE FLOW OF OXYGEN into her lungs could suspend the moment in stasis before the other shoe dropped. Not that she was afraid of Raven, of how he'd react. She was just afraid, plain and simple. Frightened of what came next as the consequence of her bad choice hung in the balance. She usually fled bad choices before they had the chance to look her in the eye and hold her accountable.

Raven simply watched her from his spot on the bed, waiting like more information was forthcoming.

Except it wasn't. Or maybe it was. Cynthia didn't know what she was feeling in the moment, just gravity. "I'm sorry," she finally croaked out, studying the scars on her arms, her unkempt nails, every physical flaw standing in for a defect of character.

"I'm confused," he said in a flat tone. He closed his notebooks and the Atlantis book in soft, careful motions. "We're halfway to Mexico. I thought we were in this together, but now you're telling me, after I brought my friends out to the middle of nowhere thinking that we were on the right track, that you know something that we don't? Something that you purposefully kept from us?"

Not a trace of anger laced his tone, which made it all worse. He was stunned. Or disappointed. Struggling to comprehend why she'd done what she'd done, because to him her choice made no sense. "Yes." She shriveled in his wake. She couldn't look at the blank shock etched on his face anymore, so she stared at the blanket to see anything but her shortcomings reflected in his appraisal. "I don't know what's wrong with me sometimes."

He rose and paced a three-foot track on the carpet. He picked up one of the notebooks and threw it back onto the bed as if surrendering hope in productive teamwork with her. She felt more alone by the second, heavy underneath her own existence.

"Look at me." He followed the firm but gentle command by crouching to capture her at eye level. "And tell me the truth. Can you do that?"

"Yes." She found him, doing her best to communicate her remorse with her own stinging, watery eyes. "No more lies. I'm so sorry."

"Why?" He scowled. "Why would you do this? And how do you know where shifters are or aren't? I can't fathom you having malicious intent, but this makes so little sense that I honestly can't make peace with any of the interpretations running through my mind."

Oh, boy. She had trouble swallowing the lump in her throat. "On the subject of where shifters are, yeah, I know. I know because I lived in a shifter colony. For years. That's what I was trying to tell you when we were in the other place, but I couldn't get there. I couldn't bring myself to open up all the way."

His lips divided. "You lived with shifters and you didn't tell me? Why? Cynthia, what's going on?"

She covered her face and turned away, speaking her messy thoughts as quickly as she could, not caring how disorganized they were, just desperate to get them out. "I don't know. I guess I thought that if I had a secret, something that I was holding back that you wanted, that I'd be retaining my value to you. I was afraid that once I told you where the shifters were, you'd go there and leave me behind. I'd have nothing that you wanted anymore. Before you tell me that's irrational because you already said that you need my magic, I know. I realize that. But it's like, maybe if you knew where you needed to go you'd realize that you didn't need my magic after all, especially after we looked at the books together and you formed all of your theories about the purpose of the Coven Daughters symbol."

After sucking in a mega breath, she filled more silence. "I was scared that as your vision of your destination took shape, you'd reevaluate what you *thought* you wanted from me and change your mind once you figured that you'd gotten enough. My mama always warned me not to give it up, not to give up what people wanted before I got what I wanted first. Otherwise they'd use me and throw me out. I never listened, of course, and she was right. I was trying to take her advice for once, trying to finally be smart." The words she spoke sounded so screwed up and twisted, so immature, when she uttered them aloud. She hugged herself like she could contract and shrink before dematerializing. "That sounded insane. I'm so fucked up."

Raven was back on the bed fast, holding her, his arms providing comfort in strength while his scent and warmth made a cocoon where she was able to temporarily forget her humiliation. "Cynthia, baby. You thought that if you gave me what I wanted, that I'd abandon you?"

"Wouldn't be the first time." She nuzzled against him, grateful to have intimacy without the raw submission of eye contact.

"With me it would be the first time," he soothed in a smooth cadence. "But the point is moot, because there won't be a first time. I don't treat people like that. And I'd *never* treat you like that."

"I've heard that line before, too." A bunch of hurtful memories that she'd stuffed way down low all floated up at once, landing blows before she could strike them down. "I've heard them all."

He rubbed the knots in her shoulders. "I'm so sorry that people treated you so badly. You deserved so much better."

"I'm devolving into what I said I'd never become." She sneered at herself, willing the hard plaque that'd once grown over her heart to reform. "A whiny victim."

"I don't think of you that way. I never would." He drew back from the hold to capture her stare. "You're incredibly strong. But you're hurt."

"Broken," she said with bitterness. Why was she never good enough? Why hadn't she figured out the right way to be a person yet? "Damaged."

"No." He wiped an invisible tear from her cheek. "Not broken in need of fixing. Wounded in need of healing."

His kind words might not reflect a principle that she'd ever find the self-worth to internalize, but they made for a nice mantra to offer a new perspective. "That's really beautiful."

"You're beautiful, Cynthia. Beautiful and strong. You're fearless, and brave, and completely committed to mastering your craft. I admire you, and that's why I want to work with you. Not because I want to take something from you. I admire you, I don't covet something that you have that I want for myself. There's a difference."

She treated herself to several luxurious, deep breaths. In and out. Lowering her guard around Raven wasn't the hardest thing in the world, and besides, relaxing her semi-permanent state of defensiveness had to be healthy for her blood pressure. "You're taking this well."

He chuckled. "I try to go with the flow when I can. I gotta say, asking questions when I'm tempted to freak out or react with strong emotion has gotten me pretty far in life."

Now there was a lesson she could stand to learn. Lightness overcame her, and she allowed herself to accept gratitude for Raven's presence. He had a good energy, mellow and philosophical. Still waters running deep. He was a gift to her, and the least she was able to do for him now was come clean. "You want to know the truth? All of it?"

"Absolutely." He stroked the pad below her thumb in circles. "But only as much as you want to share, and when you're ready. I can tell that this subject is personal to you, a big deal, and you don't owe me anything."

A generous claim, about her not owing him. The least she owed him at this point was honesty and no more lies. "The shifters live in the Peruvian jungle in one specific region in the eastern part of the state, on the Amazon river. I'm sure that I'd be able to figure out how to get us to the exact location with a little research or a little magic, or both."

While he listened, she did her best to explain more of what she'd been worried about when it came to Peru, how the colony there had been the most loving family that she'd ever known. How she'd taken off, abruptly, in the middle of one sticky summer night when the bugs had been especially vocal and the urge to unite with her witch sisters had become too urgent to ignore anymore.

She told him how she missed the shifter colony with every fiber of her being and dreamed of going back. How scared she was that they'd send her packing if she went back, and how part of the impetus for keeping the true location secret from Raven was to prevent such a confrontation, to preemptively avoid the threat of them turning her away if she came back repentant and begging for them to reinstate their goodwill. The thought of Raven and his friends bearing witness to such a failure had been too much. If he hadn't spurned her already, surely he would have when he saw firsthand how she was unwanted by her only living family—former family. "So I guess I figured that if I keep running and hiding, it's like I'm a new version of myself in every new place that I end up. If nobody from one of my former lives is there to see me, then I don't have to look in the mirror. So I might be alone, but I can't get lonely if I'm choosing not to have others get too close to me. That way, I have the power." She managed a weak laugh. "Something like that."

He gently urged her to lie down and reclined next to her, still holding her close. "So why did you choose to leave your family and take a chance on finding the other witches when you had no idea where they lived or even if they existed? Seems like quite the leap of faith."

She scooped up the slumbering ball of Buddy and placed the young dragon on her stomach, watching her sleepy form rise and fall on waves of breath. Regardless of what happened with Raven, she'd found her precious familiar through this latest phase of her life.

Content with the present, she reflected on the past. The years in Peru were close to idyllic but not pure utopia. She'd always felt like an outsider, albeit one that was close to breaching the inner circle. One example came to mind, a memory that stung even though nobody was at fault. "They'd have these ritual runs."

Raven's touches calmed her more with every brush of his palm. "Like a marathon, or what?"

The thought of a bunch of shifters jogging in racing bibs and spandex pants was a ridiculous doozy. "Sort of, yeah. On certain significant dates, like the solstices and equinoxes, they'd all shift in unison and cavort around in the jungle. Running, flying, swimming and slithering. A big, giant, animal party. Everyone was always really nice and invited me, but I stayed behind instead of being the odd one out. I told myself that those events were a good chance for me to catch up on sleep or reading or whatever, and sometimes I did take the opportunity to spend quality time with my grimoire. But there was a lot of reflecting, too. And moping."

"I've heard about those rituals," he said with a wistful sort of awe. "They're huge energetic engines, or so goes the lore. My parents were killed around the winter solstice. I've long suspected that this corporation called Scarab has a connection to the solstices and equinoxes, and uses some celestial magic in their sacrifice, but I don't have proof."

"That's terrible." She couldn't fathom what he'd gone through and wanted more details, but it wasn't her place to ask. He'd open up if he was ready. "I'm so sorry."

"I appreciate it." He threaded their fingers together in an intimate clasp that made her instinctively jerk away before she accepted the tenderness of his touch as a gift that she deserved. "But this isn't about me. You were talking about the Peruvian shifter half-marathon. How it pushed you to leave."

His dry sense of humor put her at ease. "Yeah, I mean, I was always a little jealous of this special event they had to share. It got me wondering about whether I could ever have something that special and sacred with folks of my own. My people, you know? My clan. So I started researching the Coven Daughters and prophecy more deeply, and decided that if I was to have a shot at what I wanted so bad, I'd need to find those witches. Of course, my thinking on the matter was naïve."

"Why do you say that?"

She'd gazed into the abyss but didn't have a thorough picture of what had gazed back. Which made her experience with the darkness all the more abyss-like in its frightening mystery. "Something Folly said keeps bothering me."

"Which part?"

"The stuff about rabbit holes and how if we keep chasing them, we won't find a truth or secret, all that we'll accomplish is falling into a pit without light. I worry that's what I'm doing chasing these witches. Digging myself a deeper and deeper hole."

"She could also be lying or misdirecting to scramble you."

"No doubt. I have no idea where I'm going anymore, you know? Up, down, sideways. They all feel the same and equally likely."

He spoke with good-natured teasing, "In a very literal sense, we do know which direction we're headed. Toward Peru, which, fortunately for us, is roughly the same geographical trajectory as Mexico."

She cringed, ashamed at the scope of her egregious lie and how that fib had led them astray. "You're such a good sport."

"Call it a survival skill, not necessarily a virtue."

"Whatever you want to call it, I appreciate you rolling with my crazy. And, if the rumor is true and they've taken in the water witch down there, I'd at least have an opportunity for physical space collaboration. So there's a point in the win column for us. And Helen left the door open for more outreach, so to speak. I've got at least some link to three of us, which is two more than started out with. Maybe if I build enough trust, I can start talking to them about what they know about the other three."

"I think that's all we can do at this point. Keep trying things and taking chances. Throw ideas at the wall and see what sticks."

"Yeah. Totally. And I'd like to talk to another witch about spell craft before I try anything else. That last visit with Folly shook me up pretty bad." She petted Buddy's sleepy head, throttling back the worst of her fears. Folly could have been bluffing. It was possible. "But at least I got this little nugget out of the deal."

"There's always Nerissa next door, too." He tipped his head at the wall that they shared with the adjacent room.

"That's a whole other topic." One that her gut said to stay wary of until she had a chance to run the situation past another witch or at least do more research. The subject of possession felt volatile and dangerous to her on a visceral level, and besides, she didn't understand it enough to even really know what questions to ask. "I have this nagging feeling that I ought to keep my distance from anything having to do with possession or body jumping as much as possible until I can make more sense of the phenomenon and how it works. I realize that I can't avoid Nerissa, but her presence makes my skin crawl and I'm not sure why. I don't mean for that to sound cruel. I realize it's not her fault, necessarily."

"Smart." He trailed off, the one word he'd spoken loaded with unspoken meaning. "I wish that my mom and dad had heard an inner warning like the one you describe."

His change of subject startled her. Raven's parents had sealed their own tragic fate? "How do you mean?"

His hair tickled her chin, silence thickening the air into a solid wall. "They were both anthropologists who became paranormal hunters. Except they weren't chasing Bigfoot, they wanted to prove the existence of magical creatures. Discover others like me." He rubbed the sides of his nose. His voice shook with emotion as he added, "They wanted me to be less alone. So they started chasing magic and shifters and cryptozoological phenomena. They chased all of that right into some underground lair in Florida, where they died."

Her mouth dried. This story sounded awful and painful, so she didn't want to pry and risk re-traumatizing him, yet there were major pieces of the account missing. "Do you mind if I ask what happened?"

"I'm not sure, exactly." His tone was sharper than it was a moment ago, and he peered out of the corner of his eye. "Why, do you not believe me?"

"I didn't say that. Why would you jump to such a conclusion?"

"I'm sorry." Three lines grooved his forehead. "It's a touchy subject. Their bodies were never found. Nobody's are."

"How do you know for sure that they were killed?"

"Because everyone is killed in those things, Cynthia. Everyone that chases magic is killed eventually. My mom had a background in genetics —epigenetics, specifically. She was sure that she'd isolated the magical lineage in our genetic line through some DNA protein. And if she was able to detect it, you bet that Scarab was. Which is why I know that they sacrificed them. Where else would they be?"

Everyone that chases magic is killed eventually. Now there was a chilling portend.

She didn't have an answer to his question, but she begged to differ that he knew for sure that his parents were dead. Besides, why sacrifice both if only one carried the magical gene, supposedly? At best, he had a conjecture or a theory pieced together from whatever research he'd done, plus the fact that his parents had vanished long ago without resuming contact. None of which proved "dead," let alone beyond a doubt, but she wasn't about to argue with him on what was a highly emotional subject that had motivated his quest for revenge. "I'm so sorry. I wish that I could help."

His gaze landed on the ceiling, his physical presence tensing. "Thanks," he said crisply.

She resisted the urge to get upset. "What's wrong?"

"I can tell that you don't believe me."

That interpretation didn't quite fit, but she didn't deny that his conclusion based on the facts at hand had some holes in the fabric. "It's not that I don't believe you, I just don't feel like it's time to give up all hope."

In a single, abrupt motion, he sat up, swung his legs around to plant his feet on the floor, and addressed her while facing the wall. "When you said that you could help, I was hoping that there was something you could try to possibly bring some closure on this subject. A skill that certain witches in your network have. I'd held off on asking you thinking that once we found the shifters I'd have a shot at getting answers without dragging you into this, but since we're taking about it now, perhaps you'd consider giving it a try."

She bristled, clenching her teeth. Here he went, asking for things, bringing their relationship back to the transactional. Cynthia's insecurities about Raven's motivations resurfaced, but she did her best to brush them aside. Asking people for help wasn't inherently exploitive or instrumental and didn't mean that one person saw the other as mere means to an end. People asked each other for things all of the time. "What's that?"

Before he had a second to answer, shouts and thuds in the hallway broke her concentration and jarred her upright. Multiple voices, masculine and feminine, shouted single-syllable commands like "Stop" and "Hey."

A barrage of angry knocks slammed against their door. "Come out," Nerissa bellowed in an urgent proclamation. "Quit your conspiring and come out and face me."

EIGHTEEN

CYNTHIA HAD FORGOTTEN ABOUT RAVEN'S REQUEST AND BLOCKED OUT the few seconds it took to rush out of the room and into the hallway, focused only on getting to Nerissa and defusing the crisis before other hotel residents complained or inserted themselves into the blowup. The last thing they needed was witnesses, concerned citizens, busybodies, good Samaritans, whatever.

The problem was worse that she'd thought, not that she'd had a moment to think.

Ether, yanking at his white-blond hair, flung himself into a wall with a sickening thud, his motions sloppy and boneless, painful to watch. "Get out," he howled in his own voice, his ankle bending into an unnatural position as he writhed against the patterned wallpaper. "Get out of my head."

"We tried to hold him back." Portia wore disheveled pajamas, her face contorted into a rictus of distress as she recoiled from the spectacle of self-inflicted violence. "I think that Nerissa's control over him is breaking down, or they're fighting for domination of his body."

Dragon, advancing on Ether, added, "We tried working with the cards, too. To transmute Ether into a different form that wouldn't be so inhospitable to Nerissa."

That probably wasn't the right call. Cynthia was really starting to think that when it came to magic, less was more. But what the hell did she know?

"Shut the fuck up!" some random guy yelled from behind a closed door. "It's midnight. Go to bed or I'm calling the cops."

Raven ran to Ether and pinned him to the wall, halting his motions and the threat of more loud disturbances. "It's okay, man. Calm down. Take a few breaths. We've got you." He led his friend into Cynthia and Raven's room, and everyone regrouped in there, where Buddy was still asleep and blissfully unaware.

Cynthia gingerly moved her peaceful familiar to the dresser, her arm muscles aching as she carried the growing dragon and set her down beside the television remote control. Buddy had definitely gotten bother larger and more solid in the last hour.

The possessed blond sliced Cynthia a cold, furious look before speaking in Nerissa's voice. "You did this. You sent me to the darkness of the other place and bound me to the filth that resides there. Your fault. Your doing."

A sizzle raced over her chest. She struggled to draw a good breath. "What are you talking about?"

"You witches just can't steer clear of the sixth circle, can you? Your taste for the forbidden is insatiable. Always has been and always will be. There's no going back now. What you've unleashed is unavoidable and inevitable. Her hooks are stabbed in deep. Everywhere I go, I'll bring her with me from here on out. Bring a piece of her into this world so she may take root and establish her presence with greater and greater tenacity, like the invasive opportunist that she is. Keeping Folly at bay was *central* to overcoming this prophecy, but, yet again, one of you has failed."

Facts clattered around her brain in a chaotic jumble as her spirit crashed downward like hunks of broken glass. What had she done, exactly? Who else had failed? Cynthia didn't recall Nerissa issuing a direct command to do or not do any specific magical thing. "Why didn't you warn me?"

Nerissa laughed bitterly. "I did, and you acted anyway. I warned you on that beach. Perhaps you didn't listen or didn't hear, but I warned in every way I could, from my voice to the whispering wind to the howling of the fire. You acted in accordance with other practitioners during your fire circle, overcoming my free will with your own. I fear that I am now a vessel in addition to a travelling spirit."

Cynthia had had a feeling that the fire circle ritual had gotten out of hand. But she wasn't the spell police or Raven and company's babysitter, either, and not responsible for putting limits on their practice. Which was not to say that she was passive or innocent, because she'd taken an active part in the fire ritual. "A vessel for evil."

"Close. A vessel for chaos, which nurtures and enables evil. You wanted to learn the secrets of fire and chaos? Well now you have them, dear air child. Best of luck."

Frustration lanced through Cynthia in violent intervals. "I don't know what any of that fucking shit means, Nerissa. Say something real or leave us alone to sort this out."

Ether returned to interject, "Get the fuck out of me." He thrashed his head, moaning, his eyes rolled back to show more white than iris. Perspiration slicked his bulging arm muscles.

Nerissa spoke again, hoarse and thin, "He's rejecting me, this host of yours. I'll need an exorcism. I must not take such a large piece of Folly back to one of my regular bodies. She's inside of me, I feel her, but we can control how much stays. We must excise as much as we can."

"Or else what?" Raven asked.

Ether's chest heaved. "Leave." His tone was an exhausted, childlike whimper. "Leave me now."

Cynthia felt for the guy and didn't blame him for not wanting to be possessed anymore. Becoming aware that you'd been taken over by an outside force had to be a horrifying violation. Dabbling in magic at all was overwhelming, and Ether had gone off the deep end.

"Or else we're all trapped here indefinitely." The old witch spoke through Ether's mouth. "That's the endgame. What Folly desires is a total reimagining of the world we know. For a holographic shield to form around our sphere of existence, trapping us in this realm forever so that our energies, magic, and intentions may be harvested in perpetuity by the Other Ones and their master, Folly."

Pieces started to come together. Cynthia had heard a few different versions of this account of the prophecy, this holographic prison concept explaining the source of Folly's motivation. These Scarab types were somehow urging the process on in service of their own selfish greed. "Why does she want that? How does she benefit? What does she gain?"

"Complete and total power and dominion over this earthly realm. Once she achieves that goal, she will move on to expand her godlike prowess to encompass the entire known universe, corrupting every conceivable plane of existence into a hell dimension that she may rule over with her minions in tow. The other five elemental sisters will be crushed in defeat, their pillars of support tumbling to leave Folly victorious and standing alone to rule over all that is, was, and ever will be. No one will escape in body or soul. The seas will boil before evaporating. The air will turn to poison gas; once-fertile soil will erode into a barren wasteland. The sun will die in a fiery crescendo and rain flames, and, once its death throes are spent, the next phase will usher in an endless epoch of darkness. And spirit? Forget that. Every spark of soul will be snuffed out. The new world will be utterly bereft of curiosity, art, creation, charity, synchronicity, dreams, or elevation of any kind. Hell will prevail when chaos reigns in all its Folly."

Fuck.

"What do we do to stop this?" Cynthia pressed through the solid barricade of horror standing in her way.

Ether groaned, thrashing against Raven, his t-shirt twisting around his navel to show a pale peek of midsection. "Help," he shouted. "Help, help. Someone help me. Someone make this stop happening."

Dragon clamped a hand over Ether's mouth. Everyone looked at each other in silent, grim affirmation that the situation was deteriorating faster than they could figure out how to slam the brakes on the runaway train.

Cynthia took a shot at dragging the nightmare back from the brink. "Ether, I need you to relax right now and let me work. We want to help you, but we can't help you if you're fighting and resisting and freaking out. So can you stay calm and let me talk to Nerissa long enough to send her away? Blink once for yes and twice for no."

He blinked once.

His response loosened the worst of the painful constriction wrapped around her torso. Go time was now, and she had to figure out a solution that hopefully wouldn't backfire. "Okay. Good. I promise that we'll get you back to how you were, Ether. Now, I need to talk to Nerissa. Nerissa, are you there?"

One blink.

Raven glanced at Cynthia as if to take a cue. She wasn't sure what exactly he was asking of her, but she nodded to give him the go-ahead, confident that they were on the same team.

Even if they were in way over their heads, there was nowhere to go but forward, flailing for a sign of the surface where madness broke.

"Dragon is going to take his hand off your mouth," Raven said. "But you have to promise not to yell or scream. Sound like a plan?"

One blink.

Dragon pulled his hand away, and, fortunately, Ether didn't vocalize a peep. He just stared, his complexion clammy and gray.

"I need Nerissa to come out and stay out, and to speak softly. Can you cooperate, Ether?"

"Yeah," he croaked.

"Good. Nerissa, I think that the best option at this point would be to send you back to your main body in Minneapolis. Once you're in your familiar self, I'm hoping that you'll be best equipped to help us undo whatever damage we can and get back on track halting this prophecy. Does that sound right?"

"No," she said with adamant confidence, a spark flashing in Ether's irises. "You must not move me into another life form with this much residue from Folly stuck to me. She will only grow stronger once rooted in a new physical host. This poor man may be a lost cause once he succumbs to her parasitic infection."

Cynthia swallowed hard. She didn't need bad news. But it didn't do any good to get ahead of herself, either. Fixing up Ether would have to be a bridge that she crossed if they came to it. For now, the urgent matter at hand was purging Nerissa and putting her somewhere safe, and Cynthia had a crazy idea beginning to take shape. She glanced to the books and notebooks that Raven had stacked on the nightstand, her grimoire lodged in the middle of the heap. Oh yeah, she'd studied her tome a lot, and she had a radical thought that just might work. "I'm going to put you in my spell book for now, okay? Make you into an incantation. Once we're confident that we've got this Folly issue under control, we'll speak the incantation to send you back to your body. Sound like a deal?"

Ether glowered. "Have you accomplished a transmutation of this caliber before, air witch? Have you spoken an entity into form before?"

Cynthia wasn't in the mood to be questioned, especially since Nerissa wasn't bringing any alternative solutions to the table. "Nope on both counts. You'd be the pilot project. But we've all got to start somewhere to level up, right?"

Even though Cynthia had never met Nerissa in the flesh, she was certain that the way Ether wrinkled his nose reflected one of the old woman's mannerisms, not his own. "What you're describing is energy transfer, a spirit spell. You'll have to initiate a chain reaction to draw from that element, preferably with a partner or partners to strengthen the connection enough to accomplish such a complex feat. I know that you've done partner work, so let's hope that you're halfway competent with it."

Confidence surged in Cynthia. She hailed Raven with a look. "We've got this, right?"

He placed her book and three of his own on the bed, splitting them all to reveal a jumble of words and sketches. "Absolutely. I have a theory that the dream work I've done has bound me closer to the fire element. My ability to tap in in no way comes close to a witch's, but I think that I have a slight edge over someone who has never studied the mysteries of this prophecy."

"He's not wrong," Nerissa said with a hint of begrudging respect. "Shifters can absolutely achieve synthesis with witch magic through dedicated practice, even attaining a sort of witch-adjacent ability if they work hard enough. I'm not supposed to reveal that, technically, but desperate times call for drastic measures."

Portia clapped. "Dragon and I can help. With the cards. We'll each pull one to heighten our abilities to access magic."

Cynthia wasn't all in on those cards, something about them bothered her. Maybe it was the look of them, creepy in their cultish unknowability. Maybe it was the recklessness of it all, this sense that Raven's crew played and experimented with the deck like it was a toy, flimsy cutout Tarot cards torn from a teen magazine. Not that she had a legitimate counterpoint. Nerissa might have a better idea, so she asked her, "Does it sound okay to involve the deck like they're talking about?"

Nerissa rolled Ether's eyes in that way that was very much her personality in his body. "Those cards rightfully belong to one of the Coven Daughters, so I'm not thrilled that shifters have appropriated them to enrich their own study of magic, but the cat's out of the bag, isn't it?"

Who did the cards belong to and what would the owner do with them? Cynthia was dying to know, but the timing wasn't right. "Yeah, they've pretty much made those cards their own. I hate to be the one to tell you."

A grumble that bore Nerissa's stamp heaved out of Ether's mouth. "Not the worst infraction, I suppose. At least this co-opting enhances the potency of our magical lineage, which we will likely need down the line. Do as you must."

"Thank you for your flexibility. You're a true team player," Cynthia said with a touch of salt in hopes of lightening the mood a shade.

Nerissa's glare betrayed a hint of amusement. "A real comedienne we have here. Now get on with it."

Portia ran from the room and returned less than a minute later with the battered box. "This is so cool. We get to use these in a high-stakes situation."

"It's not a game," Nerissa chided. "This is life and death. If you fail, the other place might subsume my essence entirely, and who knows what problems that will create."

"We're taking this seriously, I promise." Cynthia lobbed Portia a stern look. "And I guarantee that you have our fullest concentration."

"I'll take Spirit," Dragon volunteered. "Portia is better with the chaos factor, dancing with the dark and all. I have more of a knack for travelling through the cosmos."

Portia looked through the deck, picked two cards, and dealt them face up in front of the person designated to play them. Dragon got a card that depicted white mist flowing into or out of a simple black bowl. Portia's showed a mess of yellow tentacles with a red jewel in the middle. All of those symbol had to mean something beyond merely embodying the element in question, but, again, timing. She looked to Raven, who was busy reading from two notebooks simultaneously. "You ready?" she asked.

"Ready as I'll ever be. You?"

"Let's do this."

Nerissa bit out, "You two are so sweet that my teeth are rotting out of my head. Get on with it."

A pale pink tint spread across Raven's milky cheeks. "Do the honors, boss." He said to Cynthia. While she liked the honorific, she kinda missed *Baby*. "Once you start reading, the three of us will tune in our concentration and build the links in this chain reaction."

Cynthia thumbed to the Spirit section of her book, locating the part on energy transfer. This chunk covered everything from simple blessings like making food taste of love to heavier forms of the power such as imbuing an everyday object with a portion of one's energy to transferring consciousness of the self or other from one point to another. The highest level of the Left-Hand expression of Spirit magic was mind control—programming another person into an actual drone and coding them to do the witch's bidding. No way would she get mixed up in that kind of nastiness with all of its unethical implications.

She marked the consciousness transfer section with her index finger, and, after confirming that Raven and the others were ready to collaborate, began to read. "Hail to the four corners and the sentinels of the watchtowers. Sister Spirit, I, an air born, humbly call upon your assistance." Her head went fuzzy, like a part of her mind had broken from her body and floated away. Good—that meant that the spell was working. She pressed on, even though the words had started to bleed together a bit, spreading into an inky blob on the paper. Her ears rang as she incanted, improvising to reflect the unique elements of the situation like she always did when casting spells. "One of our own, a spirit mother, has found herself trapped in an inhospitable vessel. It is with some urgency that we call upon you to remove her from the fleshy coil that she inhabits and place her heart and soul on these very pages until we may return her to the body that nature created for her."

She looked to Raven, who was chanting under his breath. Portia and Dragon were totally zoned out, swaying as they gaped at their respective cards. But nothing much seemed to be happening with Ether or Nerissa. They stood against the wall, upright but otherwise lifeless, their stare a million miles away. For all she knew, though, the reaction was to be expected.

She read more, grasping to retain enough control of her sensory and mental faculties to read the words and fill in context. "Sister Spirit, please purge mother Nerissa from the prison of this man's flesh and bone."

"No," Ether growled, jerking. "No, no, no." The voice sounded like a blend of his and Nerissa's.

Desperation clawing its way forward, Cynthia asked any of her companions who might be lucid enough to offer feedback, "Anyone got any ideas?"

"She's resisting," Portia shouted, though she sounded like she had a mouthful of molasses. "The separation is causing her pain, but she doesn't realize that that's a good thing. Push through. You're fine, Nerissa."

Cynthia flinched. "Isn't that a little violating, to make her do this against her will?"

"It's not as bad as mind control," Portia shot back.

"Which I have never done and never will do."

Ether and Nerissa wailed, two voices merged as one disturbing chorus.

A book in each hand, Raven blinked rapidly like he as moving in and out of a deep phase of sleep. "We're losing her, I can feel it. She's slipping away on the wheel of fire."

"What the fuck is the wheel of fire?" Cynthia's hope of a successful energy transfer crumbled.

"It takes you to the astral plane or even the other place," Raven got out, his words slurred. "It's the chariot. I'm trying to steer it back to

Ether's body long enough for you to finish, but Folly is fighting me for control of the wheel. Keep going, Cynthia. Keep going."

Dragon staggered, pawing for his spirit card as he slipped and fell, slumping against the edge of the bed. "Spirit is getting away from me. Our link might break any second."

"Shit. Okay." Cynthia read on. The squeeze of pressure pushed her into a single viable choice. "Sister Spirit, the time is now. Please guide the chariot of fire back to us so that we may save our dear spirit mother, Nerissa, from the clutches of chaos." Her neck snapped back, an invisible push coming from Ether's direction. Encouraged by the change in energy and the power behind the shift, she read the final lines on the page. "Deliver her. Deliver her here, to me, essence and soul. Write Nerissa's story on the page before us, holding her safe until the magic on my breath may liberate her once again. Come to me, mother Nerissa. Come into my book."

Ether's jaw stretched wide. A pained, hideous, metallic screech issued from his gaping maw along with a dark cloud that flowed into the guts of Cynthia's grimoire. A glaze of iridescent light raced over the book to illuminate the pages before vanishing.

Ether crumpled to the floor in a heap, his jaw slack from dislocation.

The book turned a page on its own, revealing two measly sentences scrawled at the top of a massive amount of empty space. That scant collection of words was all that the incantation to free Nerissa amounted to?

"Is it done?" Portia whispered, snapping her fingers in Ether's face. "Is he okay?"

"No clue on either account." Cynthia knuckled her eyes until her focus sharpened.

She read the words again and again, at first halfheartedly convincing herself that her vision was still too screwed up to read properly. Next, she rationalized that the spell wasn't, in fact, done, and all they had to do to rectify this misstep was try again.

Finally, after reading the newly transferred text for the umpteenth time, she accepted that they hadn't done a damn thing to help Nerissa. In fact, they'd made things worse.

I'm coming closer, AiR WITCH. Do YoU FeEl mE YET?
A gap before the next words dragged out her dread.

EVIL WHITE SPACE. *SHE KNOWS WHAT SHE'S DOING.*

HavE you made yOUr chOicE? SiX moRe dAys.

NINETEEN

THOSE MOMENTS OF RESPITE IN BETWEEN BOUTS OF DISAPPOINTMENT had never been Cynthia's favorite, taunting her into believing that she had a real shot at happiness.

They had always felt like a tease, a cruel joke, a temporary bit of hope before she was dumped again, robbed, or left for dead. Good times were transient, while bad persisted.

At least this time, nobody was howling or beating their head against a hotel wall, so win?

Raven maneuvered a sleeping Ether to a more comfortable position on the floor and gently lifted his head to place a pillow underneath him. "At least Portia got his jaw back in."

Cynthia had turned away for that particular small miracle and plugged her ears to block the sickening crunch. Even she had her limits. "Does he seem okay, relatively speaking? Sleeping normally?" She'd never seen anyone taken out by a spell to this degree, but she was learning that there was a lot in the wonderful world of magic that she hadn't seen.

"He's breathing normally and will wiggle his fingers if I pinch him. I don't think he's comatose or anything like that. I suppose being possessed sapped his energy. If he doesn't wake up, we can start looking for spells to help." Raven rose to stand and walked to the bed where Cynthia had sprawled herself belly-down in front of the books. He sat on the edge, looking over her shoulder. "Finding anything good?"

The pages of her grimoire scratched against her finger pads, so many confounding secrets of witchcraft woven in with discolored flecks of pulp. "Define 'good.' It feels like the more I learn, the less I understand. I'm starting to wonder if this magic isn't meant to be figured out. Or if it's continually changing. Every time I open this thing, I swear that I see some new piece, even though I've read the entire text. Or I thought I did. I worry sometimes that this system is constructed to pull us into something very destructive, to addict us. Like how when talking about Ether a minute ago, you went right to the prospect of more spells as a solution." She flipped to her back, taking cut-rate respite in the bland slab of ceiling. From the pullout couch, Dragon chuffed a juicy snore, stirring Portia enough that she moaned and yanked the thin blanket off him. While everyone else slept off the hangover of the possession insanity, Cynthia remained terminally wired and stuck with her overactive brain. "Do you ever feel cursed?"

Raven looked off into space for a long moment, the shape of the Atlantis book drawing attention to his long, slender fingers fanned out on the comforter. "I have, yes. But I'm not sure if that line of thinking is healthy." He opened his skinny book and slowly leafed. "When I first started working with this, I was nervous about curses. I worried that it was an entire book of them, actually, and that even looking at the content was unleashing some sinister force."

Birds of a feather, apparently. "You might have been correct. Yet you didn't let that stop you."

He spoke in earnest, balancing her sarcasm. "No, I didn't. Once I discovered my ability, what made me so different, I got this unquenchable determination in me, you know? To learn as much about everything having to do with magic and the paranormal and esoteric traditions as I possibly could. I became insatiable."

Swirls and symbols from all that she'd read, recited, and uncovered danced through her head like wicked elves. "Maybe that's the essence of the curse itself. An urge to know more, more, more at all costs. To feed every one of the universe's secrets into our brains and egos like data into a computer, stripping away those sacred mysteries in our arrogant quest for mastery. That was Eve's original sin in the garden, right? An unquenchable appetite for knowledge that pushed her to steal what was meant for the gods—what wasn't hers to take?"

"If you're going to go all Biblical on me, I'd respond by saying that ignorance isn't a virtue, and that no god of mine would insist that their believers stay uninformed, passive, and compliant as a condition of devotion."

She kicked his foot. "I simply cannot fathom why you didn't fit in at your parents' church." Instantly, she regretted the flippant remark. "Shit. I'm sorry. I didn't mean to make fun of your parents."

"It's fine." He grabbed her toes and wiggled her foot. "And it's funny because it's true. My folks always had an open-minded streak, though." He opened the slender, pamphlet book to a page near the back and slid it in Cynthia's direction. "Mom found this book while travelling through Greece and Turkey. Well, found is inaccurate and overly generous. They'd go on these amateur archeological digs that were not above board and probably illegal. Most years they only came back with chunks of broken pottery or animal bones. But eventually, they hit the jackpot."

What if someone had buried the book for a reason and intended it never to be dug up? The jackpot in question might not be a prize that anyone wanted to win. "What if that's the trap that Folly's springing for us? Dangling all of these books and spells and cards in front of us to stimulate our desire to know, only to lure us into this terrible prophecy?" She gripped her ears in a failed effort to still thoughts that were rapidly spiraling out of control.

"You wanna take a walk or something?" Raven said. "Get out of this room and clear our heads, maybe see about finding that sushi that we never had a chance to stop for? It might be good to move around. Break some of the tension we stirred up earlier."

His idea actually sounded awesome, if doomed. "Sushi at midnight on a Thursday?" At least she guessed it was Thursday. Days had been running together lately, though she ought to be more cognizant of time given Folly's deadline.

He pulled her into a seated position as he slid off the bed. "We have the motorcycle. We'll find something. C'mon. It'll be an adventure."

Cynthia did love adventures, and present circumstances had gotten her so stressed that she'd nearly forgotten about the spontaneous, uninhibited aspects of roaming the country in search of witches—the ones that lured her to her quest in the first place. She pointed at the sleeping shifters. "What about these three?"

"What about them?" He tugged Cynthia to her feet.

"Not your brother's keeper, eh?" She wasn't thrilled to leave Buddy, but she trusted the three shifters well enough to at least not harm the dragon and to maybe order takeout if she got super hungry. Besides, the dozing young dragon was now as big as a medium-sized dog and equipped to defend herself.

"There you go with your Bible references again. What's next, the Sermon on the Mount?"

"Water into wine was obviously the best story. Let's go."

He threw his room key on the dresser by the pullout, so considerate, and they ran to the elevator holding hands. Felt incredible to escape, even if only from the confines of a room and the rumination inside those walls. Her heart soared at the feel of his skin and the anticipation of what they'd do, and she let herself enjoy the sensations. Permission to live in the moment was hers for a little while. Inside the the silver box, he studied her reflection. "What happened with you last relationship?"

Mirrored, her dumb face blinked and paled. Yeah, she'd lose every penny in a poker game. All she could do was parry. "That's a hardcore question."

The elevator opened to the clean, corporate lobby where they'd talked about Buddy's species with the teenage employee. Muffled pop music came from somewhere close by, but not another soul was to be found. Though Cynthia typically enjoyed the soft melancholy that tended to accompany empty spaces, this time she cursed the absence of small-talk sources to offer deflections from Raven's question.

He put his arm around her waist while they breezed through the sliding doors, a balmy breeze animating his hair. "Hardcore as in too much?" A hint of a dare rode the final note of his syllables, poking her oh so slightly.

"No, it's not too much." The rattled snappiness she used wasn't lost on her, and probably didn't get past him either. "I just don't think it's any of your business."

He whispered against her temple, his lips soft and tickly, "So it is too much." They reached the bike, keys jingling in his hand like a shot across the bow.

"I didn't say that." Damn this guy, digging around near her wounds like his mom did in the desert with her shovel and demon book. Going where he didn't belong, searching for what was best left alone. "What I meant was that you're nosy."

She took her place on the back of the bike, though, silently hoping that he'd persist in his line of inquiry. Nosy as his efforts were, at least they were interesting. Nobody else had ever cared enough to try to read her, overcome her resistance, or challenge her to open up or grow or be more than who she was. She'd always been acceptable enough to others, useful to fulfil a narrow band of their wants. In the past, the minute she threw up any kind of roadblock, the other person left. Cynthia had come to accept that she was desirable because she was easy, and if she became difficult or complicated or dared to exist once her utility had expired, well, then she wasn't fun anymore.

"Of course I'm nosy, I want to get to know you." Raven threw his keys in the air a few inches and caught them. "You can be as mean to me as you like, but I won't stop trying. Of course, if I violate your boundaries, tell me, but until you do I'm going to keep working on that wall of yours. Deal?"

Is this how relationships were supposed to work? Someone wanted to get to know the *whole you* in all of your authenticity as opposed to taking the parts that they wanted for as long as those parts were amusing? Someone stepped up to accept the worst along with the best? What sorcery was this?

"Good." He pressed his foot into the pedal a few times to rev the engine. "I'm not done with you yet, but for now, let's eat."

With that, they were off, zipping down yet another black bar of highway, the night lit only by those yellow lines slashed down the middle of the pavement and a reaper's sickle of a crescent moon that peeped through billowing puffs of smokestack clouds.

The hunt for sushi seemed destined to flop as they crossed miles of desert interrupted by the occasional shot-out strip mall, junkie motel, or greasy spoon with a few jalopies in the lot.

The bike groaned as Raven slowed to scope out a very out-of-place, Victorian-style house with two castle spires and upper decks stacked atop a wraparound porch, the entire property painted in dark colors. A pink neon sign in one of the bottom windows must've gotten his attention, igniting the night with a hue as saturated as bubble gum.

Sushi.

"You have got to be shitting me," she shouted over the wind that howled in her ears. "This is a poster child for food poisoning."

He veered to the driveway. "I thought that you liked to live dangerously."

"Salmonella is a hard no in my personal calculation of risk." However, the home was certainly intriguing, an ornate anomaly amidst run-down, rural desert atmosphere. If her stomach had its way, she'd be risking the fish, but the last thing she needed on an already rocky night was a bout of vomiting. Surely, though, there had to be some edible options on the menu. Not like they had a multitude of choices. "Looks cool, though. We could at least have a look and see if there's anything cooked."

"That's the spirit." He pulled into the driveway, a swatch of gravel hosting an old-school, Volkswagen hippie bus complete with bumper stickers promoting causes and politicians long since relegated to the dustbin of history. "Live a little."

Cynthia's reunion with impulsivity had her bubbly and laughing, taking Raven's hand again as they dismounted and walked to the front. "I really like you," she blurted out in a hideous, goofy voice before her brain had a chance to shut that shit down.

He smiled as brightly as the sign, a strangely innocent look on someone with his aesthetic. Weirder still, it suited him. She wondered about asking to call him Matthew before shutting that idea down as way too intimate.

"I really like you, too."

Steps creaked under their feet, the wood rotted from neglect. She hoped that the kitchen was better tended than the outside, though they had come more for the ambiance and experience than the food. In her peripheral vision, the sign blinked. When she looked, she swore that the word had changed, but no. Still "sushi" in pleasing, easy-to-read, pink cursive. Odd. She wrote off the anomalous occurrence as a minor hallucination brought on by too little sleep and too much time on the road, a condition that she'd experienced before and referred to as the weirds.

"You saw that, too?" Raven hesitated before ringing the doorbell.

The night got colder. "I saw it morph or move, almost. Did you read a different word for a split second?"

"There wasn't enough time for me to tell. All I caught was the movement. You wanna get out of here?"

The sensible, correct answer was yes. But they'd left the domain of sensible practicality awhile ago. Cynthia wasn't really the type to make decisions out of fear or to prioritize safety. It stood to reason that going toward bizarre stuff, not away from it, made more sense in the context of the overall philosophy of her quest. "Nah."

He laughed, the sound throaty and warm and downright intoxicating. "Damn, baby. You're braver than I am."

Baby had become a little gift that she secretly treasured and held safe, a present that she deserved even though she wasn't a good girl. "Just stupider."

"No more negative self-talk. Are we going in or not?"

She stared down the "sushi" sign as if daring it to change. Cream-colored curtains were shut behind the glowing letters, coyly covering what was inside that house. "Ring the bell."

He pushed the disc, and a faint jingle played.

Footsteps approached, slow and deliberate. It helped to have someone to share these wild moments with so at least she took solace in not riding the crazy train alone.

The door opened a crack, a cheap bronze chain offering limited security. An older woman peered through the gap, her gray hair sleek and long, filmy scarves draped over a tunic. "Can I help you?"

"You still serving sushi at this hour?"

She quirked her lips. "You answered my call. I knew that I mind melded with the ones I wanted, and that appealing to instinctual drives and impulse gratification would work well. Come in."

The sign now read "tarot," which made a boatload more sense in context with the house, its inhabitant, and her bus. "Did you use chaos magic to change the word and reach out to us?" If this woman could get inside their heads, there didn't seem to be much point in Cynthia trying to hide her knowledge or nature.

The old lady closed the door and presumably undid the chain, opening up wider this time. Her home smelled of incense and warmth undercut with a more pungent note, like mothballs or cat litter. She stepped aside and made a sweeping gesture with her arm. "Nerissa's in a book, Folly has a toehold in our dimension, and the Ballad of Capricorn draws nearer every day. The Song of Virgo has been prematurely halted, but I can't discern yet if that is good or bad. Everyone's magic is growing stronger even as we lose control of the faculties that we need to harness it. Familiars are afoot, and, if we aren't all careful, doppelgangers may manifest again. That means the prophecy is commencing its final stages. We're in end times. Please, enter."

Though it was shocking to hear such an onslaught come from the mouth of someone else, Cynthia wasn't exactly surprised, either. The proclamation made sense. Best to build some rapport to counterbalance the grim situation. She crossed the threshold, finding herself standing on a plush, Turkish area rug, and stuck out her hand. "I'm Cynthia. This is Raven."

"I know," the woman said dryly, casting a dismissive glance at Cynthia's palm. "You are by far the most...motivated of the Coven Daughters. Your zealous use of magic has pushed the machinery of fate toward its terminus faster than anyone could have predicted. You are the second to take up with a shifter as well. We suspect that plays a role in the expedition as well."

Raven put in, "Who is 'we' and who are 'anyone' in this situation?"

She threw at him the same cool, disengaged scrutiny that she'd levied at Cynthia. "I don't have any fish, raw or otherwise, but I do have chicken stew, fresh-baked bread, and a fruit salad. Are you still hungry?"

The food could certainly be drugged or poisoned, but she wanted to hear what the woman had to say. She might have valuable information to impart. Maybe they could fake-eat. Her stomach growled, one-upping her. With a look, she asked Raven to give his opinion.

He barely ticked his facial features, the movement so subtle that a casual observer would have missed it, but the meaning got through to Cynthia. *Let's do it.*

"Sounds delicious," Cynthia said before she had one second to change her mind. "Thank you."

The old woman shuffled to the door and closed it, engaging a deadbolt.

TWENTY

THE OLD LADY ATE THE MEAL SHE'D COOKED, SPOONING UP HUNKS OF chicken and carrots and chowing down on broth-soaked bread. Good sign. Cynthia tried not to stare while she mentally retraced her steps in search of a medicine dropper, pill, or baggie of powder lurking somewhere in her short-term memory. Instead of giving off suspect vibes, the lady sipped water, enjoying her dinner like a normal person.

Moments ago, Cynthia had stood in her host's retro kitchen with its farmhouse sink and watched the lady use a ladle to dole out all three portions, serving from a pot on the stove. No fast fingers slipped into the waistband of her maxi skirt or the pockets of her sweater.

The host swallowed a mouthful of food, casting a playfully disdainful glance across the long, wooden dining table. "Oh, come on. Eat. Please. I'm the coven mother of chaos. If I wanted to kill you two clowns, I would have done so already."

Raven took a bite of stew, murmuring with enjoyment before plunging his spoon in the bowl for more. "This is delicious. What's your name?"

"Don't worry about it." The chaos mother plucked a fat strawberry from a cut glass bowl and sucked on the fruit. "You're out here running around like this because you want to learn the secrets of fire and chaos, right? And find shifters and witches like yourselves?"

"More or less," Raven said diplomatically, as if still debating how much or little to reveal on the detail front. "Cynthia and I teamed up to get a better sense of how our powers work in accord. From what we've already determined, we need to combine forces to stave off some bad outcomes."

"That's a classy way to refer to ritual fucking."

Yep, the elder had to be a legitimate witch to know that intimate fact, so Cynthia didn't bother to demand how she indulged in voyeurism through remote viewing. "Sex magic called, and we listened. We're trying different things, you know? Operating intuitively. Not like there's much guidance or direction to be found in all of this stuff." Feeling safe enough to eat and too ravenous not to, Cynthia started on the stew. Perfectly cooked and generously chunky, the meat and vegetables went down heartily in a satisfying payload of starch, salt, and fat. A bite of crusty on the outside, chewy in the center bread lifted her mood instantly. "Compliments to the chef."

Their host paused from eating, swirling her spoon around in her bowl. "This *stuff* is the generational residue an ancient and powerful birthright. This *stuff* came to us as a gift from civilizations and divine beings that we'll never even begin to have the first clue how to understand. This *stuff* has withstood the age of dragons meeting its violent, untimely end. This *stuff* survived the witch trials."

"That's great." Cynthia drank the rest of her broth, holding tight to an even-keel approach despite the emotionally charged lecture. "It still would be really great to get some help with how to use it."

Raven added, "It sounds like you're telling us that magical powers are not to be trifled with or taken lightly, which I get. That's totally fair. Where we're frustrated is that we don't know exactly how to treat it with reverence or caution, what that type of carefulness looks like in contrast to recklessness and how to use discernment to distinguish between the two. I don't want to speak for Cynthia, so correct me if I'm wrong, but I think that both of us are feeling like we're stuck in a permanent trial by fire or experimentation phase and don't know how to break through to the next level."

The witch's reply was instant and assured. "You're right, you don't exercise enough discernment. You certainly don't with those cards that you and your friends play with willy-nilly, flipping and turning over as your whims dictate without due consideration for how every move puts another ripple into the ocean of destiny." She spoke in a droll, savvy way that implied that he should know better, which pretty much proved his point.

"Great example." He returned fire. "You imply that we're careless or stupid in how we handle the cards without pointing us in the direction of an alternative."

Cynthia grabbed a mango slice from the bowl and cleansed her palate with its tropical sweetness. "There's no way that we're just supposed to ignore this whole divine birthright when we feel it coming to us, right? Or, when we connect with a card deck or grimoire, put it down and run in the other direction or shove it under the floorboards? How does turning or backs on this incredible magic make any sense?"

The old witch sighed as if exhaling the weight of the ages. "You're not wrong, necessarily. None of us particularly know what we're doing, and mentorship can only accomplish so much." She checked her reflection in the spoon. "Just ask Nerissa."

"What's that supposed to mean?" Cynthia wiped her mouth, her mind clearer now that her belly was full.

The woman pushed her chair back and stood, ambling to a built-in bookshelf that spanned the majority of one wall. "I can't give you much in the way of your own magic, as you'll need a coven mother of air for that, but I'm able to provide a few general insights that might help your progression."

While their host pulled a fat brown book from the shelf, it occurred to Cynthia that the aging woman appeared to be really settled in this home. Well-tended potted plants topped end tables and other vintage furniture. Art that looked valuable hung on the walls, and she smelled cats. Her place had been decorated with care and attention, probably inhabited for many years judging by the sheer amount of possessions accumulated. This was a lived-in abode, not a temporary pit stop meant to be fled. "Are you planning to come to Peru for when we all have to gather?"

Tome in hand, the mother of chaos returned to the dining table. "Let's chat more in my den once you're done eating, shall we? I'll make tea."

Chatting more sounded good. Or better, at least, than the guesswork and circular movement to which she'd grown accustomed. Once the food was finished, Cynthia gathered up her plate and cup while Raven did the same. They silently washed the dishes by hand with a rag while the old woman filled a kettle and set it on a gas stove. "Fire is mighty, but interdependent. A product of all of the other elements." The old woman measured herbs and spooned them into the basket of a teapot and lifted the kettle, leaving the flame to curve the space like iridescent fingers. "It's strength and weakness are one and the same. Nerissa told you that, didn't she? Before you trapped her?"

Guilt came on strong as Cynthia set a plate in a slotted drying rack. "Yes, she did. And I didn't know what else to do. It was an intense situation."

"Chaotic, if you will." The woman wore a cagey expression.

Raven wiped off the counter with a sponge. "Are you saying that to learn the secrets of fire and chaos, we have to embrace their natures completely?"

She turned off the stove burner with a click. "I need you to recognize what isn't yours to take, shifter."

Tension charged the air as if a live wire connected all three of their bodies. "I need you to help me discern the tools to see what is and what isn't permissible," he said. "Because I don't have a reliable method to sharpen the type of recognition that you're talking about."

The crone went quiet for a moment, wiping her hands on her skirt. "That's fair, I suppose. And the two of you are already so far in that it's likely pointless to pull back anyway. The only way out of this is through it."

A small shock kicked into Cynthia. Though she supposed that nothing should shock her anymore, she was so fatigued on bad news that her defenses had depleted. "What does that mean?"

"It means, come sit with me." She stood on her tiptoes to reach into a cupboard and took down three mismatched coffee cups. "Don't forget your tea. You'll need the calming effect. My name is Cristabel. You'll need that, too."

Cynthia caught Raven's gaze. At least they had each other. She poured Cristabel's tea, then Raven's, then finally her own. "That's a beautiful name."

Cristabel crossed the kitchen before walking through a doorway. "It's a family name that goes all the way back to the Age of Dragons. Back then, our familiars named us during a dream ritual. They had majestic names, too, monikers fit for royalty. Much better than 'Buddy.'" She shined Cynthia off with a judgy look.

Cynthia caught up to the old woman. "So you can read my mind, or what?"

"Not exactly." They all ended up in a sumptuous den full of bookshelves and overstuffed couches, the décor basking in the soft glows of vintage floor lamps shrouded in designer shades. "Don't think of it as my conscious thought accessing yours in some simplistic, one-to-one correlation. It's more like I can pick up on your stream from a collective ocean where all of us magicals inadvertently upload our thoughts. I'm not reading your emails, so to speak, but I am picking you out of a giant morass of noise based on your metadata and IP address, if that high-tech analogy makes sense. Have a seat. Please. Get comfortable."

How comfortable was comfortable, and for how long? Cynthia had Buddy and the others to think about.

Cristabel stepped out of fuzzy slippers and tucked herself in the corner of a loveseat, folding her legs underneath her body. She set her mug down on a coffee table strewn with books, including the one she'd pulled from the dining room. "Your dragon is safe and sound, rest assured. Despite my ambivalence toward shifters, I can say with confidence that the three you travel with are decent. And not susceptible to any further possession attempts, now that my poor sister is temporarily neutralized."

Temporarily. Hey, there was a morsel of decent news.

Raven sat in an easy chair opposite Nerissa and crossed his long legs. "I'm going to take a guess and say that you chose to reach out to us with the sushi sign after honing in on our streams, as you call them, to get a better sense of who we were."

"That's essentially accurate." She hauled the big book onto her lap opened it wide. "I promise that my actions were well-intentioned and not as creepy as they may seem. I'm interested in the outcome of this prophecy, don't get me wrong, but I'm not as convinced as some others that the proper course of action is to attempt to stop the machinations entirely or even to alter their course."

Cynthia took a spot on a loveseat, finding the cushions spongy and decadent, and studied the lines on the older woman's placid, wrinkled face as she read. Cristabel didn't seem agitated or stressed about the whole prophecy debacle, certainly not like Nerissa had been. While the danger of lapsing into a false sense of security was certainly worth considering, being in the presence of such a grounding presence had its merits. Finally, an opportunity for reflection and study, minus the scares and shouts. "What drove you and Nerissa to see this differently? Aren't we all reading the same material from essentially the same source?"

Cristabel flipped a page. She sipped tea and read for a while before speaking. "One would assume, given the similarities among the books, that your instinct would be accurate. But the more I study, the more I'm thinking that the answer there is no. This scripture is a living document, updating as we go. So the spells change, and the information changes. It adapts. The magic is a living thing in this regard. It's learning. Now, the question becomes, what prompts or motivates it to change and modify? Does it have an agenda or purpose, pushing us one way or the other?"

Raven drank some tea, the golden aura of the mood lighting reflecting off his skin to create a dreamy atmosphere where every element of time and space was sensual and surreal. "Any theories?"

If magic had a texture, an ineffable presence in the air that was impossible to define with any of the basic five senses, Cynthia pinpointed that mojo for a split second. It was as if her functions of memory opened to encompass events and feelings that had happened to others in the past and, simultaneously, were going to happen to others in the future. She tried the tea, noting to herself that this was her first sip. She wasn't hallucinating or reacting to the influence of some substance that Cristabel had added to the dried flowers and crushed leaves. The liquid tasted of chamomile, lavender, and a subtle spiciness that she lacked the palate to identify. "Delectable. Perfect evening blend."

"I'm not a kitchen witch," Cristabel murmured, scanning a page. "A knack for conveying magic through cookery is the purview our earth and perhaps water lines. So please let go of this naïve notion that I'm going to drug or poison you. Like I said, my methods differ."

"How so?" Raven asked, his fingers pale against a mug as black as his jeans.

"Chaos magic rests heavily in the free will of the beholder, the role of the one who interprets as being a participant in the spell, almost. Here's an example." She held up her book, showing two pages full of symbols inked in dark, swirling loops and points. "This is a simple chaos spell. What do each of you see? You first, Raven, since you asked a question."

He leaned forward, knitting his brow. "I see a landscape. A road curving along a mountain. There's a car on it, and what looks like an opening going into the side of the mountain."

"Good," Cristabel said. "And you, Cynthia?"

Cynthia studied the drawing. She didn't see what Raven identified at all, even with the power of suggestion laying the tracks for confirmation bias. "I see the portrait of a young woman from a few decades ago. The twenties, probably, judging by her bowl haircut and round hat. She's wearing a fur with a fluffy collar and looking away from the camera. She's demure."

"Good," Cristabel used the same tone that she'd spoken to Raven. "My theory is that each of you cast a separate spell just then, a harmless one. That's chaos magic. Manifesting through hodgepodge and interpretation. Applying the stuff from your own minds and frames of reference to the symbols that you see to imbue them with a certain energy. Now watch your environment for evidence that your work is bearing out."

So this was cool enough, but not necessarily helpful. "What does this have to do with the prophecy?" Cynthia drank down another mouthful of warm liquid. Cristabel may not have drugged the brew, but her concoction sure was addictive.

The aged witch fingered a frayed corner of her book. "I don't necessarily say this because I'm biased, but I think that chaos ultimately governs this magic system or sits atop a hierarchy of sorts. Yes, the others elements have their places, even though I confess I can't yet decipher what or where those places are. But chaos magic is writing our story. Chaos magic is the sum total of all of our magical minds and efforts when they act in congress, tapping in to the sentient nature of these books and spurring them to write themselves. So the books read us, and we read the books, co-creating our own reality in a feedback loop that is ultimately leading to a set conclusion." She closed her tome and patted the cover. "The story has been told, somewhere in time and space and consciousness, but all of us confer some essential contribution. Only when the story is transcribed can it unfold in all of its fine points and nuances. Even if we don't realize that we are united, we are contributors playing a crucial but narrow role into which we've been cast."

Cynthia didn't love this. The way that Cristabel described the system had a sour, disappointing sort of fatality to it. "Determinism, basically."

"The prospect clearly bothers you."

She hummed a sound of agreement, uncrossing and crossing her legs. "It just seems like a huge waste. If the course of fate is already set and the outcome sealed, why bother with all of this pomp and circumstance and intrigue and whatnot?'

"I don't know," the chaos mother said. "Perhaps there is a lesson to be learned. If so, I don't purport to have absorbed it."

Raven finished his tea and set the cup down with a clink. "Does this get into the difference between fate and destiny?"

"What do you mean?" Cristabel returned to perusing her book.

He explained, "What if, even if the course of fate is set, if each of us has a destiny that produces a meaningful outcome, and within that destiny, we're afforded some degree of free will or agency that tweaks the program in tiny but impactful ways? AKA, the butterfly effect."

Cynthia knew that she liked this guy for a reason, always rolling in hot with his deep and philosophical thoughts. "Yeah. Exactly. So our destiny may be painted in broad strokes, so to speak, but within that programming there is room to maneuver based on what we choose. So whether I pick pizza or a burger for lunch on any given day sets off a chain reaction of who I interact with, who they interact with, who is late for work that day and who meets their soul mate when they both grab for the same cantaloupe at the grocery store."

"Who decides to send a strawberry milkshake to the weird goth at the truck stop," Raven said.

Cynthia actually, for real, fucking straight-up *giggled*. Like a schoolgirl. Some may have even described the sound as a squeak. Egad.

Instead of dropping a smartass remark, Cristabel looked on wistfully. "Young love is one of the most potent drivers of the chaos magic machinery that there is."

Cynthia closed in on herself. She couldn't allow Raven to think that she had *those* feelings for him, or he'd freak out, literally sprout wings, and fly off never to be seen again. "Oh, we're not. I'm not. What I meant to say was, um, wait, what did I say?" She giggled stupidly again, her brain flustered and her face hotter than a sauna.

"Nothing too specific." Cristabel's smile, one of a matriarch in the know, made Cynthia cringe even harder. "You didn't have to say anything to communicate your feelings. And anyway, I think that you two are close to correct in how you theorize on these foundational principles of our universe." She flipped to a different section of the book and laid it out on the coffee table. "But I'd like to try an experiment to confirm some of these theories."

"What type of experiment?" Raven craned his neck to get a better look at the pages she'd opened to, and Cynthia did the same. All words.

Cristabel face was a portrait of devious glee. "Let's just say going rogue with spell casting to shake down this Folly character for more than she's been willing to give up thus far. I can't make promises in the way of outcomes, but I have some designs on what the three of us might be able to accomplish in terms of chaos and air partner work in the Other Place. Raven, your work with those cards has essentially been chaos magic, so your presence will strengthen the circle as well. Whatever happens is sure to be an adventure of the highest degree. Do you wish to continue?"

Leaving would be a complete waste, and, besides, why wimp out when they'd potentially gotten to the literal threshold of discovering the secrets of chaos? Adventure was what they'd signed up for, and opportunity had thumped a few more knocks on their door. Cynthia asked Raven, "What do you say, partner? Up for another ride through the cosmos?"

"Baby, I'd travel anywhere with you."

TWENTY-ONE

Anywhere MEANT AN ENERGETIC SINKHOLE IN THE MIDDLE OF Cristabel's dining room floor.

A vortex, more specifically, as luminous as a galaxy, one long arm coiled around and around in a hypnotic thread that looped to infinity.

Cynthia waved her foot over the cosmic void where an area rug had once been, her toes itchy with anticipation. She had a pretty good idea of where she was going, and the direction wasn't up. "How did you do that?"

Her book open and balanced on her forearms, Cristabel snapped her fingers. The vortex reverted back to a circular, polka-dot rug. "Reconstituting matter is actually a fairly elementary level chaos spell. I'm advanced enough in my practice that I'm able to scramble the atoms and subatomic particles in physical objects and render them into portals. Are we going or not?"

One of Cynthia's first major accomplishments with her air magic was sealing a portal for the Peruvian shifters after their leader had claimed that some unwholesome mojo was slipping through. She hadn't understood the process all that well at the time but had done her best to help.

Now, however, was not the time to ruminate about the past. With

Folly's countdown clock ticking, Cynthia had to gain an advantage over the darkest of elemental sisters, even if opportunity in this case looked like jumping into a hole in the ground. The master of chaos was about to lose this freaky game. "I'm ready to go. Just getting a bit of cold feet I guess."

Beside Cynthia, Raven urged her body to his. "We're in this together, baby."

"There is nobody I'd rather dive into the pit with."

Cristabel huffed. "Except perhaps me, as I have enough experience with Folly be able to navigate her vagaries and those of the other place with some skill. I can help us stay out of her traps, unlike you." She looked right into Cynthia's soul with a glance that cut her in two.

Cristabel knew of Cynthia's bargaining mishap. The gist, if not every nuance and detail.

"What do you mean?" Raven asked.

"Never mind." Cristabel muttered a quick incantation and waved her hand through the space. The vortex portal reappeared. "Stick with me is all I'm saying. I'm somewhat adroit in moving through this place, if I do say so myself. I can help the three of us wander without getting lost, and, with a bit of moxie, get the two of you what you want."

Those were some massive promises. Would Cristabel deliver?

"Understood," Cynthia said, not wanting to step out of line by asking questions. Cristabel was doing her and Raven a favor, and they were guests in her home. Who else did they have? "Lead the way."

Cristabel dropped her book with a thump and clamped a cool, firm grip around Cynthia's wrist. "The solution for cold feet is to dive right in and get everything cold."

Before she had a chance to gasp, Cynthia was tumbling, her footing and purchase erased entirely as she catapulted through unrelenting darkness at a speed that felt deadly. Wind screeched in her ears, the temperature so cold, bone marrow cold, so cold that its stinging frigidity connected with the other end of the temperature spectrum to merge with hot. She wrenched her jaw open in hopes of relieving some of the relentless pressure closing in from all sides, but the vacuum she found herself in seemed to suck all of the air right out of her lungs.

Then, she was floating, suspended by an invisible cord of tension that connected her belly button to an unseen fulcrum up above. Her arms and legs hung limp at her sides.

"We meet again," Folly said, smooth and unbothered. "What is it that you want from me? What is it that you think that I could do for you, with you, or to you that would in any way be to your benefit?"

Cynthia didn't have answers to those questions. She wanted to know the secrets of fire and chaos, yes. And the origins of her magic. But the more she knew, the less she understood. As Folly had warned, the deeper she dug, the farther down a hole she found herself. But there really was no turning back at this point. Where would she go? At least now she had the factor of Cristabel in the equation. Perhaps Folly would take Cynthia more seriously now that the coven mother of chaos stood by her side. Well, technically, the cover mother of chaos wasn't standing anywhere that Cynthia was able to see, but she must've been energetically present. "I want to know the secrets of fire and chaos. How to master my craft and understand magic to the best of my ability. I want to know where magic comes from and where it goes. I want to know everything that is knowable about this prophecy, up to and including my role in it."

Uproarious laughter rang out through the abyss, echoing though there were no walls, the noise permeated with contempt. "Anything else, princess? A pony? A million dollars? The shirt off my fucking back?"

Cynthia squirmed, her arms and legs burning as they flailed against nothing, her back achy from the unnatural position. She was upside down in an arch, suffering in the stress pose, and supremely annoyed. "I don't get you. At all. You subject me to riddles. You ask me what I want and ridicule me when I answer. You give me a familiar to love, only to threaten to snatch her away unless I kill the first person in forever that I've cared about. Maybe I should be asking the questions. What do you want?"

An answer didn't come. The void teemed with a barely perceptible hum, that oddly metaphysical non-noise that she heard in the other place and in the dead of sleepless nights. Were Raven and Cristabel okay? Was she all alone in the dark with this infuriating trickster? "Hello?"

"Hello." Folly answered in a taunting way, drawing out her second syllable into and endless, protracted "o."

Cynthia's throat thickened. She bit her tongue to stop herself from screaming or crying. "What do you want?" she shouted.

Light blinked on with a glare so cool and bright that Cynthia squinted against white-hot, fluorescent pain. A haze of color surrounded her in every direction along with gauzy rainbow prisms glimmering on glassy surfaces. She squeezed her eyelids shut and reopened them a few times until she made sense of her environment. She floated upside down in that arch shape in a hall of mirrors. Cynthia's image surrounded her, an endless funhouse menagerie of her curved, belly-up form. The mirrors reflected the images of each other, creating an uncanny, infinite regression.

Caught in the contortion, her face swollen and red from all the blood having rushed there, none of the representations looked good. They showed her in all of her flaws and folly. "You want to hold up a mirror to me. You want to show me the worst of myself."

Folly unloaded a dramatic moan, her voice dripping with condescension. "Of course you choose the most prosaic terminology possible to describe my approach. Of all of the witches that I have had the misfortune of attempting to teach, you are by far the most tedious. I'd rather show a goat how to program a computer. Let me put it this way to best pander to your micro-brain. There isn't a 'me,' per se, in the way that you eating, shitting meat sacks understand yourselves through the lenses of your silly egos. I am a simulacrum, a reflection, and the sum total of all that is, was, or ever will be. I am the collective unconscious. Heaven and hell. I am your magic. Your law of attraction, your spells and dreams, your synchronicities and incantations and bouts of bad luck. I am there when you see repeating numbers or hear a song in your head three seconds before it comes on the radio. I am there when you chant, pray, curse, or wish upon a star. I am the dragons, the star children, the hologram, the origin. All roads lead to me and through me. Haven't you noticed, with your magic and books, how many paths to me exist? How I am the minotaur at the center of your witchcraft maze? Left-Hand practice. The dark trinity. Partner magic and the chain link system. I'm always there, forever indispensable and inherent. You can't escape me. You *are* me."

Either Cristabel was right and chaos ultimately governed the entire magic system or Folly had a god complex rivaled only by those hopelessly corrupted by extreme power. "If you're as omniscient as you say, why do what you did with Buddy? What's that supposed to accomplish?" Cynthia addressed a particularly unflattering image of herself, her ruddy face puffed up and her messy hair plastered against her lips. She really needed to get out of this twisted prison of prisms, but not until she got some more information. She was so close she could taste it. Not that she knew what *it* tasted like, but she knew in her soul that she had to keep going.

"Perhaps a short vignette will offer added clarity."

Without a millisecond of warning, the mirrors blasted into shards, a series of shattering cracks piercing Cynthia's eardrums before she could slap her palms over the holes. She wailed from the pain, thrashing as the chunks rained to the ground in a series of metallic crashes. Once she came to, she was on the floor, sitting in in a circle of jagged fragments, thankfully unharmed, the walls as blanched as bone.

One spot directly in front of her seemed to move, then another, two black specks pushing their ways out of the bright white slab in tandem. Each grew to the size of a marble, then a baseball, before sprouting what looked like limbs.

One grew into Raven, an angelic version of himself accessorized with feathery black wings that dwarfed his form. Beside him stood Buddy, as large as a tiger, her scaly skin pale and sparkly like winter's first snow. They stood still and gazed off into space as if hypnotized.

I can't have both. The thought came in as a maxim. Cynthia hugged her knees to her chest. *I've taken too much.*

"You're sharper than I initially gave you credit for," Folly said. "Since you asked about the prophecy and I'm feeling chatty today, here's some more insight. Each one of you creatures is a cog in a much larger wheel, and your personal agency, while certainly present and valuable within reason, must be truncated for maximum efficiency. That ability has to be limited for optimal function. Think of an artificial intelligence program running at its peak effectiveness. If you do too much, it won't reach its potential. Understand yourself as an avatar that's being played by someone else. That someone is me. And in order to impart the proper programming into you, you aren't allowed to screw up the system. Play your part, speak your lines, make your little choices within the parameters outlined, and we'll all get through this."

In addition to being totally insulting and radically offensive, Folly's ramblings on the importance of being a good little puppet gave away clues to a weakness in her precious system. The outcome of the prophecy wasn't predetermined, fated, or inevitable at all. In fact, the result that Folly wanted depended on Cynthia and everyone else remaining docile and obedient. And when had she ever been that?

Or perhaps Folly was counting on her ability to demoralize Cynthia so she gave up and resigned herself to the whims of fate. But she'd never been weak and pliable in that way. Never. She was the wind of fate, a witch of the winds. "What if I want to screw up the system? What if I want to defy your plan?"

Folly laughed, but this time the chuckle came out with a shaky little twinge. "I knew you'd say that. Good luck, my sweet air child. Just remember, I'm always three, six, fourteen steps ahead of you. If the world is a chessboard, you're the first pawn to die, and I'm the creator of the game."

Yeah, sure. If you say so. Folly was starting to give off major little man behind the curtain energy. Cynthia had to play it cool for a while longer and use the elemental sister of chaos's hubris against her. For someone claiming to have no ego, she sure seemed to be motivated by an inflated sense of self-importance. "Whatever you say, dungeon master."

Raven came to life in a burst of movement. "The cards," he shouted, eureka crackling through his words.

A low rumbling made the air tremble. "What about them?" Cynthia called, her teeth chattering from the vibrations.

"They do it. That's why they're so controversial and powerful. The cards screw up the system, give us the ability to take Folly's power back for ourselves, and are the ultimate keys to controlling the prophecy." He ran to Cynthia, clamped her wrist, and pulled her upright. She loved when he did that: helped her stand on her own two feet. "We have to go. Now."

The shakes increased to earthquake levels, so strong that Cynthia stumbled as she fought for balance. "How do you know?" she had to yell over the mighty groans all around them.

"The images. I saw pictures from them, scenes, in the place where I was before I found you. They spoke to me. I don't know what's in those cards or who intended for us to find them, but they're the keys. *We're* the keys, too, Cynthia. You and me. Our magic. Our partner work. That's why Folly wants me dead. I'm too powerful when combined with you. Let's go."

"How?" She jerked her head in both directions. The mirror pieces shook and slid on the ground, jostled by the event in progress. "Where's Cristabel?"

He ran with her to Buddy, who dipped her chin to the floor and presented her wide, strong back. "Folly doesn't want her in the picture either. You're right. It makes you too powerful—too much air magic, maybe. I'm not sure, but I know it's not bad. We're so close. We just need to keep our wits about us and get down to Peru. Let's get out of here." Raven slung his leg over Buddy's back and wrapped his arms around her long neck.

Unsure but low on options, Cynthia mounted up behind him, once again finding herself behind Raven and ready to fly. How this tied in with her air magic, well, perhaps one day she'd put together a well-formed theory. But for now, she gave him the benefit of the doubt. Not like she wanted to be in the other place any longer, spinning in literal and figurative circles while Folly slung insults and poked at her insecurities.

"Cristabel," Cynthia shouted. "Give me a sign if you can hear me."

The squiggle-finger, red handprint stamp appeared on one of the white walls like gore splatter at a crime scene. The sigil of chaos was Cristabel's element and very well could have been her way of announcing herself.

The floor shook harder, the walls closing in to make a claustrophobic enclave no larger than a bedroom. Mirror shards jumped off the floor and began to fly through the air, one whizzing past Cynthia's face so fast that she had to duck to avoid a slice.

"You'll need to say an incantation to get us back to our world. Quick. Before one of us is hurt by this glass."

"I can't leave her," Cynthia protested. "What if she's trapped here? We can't lose two coven mothers."

Glass was now hurtling in all directions, forcing everyone to jerk and duck.

Buddy bellowed, a red flash catching Cynthia's eye. A small piece of mirror had lodged in Buddy's toe. Not serious, but not good. "Shit. Okay. Sister Spirit, I, an air born, humbly call upon your assistance. Please bestow upon my companions and I the gift of astral flight, allowing us to transcend the borders of the other place and transport our bodies and souls back to the room we departed from."

Spirit spells were tough, but, thankfully, Sister Spirit took mercy and heeded Cynthia's desperate plea, sending the trio rocketing through a tunnel. Cynthia snapped back to herself facedown on Cristabel's rug, her head throbbing. She stumbled to her knees, whacking her hip on a table, dizzy and disoriented. "Raven? Buddy? Cristabel?"

"I'm here," Raven said, sitting on the floor with his head in his hands.

Buddy stood beside him, crouched in a defensive posture. The piece of glass lay in front of her face like she'd bitten down on it to pull it out. Her toe was bleeding, but not profusely. She'd need some care, though, to prevent the small wound from getting infected. Not like Cynthia could take the dragon to a vet.

"Cristabel?" Cynthia called, her heart sinking lower with every second that passed. The old witch wasn't around. She'd stayed in the other place, voluntarily or not.

"Take a look at this." Raven came to Cynthia with Cristabel's open book and sat beside her.

"Oh, no." Cynthia sensed the vicinity of where Cristabel had gone as she glanced down at the pages. "Is she in here? Why is she in here? I don't know how to get them out."

"This is interesting," Raven said. "Read it."

Cynthia forced her tired brain to lock in with the words on the page.

I should never have mocked your sending Nerissa to the book, for turnabout has become foul play. At least I was able to write you some directions before these pages trapped me. I'm not sure of how yet, but I think this is how we defeat the prophecy. The coven mothers rejoin the sacred texts and write our parts of the story from within. You, daughters, will incant us to channel our energies when you join hands to dissolve the hologram. Please add my book to your collection and take it, and by extension me, to Peru with you.

The passage blurred and wobbled as Cynthia's tears welled. "I put another person in a book. I killed her. I basically killed her." She looked at her feet, her bare toes scratched up and red from the glass house debacle.

"Baby, stop." Raven lifted Cynthia's chin with two fingers, bringing her gaze to meet his. "You did everything right. You didn't do anything wrong. She said herself that this is how it's supposed to be. Take the book. You have two books now, and I have the cards. Let's collect the others from the hotel, go find our tribe, and beat this prophecy."

She wiped her tears. "I just feel like I'm letting people down. What if she had goals and dreams and hopes that didn't involve being stuck in a book? What if she never gets out?"

"I think that it's not our place to question or doubt her path. Besides, all we can do is go with what we have. If we take the book like she asked, there's a better chance that we'll eventually have the skill to free her."

She rested her head on his shoulder, feeling calmer from both his words and listening to him speak. "My voice of reason. My rock."

"Ironic to call me a rock, since I'm pretty much defined by the opposite of stability."

A warmth shrouded her. She always felt a little warmer, a little more stable, with Raven around. "Me too."

He kissed her temple before looking back to the book. "Wait, is it changing?"

She returned her attention to the page. Sure enough, a paragraph of text below the one that Cynthia had just read was erasing itself in real time, fading away before she had a chance to read the words. She tapped the words on the page like her frantic scrabbling could halt the inevitable. "Crap. You catching any of this?"

"It's going to fast." He ran a finger down the page. "They look like the instructions for how to speak the words to let her out."

"No." Hope crumbled into dust. That was the worst thing that could possibly disappear. But wait. Words started to come back. Only two, though, and when Cynthia read them, she died a little on the inside.

I ERASE YOUR CHAOS MOTHER. I AM CHAOS. I AM ALL. NEVER SNEER AT ME AGAIN.

FOUR DAYS.

TWENTY-TWO

DESPITE THE LATEST WAVE OF SETBACKS, THEY'D PERSISTED IN THEIR journey, choosing momentum over inertia. At least taking steps felt like progress.

Smuggling Buddy out of the hotel had been a comical endeavor involving a stolen bed sheet and a prepared yarn about a sick dog, the entire ordeal cumbersome and messy since the dragon had grown to the size of a small horse. Apparently Portia, Ether, and Dragon had been feeding her, not that Cynthia blamed them. Fortunately, they'd all done a decent job of blocking Buddy during the hustle out of the New Mexico hotel, and none of the tired, bored employees had cared enough to ask questions. Causing a stir was probably above their pay grade.

Thanks to the deck and its ability to render everyday objects into passports and credit cards, the five travelers had landed in in a three-story treehouse cabin somewhere in Costa Rica.

The ride had been punctuated by sumptuous greenery, roadside fruit stands, and a several stay overs in motels of varied quality when the sun slipped into night. Buddy had flow high enough in the sky to elude the attention of anyone who happened to gaze up. Cynthia hoped that no satellites or air traffic controls spotted her familiar's flight path. She mentally kept track of a most grim countdown, the back of her mind worn and weary.

At the moment, at least, they were settled somewhere pleasant. Waves rumbled in the distance with their familiar, sonorous meditation, the dense buffer of vegetation having been thinned to offer residents a view of the beach. Cynthia would have liked to stay in the funky, bohemian-chic treehouse lodge for a few days, if possible, not that she had a firm sense of any timeline beyond the unpleasant one ticking off days in her mind. At least Folly had been absent and silent, though who knew anymore if that was good or bad. The culmination of the prophecy was one of many mysteries, though her trusty intuition said "soon."

She sat on the rustic, wooden floor of her latest temporary abode, her concentration captured by one of the fake credit cards that they'd used. She turned the bright blue Visa over in her hand a couple of times, its weight and finish similar to every other credit card that she'd handled. The name on the card, Brenda Montgomery, didn't ring any particular bells, nor did the string of numbers, so fingers crossed that the information was meaningless and not tied to bad outcomes for anyone with that name. But who was she to say?

Raven sat behind her, watching in silence for several seconds while she played with the card. "What are you thinking about?"

Her mind wandered to the money magic spell that she'd done to help out the man at the motel, charting the steps she'd taken in hopes of unearthing any clue as to the consequences of that particular action. There had to be some accountability registering somewhere, had to be some sense in which her choice to use magic at that moment, in that way, had instigated a butterfly effect of events and occurrences that would, without a doubt, swing back around like a boomerang. Or maybe Folly was just screwing with her. "My question about where magic comes from and where it goes. It's interesting to me that money magic is part of the air lineage. That's got me thinking about deposits and withdrawals. A banking system. Balances of magic, like balances in a checking account."

He ran his fingertip over the credit card number, his presence and the soundtrack of the ocean soothing her worried mind. "As in the system stays in balance when we give as much or more than we take so we stay in the black?"

"Something like that." She turned over the credit card so she didn't have to see the name and set it on the ground, the magnetic strip catching a ray of dim light from the bedside lamp. "I worry that everything that we're doing with this deck is taking. For example, do the names on these fake credit cards have any significance? The numbers? Is someone, somewhere being harmed by our doing this? Are we stealing? That seems even worse than taking. Even if we aren't stealing, are we draining the magic system so heavily that we're incurring a debt that has to be paid?" Perhaps Folly was acting as a debt collector by presenting Cynthia with the Buddy/Raven conundrum. In her own sick way, the sister of chaos might be trying to teach Cynthia a lesson about managing her magical assets, so to speak.

"That's a lot of moral quandaries stuffed into a few sentences." He spoke in a jesting tone, unbothered enough to bother her. Did he take their practice seriously? "It sounds mentally exhausting."

She met his stare dead on, trying not to get too caught up in his leather-and-pheromones scent or how his proximity affected her body—and heart. "Please tell me that you're at least thinking in passing about the consequences of all of this magic that we're throwing around."

He held an extended, sidelong glance. "That doesn't sound like you, to fret about all of the possible outcomes of every action."

A twinge of pain stuck in her chest, and offense rushed in to cover the stinging wound with a barbed dressing. "You think that I act without thinking. That I'm reckless."

"Yeah, I mean, aren't you? I love that about you."

Reeling as the indignity twisted through her like a corkscrew, Cynthia jumped up and walked to Buddy, who was curled in the corner looking out on the water. Cynthia fussed with her familiar's bandage, which had been cleaned and changed and didn't really need any attention. She supposed that she had to do something to make herself feel responsible for correcting a harm she'd caused, and the self-awareness made her even more annoyed and defensive about her random reaction. "That's not very kind. I'm doing my best here. I'm trying to be mature and responsible."

Buddy whined and pulled her foot away.

"Here, let me see," Cynthia cooed, gently tugging at the affected toe.

Buddy growled and swatted at her, five sharp, bone-white claws raking the empty space.

"Let me see your fucking foot to make sure it's okay. You're so damn stubborn. What's wrong with you?" She heard her mother's voice come through her mouth, which only made her more aggravated.

Buddy drew back and snarled with her lips peeled inward to bare her teeth, creating a truly terrifying visage.

"Have it your way." Cynthia's whole body tensed. Her voice sounded awful, shrill and bitter, like someone she never wanted to be. "Get an infection for all I care."

Raven circled his hand around Cynthia's upper arm and led her a few feet away from Buddy. "Let's leave her be, okay? She's fine."

Her brain soupy and misfiring, she struggled to collect her thoughts and feelings before yanking out of his grip. "Don't tell me how to take care of my familiar. Don't tell me how to feel while you explain things to me like you're all cool and calm and I'm some hotheaded idiot. You did that on purpose. It's manipulative."

"Whoa." He scratched his head. "I wasn't aware that I was doing any of those things. But clearly I hurt you, and I'm sorry."

She sat on the bed, slumping forward, a headache taking root behind her eye. Maybe someday she'd get better control of herself and stop losing her center over every damn disruption. Maybe someday she wouldn't be crazy and stupid anymore. "Forget it. I suck."

He took the spot beside her. "You want to talk?"

Buddy began to snore, long, rumblings noises of deep sleep that put her mind at ease some. The familiar was tired and crabby and needed to be left alone, which Cynthia could respect and relate to. She didn't want Raven to go away, either. Actually, having someone to talk to helped her get outside of her own head. Too bad that all of her friendships and relationships ended up being transactional and/or brief, so she didn't have the best idea of how to get to deeper levels with others or feel safe leaning on them for support. "I just have a lot of heavy stuff on my mind, I guess. I worry that we're not doing the right things. I'm frustrated that we don't have more guidance, but maybe it's entitled of me to expect that."

"Are you feeling overwhelmed?" He cupped her leg above the knee and massaged, the touch working to sand the edges off her distress.

"Yeah. You could say that."

"I do, too. Feel overwhelmed, that is." He moved his hand from her thigh to her hand, bringing them palm to palm. "And I hear what you're saying about magic. I really do. I worry quite often that my choices aren't going to generate the results that I want—or think that I want."

She gazed pointedly at him. "And yet you keep going."

"You confuse me, you know that?"

She resisted the urge to snap at him. Raven might have been the first person she'd ever met who'd put up with her as long as he had. What in the world did he see in her? She was moody, restless, and not exactly a bastion of congeniality. "What do you mean, I confuse you? That doesn't make much sense. I'm pretty easy to read."

He bent into a conspiratorial lean. "You have to promise that you won't hit me. Because I'm about to get real."

Irritated at his efforts to see and read her on a deeper level, but flattered at the same time, she knocked into him. "What, you think I'm a violent psycho? Gee, thanks."

"No, I don't think that you're a violent psycho. But I think that you're incredibly aggravating and full of contradictions. You might be the most contradictory person that I've ever met."

She glared at him, but given how open his face remained, she bet that he saw the interest underneath her attempt to erect a tough façade. Everyone who stuck around saw through her eventually. "Do tell."

"You do the cutest thing with your eyebrows when you want to open up but you're scared to, so you act pissed off instead."

Okay, she did *not* do that. Did she? She shoved him harder than she had the first time. "That's specific enough to be fairly creepy, birdman. And I don't do that. Weirdo. Do you watch me when I sleep, too?"

"Wouldn't you like to know?"

"Um, yes. Because that's terrifying."

"Of course not. Contrary to your accusations, I am not, in fact, a creep."

She knew that he wasn't a creep and didn't watch her sleep—Cynthia had perfected the art of half-sleeping with one eye open over the years and would've noticed if he was skulking by her bedside. But banter was fun. "Whatever. If I catch you doing any *Twilight* stalker type shit, I'll pluck out your feathers one-by-one. Now back to my contradictions. What the hell are you talking about?"

"I can't get enough of you, you know that? And what I mean by the contradictions is that you're fundamentally this sweet, generous person who wants to reach out and connect with others. That's evident. But you're so committed to your tough, badass act that you deny those softer parts of yourself. And you deny them so hard that you're tripping over yourself half the time, trying to keep these competing facets of your identity straight."

Stunned, all that she managed to do was sit with those words for a bit. That was a whole lot, and delivered with a generous serving of empathy that she didn't deserve. "I don't do that," she aimed for matter-of-fact, but of course the statement came out sputtering and defensive. Not for the first time, but perhaps the most seriously, Cynthia entertained the notion that it was time to stop pretending to be anyone but herself. "I totally do that, don't I?"

"You do. And I don't blame you. We all basically go through life making a series of calculations on how to keep ourselves safe, both physically and emotionally. And you've had to do a lot of both."

She blew off an exhale that felt like a ten-pound drop of garbage. "Yeah. But I'm not special or different, ya know? I'm just a person. And there's no glory or romanticism in being fake. All it means is that I have a harder time connecting to people, because I never let myself trust enough to show my true self." She hugged her arms in tight. The chip that she'd stuck on her shoulder covered up her tender parts, but maybe those tender parts were the ones that most needed to touch others' tender parts? If that clumsy metaphor made sense. Cynthia was nobody's poet.

"Look at me," Raven whispered with such conviction that she had no choice but to sweep her stare up to lock in with his. He continued, "You aren't just any person to me. I don't mean your magic, either. I mean who you are. I've never felt like this for someone before, how connected I feel with you. I want to get to know you, as difficult as the task is. Because I know that the reward I find under that hard shell will be invaluable. You *are* special, Cynthia. I don't care anymore if me saying that makes you mad or makes you want to push away. All that matters to me is that you know that I see your worth. Your value. How exceptional you are."

She wanted to bust his balls about the "hard shell" remark. What, was she an oyster to be cracked, dominated, and mined for a pearl? How fucked was that?! But, when she probed a little deeper into herself and chose to read his remark charitably, she knew that wasn't what he meant. Instead of serving up some snarky comeback, Cynthia threw her arms around Raven's taller, more muscular body and melted into his arms. "Thank you."

"For what, Baby?" He stroked the top of her head.

Her heartbeat banged against her ribcage. She felt herself quivering. "For taking a chance on me. For believing in me when lots of other people would say that my juice isn't worth the squeeze."

With one motion of swift confidence, he lowered her to her back and looked deeply into her. "I'm going to say something extremely cheesy."

She enjoyed his lighthearted, self-aware remark, time and space melting into the moment where only the two of them remained. "Let's hear it. I think that cheesy is just what we need right now."

"As lousy as this magic and prophecy is a lot of the time, I firmly believe that it brought us together. That destiny, or fate, had a role in connecting us. Every choice that each of us made for an undetermined period of time led us to that truck stop diner on that day. What started out as a random quickie turned into so much more, on so many levels. We can't deny that. We can't fight it. This is meant to be."

Cynthia had never heard something so romantic spoken in her life, let alone directly to her, and especially not in a mood-lit treehouse cabin in Costa Rica where gentle breezes animated the gauzy curtains of her bedroom. Such romantic trappings were for other people, books, and movies—until they weren't. They were for her now. She was blessed. Lucky. Grateful. All thanks to this man and his persistent, unyielding insistence that she finally claim such beauty for herself. The beauty in life that she deserved. She guided him squarely on top of her until there bodies were flush. "Kiss me. Make me forget everything but you."

She meant *everything* literally. If he could make her forget all of it— Folly, magic, the every-expanding body count of her mistakes—even for a few minutes, she'd never push him away again. This wasn't a test, or even an order. This was a plea, a prayer wrapped in a challenge.

Raven accepted the challenge by brushing his lips against hers, sending his warm breath to mingle with hers against their tongues before molding their lips together in an urgent crush.

All she heard was their breath and heartbeats, chased by the rhythms of nature. Clothes came off in graceful slips and pulls, every touch and taste reverent and slow. There was no urgency, no lust. Just the wind, carrying its song, her legacy song, directly into her heart as Raven's skin slid against hers with an intimacy that took her breath away.

She closed her eyes the entire time he moved in and out of her, not because she didn't want to look, but because turning off the visual heightened everything else. Her legs found their way around his hips, crossing at the ankles, hemming him in because she never wanted him to stop. Never wanted him to go, never could bear the thought of him leaving her.

"I love you," she mouthed the words against him, a mix of pain and joy cascading from the center of her chest down to her stomach. This was too much and not enough, a force massive enough to crack her wide open. "Please love me. Please don't leave me."

He slowed his motions to a luxurious, tortuous pace, easing her head onto the pillow.

The tears streamed down her face, and she let them flow, not bothering to hide her feelings anymore. Despite her begging, if he told her that he didn't feel the same way, or that he liked her a lot, but wasn't ready to say bigger words, that was okay. She was okay with what she felt, and could live with that. Even if he didn't return the sentiment, what she'd just confessed was poignant and profound to her, and nobody could take that away.

"I love you." The words tumbled from his lips with an impact that seemed to shake the entire world to its core. "I love you more than I've ever loved anyone, and I want to be with you forever. Do you understand, Cynthia? Do you understand how much you mean to me?"

Was this the whole soul mate thing at work? Two lonely, lost hearts connecting through serendipity and a series of coincidences until they found themselves in the middle of a jungle, bodies joined and riding a wavelength that was more spiritual than any meditation?

"As much as I can understand what it means to be loved, to accept this thing called love, then yeah. I do."

"Good." He resumed pumping into her, harder and faster, the depth and pleasure of his strokes prompting her to arch her back and bounce her hips in response. "Because you are mine, Cynthia, and I'm yours."

"Yes," she cried, checking the volume of her voice so as not to wake the snoring dragon. The blissful sensations became too much to bear, and she spilt into ecstasy, riding burst after burst of climax until she had no more energy left to spend. "Yes. I'm all yours."

Boneless, she fell back in a supreme surrender of tension while he thrust away, his speed picking up as he raced to the end. Once he got there, he withdrew with a jerk, spilling into her hand while she massaged the crown of his erection, the length of him wet from her.

They lay in silence for a bit, caressing arms and collarbones and the spaces between ribs. She tucked herself into a spot underneath his arm. "I don't think that it matters."

"What doesn't?" He ran the backs of his fingers down the side of her face.

"Where magic comes from and where it goes."

"Why doesn't that matter to you anymore?"

"Because I think it just is. It's a gift to be treasured. Regarded with wonder and not necessarily analyzed or deconstructed. Too much picking at it ruins it."

"Epiphany?" He dropped a kiss to her forehead.

"Yeah. I guess you fucked it out of me."

He laughed like he was caught off guard. "I thought that we made love just there."

"We did. I'm just delivering my obligatory smartass line. I'm not a completely transformed woman. It's not like I had a personality transplant."

"Good." His breath tickled her ear. "Don't change a thing."

On that note, she dozed for a bit, satisfied enough to sleep with Raven chilling behind her. Cynthia had no idea how long she'd been out when she awoke with a jerk, jumpy, her calves tight. A shadowy figure lurked in the corner. "Who's there?" Maybe one of the others had wandered up the spiral staircase that connected the two levels, looking for a toothbrush or bottle of water.

But there was nobody there expect Buddy curled up in the corner, her breath rumbly, her back rising and falling in time with the flow of oxygen. Raven was out cold, sleeping on his stomach, his black hair spread out in a fan.

Piqued and antsy, she got out of bed and walked to the edge of the open-air bedroom, the curtains drawn across the wooden deck to block the sunlight and keep out any bugs or birds. She parted the heavy fabric and took in the view, the waters glistening like an obsidian jewel through peekaboo gaps in swaying leaves.

A few grounding seconds got her centered enough to think about returning to bed. She must've had a nightmare that she'd forgotten. Her brain was overloaded and overstimulated lately.

She turned around, the trespass of an unwelcome sight freezing her with shock. A figure stood in the corner where Buddy had lain. A nude person, female judging by the slight build, though she didn't see any breasts. "Portia?" she hissed, a high-voltage current of fear yoking her scalp to her toes.

Whatever stood there wasn't Portia, nor any person. The entity was translucent, an apparition, a form made up of faint, glimmering energy like static. Where a face should have been, there was only a smooth slab like a bald head. No hair. Its hands were outstretched in a gesture of supplication or grasping, Cynthia wasn't sure which.

"What are you?" Could this thing harm her? More importantly, what had it done with Buddy? It appeared to be made from pure energy and was as wispy as expected, but that didn't mean it was benign. "Where's my familiar?"

The light-figure advanced, floating instead of taking clear steps, its blurry feet hovering several inches off the ground. "I'm here now," Folly said with victory. "I've begun to manifest in your world, and soon I will be corporeal. Then there is no telling what I'm capable of. Until then, you have one more day to make your choice. From sunup to sundown tomorrow is your last chance. You must pick. You must."

"No." Cynthia balled her fists and stood her ground. There had to be a way around this ultimatum. Besides, in her current form, Folly was hardly a fearsome force to be reckoned with. This was the best she could do in her manifesting in the material world? Pathetic. "Fuck you, you insignificant spark of static electricity. You don't scare me."

Folly's ghostly self advanced, her hands sinking into Cynthia's throat like two spears. "You must. You must, you must, you must."

Cynthia screamed, the high-pitched wail of her voice wracking her from the inside out as an explosion of bright light erupted in her face.

TWENTY-THREE

"Baby, baby, it's okay." Raven's assurance shook Cynthia from her stasis, though her rigid limbs resisted her brain's efforts to zap them alive. Finally, she forced a kick from her stony legs, her body and mind struggling to process where she was and if she was dying. He spoke more phrases of comfort, "Take a few deep breaths. You're safe. You had a night terror. You're in the treehouse cabin with me, Raven, and Buddy."

The words slid off her brain, but the basic, emotional concepts stuck despite the tsunami of stress flooding her system. "Okay." She twisted in bed, clutching at wads of sheets, pressing her bare heels into the mattress. "It's okay." It wasn't, but she wasn't sure why. But it was okay in the sense that she hadn't died and gone to hell. "Sorry to scare you."

"No worries, it happens." His speech laden with sleep, Raven rolled out of bed, yanked on his boxer shorts, and swiped a bottled water from the bulk package that they'd bought. He handed her the bottle. "How are you feeling now?"

Nature's rich darkness surrounded her, primordial and ancient, as she sat up in a daze. Her pulse ran on overdrive. Sweat dampened her neck and hairline, the odor musty. Buddy watched her with golden eyes that glowed like headlights in the otherwise blacked-out room. A long drink of lukewarm water helped her regain a bit of composure and tee up a choppy, unwanted memory. "She's here."

Next to Cynthia on the bed, his long legs folded underneath his body, Raven surveyed the room. "Who is?"

More recollections arrived to knit together a coherent framework. "Folly." She strangled the bottle, flimsy plastic crunching in her grip. "She came to me in a dream as some kind of light being and reminded me of the deadline. Buddy disappeared when she did that, like they traded places. I want to believe that it's just a bluff, but I'm scared. I'm scared and I don't know what to do."

He swept her into his embrace in a fluid, automatic movement. "If she came to you in a dream, she's not here, strictly speaking. She's in the astral plane or wherever dreams happen."

"Fair. But she's still advancing, though. Doing more. Interacting with me on her own terms in a form that's approaching corporeal. That's a new development. The situation is getting worse, not better."

"There has to be a spell for this, some incantation to block unwanted entities or thicken the veil between us and them."

Slices of daybreak pierced the gaps in the drapes the same way that Folly had figured out how to cut herself a pathway through the barrier that separated the earthly world from the spirit domain. Raven was right: there was a spell that existed to seal the opening in the metaphysical curtain. Cynthia was growing leery of magic, though, and especially apprehensive about drawing from elements other than her own. Borrowing, or taking, or whatever the practice was at its core, really seemed to be a big part of the problem. Yet her range of choices kept dissolving, leaving behind a throbbing, juicy core of magic. Magic, magic, magic. "There is. There's a high-level Spirit spell called Banish Intruders that fits our needs."

"But you'd rather avoid it. I hear it in your voice."

She'd rather do a lot of things, but lately she felt that she didn't have a choice, or that her choices were so heavily circumscribed that the entire notion of free will was a joke. Which easily could have been part of the mindfuck. She jammed her fingertips into her temples as if pain and pressure could straighten out her thinking. "That's correct. The last time we traveled to the other place, I guessed that doing partner work and building a chain link with other elements is empowering Folly to do more of this kind of stuff, gain power and influence in our world. She said that all roads lead to her, and it certainly looks like she's in the process of paving those roads for easier access. So yeah, I'm leery of enabling her."

"Unless that's manipulation or reverse psychology on her part. What you described could be exactly what she wants you to think is happening."

Also a valid point. "As in, she's using lies and trickery to dissuade me from doing collaborative spell work because that practice might, in actuality, stop her?"

"Bingo."

"How do you figure?" She didn't mistrust him. She needed all of the help she could get in figuring out the maddening maze of a crucible.

"A hunch. Intuition. From what we've seen, Folly functions in this really diabolical manner involving deceit and changing ground and the mingling of lies with truth. So we're always unstable in reference to her, trying to figure out someone or something that has no center or foundation. So the theory of her trying to fool us out of doing partner work fits with that hypothesis."

"Okay. I can see that. But how do we know?"

He laid down. "I don't think that we do, or that we can. What if surrendering the fantasy of certainty is part of the test, or an uncomfortable reality that we have to accept?"

She crashed next to him and groaned an impotent protest. "Then that sucks. That's awful. If what you described is true, it means that all we're ever doing is taking chances, trial and error, wishing on a star and hoping for the best. We're never empowered to act with complete confidence."

An unanticipated pause lasted until he said, "I don't like the idea of hope."

Aspersions for Raven incoming. "Excuse me?"

"The feel of it. I don't like it. It feels grasping to me, desperate, wanting an outcome so badly that you lose sight of the process along the way. Hope doesn't attach to a positive state, in my opinion. It attaches to fear and attachment to results. From what I've learned at least, that's a surefire way to guarantee unhappiness and an inward sense of defeat. Sacrificing the joy inherent in process for a fixation on getting a certain kind of result."

His musings, aptly, got her thinking about the spirit spell again. "That sounds like something Helen would say."

"Who's that?"

"The spirit witch. I stalked her online. She's super into all of those heady spiritual and meditation concepts."

"Sounds about right for a spirit witch."

"Yeah." Cynthia eyed her book, the big old compendium looming in the corner along with her backpack and shoes. "Let's go ahead and do Banish Intruders, see if that holds her back for a little while at least."

"Okay. I'll get the deck and the others so we can make a chain to Spirit."

Nervous energy compounded to juice her up, her focus pinned on her book. "I want to try something else." If Folly was telling the truth about the consequences of partner magic, Cynthia would be wise to attempt a workaround. And she had one in mind.

"Elaborate?"

"I'll show you." She padded across the floor, hauled her book back to bed, and opened it to the index. Once there, she flipped to the hexagon graphic with each of the elemental symbols marking a joint between planes. The handprint tattooed the middle of the shape. "Notice how Spirit and Air are directly diagonal from each other." She used her finger to trace a direct line between those two points.

"Which means what, exactly?" He asked with interest, looking on.

She chewed on her lip as if the repetitive motion could draw her hunch closer to the surface of her understanding. "I think it means exactly what it looks like. That there's a shortcut available between these diagonal elements, and that finding it allows the practitioner to bypass the need for chain link partner work."

"Except that the shortcut goes through Chaos." He pointed at the handprint. "They all do. Which supports Folly's point about Chaos underscoring the entire system."

"True. The thing that bugs me is that she kept talking exclusively about partner work and didn't mention this alternative. So I wonder if there's a way to *harness* the force of chaos through this approach and in the process neutralize it. Take control of it as opposed to relying upon it or borrowing from it, both of which feel more passive to me."

She could feel the foreboding of his next words a few seconds before he spoke. "What if it's a trap?"

Perhaps embracing the chaos inherent in her magic was the only true solution, the final pathway to mastery. If there was someone out there who knew the secrets, it sure wasn't her. "There are traps everywhere. I'm starting to think that the key isn't ducking them or running from them, but tapping into the wisdom or skill to escape them once they spring."

"It feels a lot of times like this game is rigged, though. Just ask Nerissa and Cristabel."

As her determination grew, she lobbed him daggers. "Do you have a better idea? Because the contrarian angle isn't helping."

He matched her pointed glance and raised with a question, "Are you sure about that? Because the deeper we go into this, the surer I get that this is absolutely, hands-down, a process that needs to be forced to withstand doubt."

Some time ago, she would have, in one of her infamous knee-jerk reactions, balked at the bundling of the two of them into a "we." Now, however, Cynthia accepted that she and Raven were very much a team— a bonded pair. She was sick of going at the world alone. Which didn't mean that she'd meekly capitulate to his every pushback, either. "I don't think that the scientific method applies here, Raven."

"Yeah, well, maybe it should."

"So what's your idea? How do we stop Folly and get the upper hand on this prophecy before anyone dies? Before the world as we know it ends? What's your solution? Because, in my humble opinion, we don't have an endless amount of time to test and research and hypothesize and otherwise pull back and wait. We have less than twenty-four hours, specifically, before she strikes again. The clock is ticking."

"Look, I don't want to argue with you. About this or anything else." Slowly, he reached over and pushed her knuckles, separating her flesh from the book. "I'm just not convinced that full steam ahead with this is a best practice. We ought to be careful of faith morphing into zealotry."

Now she was actively annoyed. Who was he to tell her how to do her job, how to practice her craft? If Raven was out to hold her back, they were gonna have a problem. "I don't want to fight, either, but I will. Because right now, you're giving me questionable vibes. This feels like you telling me to scale back on my exploration of a craft that is very much my birthright, and I won't stand silently and bow my head while you shrink my world piece by piece."

He made a noise that was very much in the vicinity of a scoff. "My apologies. I didn't mean to step on a trigger."

A knife of outrage pierced her. "Don't patronize me. I heard the condescension in your voice and that huffy noise you made. I'm not 'triggered,' I'm standing up for myself."

"You talk about standing up for yourself like it's some huge breakthrough even though you've never had a problem defending your choices. I do think that you'd be remiss not to examine closely what it is you're standing up for in these moments."

Her skin was raw. Calm thoughts fell back, subsumed in a wave of offense. "Fuck you. Don't tell me what to do. And don't you dare imply that I'm stupid." Instantly, she felt dirtier, smaller, and hollowed. Like she'd regressed, and rapidly, without thinking.

"Fine. Message received. Have at it. Dig your heels in and do whatever the hell you want regardless of what anyone who loves you says." He jumped out of bed and yanked his pants over his hips in a hard, aggressive pull. "That's what you do, right? Whatever you want, like self-absorption is some noble principle."

A plume of rage erupted between her eyebrows, though deep down she trembled. What happened to the special moment where they'd held each other and shared precious words and touches? How had she poisoned that? She figured that it didn't matter what she'd done or how she'd done it, just that she *had*. Cynthia was who she was, and the ugly truth of her came out eventually. Though ugly, at least her familiar pattern fit comfortably, like a worn out old shoe. "Miss me with the lectures, birdman." She pointed at the door, her insides twisting into knots. "Get out."

"Your wish is my command." Following the sarcasm-laced comeback, he turned away from her, snatched up his shirt in a violent grip, and stormed down the spiral staircase that connected their loft to the downstairs room. "I'll be downstairs. Have fun with your book. Say hi to Folly for me."

"I'm trying to save your life, you idiot," she shouted at his back. "I owe you that much."

"Don't bother. I'm not interested in whatever it is that you think you owe me." The top of his head slipped from view as he reached the base of the stairs before a door opened and closed with a click.

He'd been considerate enough of the others' rest not to slam the door, which somehow made her more upset. Where were those kid gloves when it came to *her* feelings?

Oh well, at the end of the day Raven and his motivations didn't matter. Once again, Cynthia was alone. She sneered at the darkness, a black, hateful aura filling her from the inside out. Alone was how she always ended up eventually, so there was no point in fighting it. Solitude was her fate, her destiny, her path. She pushed everyone away and invited rejection. That was simply who she was. She looked to Buddy. "At least we have each other."

The dragon chuffed. "We have each other."

"You'll never leave, right?"

Chuff. "Never leave."

Buddy could have very well been parroting, as her communicative ability hadn't advanced past the level of mimicry yet, but Cynthia needed validation so badly that she took the comments as affirmations. "Thank you. I'll never leave you behind, either." Meaning that she needed to get cracking on Banish Intruders and save Buddy, her only friend. Who knew how much longer Raven and his pals would stick around. Not that she'd let him die without putting up a fight, as she didn't hate him or anything, but Buddy was her top priority.

On that note, she went to the end table and flicked on the lamp. The soft glow was just enough light to read by. Cynthia dressed in her pajamas and curled up in bed with her book, getting into the zone. For all of her foibles, she was still a powerful witch. She had the ability to cast a formidable spell to save her familiar and stop the encroach of ultimate evil, and she was damn sure going to apply her abilities to the fullest extent. No holds-barred, no holding back. Hell, without Raven in the picture, she didn't have to rely on anyone else for partner work at all.

She could cut right through Chaos herself and get to Spirit, leveling up significantly. If she was going to be a confirmed solitary practitioner and person, solo work was a skill she'd better advance at fast. An ache unspooled in her chest, and she promptly pushed the hurt down deep where it belonged.

Once emotionally squared away, she fixed her intention on the hexagon symbol, occult authenticity radiating from the ink that bled down the page like leaky watercolor paint, the script rendered in jerky, arcane penmanship from a stranger. Screw Raven, screw him, forget him. She didn't need him. Didn't need anyone except Buddy, magic, and her book.

She flipped to the incantation to hail Sister Spirit, visualizing a straight, paved blacktop road through a town called Chaos while she spoke the spell, improvising for her precise purpose. "Sister Spirit, I, an air born, humbly call upon your assistance. It seems that a malevolent force has infiltrated my world, one with great power and prestige. I ask you today to banish this intruder and send this one who loves me not back to its natural abode."

"It?" Folly's rejoinder came back at once, soaked in incredulity and followed by a cackle that could crack glass. "You have got to be fucking kidding me. *It?!* And you dare to erase my name and station under this neutered, faceless moniker of 'malevolent force?' As if I'm some lesser demon hiding under your bed, scurrying around like an imp and capable of only going bump in the night. How dare you? Seriously, how dare you? Just for that, we're going to have some fun."

Cynthia stood on a dirt trail, the pathway covered in fallen leaves painted in the red-gold palate of autumn. Trees in various shades ranging from beige to russet to brilliant maroon surrounded her in all directions and for miles ahead, shedding leaves of similar coloring in a gentle, sustained watercolor rain. A crisp breeze made goosebumps burst across her bare arms, but as far as other place options went, this landscape wasn't bad. Unaided by trail markers, she forged ahead. So far, Folly's ominous threat of "fun" wasn't particularly insidious, but who knew what lay ahead. The best Cynthia could come up with was to stick with her instinct to keep going and operate from the assumption that the most pernicious of the elemental sisters was made of more bark and bluster than she cared to let on.

An unseen sun must've retired for the evening in a sudden drop, because night fell quickly, blanketing the trees and dirt. The air was much, much colder, chilling the soles of feet that Cynthia now realized were want for shoes. She contracted her muscles and folded her arms over her front, her steps tentative but not fearful. Wind bit her exposed skin from all angles. She glanced at her body only to discover with a shock that she was naked.

"You pass through me and become me," Folly's whisper blew through dancing leaves the same as a breeze. "You are me, air born. We all are many, and we are one."

Yeah, okay, whatever. Cynthia was over it, the opaque riddles and senseless parables with no point or moral. All she had to do was trek her bare ass across this trail and come out the other side to reach Spirit.

Moonlight, or a light reminiscent of the lunar glow, filtered in to drape the tree trunks in phosphorescent silver. Movement undulated in the spotlight, sinuous, as serpents as fat as thick thighs curled up the bark in muscular coils. "There is no passing by this element, air born. Only passing through. And a witch who passes through, will inevitably absorb."

Cynthia halted her steps and met the beady leer of a spotted snake wrapped around the trunk of an oak tree. "What do you want from me? To scare me? To drive me insane? Because your games are getting old. If I knew the rules or even what the board looked like, this might be fun, but since I don't, it's just tedious."

A forked tongue as red as a cherry split the air. "What makes you think there are rules?"

"You know what? I'm tired of you. I don't want to hear one more weird solipsism. They're exhausting. Have a great night." She broke into a run, pushing forward though no light at the end of the dark tunnel offered salvation. With no endpoint or goal, she ran from a place of frustration, feeling herself tire sooner than she would have on a treadmill.

A chorus of hisses split her ears, primal and chilling, so invasive that her brain flared up in a self-preservation instinct and lost the ability to reason. All that remained was a drive to run from the predator, so Cynthia ran and ran. Into darkness. Into nothing. The path was never ending, tunneling into a cavern, the whole damn hole infested with angry, hissing snakes.

The rabbit hole that never ended awaited Cynthia, eager to swallow her entirely. Exactly what Folly had foreshadowed was manifesting.

Still, piloted by her stubborn drive, Cynthia ran and ran into darkness, her legs screaming for relief, a howl born of both determination and failure erupting from her throat in a plea to drown out the goddamn hissing that was driving her mad.

"Stop," Cynthia screamed at everything and nothing, her demand ironic given how she *couldn't* stop and kept right on running. "Stop, already. Stop right now."

Pain ripped Cynthia from her momentum, and the next thing she knew, she was floating midair. Except now, unlike in the house of mirrors, she was somewhere decidedly mundane. Cynthia levitated in the middle of someone's bedroom, looking down on a man and woman sleeping in each other's arms.

Long, brown waves spread out to cover the woman's face, but Cynthia recognized her. She recognized the energy of one of her coven sisters. "Helen," she whispered, loud enough to rouse her but hopefully not to scare her too much.

Helen turned her head, and her eyes popped open.

TWENTY-FOUR

THINK FAST BEFORE SHE SCREAMS! CYNTHIA SEALED HER PALM OVER Helen's mouth, staring into eyes stretched wide enough to split the darkness white. The surge of forward momentum sent Cynthia's legs pivoting upward in the air, and she swung them feebly against open space. She would have enjoyed the fantastical, astronaut novelty of it all more had she not been worried about Helen freaking out, shrieking, and waking her partner. Not that she preemptively judged Helen for this possibility, as she could see herself doing the same if the roles were reversed.

Fortunately, the spirit witch seemed to quickly register who was floating above her and had covered her mouth, because she stopped struggling right away.

The shirtless man groaned and stirred before dozing back off.

Cynthia nodded at Helen, who nodded in reply. Cynthia slowly removed her hand, wincing from the guilt of having woken Helen with such a violating scare, but what choice did she have? The alternative would have been a shitshow.

It occurred to Cynthia that she spent a fair amount of time rationalizing her actions on the grounds that she lacked the luxury of legitimate choice. Maybe free will really was a lie. Or maybe that was

Folly screwing with her perceptions again, burrowing into her brain matter like a parasitic worm.

On that note, Cynthia whispered, "Come see me in the other room. It's an emergency."

Helen sat up, her hair messy, a frazzled look contorting her face. One strap of a camisole top slid down, the disheveled intimacy motivating Cynthia to look away while the other woman straightened herself out. She owed Helen a meal and an apology. "It better be. I thought that I was gonna have an actual heart attack. Just so we're clear, when I invited you to come see me again, I did *not* mean in the creepiest way possible."

"I'm so sorry." Cynthia looked down at her still-levitating self. At least she wasn't nude anymore. Materializing in one's birthday suit in the middle of the night had serious predatory vibes. "I was on the astral plane dealing with Folly. I think that I finally mastered flight along the way." She drifted to a corner, swinging her legs and arms in a futile attempt at stabilization, ending up with her butt in the air and her elbow jammed awkwardly between the wall and ceiling.

"You haven't mastered shit, from the looks of the position you've wrenched yourself into." Helen swiped a sweatshirt out of a dresser and layered it over her filmy top. "Did your book travel with you?"

"Not that I'm aware of." Cynthia shimmied down the wall until she got her feet on the floor. Grounded at last, she familiarized herself with her surroundings. Spacious bedroom with an antique dresser that Helen stood at, rubbing her eyes in a vanity mirror and twisting her hair into a bun. A couple of retro end tables covered in crystals, candles, and small jars imbued the décor with personality, the ensemble rounded out by a king bed occupied by clueless man. "Will he be okay?"

"My husband? Yeah. He's a heavy sleeper. Don't worry about it." Her words and movements shot through with urgency, she took Cynthia into a chic living room where shiny discs hung mounted on the walls, reflecting specks of light from beyond the front windows. Right, her husband was a famous musician dude. There was some connection to magic in the story of their relationship, too. Curious and curiouser, but the time was not appropriate for asking personal questions. They had more important matters at hand. "Now what's going on that's such a big deal?" Helen led the pair to a white sectional couch and motioned for Cynthia to sit.

She spotted the unmistakable spine of Helen's book right away in a built-in bookcase, the familiar sight of a specific shade of weathered, creased brown leather ushering in a cascade of relief and excitement. Thank goodness they had at least one to work with. They'd do magic, and soon! "I've been meeting with Folly quite a bit lately to get the drop on this prophecy situation. But it's gotten a little out of control, and she put a curse on me. I think it's a curse, at least." She stared at the book. She had to get her hands on that tome, the fat girth of it packed with juicy, crucial insights.

Helen's lips parted. "We aren't supposed to be touching the sixth circle, let alone taking deep dives like you're describing. The consequences could be devastating."

"Yeah, about that. I've never been one to follow the rules and listen to authority. Oops." She hoped that a dose of self-deprecating humor would defuse some tension with levity, but Helen's dour expression suggested otherwise.

Helen got her book. "So you ignored the warnings and it's gotten bad."

Helen's disapproval stung, though the spirit witch was right. Cynthia had broken the rules and paid the price. "Do you hate me?"

"No." She opened her text, releasing the faint, nostalgia-sweet smell of old paper and glue. "I'm sympathetic, because I've been there, and I understand the addictive temptation of magic. How this gift, if we can even call it that, pulls you in and draws you deeper until you're obsessed with getting, having, and finding more. It's insidious that way. Gets into your entire self, your soul, and won't let go."

Right on the money. "So how do we prevent that addiction from taking over?"

Helen's facial features sagged. "By not using magic. I even managed to take a sustained break until this prophecy stuff ramped up. And it's not your fault. I've been having weird dreams again and sensing disturbances in the energetic field. So has Nerissa. Besides, here I am leafing through this book like a total hypocrite, so I'm not exactly taking my own advice, now am I?"

"Do you think that could be one of Folly's tricks? Manipulating us into thinking that our birthright is so volatile and dangerous that we're best served by pushing it away?"

The spirit witch looked up from her pages, a savvy look in her weary eyes. "I think that thinking and talking about her constantly is part of the problem, because once she's in your mind like that, she has a toehold to infiltrate your psyche and instigate all sorts of possession-based invasion that I can't even begin to understand. I should have listened to my mentor from the very beginning when she said to stay away from the sixth circle in every respect. But of course I didn't, and that choice nearly ended in the death of an innocent person."

Real talk about the state of Nerissa might be incoming shortly, with Helen continuing to bring her up. The whole matter of Cynthia flouting the warning that Helen mentioned wasn't to be taken lightly, either. "Hindsight is always twenty-twenty, right?" Out of fear of having to drop the bombshell about Nerissa before the time was right, she didn't give Helen a chance to answer the rhetorical question. "So what do we do to drive her back at this point? I came here to talk about casting a Banish Intruders spell. That's all I can think of, and I don't trust that my level of expertise is sufficient to work with it on my own."

"I've done that spell successfully." Helen rubbed the center of her chest in a circular motion. "On two much lower-level entities, though, and I'm out of my depth when it comes to wrangling elemental sisters. What you're describing sounds as big to me as controlling the weather or starting fires with my mind. I need to call Nerissa for advice before I proceed."

Fuck. "Wait." The word came out pinched. "There's a complication with her."

Helen grimaced. "Excuse me?"

"She's stuck in a book now. My book, which isn't here."

Her scowl hardening, Helen tilted her head. "Stuck in a book? My mentor? What the hell did you do to her?" Pain, anger, and worry ripped through her words.

"I'm sorry. It wasn't intentional. It was a bad situation. She'd possessed one of my friends—she'd been body jumping—and he basically freaked out about it and had a panic attack. We were afraid of losing him, so we did a spell to exorcize her in hopes that we'd get her out of his body and back into her own." It all sounded so chaotic and stupid when said aloud.

Helen gaped. "What the fuck are you talking about? Body jumping? She'd never do that. Nerissa would never mess around with possession-based magic. Her moral principles are too strong, and besides she knows the danger." She pointed an accusatory finger in Cynthia's face. "You're lying."

"I'm not. I swear. When I first met her, she was in the body of some truck driver named Denise. She talked about moving into other people, too, six of them. One for each of us. Then, we did a ritual circle around a fire. Folly showed up, and, after, Nerissa moved into the body of this guy."

"Oh, no," her words wet and wobbly, Helen brought her knuckles to her lips. "She's been compromised somehow by all of this sixth circle involvement. Seduced into doing possession. That's the only explanation. That's how Folly got her out of the way and into the book, by luring her spirit into other bodies before tucking her away on those pages. Rendering her harmless. Once our elders are taken out, we're much weaker. If she's still breathing, we might be able to reunite her flesh with her spirit."

Same logic applied to Cristabel, unfortunately. Cynthia felt awful for leaving New Mexico with Cristabel unresolved, assuming that her entire self had been captured by the book without examining the situation from different angles. "Do you think that their bodies are somewhere on the physical plane still?"

Helen looked ready to puke. "Their? Plural?"

"The chaos mother got stuck in a book, too. Also mine. Four of us went to the Other Place to see Folly, and the chaos mother, Cristabel, didn't come back. Not as a person at least." Cynthia was not exactly coming up roses here, all of the mistakes and mishaps leading back to her choices. She didn't even have Raven anymore. She'd screwed up royally on a few different levels.

"Who are all of these other people that you keep mentioning as involved in magic with you? Please tell me that they're the four other witches. Though you said that one was a guy, and as far as I know the coven mothers and daughters are all female, so I'm extremely concerned that you've rounded up a cast of unauthorized individuals who've been screwing around with magic and causing some real, everlasting damage."

The indictment was harsh and not unfair. "Cristabel was one of us, yes. The coven mother of chaos. The others are four shifters. They have some kind of blessed card deck that gives them access to our magic and a heightened ability to do chain link partner work. So it's that group and my familiar, a dragon named Buddy."

Helen scowled. "Blessed my ass. I'd bet all of my money that those cards are hexed. Where did you meet these four? I hope that you vetted them carefully before doing any spells. You didn't, did you?"

Cynthia looked away, a whirlpool of shame sucking her into an imaginary drain. "No. I didn't, and I'm sorry. The entire situation felt very auspicious, and I went with the flow thinking that spontaneity was central to the process. At least that's what I told myself to write off my own dumb impulsivity. I see now how it was likely a trick, a trap, and I played right into it."

"I've been where you are, so I can't come down too harshly on you. That's part of the game, it seems, getting us so swept up that we don't think through our actions too clearly." She shut the book, hard. "I'm not angry at you. I get it. But the point is that we need to do some damage control before we try Banish Intruders, and undoing possession is above my pay grade. It was above yours, too, which is why you got Nerissa put in a book. To answer your earlier question, I'm hoping that their bodies are in a state of deep sleep, like a coma, and that they aren't physically dead. Nerissa lives across town from me, so we can go check on her. Once we figure out what's going on, we can see if we can somehow do the same for Cristabel. Bottom line is that they both need water ASAP."

"You're so practical." Cynthia managed a measure of deescalating kindness. "And you have such a warm, healing energy."

"Thanks. The practical side has been a new development that arose out of necessity. Or maybe it's my Virgo Moon finally showing itself."

"I'm an Aries." Cynthia played with her nails following the meek attempt to commiserate. She knew enough about astrology to fake interest. "Headstrong and stubborn with a propensity to act without thinking."

"Checks out," Helen said in a jesting way that smoothed some of the rockiness. The spirit witch walked to a closet and took out a fluffy white coat that swished gently above her knees when she stuck her arms in the sleeves. "Your season can't come soon enough. I love spring. It's cold here, so I have something that you can borrow." She tugged a tan pea coat off its hanger. "You're from where, California? That beach you plopped me on had a West Coast feel."

"Missouri, originally." Cynthia wrapped herself in the wool coat, grateful for the cover of added warmth. A poor substitute for a hug and reassurance that everything would be okay, but good enough for now. "But I've travelled a lot and lived all over the country. South America, too."

"Where'd you get the familiar?" Keys jingled in Helen's hand, and she hoisted up a big purse before pushing buttons on a security system mounted beside a large front window.

Cynthia clenched her molars. "Gift from Folly."

"Oh, girl." After speaking the words with resignation, Helen opened the front door, letting in a gust of air that brushed Cynthia's nose. "Let's see if we can get Nerissa and Cristabel out of your book and un-fuck as much of this as humanly possible."

✳

A SHORT DRIVE LANDED THE PAIR IN A TREE-LINED NEIGHBORHOOD full of large, vintage houses with brick facades and other inviting details. While Helen parallel parked on the street, squeezing her Mini Cooper between two cars, Cynthia begged source or God or the universe or whomever to save Nerissa and Cristabel's lives. After Helen called and texted Nerissa numerous times to no avail, Cynthia's optimism deflated.

"I felt that." Helen cranked the steering wheel to the right.

"You kiss their bumper or something? I'm sure it was barely a ding." Cynthia hadn't felt a thing, but Helen obviously knew her car better.

"No, I mean your energy just there. When you reached out to source. Your vibrational field lifted, and it was really beautiful. It was only elevated for a few seconds before it dipped again, but for a little bit there, you were riding high on some good mojo." She put her car in park and turned the key in the ignition, shutting off some classical music that'd been playing on the radio.

Helen felt vibrational fields? Interesting. "You can tap into other peoples' energies as part of your powers?"

"'Tap into' isn't the most accurate way to put it. I can sense how high or low someone's energetic state is if they're in close proximity to me, and along with that, I can tell if their state rises or falls."

"Like empathy but more precise." What she'd described made sense as part of the lexicon of spirit powers.

"Yeah. More or less." She opened her car door and grabbed her purse from the backseat, the bag stuffed full with the grimoire.

An urge for more information, darker information, pulsed in Cynthia. Before she had a second to stop herself, she blurted out, "Can you read minds at all?" Instantly, she regretted the question. It was uncouth, greedy.

Helen's aloof, detached look confirmed Cynthia's hunch.

"Sorry." She scrubbed a hand over her face. "I don't know why I asked that when I knew it was wrong. I don't know what's wrong with *me* sometimes."

"It's okay." Helen patted Cynthia's upper arm. "It's not inherently wrong to ask questions, in fact it's normal and healthy. We just have to be really careful. We're all stumbling our way through this and learning as we go. I learned the hard way, making what seemed in retrospect like every mistake possible on my road to some semblance of wisdom."

"I'm glad you're here. At least I'm not having to fumble around on my own at the moment." Cynthia followed her across the street to a two-story bungalow with a bare-branched tree in the front yard.

Helen asked, "What happened to your four shifters and familiar?"

Once on the doorstep, Cynthia shoved her hands deep into her pockets. "The familiar is in a cabin that we rented. I was...involved with one of the shifters. Things were going really well, but then we got into a huge fight about magic. Of all things. I told him to get lost, and he did."

Helen rang the doorbell, waited, then cupped her hands around her face to peer in one of the windows. "Shoot, the blinds are drawn. Do you care about him?"

"Yeah." Cynthia looked around in case a cop car showed up and noticed their sketchy behavior, but thankfully all she saw were tree branches glazed in the eerie, halogen glows from streetlights. "We'd gotten really close. We even said 'I love you' to each other on the night of the argument. But I drove him away, because that's what I do."

"Well, look." Helen took a break from peeping in the windows to face Cynthia. "If you truly love each other, then you won't let this be the end. You'll reconnect and reconcile. I know that the aphorism about loving something and setting it free is a cliché, but I think there's some wisdom there." She rocked on her heels. "And, if I may be so bold and presumptuous, a lesson."

Cynthia had been humbled enough to accept any advice or help that anyone had to give, especially one of her coven sisters. She couldn't always face the world alone. It was just too hard. Everyone needed friends, allies, and all-around good people in their corner. Why hadn't she realized this sooner, during all of the time she'd wasted being a bitter loner with an edge hard enough to break rocks? "What's the lesson?"

"Chill out on the magic, okay? When you reconnect with this man, find something else that the two of you can enjoy together or have in common. Go to a concert. Or to batting cages. Dance in the rain, take a sewing class together, whatever. Just not this. Just be people, together, enjoying each other's company. It sounds cheesy and naïve, I know, but trust me. That kind of break is crucial when you're followed around all of the time by the type of burden that you and I have."

Helen was clearly sick of magic, and Cynthia had sucked her back in. Cynthia threw her arms around her coven sister and hugged her mightily, delighted when she felt the squeeze returned. "Thank you for everything. For putting up with me and being so understanding." She bit back tears. "For not pushing me away."

"You're welcome. And I want to help. I've been where you are, more or less, and I didn't have any help. We witches have gotta stick together. Like, for real. Blood is thicker than water, and whatever binds us is thicker than blood. So we're good, okay?"

"Okay." Cynthia came to her senses in the moment. "Any sign of Nerissa in there?"

"No, we'll have to break in." Helen rummaged in her purse and withdrew a pink wallet.

That escalated fast. "First attempt is the credit-card-in-the-door-jamb method?"

Helen slipped a blue card from the sleeve that held it. "I love that you know that. We're going to get along just fine, my friend."

This woman was a saint. And actual one who deserved to be consecrated and made into a marble statue. "This isn't my first B&E rodeo." At least the previous times had been out of shelter necessity and not motivated by petty theft, so Cynthia didn't feel like too much of a criminal.

Helen pressed her hip against the door, grunting as she wiggled the card in an effort to pop the lock. A click sounded, but the door still wouldn't give when Helen turned the knob. "No dice. We've got a deadbolt in the way. Any more ideas?"

Cynthia walked to the front windows, leaves crunching underneath her steps. She touched the panes, examining what she could see of the tops and bottoms in the darkness. "These are older, and the one in the middle doesn't have the storm glass down. It's not locked, either, so we'd just need to cut the screen and push the pane up."

Helen stepped to Cynthia's side. "Damn, I'll need to help Nerissa upgrade her home security. But for now, yeah, this might work. Good eye." She cut off the screen with a nail file from her bag, the ripping sound of Nerissa's property being destroyed causing an invasive and brutish discomfort. But it was for the older woman's own good.

Working together with all four of their hands, Helen and Cynthia got the window shoved up. Helen insisted on going in first, so Cynthia gave her an assist by holding on to her legs, then watched the window swallow her from head to torso to feet until she landed with a thud.

"You okay?" Cynthia asked in a hoarse whisper. This would all be funny if it weren't so dire.

"Yeah. Give me your hand, and I'll pull you up." She stuck her arm through the gap.

Cynthia accepted Helen's tug and moved herself into the opening, bracing her feet against the outside wall of the house for support. With an awkward tumble, she landed on the floor of a cozy living room that smelled of roses and incense.

"I'll check the bedroom. She may have gotten into this mess through dream work." Helen cut a confident path across the floor. "How long ago did you meet this Denise woman that Nerissa claimed to be inhabiting?"

A bleak thought struck Cynthia. People died after three days without hydration. "Several days. She needs water."

But Helen was already several steps ahead and unseen. The next thing Cynthia heard was a creak, followed by Helen unleashing some scary cross between a moan and a gasp before saying, "That is not what I expected to see."

TWENTY-FIVE

CYNTHIA RACED AFTER HELEN, HER TONGUE DRYING AS HER THROAT vaulted into her mouth. She wasn't quite sure what she'd expected to see in the bedroom, but the shock that she got certainly wasn't it.

The person who must've been Nerissa floated a few feet above her unmade bed in an arch shape, her belly bowed upward and limbs dangling until her fingertips and the endpoint of her gray braid hovered above a tangle of blankets. Her head and neck hung passively as she rotated slowly in a circle in the same position that Cynthia had found herself in during her stint in the wilderness of mirrors.

Cynthia took solace in the rise and fall of Nerissa's chest. She was breathing. Alive.

Helen was already fast at work in her book, shoving makeshift bookmarks into a couple of sections before flipping forward and back. "No offense, but I think it's best if we avoid partner work for the time being. I can't be sure yet, but I think that I've found a mid-level spirit spell that can unite bodies with wandering spirits. We may need to join forces to make Cristabel whole, since we don't have access to her physical body, but first things first."

"Understood." Ego had no place in this. The priority was saving Nerissa and Cristabel.

Without so much as a throat clearing, Helen dove right in. "Sister Spirit, I, born under your auspices, humbly request your assistance. The flesh of one of ours, Nerissa the Coven Mother of Spirit, has been cleaved from her soul, a separation which causes much duress throughout the sisterhood and puts our dear elder in the way of harm. Please unite the witch before me, matter and essence, so she may walk, love, and breathe as one."

Following some chanting, five fingers of glittery golden light erupted from the center of Helen's book and shot toward Nerissa. Once the beams made contact with her body, they seeped into her skin until she glowed like a freaking human nightlight. Helen read some more, then more, frenetically flipping pages. Shit. The spell might've flopped. Then what? Partner work after all, and the risks that entailed? Cynthia wasn't eager to take any more potentially harmful risks.

Finally, finally, just as hope seemed lost, Nerissa crashed to her bed, gasping and moaning, golden sparkles flittering around her like flecks of static electricity.

Cynthia dashed to the kitchen, fumbled in a cupboard until her trembling fingers closed around a plastic cup, and filled it with water from a pitcher in the fridge. She ran the water to Nerissa, who accepted and drank.

Helen sat beside her mentor and watched while she hydrated herself.

Nerissa put the empty cup on a nightstand. "I've been to a realm that I can only describe as hellish. The Other Place has levels and layers of misery that our most depraved nightmares are unable to conjure." The delivery of her words matched the grim declaration. "Chaos, deceit, and treachery reigned at every turn. How did I get there? How was I separated from myself, and for so long?"

"It's my fault," Cynthia said. "We haven't met. I'm the air witch, and I've been spending far too much time in the sixth circle than I care to admit. I didn't know it could get this bad, but that's no excuse. I'm so sorry."

Nerissa smoothed the frizzes out of her hair and straightened her clothes. "Yes, that's right. I have a fragmented memory of you. We met, I believe, in some form or fashion. While I was away, I somehow remained partially tethered to this world in my human format. Did a part of me inhabit another body for a time?"

"Yeah." Cynthia sat on the edge of the mattress. "That's exactly what happened."

"I would never possess anyone intentionally. How did this happen?"

Helen saved Cynthia with an overly generous interpretation of the truth, "There's been a lot of sixth-circle activity and Left-Hand magic in the field lately, and it managed to overpower and control you. Which is why I'm starting to get onboard with the idea that all of us witches need to get to one location, and soon, to put our heads together about this prophecy. We need to be on the same page with the rules and best practices of our magic, and in-person communication is the ideal way to achieve that."

Nerissa loosed a litany of unhappy sounds. "Yes, I can feel it. Sixth-circle recklessness everywhere. Money magic undertaken for self-interest and without balance. Shapeshifting. Sex rituals. No blood sacrifice that I'm aware of at least, thank goddess."

Bad to worse, minus the sliver of a silver lining about nobody having made a blood sacrifice. Small miracles? "Money magic is listed in the air section, though. How is that a sixth-circle practice?" She hoped that her question didn't sound defensive. She genuinely wanted to know the answer.

"It's not entirely your fault," Nerissa said in a kinder tone than Cynthia likely deserved. "Money magic is a fickle and capricious mistress that somehow always finds a path back to the sixth. I've been practicing the craft since my first menstruation, and I still don't fully understand the baffling, occult techniques involved in mastering the flow of financial currency. Few do, I'm guessing, which is why the world isn't overrun with billionaire witches and their disciples. I thought I understood, but I didn't, and that's how this one unleashed a demon and doppelganger into this world and nearly got us all killed." Nerissa patted Helen on the knee. "But that's a different story."

Helen puffed up her cheeks. "Indeed it is."

Cynthia would love to hear that story—someday. For now, they had both short and long-term problems to wrangle. "The coven mother of chaos is in the same situation as you. She's in a house in New Mexico with her spirit stuck in a book. What should we do?"

Nerissa rubbed her face until it reddened. "I felt her. She's crying out, hanging on by a thread as death closes in. We don't have time to try to get to her physically. Someone will need to find her in the Other Place and attempt this reconnection spell while there." She didn't exactly speak with confidence that any of the people in the bedroom had the chops to pull off such a feat.

"You don't make it sound easy." Helen confirmed Cynthia's suspicion.

"It's not," Nerissa admitted. "Without access to the body of the person whom the practitioner wishes to reunite with its spirit, the risk of failure is high. Cristabel could end up in an even deeper layer of the Other Place, subsumed forever, or even in the body of some random creature like the stray cat down the street. Then, of course, there's the matter of the practitioner."

Cynthia didn't see any other choice. "But the alternative, if we don't do it, is that she for sure stays trapped in the Other Place when her physical body dies in that house."

"Correct," Nerissa said.

Cristabel had cats in her home, Cynthia had smelled them. The pets were of less importance than the person, of course, but Cynthia had a moral obligation to save those animals whose innocent lives she'd gambled with when she cracked her grimoire, too. "I'll do it."

"You didn't even ask what the consequences of failure would mean for you."

It was time for her to stop being so selfish. Who cared if she lived or died? Nobody else did. The least she could do as her last act was try her best to save someone else's life. "Some really awful fate worse than death, right? I get stuck in the body of a rotting corpse for all eternity? Ten demons take turns using me as toilet paper? The psycho queen bitch of the sixth circle wears my skin as a suit every third Friday to her dinner party?"

Helen snorted. "Sorry. That laugh was inappropriate. But that was funny. Please don't die. I'm starting to like you."

Cynthia smiled. Well, maybe one person cared if she lived or died.

Nerissa moved her palms up and down like she was balancing scales.

"Sure. Those are all viable options. Or your eternal soul might end up screaming in a dark pit for all eternity."

"I don't care. I'm going to try." She'd messed up so much and so badly with magic, and now she had an opportunity to fix at least one of the problems that she'd caused. "How can I begin without my book?"

"Are you sure?" Nerissa held Cynthia in a stern look. "This is dangerous, Cynthia." Maybe two people cared if she lived.

And speaking of danger, Cynthia thrived on its edge. This was her wheelhouse. "Positive."

"Sit in a circle with me." Nerissa motioned for the younger women to scoot closer on the bed. "I'll cue you."

They did, and Cynthia grabbed a hand in each of hers to complete the circuit.

Instantly, Nerissa pumped the brakes with a warning, "No, no. The energy field is dark and tumultuous. The influence of chaos is too thick and powerful. Our most nefarious sister has been unleashed, and she runs free. With the ether in a diseased state like this, a spell like the one under discussion is nearly impossible. Chaos will surely take control."

"How do we banish her and clean out the space to save Cristabel?" What a bonus that would be, kicking Folly to the curb and rescuing the chaos mother in one fell swoop. Talk about a good day.

Nerissa said, "We'd need to do the Banish Intruders spell through partner work, using her element against her to return her to the Other Place and seal the rip that's been torn in the veil that keeps her at bay. Incredibly difficult."

"I have some experience with it, as you know," Helen volunteered. "Will that help our odds?"

"Certainly," Nerissa said. "It'll raise them from absolute zero to one in a million."

"So you're saying there's a chance." Helen affected a jaunty tone, her wry humor coming through loud and clear.

Nerissa looked at her protégé the way an annoyed teacher might glance at a naughty but precocious student. "An infinitesimal one."

"So let's go," Helen said.

Cynthia adored her coven sister's bravery, good humor, and the graceful way that she had Cynthia's back. Helen was awesome.

Nerissa harrumphed. "Well, the plus side is that, if we make it out of this, we'll all gain valuable experience and a boost to our powers in ways that we've only dreamed."

"See?" Helen nudged Nerissa. "High risk, high reward."

"Fine." Her word weighted down with both apprehension and hope, Nerissa gestured to Helen's book, open on the floor. "Place your grimoire in the center of our circle and flip to Banish Intruders. If nothing else, at least we'll be together."

Cynthia choked up at the bittersweet confession, fake-coughing to block a sob from escaping. "Thank you. Thank you to both of you."

It was Nerissa's turn for a sarcastic snort. "For what? We haven't even begun, let alone prevailed."

"For accepting me." She squeezed both of their hands, tightening her hold when they squeezed back. "For letting me stay. Nobody really has before."

Helen interjected, "You're stuck with us now. If we all die here tonight, you're probably stuck with us in some terrible afterlife, too."

"Exactly." Nerissa gave Cynthia's clenched grip a little shake. "I'm not going back to that poison pit of an Other Place alone. I'm taking the two of you with me, and we're all staying if it comes to that. On that note, are we ready?"

"We're all in this together." Cynthia sat up tall and evened her breath, clearing her mind.

"All for one and one for all," Helen said.

"Alright, then. Read now, spirit born. Your sister and I will apply our intuition to best assist the spell using the application of our energy. Air born, the goal is not to think too much. Simply feel and intuit. Follow the calling of the deepest energetic force inside of you, the song of your magic. Does that make sense?"

Beautifully put. "Yes."

Part of her was giddy. She'd never done authentic partner work with her fellow witches before, and what a spectacular opportunity. The spells she'd cast with Raven and the others had felt potent and huge, but this was the real deal. And now, she was taking her best shot at setting things right and knew enough to not be completely flying blind. At least, that was the optimistic read.

An even more optimistic part of her held hope that she'd find a way to turn a magical success into repairing the damage with Raven, but it wasn't wise to get ahead of herself. And Cynthia had to start using wisdom. Which meant, for starters, hanging back while Helen took the lead and doing her best to help once her assistance was needed.

"That's my cue." Loose strands of brown waves tumbled forward to shield Helen's face when she bowed her head and began to read the words to Banish Intruders, riffing and improvising to mold the spell to the particularities of the situation, as was common practice.

A loud, bass-note frequency vibrated in the atmosphere, penetrating Cynthia down to her bones and organs. The hum increased in volume, and she gave herself over.

The world was far away, so far away, as Cynthia's consciousness seemed to seep and spread out until the core of her selfhood touched hidden, fantastic dimensions. She was blinded, but aware of her surroundings. She knew for certain that she could still hear once Helen raised her voice to a shout: "Banish her! Banish the elemental source of chaos and exile her to the realm that she rules and governs. Sister Folly, you are unwelcome here, with your lies and tricks. You take, you break, you tear down and ruin. You slander, poison, corrode, and sow doubt and malice. We cannot sustain your energy, so we banish you. Banish! Banish!"

Cynthia stood in an empty room that sparkled like pure gold from floor to ceiling. She wore a jet black cat suit made of some kind of latex, judging by the kinky, decadent gloss. Platform heels tricked out with a stiletto spike grew out of the pants like natural extensions.

Helen and Nerissa were nowhere to be found. This scenario didn't feel like one that would occur in the wake of a successful banishing. She wished for something to happen, an action or event to break the foreboding stillness with an indication that the spell had worked.

A black dot the size of a grape appeared in one shimmering wall. It grew to a hole large enough to push out a basketball and began to eject a tube of black goo that slunk around the perimeter of the room like a scaled-up version of those cheap Fourth of July snakes.

"Snakes?" Folly's taunting voice, of course, as the hole excreted an ever-growing quantity of the cylindrical, serpentine mass. "You're quite fond of those, aren't you?"

A mere few days ago, Cynthia's heart would have sunk at this depressing but familiar turn of events to remind her that she wasn't in control and that her magic wasn't good enough. Now, though, she was just pissed. "Fuck you. This outfit is ugly. Where are my friends?"

Details took shape in the tube along the golden floorboards, a snake's head at the emergent end followed by a body of scales. "Don't you want to know the significance of the golden room?" She sounded like she really wanted to talk about her eyesore paint job, her obvious desire stimulating the oppositional-defiant side of Cynthia to cause as much frustration as possible. At least she could gain leverage by being a pain in the ass. She'd always been good at that.

"No. It's stupid. Where are Helen and Nerissa?"

Folly hissed, baring fangs. "Somewhere else. They should have thought through the list of possible destinations before they tried to *banish* me. And my symbolism is *not* stupid, you smelly bag of flesh."

Cynthia faced off with the angry demon, taking stock of her proverbial arsenal. This asshole had a weakness—her ego. But narcissism didn't provide enough ammunition to take her down. Cynthia needed more, and the solution was close. But not close enough. She mentally recited what she remembered of the Banish Intruders spell. The answer was in there somewhere.

"Cat got your tongue?" More and more of Folly slithered out of the hole. She was layering on top of herself now, climbing the walls to smother them with a claustrophobic layer of dark, scaly padding. "Or are you, shall we say, feeling the squeeze as you collapse under the crushing pressure of your own unsanctioned inquiries?" She mocked Cynthia's voice, "Where does magic come from? Where does it go? Stupid questions. *You're* the one who is stupid, Cynthia Fields. Everyone agrees. Your teachers. Your mother. All of those boys and men who used you as a sperm toilet but would die of embarrassment if their friends assumed that you were their girlfriend."

"There are no stupid questions." Cynthia stuck out her tongue. "Only stupid answers. And stupid looking rooms and outfits." She lifted her leg and wiggled her foot in the air, buying time with banter while she wracked her brain for something better than rattling Folly's cage with cheap insults. "Seriously, why do you dress me in this weird shit when I come see you in the Other Place? This is, like, stuff that a teenage girl assumes that Satanists wear to sacrifice puppies in the woods."

"I'll be sliding into your skin soon enough, don't you worry. In case you must know, I dress you to live vicariously. Once I'm wearing your shell as I please, I'll drape your hollowed-out meat suit in furs, leathers, and silks. The finest fashions. Cheap thrills, too. Lingerie. Fetish wear. Because those wrinkled parkas and khaki shorts you choose are *hideous*, honey."

"Oh yeah?" Cynthia circled the room to keep tabs on the ever-expanding Folly, who now filled half the walls in a striking contrast of black-on-gold. A whirlpool swirled up from her depths, an epiphany of sorts. Folly needed to possess other bodies to stay viable. That was part of it. Had to be, given how heavily she leaned on that particular ability. But there was more. "Why me? You don't seem to like me or find me interesting or important, let alone a threat. Why are you so obsessed with me, and so much that you put Helen and Nerissa away just to deal with me directly? If I'm such a worthless piece of shit, why won't you leave me alone?"

"Never you mind." Her hissed reply was undeniably tense. On the defensive. Good.

"Oh, I mind very much. I mind because my friends and I are grasping at straws trying to figure out how to save the world from you. What's your problem, anyway? It's not just that you enjoy hurting people for the sake of sadism, is it? You crave something that you can't have. You desire. I feel the void in you, aching to be filled. I can tell that there's an object that you want badly, because you're always so mad and thirsty. You aren't just mean, you're unsatisfied. What are you after, Folly? What do you want?"

"Shut your whore mouth."

Cynthia laughed, freshly empowered by this dumb serpent's worn out attempts to debase her. "Never."

In that moment, her glossed heels clicking across a tacky, lacquered floor the color of a spray tan, Cynthia tapped into a grand sentiment. She held the cards with Folly, fundamentally. She always, inherently did, and so did the other witches. Because like Helen implied, despite all of the harm she was capable of causing, Folly could never create. She was only able to take, break, covet, copy, mimic, commandeer, possess, steal, and spoil. She lacked the ability to generate anything new, and this shortcoming drove her crazy. She never stopped overcompensating.

Successive taps echoed off iridescent walls as the witch and the serpent circled each other. There was more. Folly was obsessed with possession because the only way that she retained her power was by stealing it from others. Folly hated the witches because she coveted what they had. What she could never have for her own in pure form. That's why she wanted inside of everyone so badly all of the time.

More revelations landed like thunder: Folly had no inherent element of her own. Chaos was a parasitic force that latched onto other elements only to tear them apart in perverse pursuit of entropy. That was the secret of chaos.

"What are you thinking about?" An unchecked tremor shook Folly's voice.

"None of your fucking business, you leech."

She drew back her bulky head. "What are you talking about?"

"I'm on to you." And was she ever. There was one final, tiny but crucial detail. Folly had first appeared to Cynthia soon after her million-dollar questions—*Where does magic come from? Where does it go?*—had come to her.

The hairs on the back of her neck stood at alert, euphoria fueling her. She got flesh bumps as the last piece clicked into place. Folly didn't know the answer to those questions, either, and she wanted them obsessively. And she'd jump from witch to witch to shifter until she ended up in the skin of someone who did know.

Why, well, that was a puzzle to solve in the future.

In the present, Cynthia had a good guess for how to complete the Banish Intruders spell. Given how dependent Folly's existence was on her external environment, it stood to reason that Cynthia could use that environment against her.

Improvising, Cynthia held out her arms in one long line and focused her stare on a spot on the golden wall. "I banish you, intruder. Your chaos is unwelcome here, so I send you back to your realm where you will stay. Sow division on your own time and terms, for this realm belongs to the sisterhood."

After some screaming from Folly that failed to break Cynthia's focus, the hole began to suck the snake back up, the walls spitting out sparkle bursts as they flexed and pulsed. Foot by grotesque foot, the elemental sister of chaos slunk backward into the pit from which she'd crawled.

"Cynthia," Helen shouted. "It's working. Reach into that hole once she's all the way in and pull us out. Cristabel is here, too. I think that we managed to rejoin her with her body."

Once the last of the serpent vanished, Cynthia winced and stuck her hand in the gap that'd started to shrink. Sure enough, she pulled out Helen, Cristabel, and Nerissa, each of whom stumbled out. "It worked!" Cynthia hugged them both.

"It worked." Nerissa laughed and cried at the same time. "By goddess, it worked."

"What a wild ride." Cristabel blinked like a stunned deer. "I need to call my sitter to stop by and take care of my kitties. I have a feeling that I'll be away for a while."

"Let's go to my place so you can take care of that, dear one." Nerissa stroked the other elder's arm. "It's wonderful to finally meet you. I can't wait to show you my books."

"Not so fast," Folly's voice echoed through what remained of the closing gap. "We still have a bargain to settle up. You owe me."

"I wouldn't owe you a cup of piss if you were on fire," Cynthia said to the hole in the wall, holding Helen, Cristabel, and Nerissa close. "Go away."

"Oh yes you do," she taunted. The opening contracted to the size of a pinprick. "And if you attempt to banish me and seal the rip in the veil before you pay your debt to me, your spell is null and void, as I have a clear pathway to return to you. Now make your choice."

Just as the gap sealed and Folly, silenced, slipped into banishment, Raven and Buddy appeared in the middle of the room.

TWENTY-SIX

Folly's final act had rendered the other four women immobile and mute, leaving Cynthia effectively alone in the crucible of her own making. Alone except for Raven and Buddy, staring at her with all of the severity of a ticking time bomb.

"Cynthia, baby." Raven wore black jeans with a rip in the knee and looked happy—and relieved—to see her. Her heart broke as panic set in. Would she end up hurting him again and in the most awful, final of ways, coerced into making a terrible choice? "What's going on? Why did you hail us to this place? Don't get me wrong, I want to talk things over, but I'm trying to get my footing."

Buddy arched her back like an angry cat, swishing her magnificent tail side-to-side. "Danger. Buddy dragon smell evil."

You got that right, Buddy. I smell it too. How to halt and banish the force once and for all, though, eluded her. But she had to find a way to save the ones she loved.

"What's she talking about?" Following a troubled glimpse at the familiar, Raven gestured to the frozen women. "And what's the deal with them? Does all of this have anything to do with how you saved Cristabel?"

"More or less." Worry ate her up. Her vision sharpened, hyperfocusing on Raven, then Buddy, then Raven again as she waited for some sign that the other shoe was about to drop. What was she going to do? With Folly invisible and, presumably, plotting unseen, she didn't know how to spar with her. For starters, though, she'd come clean. "Look, I haven't told you the entire story. I told you how Folly wanted you dead, but there's more. The worst part. That night that I came back with Buddy, she'd blackmailed me at the very end. She said that unless I killed you, she'd kill Buddy. I should have known that there would be strings attached. I'm so sorry."

His mouth dropped open. "You've been planning to kill me?" The shock that slammed into his face—devastating didn't even begin to describe it. He'd trusted her, and she'd sabotaged that most precious of gifts. She felt so sick. She wanted to die, right there on the spot, in her absurd, trashy outfit.

Die so Raven and Buddy didn't have to.

"No," she cried. "Of course not. I would never. That's why I waited until the last minute to make a decision. Because I didn't know what to do, and it was tearing me up."

"Fuck!" He buried his hands in his own hair, doubling over before righting himself. "I want to believe you. I want to trust you. But I can't get close enough to you, Cynthia. You've been pushing me away this entire time, tender one minute and harsh the next. We make love, and confess our feelings, and right after you drive me away. And now this. I honestly don't know what to believe or trust anymore." He tapped the side of his head in a frantic motion. "Is she in here, Cynthia? Has she taken control and possessed you?"

"Of course not." She ran to him and grabbed on, not letting go even when he tried to pull away. "I know that this is insane. I don't blame you for having doubts about my trustworthiness or motives. I'm aware that I fuck up constantly, and in ways that hurt other people. I'm not that great of a person, and I know it. But I'm trying to be better. But I meant what I said in that cabin. I love you, as much as I'm able to love. Those feelings that I felt, that I feel, are real and true. I don't know yet how to undo this curse, but I'll figure something out. I'd never hurt you." She poured all of her sincerity right into him. "Never desert you. Never betray you."

She'd never again treat him like she'd been treated. She'd break the cycle today, here and now, in the center of the golden room.

His Adam's apple bobbed up and down like swallowing her promises was a struggle. Not that she blamed him. She was a tough pill. "So why are we here, in this place?" his whisper baffled, he continued, "Why are you dressed ritualistically? Why are the others frozen in place? If Folly is pulling the strings, why isn't she with us?"

The fight-or-flight instinct having ebbed, Cynthia found herself better able to think, so she anchored her spinning thoughts with her insights from earlier. "She isn't pulling the strings at all. It's a mirage. An illusion. She's the tiny man behind the curtain."

"I'm sorry, what?" He shook his head. "That flies in the face of literally every assumption we've been going on since we met."

"I know." She brought their intimate knot of interlaced fingers to rest between their chests. "We had it wrong. Backwards. She isn't mighty at all, she's a copycat and a follower, feeding off preexisting energies. The only way to win her games is not to play, because once I step off the board, she has no more moves to make."

He liberated a pinky to scratch his pierced eyebrow. "I think that I follow the metaphor there, but I'm not positive."

She said with a touch of humor, "Sometimes when you're hoisted on the horns of a dilemma, you've just gotta step off and fly."

"Okay, that was definitely a mixed metaphor. I thought that we were stepping off a game board."

"We are." She drew in an inhale, releasing with her exhalation about a million pounds of toxicity, negativity, sorrow, and grief. She released Folly, her threats and lies, and all of the anguish caused by the ultimatum.

While she was at it, breathing out more breath than she thought she'd had in her, Cynthia let go off all of the pain she'd accumulated over the years, all of the residue accumulated from the hurts, betrayals, humiliations, and letdowns caused by other people.

All of the times she'd let herself down by having weak boundaries or compromising her values or principles for a shot at being liked, securing a warm bed for the night, or winning a fleeting bit of attention. She released that heaviness, too.

All of the guilt and shame she carried for not valuing and loving herself with the ferocity that she deserved. All of the times that she'd mistreated others because, well, if she didn't deserve love, then nobody else did, either. Gone.

On the wings of her never-ending gusts, she let all of that shit go. Gone, gone, gone. At the bottom of her final out breath, when her lungs could expel no more, she felt a subtle but massive shift in the energetic field. Folly had left their presence and their lives and gone far away, taking Cynthia's accumulated burdens with her. Maybe she'd eat what Cynthia had purged and grow stronger. Maybe through some alchemy, a part of her elemental evil would dissipate.

Who knew? The course of future events, and for how long she'd stay away, was anyone's guess, but in the moment, the liberation was pure and sweet. Cynthia said, "I'm free. You're free, and Buddy is free. We're free to go."

Buddy spread her wings as widely as they'd stretch in the cramped room. "No more evil."

"How did you do that?" Raven gazed upon her with such adoration and respect that she never wanted the moment to end. "How did you just release?"

Helen had it wrong. Or at least was being overly pessimistic. The witches did have a gift, if they used their power correctly. "Air magic."

"I knew that you were an angel."

"Let's not go that far."

"How about you're my angel. My fallen angel."

"Not overtly cheesy and kinda badass. I'll allow it."

"Okay, good." He leaned in close, closer, until their lips brushed. They weren't even kissing, and it was the most tender moment that Cynthia had ever experienced. "I love you."

"I love you too." She gave herself over to those words, at long last and for the very first time. The power of her speech, the declaration of loving someone else, filled her wholly. "I love you." With no defenses left, she collapsed into his arms.

He held her. Rocked her. Did all of the things. Time lost all meaning while Cynthia soaked in all of the love that Raven offered and gave back every morsel that she had to give. Miraculously, the more she gave, the more she *had* to give, so she kept giving.

Amazing, that love wasn't as scarce as she'd grown to assume.

"I'm really sorry to interrupt your beautiful moment." Helen punctuated her sentence with a theatrical, fake cough. "But is it okay if we leave in a minute? This place is kind of headache-inducing."

Oops. Time hadn't *actually* lost all meaning, and the others had been waiting patiently for a while.

"Of course." Cynthia got herself together, stepping out of Raven's hold. "Let's go home."

Nerissa added, "Let's regroup at my house. Cristabel can arrange a cat sitter, and Helen can call her husband. Then we'll look at some books and figure out our next move."

Her expression somber, Cristabel said, "She isn't gone. Not forever. She's dormant, but planning. We have to get to Peru and convene with the others. Witches. Shifters. Familiars. Conduits. We must be in the same place to confront the prophetic unfoldings head on."

"What are conduits?" Cynthia wasn't jazzed by the prospect of having to figure out some whole new magical thing, but this wasn't about her.

Cristabel leaned against a shiny wall, fidgeting with one of the scarves around her neck. "These are humans who are serving as receptors for messaging codes. I'm not quite sure yet what purpose they serve or how they'll be needed, but my intuition tells me that they're absolutely crucial."

"It's Fyre," Raven said with certainty. "Transmitting messages through their music. I have a lot of it written down. It's like programming codes for astral travel."

"Wait, wait." Helen didn't appear to be taking the latest piece well. "You're saying that Brian has to be a part of this again? That doesn't seem fair. He never asked to have a role. He's suffered enough and just wants to live as normal of a life as possible."

"Well, to be fair, none of us asked for this," Nerissa said. "But if he's been duty-called, refusal to heed the call will create even more problems. On the plus side, the two of you will be together in Peru."

Helen was not, as far as Cynthia could tell, an inhabitant of this plus side. "I feel so torn. It's like I want to protect him, but I'm aware that I have a duty to this prophecy, too. I'm just tired of dragging more people into this."

Cynthia went to her coven sister. "I understand. But you aren't dragging anyone in. If anything, we're all being dragged into this by some presence that's bigger than each of us individually. But we're stronger together."

Her features softened. "You're right. Thank you."

Nerissa said, "Let's leave. There's sixth-circle residue here that's causing pain, and we can't have anyone excessively compromised while we're undertaking a transport spell."

"You don't have to tell me twice," Cynthia said. "Let's tune in."

Nerissa recited a spell from memory, everyone else tuning in with their meditative focus and attention. Following a blackout period, Cynthia awoke slumped on one of Nerissa's living room chairs. She did an immediate headcount. Everyone was accounted for.

Cristabel made a plan with her sitter, who fortunately was able to stay at her house indefinitely. The elders relocated to the den to look at books while Helen walked down the hallway, called Brian, and explained the latest development.

Buddy seemed content to sniff a scented candle on one of Nerissa's end tables.

Raven got in touch with the others down in Costa Rica, standing by the fireplace as he had a hushed conversation with someone. Once off the phone, he pocketed his cell. "Want to step outside for a cigarette?"

"I assumed that we'd quit somewhere along the way."

"We'll quit tomorrow. Today is an exception, wouldn't you say?"

"Fair. We'll share it. Deal?'

"Deal."

Nerissa had a stone bench in her front lawn that Cynthia hadn't noticed before, and Raven led them to it and lit up, igniting a tiny signal flare in the velvet night. "Portia is all gung-ho to bring the deck."

"The deck that's caused more harm than good?" She accepted the cigarette and drew smoke into her lungs before blowing it out.

"That's the one," he said sardonically.

"I'm guessing that you figured out pretty quickly in the conversation that there was no talking her out of it."

"Correct." He took the cigarette. "Besides, I wonder if throwing it away or giving it away would ultimately cause more trouble, you know?

By creating the very real possibility that it will end up in even worse hands. At least if it's with us, we can keep tabs on it."

One cool thing about having other people around was that they had different perspectives and ideas in difficult situations. Cynthia didn't have to solve every single problem in her life all by herself. "Good point." She took a drag, watching the smoke mingle with the predawn air, dew already kissing her tongue. Morning would come soon. They ought to get whatever sleep was possible and then start the wheels turning on the Peru trip. "Maybe Helen or one of the elders can diagnose it. Clean out its energy."

"Good thinking." He took his last hit off their shared smoke and offered her the rest.

She polished it off, crushed the spark against her heel, and stuck the butt in her back pocket. "I'm glad we're together." She leaned her head against his arm and soaked in a moment of silence that followed.

"Me too." He spoke with a gentle aura of authenticity. "Whatever happens, we're together and have each other."

It was funny to Cynthia how the twists and turns in her path had landed her farther away, physically, from her destination, though from a mental standpoint she felt closer.

From an emotional standpoint, she absolutely felt closer. To Raven. To Helen and the other witches. To Buddy. To magic.

She even felt closer to herself, the scared, broken, resilient, tough, and vulnerable woman whom she was finally learning to love. Before she could love others or be loved, she had to learn to love herself. Cliché, but true. Since Cynthia was apparently all about clichés now, while she was at it, she embraced the principle that life was about the journey, not the destination. Because along that journey, if a person surrendered to a moment without resistance or expectation, allowing the present to simply *be*, that's where the beauty blossomed. In that space, growth occurred. Love formed. Magic happened.

Where does magic come from? Where does it go?

Cynthia had always known the answer, deep down. Even when she'd thrashed and struggled and fought, she'd always known that true magic came from her heart.

***

Thank you for reading! Did you enjoy? Please add your review because nothing helps an author more and encourages readers to take a chance on a book than a review.

And don't miss more in the *Coven Daughters* series coming soon! Until then read EMBERS, the first novella in the *Coven Daughters Origins*, available now. Turn the page for a sneak peek!

Also be sure to sign up for the City Owl Press newsletter to receive notice of all book releases!

SNEAK PEEK OF EMBERS

Thom James couldn't pinpoint, with absolute certainty, when awareness of a void in his heart switched from minor nuisance to undeniable ache. On the latest routine morning in a long string, though, the abyss had stolen more than usual.

He pulled in a drag of cigarette smoke, the woodsy flavor more rote than satisfying as a rush of chemicals cancelled out the minty flavor of toothpaste. An exhale left his lungs in a choppy whoosh, his breath ejecting filmy gray residue. Here he was again, going through the motions.

He touched the cold glass of his hotel suite window and stared down at Nashville. Or Raleigh. Or perhaps his band had played Atlanta last night. Maybe they'd delivered their music to an arena of thirty-thousand cheering faces in Orlando or Dallas.

Didn't matter. This midsize city at morning was the same as any other: paper doll cutouts of buildings, drab redbrick and concrete tones, crumbling infrastructure. The theater of the mundane unfolded twenty stories below while he watched in a fruitless search for affect or even inspiration. A smattering of affordable cars lurched to jobs. A man wearing a backpack scurried down a sidewalk, prompting a cluster of pigeons to lift off in frantic flight.

Nearing the end of his forties and having played cities like this since his teen years, Thom had seen it all.

He'd felt the previous night, yes he had, high on the usual maelstrom of lust and fame.

At night, cities were sexy, glitter-sprinkled light shows teeming with promises, spectacles tailored to cater to the appetites. Come morning, though, they were little more than blight on the landscape. Interchangeable, half-real, used.

He spied a silver arch not far off in the distance, an artistic piece of architecture curving toward the clouds amid downtown buildings that weren't quite skyscrapers. Right, they'd played St. Louis the night before. That's where he was, not that it mattered.

A cynical bark of a laugh jumped out of his lips. Hollow mornings were the price he paid for his indulgent nights. The rock star's debt always came due.

From behind him came a soft, feminine moan. The bed squeaked, and the latest woman occupying whatever he called his bed sighed. The tomb in his chest gaped wider, a mocking reminder that a well-adjusted man would feel tender emotions right about now. His stomach tightened as his head spun. He stubbed out his smoke on the windowsill, snuffing his ennui.

Water rushed from the bathroom sink. Bodily noises of teeth getting scrubbed, gargling, and spitting followed. Thom smiled sadly. If their time together had been intended to be more than one night, the sounds of her freshening up might inspire intimate anticipation.

"Hey." Her voice, thick with sleep, belied a lilt of hope that toppled dominoes of guilt and regret inside him.

He turned to where she stood. A thin, white sheet swaddled her supple form, shielding the soft breasts that he'd enjoyed to the fullest. Her full-chest tattoo peeked out from the top of the material in coy glimpses of flowers crawling through emerald networks of jungle foliage.

His gaze travelled through the artwork on her chest and up to her lips, across freckled cheeks and northward to eyes as green as fresh-cut summertime grass. An inferno of chaotic red waves blazed past her shoulders.

She was quite pretty. Beautiful even, in an unconventional way with her strong features and robust bone structure. Ultimately, though, just another groupie. Another American woman in a city he couldn't place.

He didn't even know her name.

God, she deserved so much better than an empty fuck from the lowlife likes of him.

"Hi." He slid a piece of her hair through his fingers, appreciating the silkiness as he reminded himself not to be a dick. Quality aftercare in these situations kept his reputation sterling. "Sleep well?"

"Yeah. You knocked my ass out. I think it was that second orgasm that did me in. Or maybe the third. I'm pretty sure I'll have sweet dreams of the sexy British rocker for the rest of my life." With a siren's smirk, she snagged his pack of smokes off the nightstand and lit up.

Blowing rails through her nostrils, she jutted her chin in parry. Or defiance, daring him to condescend to her. Bloody hell. This bird was a live wire like none other, crackling with white heat.

Thom tilted his head to one side. Her brazenness, a shameless quality to her, piqued his intrigue. He slipped a finger into the swell of her cleavage and loosened the fabric concealing her breasts. "What's your name?"

She blew smoke in his face, the blast making him cough and blink as his eyes burned, though she didn't resist when her sheet fell to the floor. "You're an absolute pig." A touch of levity to her true statement betrayed affection. "Luckily for you, the accent *almost* makes up for it."

"You're still here. And naked again, I might add." Beneath his unbuttoned jeans, his prick swelled. He plucked the cigarette from her mouth, laid it in the ashtray, and guided her back to bed with two firm hands pushing against the velvety slopes of her shoulders.

"Touché." She walked backward in accordance with his motions, running slender fingers through the mat of hair covering his bare chest. The redhead flopped on the bed and spread her legs, her crooked smile both vulnerable and caustic. "I have a lot of problems."

His hands were busy attacking his zipper when fresh waves of shame and disgust pummeled him. Christ, what was wrong with him, screwing women as if they were mere objects? What a scoundrel he was.

"I'm so sorry." He slashed a hand through his hair, the strands as unkempt as the rest of his life, and pulled his thick mess into a ponytail in some pitifully symbolic effort to order his chaos. "Are you hungry? I can have some room service sent up if you'd prefer discretion, but if you'd like to go out, that's fine too. Or I can call you a car if you're ready to get out of here."

Her smile spread while she appraised him with a knowing, green-eyed gaze. "You don't need to pay me with food. I'm a slut, not a whore.

Nothing against whores, but judge me correctly." Though she spoke in a jesting tone, her words cut like a scalpel.

She hadn't closed her legs—gorgeous pink pussy, trimmed strip of red hair—but now Thom wasn't sure if he felt aroused, embarrassed, ashamed, or some unwholesome mix of all three. He stood there blinking like an idiot, his face hot and a nest of brown pubes sprouting through his open fly while a spotlight shone on his mortified conscience.

"You aren't either one of those." He stammered, his mouth dry. Though he meant what he said—his promiscuous arse had no right to pass judgment—the words came off forced and ridiculous. "You're a beautiful person. I wished I would have gotten to know you a little better before we ended up naked."

He meant that too. Yet some unseen force stopped him, time and again, from seeking out a deeper level of intimacy with women. It was easier to approach them as empty conquests.

Easier to forget them. Easier to keep his emotional wall high and solid.

She smacked her forehead. "A beautiful person? That's the cringiest platitude I've ever heard. Can we please fuck? I don't need to witness you thumping every branch on the way down to rock bottom."

Tension and self-consciousness flew out of him in an inexplicable gust. For all his cavorting and playing the part of boorish lout, Thom never quite felt at ease or at peace. He envied the woman on the bed, how she lay there open and free, unshaken.

"Nice metaphor." He swiped the half-burned cigarette out of the ashtray, drew down a hit, and handed the smoke to his temporary partner. "Were you an English major?" She had to be in her mid-thirties and was articulate enough to be a college grad.

Her ample chest swelled as she partook, falling when she blew out three wobbly smoke rings. He studied the multicolor splash of ink capping her breasts and marveled at the way those inquisitive eyes of hers tracked the vapory hoops as they floated before dissipating. "I'm an English professor."

He sat next to her on the bed, and she scooted over to accommodate. Considering her cue, he trailed three kisses from her shoulder to her collarbone, seeking her scent. Floral and spicy notes mixed with her tang from below. Her exotic scent suited her perfectly, even in the stark light of day. "That's sexy. Will you read to me?"

"Why, can't you read?"

For the first time, he noticed precise details of her voice. Beneath the smokiness and snark lay a melody. She spoke like a song, her rhythm rising and falling. Thom buried his face in her neck, sampling her flesh with teasing flicks of his tongue. She whined a little pleasure noise, and with that he was stiff as a bat again. "Tell me your name. Please."

"No. It's more fun this way. Anonymous."

He urged his cock from his pants and rubbed the swollen head against the soft expanse of her outer thigh, seeking relief from the pressure building in his lower belly.

"Well, you're anonymous to me, sweetheart. I'm a famous bassist, and you know exactly who I am."

The feel of his own hot breath against her skin, the arrogant truth of his cocky words, made boiling cum swirl in his balls. Sure, he got off on his own fame, notoriety, and status. No fool would dare nominate him for sainthood.

"Your ego is out of control." She punched her hips up, and he took the cue and danced teasing fingertips down her smooth stomach. "And I actually don't know you. Right now I have the idea of you, the fantasy. Which is precisely what I want."

"Fair enough." His pulse accelerated. Blood fled his brain and filled his engorged cock. As his eyes feasted upon his partner's inviting form, he took a moment to admire the length and girth of his impressive member, the healthy purple coloring of the swollen tip. He could not wait to feed this luscious, vexing piece of feminine excellence to his hungry beast.

But for now, her pleasure was his priority. Thom might be a cad, but at least he left his bedmates with fond memories of his skills. "What do you want me to do, love? Finger you? Eat you? Rub my dick over your clit?"

"Damn, I'm all about your dirty talk." Her thighs quivered, the musky smell of her arousal intensifying.

He played with the soft curls on her mound, kneeling between her legs to admire her swollen folds and the visible bulge of her sensitive nub. He sunk two fingers inside her, licking his lips at the first touch of pussy, a tease of what his prick wanted so bad. In smooth motions, he moved those two fingers in and out, every ounce of his being committed to holding off on the raging urge to plunge inside of her and take, take, take.

"Yeah," she said, eyes glazed and lips parted.

"You want me to use my fingers?" His rod flexed, a bead of pre-cum leaking out.

Driving women crazy with his talents made him feel like a god. The potent rush of ego beat a quick one-off any day.

"Please." She sat up, her eyelids and pale lashes hooding her eyes when her gaze fell to the piston work of his hand.

"Jesus, I can see your clit. I can see how big and full it is, ripe." He withdrew from her opening and used the two slick fingers to spread her folds, making a V through which the glistening button popped like a red candy apple.

She moaned a reply and began to pinch and rub her own stiff nipples.

"I'm going to stroke your clit now, slowly with my thumb. I don't want you to come too fast, but you're so round and red I don't know if I'll be able to prolong your climax. Forgive me."

Another unintelligible grunt from Ms. Articulate English Professor. Christ, this was fun.

He'd circle back to this very moment every time he felt a flare of remorse about how freely he fucked around.

He brought the pad of his thumb to her target, admiring the smooth, slick feel of the bump as he stroked in a big circle. A few passes around, and her clit went into spasms. She lost control, bucking and moaning as she came apart.

Using his opposite hand, Thom slid a finger back into her, hooking his digit on her equally flush G-spot, and rubbed methodically. Her inner muscles clenched and released all around his plunges, her body's responses proof of orgasm.

With a sharp cry, she froze. Her eyes stretched wide, and her jaw dropped. "Oh fuck, I'm coming."

"You sure are." Once she was done, he grabbed his dick and stroked up and down, slowly, offering a little show. "You ready for more?"

"Hell yes."

"Ah, give me that fiery red pussy, baby." With an unbridled growl, he fell on her and plunged inside her pocket of warm, liquid heaven. She'd sworn last night that she was on the pill, and he trusted that she was telling the truth.

Firm walls molded around his cock, sucking like hungry mouths as he mindlessly thrust in and out. "Goddamn, that's some bloody good snatch." He cupped one of her large breasts, pumping hard and fast in selfish pursuit of release.

"Thanks." She wrapped her legs around his hips and dragged her trimmed nails down his back. "I take good care of it. Only the best."

A laugh, this one earnest and bereft of the poison of cynicism, sprang from his lips. A weird, bubbly sensation cavorted in Thom, unnerving but not unwelcome. He slowed his strokes and gazed deeply into his partner's pretty eyes. "Does this feel good?"

"Yes," she whispered, squeezing his shoulders. His lover smiled at him, and the bubbles in his chest and abdomen swelled larger.

He kissed the tip of her nose before resuming his work, taking care this time to angle his pelvis so the root of his shaft connected with her clit when he withdrew on the down stroke.

When she began to moan again and her walls tightened and released in time, Thom closed his eyes and savored her. Her smell, her sounds, the comforts of her softness and sex. A lump lodged in his throat, and the inside of his nose stung. He'd never made love, but perhaps his current experience of the sex act amounted to a poor man's version.

"Thom, you're so good." She fell limp.

Before he could think too much about those false words she spoke and what it would mean for them to become true, he sped his plunges to the frantic, needy pace required to bring him home.

Her eyes darkened into a dirty, sinful stare. "You're about to come. Your balls are high and tight now, huh? Full of a big load you can't wait to blow."

"You're so fucking hot I can't stand it." He clutched her tit, his skin tingling as he rushed to the end. Base, unspeakable need overcame him, the tension below his waist ratcheting to a fiendish craving.

"Come all over me."

Heat unspooled near the base of his shaft. He gaped at the spot where their bodies joined, marveling at the wonder of his prick slipping in and out, his rigid flesh coated with the glisten of her juices. The second relief tore in, he pulled out and gave three final tugs right below the ridge of the head.

Thom cried out while he splintered into shocks of ecstasy. Blank and blissed with awestruck emptiness, he gawked as thick white ropes splashed her breasts, hair, and cheek.

"Fuck." Aftershocks reverberated through his body. He rubbed his stomach and squeezed his still-stiff member until the final drops of fluid eked out and dripped onto her chest.

"Now lick it off me and feed it back into my mouth."

"Pardon?" He struggled to regulate his breathing, clobbered by the double whammy of a life-erasing orgasm and her request. No woman had ever asked *that* of him.

"You heard me."

Lost in the haze of her thrall, he obeyed, scooping up his own bittersweet semen with eager lips and tongue. When he took her mouth, he forgot all about the nasty, kinky deed and melted into their first kiss.

And what a first kiss it was.

Her effort was predictably assertive, skilled from practice, though more sensual than he would have guessed. But as their tongues stroked, played, gave, and took in a series of caresses and lazy searching, a frighteningly glorious thought sunk hooks into Thom's mind and heart.

I could get used to this.

"Oh, shit." She broke the kiss with a start and lunged for a bedside table, grimacing when she palmed her wristwatch.

"What's wrong? Are you alright?" He reached for her, overcome by an irrational worry that he'd bolloxed something up and caused her to hate him. Absurd that he cared, because if she hated him, she'd leave without a fuss.

She shook her head while bending over, her pale and naked bottom a curvaceous temptation dangling just outside his reach. Last night's clothes flew onto the bed—the red bustier, black leather miniskirt, and matching jacket she'd worn to the Chariotz of Fyre after-party where they'd met. "I missed my flight."

Her body in that outfit had turned his head hard and made his tongue wag with an unspeakable urge to have her. But by now, he ought to have been feeling profound relief when faced with her impending departure.

As his nameless lover shimmied and wiggled into her clothing, the reality of her slipping away lanced him. He glanced at his hands, then the floor. *I do not want to lose her*, Thom thought with an odd and startling clarity.

Normally, he lost interest in a woman after the two of them had had their fill of sex and laughs. Yet here he was moping like a schoolboy in puppy love when he damn well ought to be thanking the good lord above that the groupie of the day was about to bolt without tears, begging, or his insistence. "Can I help?"

"No." She took a cell phone from her purse and rang someone while sliding her pretty feet into danger heels.

"What's up, Megan?" A faint male voice spoke through the line.

Thom clenched his teeth and glowered at a random spot on the wall. Megan. The stupid bloke on the phone got to know her name, but he didn't. What had this wanker done that Thom hadn't to earn the privilege?

"I'm so sorry, Gary, but I'm gonna be late for the setup tonight. I travelled to St. Louis for a work thing, and I missed my flight out. I'm going to rent a car and jet up there right now, so if the drive goes okay, I'll be onsite in time to help with equipment."

What sort of equipment did an English professor need? If he'd conversed with her in more depth than his usual flirtatious small talk allowed for, the context would have meant something. Since he hadn't tried, though, he got to sit on the bed as a clueless outsider, cursing his thoughtlessness and stupidity.

Worse, he was nothing to her. Less than nothing. He was a lie, a "work thing." Served him right, he supposed. She was using him just like he'd assumed that he was using her. Karma was having a right-and-proper point and laugh moment.

Megan popped open a tin of mints and tossed three in her mouth before chucking the box in her bag. "Thanks for everything, stud."

She dropped a chaste kiss to his cheek, a literal kiss-off. He actually felt himself shrink.

He caught her fingers and thought fast. "It's already noon, and the sun goes down so early this month. Please, let me arrange a flight for you." That way he'd learn of her destination, her home state.

"It's only a five-hour drive to Iowa from here. I'll be fine." Glancing at the door, she slung her purse high on her shoulder.

Iowa. Noted. Megan the English professor from Iowa. Might be able to piece a puzzle together from those scraps. College departments had directories with pictures, and with any luck, there was a syllabus floating around out there somewhere with her cell number on it. "Why the rush? Aren't most universities still closed for the holiday?"

Though he'd graduated college over two decades ago, he hadn't forgotten about the existence of a winter break.

"Oh, I'm not going home for my professor job. I have a side gig." She slipped free of his hold and made haste for the exit.

"What's that?" He laid his empty hand to rest on the mattress, clinging to the phantom sensation of her final touch.

"I'm a paranormal investigator. And just so you're aware, when we were at the party I detected a negative entity or presence near your band. I don't say this to scare you, but you may want to think about getting in contact with someone who deals in exorcisms. Thanks again for last night and this morning. Bye."

Before he could ask the first of about a hundred questions invading his confused, vaguely horrified thoughts, Megan dipped out and shut the door behind her.

✳

Don't stop now. Keep reading with your copy of EMBERS available now.

Don't miss more of the *Coven Daughters* series coming soon, and find more from Kat Turner at katturnerauthor.com

Until then, discover the *Coven Daughters Origins* with EMBERS

✳

Thom James is tired of his wild but empty rock star life, so when he meets a fan who is as uninhibited and unapologetic as he is, he falls hard. Problem is, she's busy chasing ghosts and has no interest in a serious relationship. Before she says goodbye, the enigmatic groupie leaves Thom with a dire warning about dark forces that are attached to his band.

Freshly fired from her professor job, Megan O'Neil is strictly focused on pouring herself into her side gig: ghost hunting. She can't get her latest hookup out of her mind, though, and her connection to notorious rocker Thom James inconveniently persists when she forgets her demon-trapping watch in his hotel room. When he tracks her down to return the lost object, she confronts her growing feelings for the famous bassist along with a realization that she must tackle a nasty curse that's way above her pay grade. Too bad the curse, which has followed her since childhood, is *not* about to be neutralized without a fight.

Now, Thom and Megan must battle not only a malevolent spirit, but a fierce attraction that feels doomed by the demands of their incompatible lives. When Megan excavates a strange book of witchcraft and taps into a world of magic with ties to a terrifying prophecy, she and Thom face down not only the challenges of making a relationship work, but of somehow halting the machinery of magical fate before everyone pays the price.

✳

Please sign up for the City Owl Press newsletter for chances to win special subscriber-only contests and giveaways as well as receiving information on upcoming releases and special excerpts.

All reviews are **welcome** and **appreciated**. Please consider leaving one on your favorite social media and book buying sites.

For books in the world of romance and speculative fiction that embody Innovation, Creativity, and Affordability, check out City Owl Press at www.cityowlpress.com.

ACKNOWLEDGMENTS

Huge thanks to Rosanna for being an early beta reader of this story! I'm so blessed that you connected with Raven and Cynthia, and I love how you pictured Raven.

Also, a shout out to the Owls' Nest group! There's nothing quite like a group of supportive authors to supply the laughter, shared joy and tears, feedback, and advice that it takes to get through writing and editing another book.

Last but certainly not least, thank you to my readers! Every message, post, review, and video shores up my motivation to keep creating. So grateful for all of you!

ABOUT THE AUTHOR

KAT TURNER is an award-winning author of paranormal romance and urban fantasy as well as the occasional thriller. Her favorite stories to write are those that combine action and adventure with magic, dry humor, and steamy romance if the situation allows. She lives is Kentucky with her family, where she can mostly be found practicing yoga, taking nature walks, or getting lost in the corridors of her own imagination. Kat loves to connect with readers, so don't be shy about getting in touch!

linktr.ee/katturnerauthor

ABOUT THE PUBLISHER

City Owl Press is a cutting edge indie publishing company, bringing the world of romance and speculative fiction to discerning readers.

Escape Your World. Get Lost in Ours!

www.cityowlpress.com

facebook.com/YourCityOwlPress
twitter.com/cityowlpress
instagram.com/cityowlbooks
pinterest.com/cityowlpress